Book 2 of the *Plug and Claim* Duology
Featuring Kira and Nathaniel

DARCY FAYTON

Book 2 of the *Plug and Claim* Duology
Featuring Kira and Nathaniel

DARCY FAYTON

Welcome to *Plug and Tame!* Before you begin, please bear in mind the following:

- This dark romance duology was written with the intent of providing escapism. However, it contains elements that may be triggering for some readers.

- **Themes explored in both books include:** BDSM, D/S, pet play, CNC, dubcon, virginity trope (central to plot), kidnap, anal play, bondage, plugging, gagging, humiliation, degradation, praise, vampire feeding, grooming, gore, blade weapon, and scenes involving other characters. This sequel also features breath play, other woman drama (not cheating), SA (one active scene, not with MMC), and a flashback scene depicting death of children. This list is not exhaustive; reader discretion is advised.

- This is a work of fiction. It is not a BDSM handbook. For useful information on BDSM lifestyle including safe play practices and health, please reach out to a safe online or local BDSM community.

- The story is written in British English with minor

exceptions, leading to variations in spelling and expressions (eg. realise, sceptical, burnt).

- Whilst this manuscript has been professionally edited, it is not the final copy. As an indie author, I rely on early readers to help find any remaining typos/errors. If you notice any issues, please send a screenshot via email or Instagram.

Follow me on instagram @darcyfaytonauthor
Author website: linktr.ee/darcyfayton
Add it to your Goodreads shelf

Get ready, the spicy adventure continues.
—**Darcy**

You may begin, slut. Let us see what you are good for.

CHAPTER 1

Grooming Her

NATHANIEL

NATHANIEL STRUGGLED TO CLIMB to his feet. He'd given too much blood yesterday, and it had sapped him of his strength. His father, Henrikk the Vampire King, had thrown him aside as if he were a ragdoll.

Panic surged through Nathaniel as he watched his father's brooding figure tower over Kira. She had retreated as far back as the office wall allowed, trembling as Henrikk held her by the jaw. The King shared Nathaniel's height, and he forced Kira's chin up so they were eye-to-eye, his lip curling in a contemptuous stare that was only rivalled by Kira's own.

"Say that again," she growled, her golden eyes flashing dangerously.

"I am not in the habit of repeating myself," Henrikk warned. His tone was clipped, but he smoothed his voice. "But just this once...I will make an exception." His grip tightened on Kira's face and jaw, his fingernails visibly biting into her face and causing her to yelp in pain. "I said, kneel for me, *slut*." The last word spilt from his mouth with venom.

Nathaniel wished he could shield her from the terrible truth his

father had revealed to her: that he, Nathaniel, had been grooming
her to be his father's whore.

Kira looked horrified, and the hurt look she shot him stabbed him
like a knife to the chest, causing the guilt that had been welling up
to pour free. He hadn't expected to find his father here, and now, it
was too late, because the damage was done. Kira would never forgive
him.

Except there was more to the story.

I should have told her when I had the chance.

He'd brought Kira to his office for that very reason—to tell her
everything. He'd decided he was done keeping secrets from her.
She was more than a pawn to be moved around on a chessboard.
Granted, he was one too, but together, they had a chance of surviving
the trials ahead.

Nathaniel jerked into action, ignoring the pain in his jaw from
where his father had struck him as he leapt to his feet. "Get away
from her," he seethed, advancing on his father.

An icy chill filled the room as the humour left Henrikk's face. He
released Kira with a rough push that sent her stumbling sideways.

"Watch yourself, boy. Have you forgotten who she belongs to?"
He gave a short, harsh cackle. "You might be using her now, but you
know you cannot keep her. It is *my* offspring she will carry."

Nathaniel hissed, fangs bared as he leapt at his father, fists drawn.
But his father was faster, stronger—always had been—and he only
landed one strike before his father hit him square in the jaw and sent
him toppling to the ground.

He landed hard on his back, the wolf pelts that thickly layered the
ground doing little to cushion his fall. It knocked the wind out of
him, causing him to wheeze for air. A moment later, he felt the hard
press of his father's shoe on his chest.

"She's mine, boy. Pull yourself together. I'm prepared to hand you
my empire in just a few days' time. You and Gloria can rule to your

heart's content. But Kirabelle is *mine*, now and forever. Remember that." His shoe pressed down, and Nathaniel winced as his ribs bent beneath the pressure, threatening to crack. "Is that understood?"

"Yes, sir," Nathaniel rasped.

"Good. Now..." His father removed his foot, and his voice turned pleasant once more. "I will see you at Wintermaw Keep for your birthday and wedding, where I expect to see Gloria on your arm wearing a veil—and Kirabelle on a leash."

Nathaniel hardly heard his father. His heart was pounding as he whipped around to look at Kira—but she was gone, the door to his office left wide open.

"You best go after her," his father said absently, but Nathaniel was already out the door, running as fast as he could through the school corridors. He caught a brief glimpse of Kira's long brown hair whipping round a corner as she descended the grand staircase.

Nathaniel fought exhaustion as he hurried after her, forcing his legs into long strides. He descended the stairs, clutching at the bannister for support. He was halfway down when he caught a glimpse of Kira beneath him in the foyer.

"Kira!" he yelled. "Kira, wait!"

She threw a terrified glance up at him before running out of sight.

Cursing under his breath, Nathaniel swung himself over the railing and plummeted down several heart-stopping feet to the foyer below.

He landed heavily, causing his knees to give out, sending him sprawling across the tiles. He picked himself up and spun around, ignoring the shocked students near him.

Where is she?

Kira was nowhere in sight, but she'd set off in the direction of the front door.

Of course. Where else would a terrified mouse go?

He hesitated at the large oak doors, however. His Kira was no mouse. She was a wolf and not so easily frightened. And she was only half wolf. Vampire blood ran in her veins, and she was just as capable of being as calculating as the best of them.

He backtracked and reassessed.

The hall leading to the cafeteria was also here, as were the stairs leading down to the dorms. Surely, Kira hadn't gone to her room? There was only one way leading in and out, and down there, she would be a sitting duck.

Except that there *was* another exit. Not the portal that led to the beach cove—no, the cliffs there were too steep even for a wolf, and the tiny tropical island was the only landmass for miles around. If Kira had gone there, she would be easy to find.

But there was another exit, one that was hidden in plain sight. Had she figured it out?

As he debated, a voice broke through his thoughts.

"She went that way," a wolf with black pigtails said, pointing to the cafeteria door.

"Thank you, Chelsea," Nathaniel said, giving her a small smile and a stare that could have frozen ice, "for eliminating that option."

Chelsea went white.

The wolf had lied to protect Kira, but she had lied badly. Feeling confident, he took the door to the dorms and pursued Kira downstairs.

Nathaniel couldn't see her on the curved stairwell, but he could hear her hurried footsteps echoing from far below, and he could sense her fear.

His heart squeezed tightly at the thought that Kira was running from *him*.

He didn't have a chance of keeping up, but he pursued her nonetheless. She could not run forever. And he had a vampire's careful patience. Sooner or later, he would capture her.

The door to his bedroom was wide open. There was no one

inside, but the window was broken, the glass pane smashed from the inside. Nathaniel peered through the window. Grey clouds overcast the country lane, and the trees were unnaturally still except for the persistent rain rustling their leaves. Broken glass shards lay in the muddy ground before him, where sure enough, there were several wolf paw prints.

Kira had figured out that it was a portal.

Clever girl.

He delayed only to collect a few items before climbing through the window into the lane beyond.

There were two sets of paw prints. One for each of Kira's wolf selves. She was one person, but when she morphed, there were two wolves. He assumed they each had their own personality, and he longed to meet them. He hoped he would still have that privilege one day.

He walked at a steady pace, his polished shoes crushing the mud and shrubs. There was no point running, not when Kira had morphed. He could be as fast as any wolf after drinking blood, but in his current state, he didn't have a hope of keeping up with her.

It didn't matter. He was not in a hurry.

He pursued her with the steady endurance of a wolf, his footsteps slow and relentless through the woods. The black collar and leash swung by his side, echoing the sickening roll of his stomach.

He was hungry, and he kept his eyes peeled for food to abate his hunger pangs—plants, fungi, small animals. Kira had offered to let him feed from her last night, an offer that he'd barely been able to resist. An offer that made him ache for her now.

He had a feeling she'd rescinded the invitation.

CHAPTER 2

On the Run

KIRA

FEAR SPURRED KIRA'S FEET faster as she rushed towards the front doors of Volmasque Academy, her heart thumping in her chest. She was nearly at the exit when, out of nowhere, the image of the country lane she'd seen outside Nathaniel's window appeared in her mind. She'd assumed it was an illusion, her gut feeling told her otherwise. It was literally a window to another place.

A portal.

And it didn't lead just anywhere. Subconsciously, she'd recognised the lane with the row of birch trees, but its significance had only just clicked into place amidst her terror. The lane was not far from where she'd grown up in the cottage with her foster parents. Her mind jarred to a stop. The old wise wolves were exactly who she needed to be with right now. She was barely holding it together, her insides churning with turmoil, and she needed their counsel more than ever.

She didn't have time to contemplate *why* Nathaniel had a portal in his bedroom that led to the outskirts of Nordokk, not when he was in hot pursuit, his voice calling her name from some landing above. There were other students about, and she was too afraid to shift into her wolf form just yet.

Her shoes squeaked on the tiles as she skidded to a halt by the front doors and changed direction, darting towards the dorm door. She shot down the stairs, hoping Nathaniel hadn't seen her. Earlier, she'd feared for how weak he was. He'd been so selfless, saving two unlikely people by giving them his blood: Barbara, an illegal witch hiding in the city, and Susie, Kira's closest friend at the academy.

She'd taken it as a proof of his generosity and kind-heartedness—qualities she was no longer sure he had. How could that same person have been manipulating her all this time? To have sex with her, and toy with her heart, only to betray her?

Vampires are manipulators. Everyone knows that. I know that. I should never have trusted him.

A minute later, Kira was standing outside Nathaniel's bedroom. This was the last place he would expect her to go. She smiled grimly as she kicked in the door.

The portal was disguised and bordered by a window frame complete with real glass. She nearly kicked that in as well, but she didn't want to risk cutting her leg up. She found a whip in Nathaniel's chest of interesting taboo items. She shivered at the feel of the smooth plaited leather, but it was the hard cane handle she was interested in. Perfect for breaking the window.

Although...

The twinkle of a gem had caught her eye by the bedside table. It was one of the plugs Nathaniel had made her wear. This was the larger of the two, a bulging mushroom-shaped toy made of steel. Its base was decorated with a red, heart-shaped gem that gleamed in the grey light filtering through the window. She dropped the whip with a clatter and hefted the heavy plug in her hand.

Even better.

The plug made a satisfying sound as it broke through the glass. Instead of creating a hole like she'd expected, it caused the entire pane to shatter into tiny fragments.

She morphed into her wolf form, her human form separating into two dark-furred wolves with long vicious fangs. Each wolf had nine whip-like tails with barbed ends at the tips hidden in tufts of fur. She did not understand why she looked so different to the other wolves, but Mary and Byron had taught her to keep her true form a secret. To this day, she'd never shown anyone her wolf forms, not even Nathaniel, although there had been a moment last night when she'd been tempted.

And she'd woken in his arms, aghast to realise she'd morphed while she'd been sleeping. Nathaniel had not seen, but even so, her life had spun out of control the moment they'd entered his office to find the Vampire King waiting.

Fear coursed through Kira as she tore across the lane and down a steep bank, her paws kicking up dirt and leaves as she plunged into the dense forest below. The heavy rain pierced the dense canopy, battering the leaves and dripping large droplets onto her snouts.

She'd bolted the moment Henrikk had revealed his intent to use her for breeding. The knowledge that Nathaniel was complicit in that scheme made bile burn her throat and her chest ache. Now that Henrikk had set his eyes on her, she would need to rethink her plan. But right now, all she could think of was Nathaniel's betrayal.

I thought he was different. I thought... She shook her head. It no longer mattered.

It was all bullshit.

And it serves me right for trusting a vampire.

She increased her pace, trees whipping past her as she tried to leave her mistakes behind her. She had no idea what she was doing, or where she would even go. All she knew in that instant was that she needed to put as much distance between herself and the two vampires as possible.

Her first impression upon meeting Henrikk was that he was pure evil. *A tyrannical cunt.*

But Nathaniel was worse than his father, because he'd lied to her and made her feel like she was special. Fool as she was, she'd let herself believe that he might actually care about her.

Idiot. Look how that turned out.

If she could have wiped him from her mind, she would have. Instead, her thoughts kept circling back to the horrifying revelation that he'd been grooming her to be his father's sex slave. Both father and son were repulsive.

She pushed her limbs to run faster. The last person in the world she wanted to see was Nathaniel. Any romantic inclination she may have had was dead and buried, even if the pain of his betrayal remained, digging into her like claws. She would not let him close again. From now on, her heart was cold as stone, her body off limits, her mind and thoughts her own.

Prince fucking Nathaniel could suck a royal dick.

Once Kira had put a quarter of a mile between her and the portal, she lifted her head to the dark clouds and howled. The sound had a haunting beauty, echoing for at least ten miles with the wind still. There was a small risk that Nathaniel would hear her, but she doubted he'd tracked her this far. Even if he had, he would never keep up. She was in her element.

Kira howled again, then paused, panting as she waited to hear an answering cry.

A deep, distant howl answered. Her spirits lifted as she recognised Byron. The old wolf's voice held a gravitas that commanded respect, and a familiarity that tugged at her heartstrings.

Moving in the direction of the sound, her wolves' powerful muscles traversed the rocky foothills with ease. The earth was dry here, and she took comfort knowing that even if Nathaniel tried to follow her, he could not track her without pawprints.

As she climbed higher, a cool breeze picked up, refreshing her as it seeped through her damp fur. By the time she cleared the steep slope and the ground levelled out, the rain had reduced to a mild drizzle.

Tall cliffs stretched above her, and she wove between large boulders. The smell of charcoal and smoke reached her nostrils as a campfire outside a cave entrance came into view.

A rush of joy flooded her when she caught sight of her foster parents. Byron had clearly shifted back, because he and Mary were in human form. Both her wolf selves ran to embrace them, standing up on hind legs with front paws lifted.

Mary was a short woman with short, curly, red hair and a face that was almost perfectly round, whilst she'd always thought of Byron as a gentle giant—tall and brawny with black, close-cropped hair, a short thick beard, and large calloused hands. They both looked surprised to see her as they hugged each of her wolf forms.

"Kira, what are you doing here?" Mary asked in astonishment.

Kira's wolf selves stepped back and blended into each other, forming one wolf as golden light oscillated around them, growing brighter as she morphed back into a human. She combed her thick, brown hair out of her face with her fingers and wiped her muddy hands on her pants.

"I had to come," Kira answered, smiling in relief as she looked at the couple. "And I'm so glad I found you. I've missed you both."

"We've missed you too," Mary said, licking her thumb and using it to clean a spot on Kira's cheek. The gesture was tender and motherly, but Mary's expression was worried. "But why have you come?"

Kira gave a bitter laugh as she knelt to wash her hands in a water basin. "The reason begins and ends with the jerk the academy sent to get me," she said, shaking her wet hands at the fire and causing flying droplets to evaporate with a *hiss*. "His name is Nathaniel, and he just so happens to be the fucking Vampire Prince—can you believe it?"

"I can believe it," Byron murmured.

"Yes, well...you won't believe what a royal prick he is, *every* pun intended."

Byron and Mary exchanged a look, and Byron rubbed his bearded chin as he turned his concerned eyes to Kira. "And Nathaniel knows you're here, does he?"

The smile slowly faded from Kira's face. She didn't know what to say to that. Byron's comment was strange. He'd never mentioned Nathaniel before, and had not even mentioned the Vampire Prince.

Confusion spread across Kira's face. "How do you know Nathaniel? You've never once mentioned him to me before."

Byron's guilty expression made her heart sink a fraction more.

"If Nathaniel hasn't told you, then I'm afraid it's not for me to say," he said.

Kira crossed her arms. "What's going on?" Why was he acting so stand-offish?

Byron shook his head in silent refusal, even though in all the years she'd known him, he'd always been loath to refuse her anything. Out of the wolf couple, Mary had always been the strict one.

Desperate for answers, Kira now turned to her. "Mary, why won't you just talk to me?"

Mary sighed. "Oh Kira, you shouldn't have come. You were supposed to stay at the academy. We didn't expect you to return."

Kira frowned. "But going to the academy was my idea." She was struggling to find the words to voice what should have been obvious: that Mary and Byron had raised her to appreciate a simple life in the countryside. The couple who had once been guards for the royal wolf household of Wintermaw Keep, but they'd only trained her to fight at her insistence. Mary had fought her tooth and nail, never truly accepting Kira's ambitions to fight for reform. Byron had been far more supportive, but the older she'd gotten, the more he'd tried to talk her out of her plans for revenge. "It was *my* idea," she repeated.

Wasn't it?

Silence.

Kira shook her head in exasperation. "I thought you'd both be happy to see me."

"We are," Byron replied.

Mary only pinched her lips and said nothing.

"I...I made sure I wasn't followed, if that's what's bothering you," Kira said.

Mary buried her round face in her hands. "Oh, Kira..."

Kira frowned. "What's wrong?"

The woman slowly lifted her head. "You cannot stop what has been started. You cannot run from this."

"Run from what? Nathaniel? But I just said I made sure I wasn't followed—"

"He will find you," Mary said, her voice growing high pitched as she turned to Byron. "She shouldn't have come back."

"It's all right," Byron soothed her.

Kira watched in disbelief as her foster parents consoled each other. "What the hell is going on? I never said I was running away from anything, I just...needed to get away and clear my head."

Right?

She felt foolish as she continued. "I just wanted to see you and hear your advice."

And some reassurance would be nice.

Byron rested a heavy hand on her shoulder. "Kira, you know how much I love you, kiddo. I would do anything for you. Mary and I, we're both prepared to die for you. But we cannot be the ones you turn to now."

The words stabbed and twisted. "Why not?"

"Because, you are not ours anymore."

She was too stunned to speak. Her body turned cold as the last threads of support that had kept her grounded and helped her survive the academy's insanity were ripped away. Her voice was thick as she said, "You better not be saying I belong to *Nathaniel.*"

No answer.

She changed tack, if only to stop herself from tearing her hair out from sheer frustration. "How do you know him, anyway?"

Byron's thick brows lowered, and he looked as if he dearly wanted to tell her whatever it was he was holding back.

"You're my family," Kira whispered.

"We love you as our daughter, Kira," Mary said, her cheeks red and streaming with silent tears, "but we cannot be your parents in this stage of your life. We can only serve you."

Kira's head was spinning. None of this made sense. Why were Mary and Byron acting so strange, as if they were different people—mere shadows of the happy couple who'd raised her? Her entire life was being turned upside down, and she felt lost. It all felt like a bad dream. It had to be.

She hugged herself as a terrible emptiness set in. "Well...*you* might not want me as your daughter anymore, but I don't belong to *him*, either."

Long seconds passed where the only sounds were the crackling of the fire, and her vision grew blurry as heavy tear drops fell to stain her dusty shoes.

What was her life worth, if everything that had preceded it was a sham, and the few people she'd depended on were rejecting her? Horrible suspicions swirled in her mind, and a sense of abandonment began to set in, clawing out her chest and leaving it hollow.

She jumped when a male voice spoke behind her.

"No, you don't belong to anyone, Kira."

She spun around and found herself face to face with Nathaniel. His shoulders were draped in a dashing black cloak that emphasised his height. Had he not looked so tired, he would have been intimidating.

"Nathaniel?" she asked, trying not to fixate on his eyes, which sparkled like sunlit snow.

"You don't belong to anyone," he repeated. "You do, however, belong to the cause, just as we do." He stepped closer and took her hand. "And believe me when I say that you are very much wanted."

Before Kira could snatch her hand back, Nathaniel went down on one knee, lifted her hand to his lips, and kissed it, stealing the air from her lungs.

CHAPTER 3

Traitor

KIRA

"How did you find me?" Kira exclaimed, finally snatching her hand from Nathaniel. The top of her hand still tingled from his kiss.

"It wasn't that long ago that I fed on you," he replied. "It made you easy to track. I was able to sense you—it's a talent of mine that was heightened by hunger."

Kira gaped at him, but she shut her mouth and lifted her chin. "I'm surprised you didn't drop dead from the journey."

Mary gasped, but Kira kept her focus on Nathaniel, whose lips twitched with amusement.

"I fed on an animal en route. It was...enough to sustain me."

"Probably a very small animal," Kira sneered. "Something slow. You don't look like you could have caught a deer."

Nathaniel tilted his head, studying her in a way that reminded her of an owl. His scrutiny made her insides shrivel, but she held his gaze.

Finally, he said, "It was a hedgehog."

Kira scoffed, the tension between them easing slightly. "Sounds very appealing."

Nathaniel's smile widened, but it wasn't a friendly smile. His upper lip was curled up, revealing his fangs. "Not as appealing as you, dear Kira."

As his meaning sank in, she took a step back. "Forget it. You said you wouldn't bite me again."

Nathaniel licked his lips. "At this stage, I don't have a choice."

"I thought vampires didn't need blood to survive."

"Vampires in my condition don't chase wolves several kilometres across the country. I must feed now. The alternative would mean death for me."

"Death it is," Kira shrugged, taking another step back. If she could put a little distance between them, it would give her a chance to morph if the vampire tried anything. It also brought her a step closer towards Byron and Mary. Regardless of how strange their behaviour, she would not hesitate to defend them. "After grooming me to become your father's plaything, I think death is almost too good for you."

"You haven't been told everything," Nathaniel replied. "I was not the only person to groom you."

Kira felt as if he'd slapped her. "Fuck off." She glanced at Mary and Byron, who were still stonily silent, before looking back at Nathaniel. "Who else? Victoria? Felix?" She wracked her brain. "Chelsea?"

Nathaniel shook his head. "No. Someone closer to you."

She swallowed. "Not Susie?" *Please, tell me it wasn't her.* The wolf had become something of a big sister to her.

"Not Susie."

Kira shrugged helplessly. "Then who?"

"Us." Byron's deep voice rasped the word, but he might as well have screamed it for the way it carved a hole in her heart.

"What?" she whispered.

Mary spoke up. "It was us. We were grooming you." She placed a hand on Byron's arm to console him.

What about consoling me? Kira's head spun. The world had gone mad.

"We were preparing you for the uprising you are to lead," Mary continued, "And the duties you would face along the way."

"What. Duties?" Each word felt like a death sentence.

Mary glanced at Nathaniel—she fucking *glanced at him* for permission to fucking speak—before turning back to her. "Kira, your duty is to help Nathaniel take his father's place on the throne—"

"*By sucking his father's cock?*" The angry words burst out of her before she could stop them, but she didn't care. Everyone else was dancing around the topic as if it were a minor detail, and no one had acknowledged that she'd been kept in the dark all these years. For her, the worst was still ahead.

"Kira..." Mary began.

"Don't. *Kira. Me,*" she snapped, forcing herself to stand still when all she wanted to do was rip Nathaniel's throat out. Or sink to her knees in defeat. The only thing holding her together was the desperate hope that this was all some cruel prank. "Someone tell me what the *fuck* is going on right this instant, because none of you are making any fucking sense!"

"We're trying," Byron said. "We didn't want you to find out this way."

"It sounds like you didn't want me to find out at all! Did you know what Nathaniel's done to me, Byron? Do you have any idea that he's made me wear a...a..." her anger stalled and fizzled out. She couldn't bring herself to tell her father-figure that Nathaniel had made her wear an anal plug. It was too humiliating.

But she could tell from Byron's expression that he already knew. She jabbed an accusatory finger at him, her voice a low warning growl. "Tell me this is all some sick joke."

He was the only person she wanted to hear from. He was the person she trusted most in the entire world. Mary had always treated her warmly, but Byron had more empathy than anyone she knew.

Every girl needed a father. And he was hers. Even if he wasn't her biological father. He was her person.

Byron grew ashen-faced, his fists clenching as he turned to Nathaniel. But rather than tear the vampire a new one, he pleaded. "Please, allow me to tell her, Nathaniel."

Her insides boiled to see the large man with his tail between his legs, taking his orders from the Vampire Prince he was supposed to hate.

Nathaniel shook his head. "No. It will be better if I show her."

Kira threw him the middle finger and turned to Byron, her voice rising in pitch as she beseeched him. "Byron, *you* tried to talk me *out* of leading a revolution."

"I did," he admitted. "I pitied the road ahead of you. I wanted you to have a peaceful life."

"Byron, you've always had a tender heart," Mary chimed in.

Kira's jaw muscles tensed, her teeth growing sore from clenching. She had absolutely nothing to say to Mary, the woman who had taught her how to bake and hunt in the woods. Nothing at all.

She turned tearful eyes to Byron in one last attempt to find the man she'd looked up to. It was a struggle to speak from the tight knot in her throat. "The revolution was *my* idea."

"No," Mary said, "It was ours. We prepared you from a young age, telling you stories about the revolution, and the wolves and vampires involved—"

"I remember," Kira said tightly, cutting her off. She got the picture, she really did, even if it was actually millions of pictures, the memories flashing through her mind faster and faster until she felt queasy. She would have to sit down and reflect on her entire fucking childhood to retroactively identify those tiny moments of betrayal.

Silence.

Everyone was looking at her, waiting for her to speak. Nathaniel hadn't moved except to fold his arms inside his cloak. Was he cold?

Not that she fucking cared.

"Kira," Nathaniel began, "Please, come sit down by the fire. Allow me a chance to explain. The plan is so much bigger than us."

"Us," Kira repeated softly. The word encompassed three people she would never in her wildest dreams have imagined would work together to deceive her: her foster parents, and *him*.

"You're part of this, too," Nathaniel said.

"No," she sniffed, wiping her eyes with a damp sleeve. "I'm not."

"Kira, please. Stop."

She ignored him and took another step back. "Fuck. You."

"Kira..." Nathaniel warned, his voice growing low and threatening. "Do not run."

She didn't reply. There were no insults left inside of her. 'Fuck you' really said it all. It was time to leave, and even her wolf forms could not run fast enough to leave this tumultuous day behind. She spun on her heel, the wolf hairs already sprouting on her forearms as golden light whirled around her—but she never had the chance to morph.

As fast as lightning, Nathaniel threw something at her—a length of thin rope he'd been hiding beneath his cloak.

The rope covered the distance between them, flying over her head. She shrieked and managed to dodge it, fleeing the campsite on foot.

She'd been forced to run towards the base of the cliffs. Was she trapped?

Noticing a small cave between two large boulders, she shot towards it with escape firmly in mind.

At the last second, Byron stepped in front of her and she slammed into his chest, reeling from the impact.

Traitor!

Stunned, Kira tried to regain her balance, her vision distorting. A second later, she was running, but a loop of rope flashed above her, and she wasn't fast enough this time. It tightened around her neck, constricting her airway. Firm hands seized her shoulders from behind.

"Do not struggle, or the lasso will tighten," Nathaniel spoke in her ear, dragging her back against his chest.

"*What the fuck are you doing?*" she yelled, trying to get away from him as panic set in.

His hold tightened, his fingers digging into her shoulder muscles. "Shh, calm yourself."

"Let me go!" she screamed, kicking as hard as she could at the air, trying to throw him off balance. She threw her head around to look at Byron and Mary. "Why aren't you helping me?!"

"Because, darling, he's not our enemy," Mary said gently.

"Well, he's fucking mine!" she spat.

"We're just going to have a conversation," Nathaniel explained, dragging her towards the entrance of the cave.

"I have nothing to say to you, fuckface!"

He ignored her insult. "You can do the listening, then."

"If you think I'm going to listen to what you have to s-"

Her voice cut off as a firm, rubbery object was forced into her mouth, and as the collar tightened around her neck, she realised too late that Nathaniel had gagged her.

He appeared in front of her, tugging sharply on a leash, the rope visible for only a second as he tucked it inside his cloak. He'd removed the rope so quickly she hadn't even noticed it was gone, and as for the gag, she reacted the only way that made sense.

She screamed as if her throat was on fire, and even the gag could not quieten the noise.

"You will listen to what I have to tell you," Nathaniel said, his words eerie like a winter chill as he dragged her into the cave. "But first, I will take what I need from you."

Kira threw a desperate glance back at Mary and Byron, but the couple were standing motionless by the fire.

Doing nothing to help her.

She yelled, her words garbled like a madman's, and she watched in horror as Byron turned away, as if he couldn't bear to watch her plight. Sorrow and disbelief built up in her chest, shredding the remaining tissue of her heart.

And then the darkness of the cave swallowed them whole, dousing her rage until the only emotion she had left was stark fear.

Nathaniel took her deeper into its depths until the bright entrance was out of sight.

Kira stopped screaming, partly because the cave amplified her voice in a terrifying echo, and also because she was too busy trying to suck in air past the gag. But she fought Nathaniel every step of the way, and his laboured breathing made her cling to the hope that she could overpower him in his weakened state.

She tried to morph, but Nathaniel yanked her hair painfully, interrupting the process.

"Not now, pet," he said in a ragged voice. "Not now."

They came to a standstill in the pitch-black, her entire body clammy and paralysed with dread as her heart thumped sickeningly in her chest.

"I just want to talk," Nathaniel whispered into her ear, loosening the gag. "Be a good girl and show me how quiet you can be."

She gasped for breath as the collar and gag fell away, wheezing and spitting excess saliva out. Her body was shaking, but she froze as he gently brushed her hair off her shoulder.

"Please," she whimpered. The word sounded small and useless in the dark void where the only one who heard her was *him*. The quiet, meek wolf of her personality took over as the strong one receded. "Please, Nathaniel," she repeated, "you said you wouldn't bite me again."

"I made no such promise." His lips grazed her neck as he spoke, sending chills through her. "What I said was that feeding from you again would represent love." He dragged his hand through her hair, his fingers snagging the knots as his grip tightened, forcing her head to tilt back. "And make no mistake, Kira, I might be hungry and an inch from death, but this *will* mean something to me...because I am hopelessly, desperately in love with you."

She couldn't see him, but she could feel his breath on her throat, and the sensual brush of his lips.

"Forgive me," he murmured.

Her vision flashed white with hot pain as sharp fangs pierced her skin.

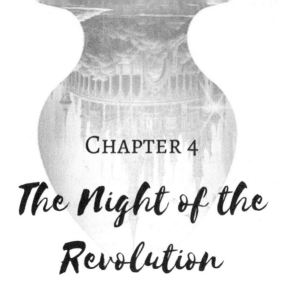

CHAPTER 4

The Night of the Revolution

KIRA

THE PAIN OF NATHANIEL'S bite vanished almost immediately, replaced with a warm cloudy feeling that quashed Kira's terror and lulled her into a state of calmness. Her muscles relaxed, and she stopped resisting altogether as Nathaniel drank her blood. His lips and tongue were hot on her neck. Gradually, his grip loosened on her hair, and he wrapped his arm around her waist and drew her close, holding her tenderly as if they were lovers.

All of a sudden, the words he'd spoken hit her. He was in love with her.

But he's a vampire.

She would never have believed that Nathaniel was capable of feeling anything other than lust. But then their minds had touched, and just like the first time when he'd claimed her, a new feeling dawned over her.

Surprise.

Because unlike the first time he'd bitten her, his thoughts were not closed. Instead, the walls were down and gates wide open as he shared his emotions.

She had expected arrogance and contempt. Instead, she was overwhelmed by affection. It poured from him like sparkling light, filling the darkness that had consumed them both.

With their minds connected, she noticed other things. Alarm bells rang when she sensed his weakened physical state. Nathaniel wasn't simply hungry. He was starving, his body on the verge of collapse as it waited for a sustenance he could not replenish.

He needs my blood.

Not wants. Not craves. He needs it like the air we breathe.

Her worry for him grew. Nathaniel's thoughts brushed hers like a gentle caress, his gratitude washing over her as he drank.

"Thank you," he said, the words tumbling around in her mind.

Kira licked her lips. She wasn't about to say *you're welcome,* but she no longer begrudged him for biting her, not if the true alternative would have been to let him die.

"Don't you have some back-up plan when you run low on blood?" she asked.

"Yes. As you can see."

Kira exhaled through her nostrils. He meant *her.* "You should stick to hedgehogs next time."

He laughed, his breath warm on her neck.

She didn't join in. Despite everything, the thought of losing Nathaniel made her seize up.

If he dies...

"No one is dying today," he said.

"Stop reading my thoughts," she snapped, with only a shadow of a growl.

His chest rumbled with a chuckle, and Kira almost smiled, but then the chill of the cave caused her to shiver.

"Cold?" Nathaniel asked, the gentle pull of his hand on her waist inviting her closer.

Reluctantly, Kira settled against him. If they were going to be here a while, she may as well get comfortable. Besides, the warm press of his body wasn't so bad compared to the hard cave floor.

He fed from her in silence, the act more intimate than a kiss. She wasn't sure how she felt about the fact that she was enjoying it, when logically, she'd been angry at him only a few minutes ago.

Suddenly, Nathaniel stopped drinking and drew his head back. His arms were still looped around her, and their minds remained connected.

"Why did you stop feeding?" she asked in confusion. She could feel the sharp pangs that raked through Nathaniel. He was still so hungry.

"I took only what I needed."

Kira could sense his guilt through their bond as he continued.

"Usually, I do not drink blood that is not given freely."

"Lucky me," she said sarcastically. *"But you may as well finish what you started."*

Nathaniel's amusement rolled over her. *"Such a tempting offer."*

His response was casual, but there was real hunger behind it, raw and edged with nausea. He was trying to mask it from her, but she could sense it.

Her worry deepened. *"What will happen to you?"*

"I will rest a while. Then I will go forage for something. But first, I need to talk to you now."

"Most people just talk normally, you know. Without the blood sucking."

"Most people are not us. And this way, I can show you what happened the night of the Revolution, and the role I played."

"Why now?"

"Because I should have told you sooner. You deserve to know about your past."

"My past?" Did that mean he knew who her parents were?

"I must warn you, it may be difficult for you to witness the events of

that night."

He waited for her assent.

She nodded. *"Show me."*

Dark smoke of midnight blue filled her vision. It swirled thickly before parting to reveal a fortified castle silhouetted against a starless sky. She was standing at the edge of a forest with Nathaniel, her view of the castle partially blocked by tall trees.

"Wintermaw Keep," Kira murmured. *"I've never seen it with my own eyes. At least, I don't remember it."*

"It's a mercy that you have no memories of that night," Nathaniel said. *"And I am sorry you have to relive it now."*

Before she could respond, several dark figures emerged from the shadows of the trees. Henrikk was there, his blond hair gleaming in the moonlight. He smoothed his sharp moustache as he regarded the Keep with a smile.

Kira drew a sharp breath and stumbled away from Henrikk. Had she truly been here, she might have stumbled over the tree roots. As it was, she drifted through them like a ghost.

Nathaniel took her hand and drew her close. *"They can't see or hear us. It's just a memory."*

Henrikk addressed the ranks of cloaked vampires, his voice a commanding hiss. "I can taste victory."

Kira noticed a young man standing behind Henrikk. She did a double take. He was in his mid-teens, and his stature and facial features were strikingly similar to Henrikk's.

Nathaniel.

It was obviously him. She could tell from his furrowed brows and the tense set of his jaw that he did not seem to share his father's anticipation.

The real Nathaniel leant close to her. *"Let's skip ahead. Brace yourself."*

Blue smoke descended upon them again, and when it cleared, they were inside a corridor with a high vaulted ceiling. Elegant carpet runners stretched from one end to the other, and the walls were lined with doors and tapestries. Two guards were stationed before each door.

"The east wing, where the royal family's living quarters are," Nathaniel said, stopping before a white door with mouldings. *"This is where the children slept."* He peered at her with concern. *"We can skip this part if you wish. What happened is...very disturbing. I don't think you would ever be able to erase it from your mind."*

Kira chewed her lip. She had a general idea what would happen next. *"It's better that I know."*

"Very well," Nathaniel nodded. Before entering the room, he gestured at the guards. *"They both fought bravely. This one on the right nearly killed me."*

"Oh." There were no words she could say to that. She stared at the soldiers with respect, her heart aching as she tried to comprehend that they were about to die.

The guards tensed as a distant commotion sounded from far away. People were yelling, and there was a loud crash that made the guards draw their weapons.

Nathaniel grimaced, causing deep lines that she'd never noticed before to appear on his face. *"I'll be arriving soon."*

It took her a moment to realise he meant his younger self. *"If 'you' weren't here yet, how can you remember what the corridor looked like before you showed up?"*

"Because the corridor is how the guard remembered it."

Realisation dropped like a lead weight in her stomach. *"You drank the guard's blood."*

"Not merely drank." Shame flooded their bond like a dam had burst, and Nathaniel tried frantically to hold it back from her. *"I drained him, and his final memories were transferred to me. It is something that can happen. They are a curse, a reminder that I carry*

with me always."

Despondency overcame her. She felt sorry for the guard's death, but she also felt sorry for Nathaniel, whose guilt seeped out of him like poison.

He exhaled sorrowfully. *"Come. I want you to see them before...before I arrived."*

Nathaniel pushed the door open, but his hand and body passed right through it as he strode inside. Kira followed, unsettled by the way her own body passed through the wood as if it were nothing.

Inside was a nursery decorated in creams, pale blues, and pinks. One side of the room was lined with lavish beds. They were empty, their almost-pristine state suggesting they were rarely used. Some of the pillows had been chewed, the feather stuffing strewn across the floor amidst baby toys and dog bones.

The children—or pups—were all sleeping together by the fire on a large square mattress. They were all in wolf form, some curled up with their snouts hidden behind their tails, others stretched out on their backs with the golden glow of the fire warming their tummies.

The seven pups looked to be four or five years old. They were still young, their tan-coloured fur and dappled white spots. Each had a cluster of fluffy tails—the nine tail puppies she'd seen mounted on Nathaniel's office wall were all here, alive in the flesh.

"Alive only in memory," Nathaniel said sadly. *"They were the offspring of King Bakker and his first wife, nine tails Queen Hannah. How it would have pained her to know what became of her children."*

Back in the cave, Nathaniel's grip had tightened so much it hurt, his mounting dread adding to hers. Kira squeezed his hand back, silently consoling him when, perhaps, she should have condemned him.

It was only then that she noticed something peculiar in the memory: there were nine more puppies. They were nestled in amongst the tan-coloured one, but they were much smaller and with dark fur. Their appearance was distinctly wolf-like, and yet eerily different. Long, sabre teeth protruded from their snouts, and they had large claws like a lion. Each pup had nine whip-like tails with tufts of fur on the tips.

"They're like little versions of me," Kira thought.

"Not 'like'," Nathaniel corrected. *"They are you. All nine of them."*

"Me?" Kira felt her stomach tighten. She moved to get a better look at the pups, treading lightly even though she knew they couldn't hear her.

"Yes, you. What you see are your nine selves."

She was shocked that there were nine.

She was even more shocked that Nathaniel knew about her true form. *That's what he's implying, isn't it?*

Her heart lurched, and had she not felt his gentle thoughts now, she might have bolted from the cave. But he calmed her, and she became sure of one thing amidst her confusion; he had no intention of harming her.

She eyed one of the hybrid pups, whose snout was resting on a bone, his ears pricked as if he heard a disturbance. "How long have you known?"

"I've always known," Nathaniel said quietly.

"This morning, in your bedroom. When I shifted by accident, you saw me."

"I did. But I already knew."

Her throat went dry. "It can't be me." Those nine dark-furred pups couldn't possibly be her. She only had two wolf forms, whereas... "There are nine of them..." she began.

"Yes. Only two survived the night."

She swallowed hard, her gaze roaming over the pups sleeping peacefully. The children of the Wolf King and Wolf Queen—her half brothers and sisters with the light-coloured fur—and the dark ones that were *her*, nine pups that made up one person.

All the pups' eyes were shut as they slept, unaware of the fate awaiting them.

All except one. The dark-furred pup whose ears had pricked now opened her eyes, and she lifted her snout from the bone and scented the air.

Kira's heart jolted as she recognised that part of her—the one who was feisty and wary of strangers.

"Perhaps, we best skip this part," Nathaniel said quietly.

Dark smoke billowed at the edges of Kira's vision, but she seized Nathaniel's arm, her hand passing right through in the dreamlike state even though she gripped his shirt in the cave.

"Wait," she said, her gaze fixed on the awake pup. The pup was now on all four paws, pulling the dark ear of another one to rouse her.

The second pup lifted her head blearily, blinking sleepy eyes. Kira immediately recognised her as the shy, sensitive one.

The first pup whined and pulled at her coat, urging her to rise.

Other pups were stirring as the sound of commotion outside in the corridor grew louder.

"Kira...you do not need to see this," Nathaniel said.

"Yes, I do."

The swirling smoke receded just as a door opened and a guard burst into the room. All of the cubs looked up as the guard shut the door and barricaded it.

Kira's insides twisted as the shouts on the other side grew louder.

"All of you, hide!" urged the guard, his face slick with sweat. *"Now!"*

Fear stabbed through Kira. The two pups she'd been watching were the first to move, scampering away to the far end of the room. The others merely blinked in confusion.

"Run!" Kira shrieked, running forward as if to shepherd them, but they did not see her. Her eyes welled with tears, her heart breaking

and the air too thick to breathe as she desperately tried to prevent what had already happened fifteen years ago.

A second later, the door crashed open.

A young, fourteen-year-old Nathaniel walked in, his build more gangly than it was now, his blue eyes carrying uncertainty as he surveyed the pups.

He was flanked by several adult vampires in black cloaks that hung open, revealing blood-red clothes. There was something unearthly about their appearance; their skin was grey, their hair dry and brittle, the shadows under their eyes purple like bruises. They stood straight-backed and eerily still, but when they did move, they were quick and precise.

"Made vampires," Nathaniel said with dismay. *"My father's creations."*

Kira stood in front of the pups, trying to shield them.

"What are you waiting for, Nathaniel?" leered one, his voice harsh and wicked. "Easy prey."

Kira tensed as she realised what that made vampire was asking. She snapped her head to look at the adult Nathaniel beside her, silently asking if he'd really killed the cubs himself.

His jaw muscles flexed visibly. *"No, I did not. Could not. But...I stood by and did nothing."*

Wide eyed, she returned her gaze to the young Nathaniel who had not moved.

The made vampire made a disapproving sound. "Your father will not be pleased," he remarked absently, scooping up a cub who was trying to get away. Without warning, he bit the pup, who yelped in pain, his shrill howls sending the other pups scattering.

"Enough," Kira whispered, panic filling her like wildfire as the made vampires advanced on the fleeing pups. *"I've seen enough. Please."*

Nathaniel squeezed her hand.

Blue smoke swept the scene away, but not before she saw the made vampire who'd spoken discard the drained pup at the young Nathaniel's feet.

"You can take credit for that one, if you wish," the made vampire mocked.

Young Nathaniel looked green as he stared at the lifeless pup.

The memory dissolved.

They were back in the pitch-black cave. Kira's heart was beating rapidly in her chest. Nathaniel pulled away, severing their connection. She wiped her teary face with her forearm.

"That was so much worse than I imagined it would be," she said with a shaky breath.

Nathaniel didn't respond straight away, sitting beside her without touching her. "I've been waiting a long time to tell you how sorry I am. I should have tried to stop them."

Kira gave a tearful laugh. "It didn't seem like you had much of a choice in that situation."

"There's always a choice. But...I fear the outcome would have been the same."

Kira slid her hand up his back. She could feel the striated scars through his shirt.

"Is this when your father did this to you?" she whispered.

"More or less. He punished me a week after the Revolution, once the high of his victory had worn off. The councillors were discussing my...inaction. My father summoned me to the council chambers, where they had a middle-aged wolf tied to a post. He was a surviving member of Bakker's Royal Guard. My father expected me to kill him. It was meant to be an opportunity for me to redeem myself."

"And did you?" she said in a hushed tone, stroking his back. "Kill the guard?"

Nathaniel swallowed hard. "Yes."

"And then?"

"And then my father whipped me."

Her fingers stilled on Nathaniel's back. "Why? You did what he asked—"

"He said that redemption does not save me from facing the consequences. And so..." His jaw clenched. "I don't remember how many lashes. I fell unconscious. When I awoke, I was on the floor, and the room was empty."

"Oh, Nathaniel."

"I've thought about killing him," he said quietly, his eyes unfocused. "But I cannot."

"Because he's your father?" Kira whispered.

Nathaniel gave a bitter chuckle. "Yes, but not in the way you might think. I cannot kill him without forfeiting my own life. Vampire families are tied together by an ancient magic that lives in our blood. If I killed my own father, I would be defying the sacred bond that binds us together as a family. I would be forever marked as a betrayer of my bloodline, and my soul would be tainted."

She tensed. "What does that mean, 'tainted'?"

"My body would become little more than an empty shell, doomed to walk the earth for endless days and nights without purpose. We sometimes call it a 'living death', because it's a fate worse than death. It is likely that I would not recognise you. Most who befall that fate do not even know themselves."

"That's...terrible."

So that's why he needs me to assassinate Henrikk. He cannot do it himself.

Nathaniel cleared his throat abruptly. "I have one more memory to show you. May I?"

"Does it involve biting me?"

"Oh yes. But it need not be your neck, and I will not drink your blood."

"So, I'll have bite marks everywhere? Great."

But Kira found Nathaniel's hand in the darkness and placed her hand in his. She braced herself for his bite as he lifted her hand to his mouth.

Sharp pain stung her wrist, his lips grazing her skin for the briefest of moments before drawing back. He kept hold of her hand, their fingers interlaced. As smoke appeared once more, transporting them back to Nathaniel's memory, Kira was disappointed that his lips did not stay on her wrist to drink.

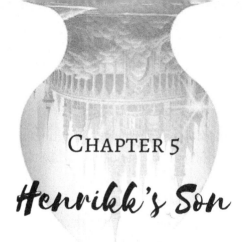

CHAPTER 5

Henrikk's Son

KIRA

THEY APPEARED AT THE far end of the children's long bedroom. They were far from the bloodshed, but the metallic smell assaulted Kira's senses, making the memory feel very real.

Nathaniel guided her so she faced away, but not before she'd glimpsed the far end of the room. The made vampires were gone. Small bodies lay around the room as if they'd been tossed aside carelessly. The floor was bathed in red.

Kira tore her eyes away from the heart-wrenching scene. A few feet away, the young Nathaniel was sitting in a shadowy corner. His knees were drawn up, his head bowed, and his hands scrunched his hair, mussing it up as if he were ready to tear it out.

"What is he...I mean, what were you doing?" she asked.

"Just watch," Nathaniel said.

A clinking sound made young Nathaniel look up. He wore a harrowed expression, it looked as if he'd been crying. Suddenly, his head whipped around as a brief scuffling sounded near him.

Wiping his eyes, he rose and crept silently to a dumb waiter on the back wall. He slid the door aside, revealing the source of the noise: two dark-furred pups curled up on a tray of plates and cutlery.

The adult Nathaniel beside her spoke. *"The two of you that got away."*

The pups startled when they saw the young vampire, and the fierce wolf leapt before the other and growled, sending a metal goblet clattering to the floor.

"Shh, it's all right," young Nathaniel said, his soft tone strikingly familiar. He extended his open hands to the pups. *"Let me help you."*

The shy one whined, her tail tucked beneath her. The fierce one stopped snarling, but remained wary as Nathaniel leant inside and craned his head to peer up the shaft.

"Do we go down, or up?" young Nathaniel murmured, before leaping up into the dumb waiter with the pups.

"We went down to the servants' quarters," Nathaniel explained. Blue smoke swirled around them as he skipped forward in his memory.

"Hey," Kira complained, batting at the smoke between her and Nathaniel. *"I wanted to see what happened."*

"It wasn't important," Nathaniel told her.

"Yes, it was! It was a chance to see you being nice for a change."

"Am I often not nice, Kira?"

"I think you pretend to be someone you're not."

"Don't we all?"

She shrugged a shoulder. He had a point. Wasn't that what she'd been doing from the moment she stepped foot in the academy? Trying to reinvent herself?

Except Nathaniel had gotten in her way.

Now, he was finally sharing his deeper secrets with her, like the fact that he was ashamed of his past. All this time, she'd condemned him for his involvement in the Revolution, never imagining how heavily it weighed on his heart.

"You've gone quiet," Nathaniel murmured.

The clouds still surrounded them—was he waiting for her answer before taking them to another memory?

"You are a mystery," she finally whispered. *"And I think I've been trying to figure you out from the first time I met you."*

"And?"

Kira didn't respond. She didn't have an answer, not yet, but seeing his younger self speak kindly to her childhood selves had made her heart yield a fraction.

Nathaniel took her silence as an answer and plunged them into the next memory. They appeared in the servants' quarters and saw multiple corridors with doors bearing nameplates.

"This is when I was trying to get you out," he explained, leading her down the hall.

"Trying?"

Nathaniel gave her a rueful smile. *"I got caught."*

Kira felt a jolt as Byron and Mary barrelled around the corner wearing guard uniforms. Byron's was decorated with gleaming badges that he'd never spoken of before. Mary's was bloody, one arm dangling limply by her side as if it were broken, her face contorted.

The couple skidded to a halt, staring at her with fury. Byron raised his sword, and for one bloodcurdling moment, Kira thought he would cleave her in two.

Except I'm not really here.

"Stop, please!" gasped a voice behind her.

Byron's sword halted mid-swing.

Spinning around, Kira noticed young Nathaniel standing just behind her, the two cubs bundled in his cloak.

"Please," young Nathaniel continued. *"I need your help."*

"Help?" Byron scowled.

Mary was eyeing the wriggling bundles in Nathaniel's grasp. *"What have you got there?"* she demanded.

The couple startled as Nathaniel fell to his knees in a show of deference. *"Help the pups, please. I beg you."*

For a vampire to beg was unheard of. To do so in the defence of another creature...

"*It's a trap,*" Mary warned.

Byron grunted in agreement. "*Lift your head, boy.*"

Gradually, Nathaniel lifted his head. His face was pale, his eyes an endless blue like a ship lost at sea.

"*It's Henrikk's son,*" whispered Mary.

Byron's expression grew hard. "*You look like your father, boy.*"

Shame crossed Nathaniel's features. "*I am. But please. The pups...*"

One puppy squirmed and tumbled out of his hold, landing on its back with a small yelp.

Byron's eyes widened as the dark-furred pup righted itself, its whip-like tails flaring out to help it regain balance.

"*Kirabelle,*" cried Mary, scooping the puppy up. "*Where are the others? They should be nine, they must not be separated—*"

"*The others are gone,*" Nathaniel grimaced.

Byron's face turned red. "*Gone?*" he breathed, the word low and deadly.

Nathaniel looked sick, his jaw quivering, but his voice was firm as he faced the large man. "*Dead.*"

Byron froze but Nathaniel pushed the second pup into his arms. "*You have to take them away to safety.*"

"*We cannot desert our post,*" Byron began, but Mary gripped his shoulder.

"*It's over, Byron. Wintermaw has fallen.*"

"*What about him?*" he replied, glaring at Nathaniel, who was still on his knees.

"*Do as you wish,*" Nathaniel said. "*Kill me. I deserve it. I killed a guard back there.*"

Byron's scowl deepened, but Mary tugged on his arm. "*Leave him. The princess is more important.*"

"*Princess?*" Kira asked in confusion.

Byron shot Nathaniel one last suspicious look before he and Mary morphed into dark-furred wolves. They scooped up the two pups by the scruffs of their neck and left via an adjoining courtyard, Mary limping after Byron as they ducked under hanging sheets and disappeared into the night.

The young Nathaniel remained on his knees, watching them go. He spoke softly to the night. *"Good luck, Kirabelle."*

CHAPTER 6

Confession

KIRA

THE MEMORY DISSOLVED.

The cave was silent, and Kira sat stunned for a few moments. Concentrating on her breathing, she contemplated what she'd seen, and all that Nathaniel had done.

There was an enormous amount of pressure on him to follow in Henrikk's footsteps. She was only now starting to appreciate the sacrifices he had made.

Kira twisted to face Nathaniel. Even with her night vision, she struggled to make out his features, but she could tell he was watching her, waiting for her response.

"You saved me," she breathed.

"I only saved two of you."

"I'm alive because of you."

"You're alive because you got away. Because you're strong, and you're a fighter. If you hadn't hidden..." He grunted, clearly exhausted. "As for me...I should have done more to stop the slaughter."

"It's not your fault. There was nothing you could do."

"I could have done something," Nathaniel stated, his voice full of anguish.

Kira thought of the other pups who had died; her seven wolf selves, as well as her half brothers and sisters with the tan coats.

"I never knew I was missing seven parts of me," she choked, placing a hand over her heart. "I never knew that I was deficient."

Nathaniel drew her close. "Listen to me. You are not deficient. The death of your other selves is a failure on my part, but make no mistake, you are no less whole for it. You are so much more than a wolf."

"I know," Kira hesitated, before admitting the question that had plagued her all these years. "But I don't know *what* I am."

"Don't you?" he asked softly, caressing her face. "Don't you remember our lesson?"

The memory of his so-called 'lesson' ruined the tenderness of the moment.

"A lesson where you were spanking me," she snapped, brushing his hand away.

"Is there any other kind?"

She was glad he could not see her blush. "I can't say I absorbed much of the reading material."

"Then let me enlighten you, dear Kira. *You* are royalty."

She sat up straighter. "I don't remember you telling me that."

"Not explicitly. But Wolf King Bakker was your father. A few years after his wife, Wolf Queen Hannah died, he took a new wife: the Vampire Queen, Liddia."

Her head was spinning.

"Are you saying Queen Liddia is my mother?"

No. She couldn't believe that. If her mother was a vampiress, then that would make her a...

She crossed her arms. "No. Fucking. Way. I'd rather kill myself."

She could practically hear Nathaniel's eyebrow lifting.

"Do not sound so disgusted."

"Trying very hard," she said through gritted teeth.

Mary and Byron had always told her she was special, destined to unite the wolves, but they'd failed to mention exactly what she was. She hadn't realised she was half-vampire, the enemy she'd grown up hating.

"And before you ask," Nathaniel continued, "Liddia was not my mother, so you and I are not related."

Kira tensed. "Good to know."

It hadn't even occurred to her to worry about that. Her mind immediately jumped to yesterday, when he'd taken her to the jewellery shop in the Capital. He'd discovered she'd taken the plug out and punished her...by fucking her ass. She'd even sucked his cock.

If he'd been her brother...

She groaned and covered her face.

Nathaniel was shaking with silent laughter—evidently hearing her thoughts through their mind link.

"It isn't funny," she growled, crossing her arms even as doubt crept in. "Are you *sure* we're not related?"

"Positive. My father was a nobleman, but there is no royal blood in his veins. He is the King simply by virtue of his conquest. But there is one more thing you should know..."

"He killed my mother," Kira said sullenly.

"Not just your mother, but the entire royal vampire line. My father was not satisfied with eliminating the royal wolf family. He wanted to dominate the world, and so he made himself the King." He paused. "Kira, there are no words that could ever be enough...but please know how sorry I am for what happened to your family. Your parents, your siblings, your wolf selves, the people living in the Keep...and every single person who is still suffering because of that night." His voice grew thick with emotion. "Words fail me. But I am so very sorry."

"You need to stop apologising for your father's crimes," Kira said. "The Revolution was—"

"It was not a Revolution," he said vehemently. "It was a massacre."

Kira fell silent, stunned by the passion and grief behind Nathaniel's words. He sounded as vulnerable as his fourteen-year-old self had.

"For what it's worth," he continued, "you should know that the history books are wrong about Wolf King Bakker. He did not abduct your mother. He truly was in love with Liddia, and she felt the same for him. She came to the Keep voluntarily, and their wedding was a much-celebrated occasion."

"They were in love," she murmured.

At least there was one thing Mary and Byron told me that checked out—even if they kept who my parents were from me. It made her feel a little more whole to know her parents had loved each other.

"Your father killed a lot of people to get to where he is," Kira noted.

"Yes. And then he rewrote the history books to justify it all."

"I'm glad you're not like that."

There was a long silence. And then...

"I hope not," Nathaniel said.

"You're not," she insisted, realising that she believed it. She changed the subject. "So...your father had a lot of supporters," Kira finally said. "Other vampires who wanted to see my family dead."

"Yes, that's correct. Some were vampires he had made himself with the witches' help. He had been amassing an army for some time, and he used that army to annihilate the very witches who had brought them into existence."

"Does he still have his armies?"

"Most of the made vampires perished that night, but my father was victorious, and he climbed their carcasses to ascend the throne."

"Why didn't Mary and Byron ever tell me any of this?"

They have a lot of explaining to do.

"They were forbidden from telling you until you came of age at eighteen. It was for your own protection, and theirs; children aren't the most reliable at keeping secrets. They feared you would confide in the wrong person and alert the authorities to your existence."

"But I'm nineteen now, and they still didn't tell me."

"Mary and Byron deviated from the plan. I was meant to take you away when you were eighteen to join the academy. Except when I arrived at the cottage, it was empty. They had whisked you away to safety in an attempt to change your mind."

"We travelled," Kira murmured as the memories came back. "Byron took us on an extended hunting expedition to see the countryside."

"Not far enough. I eventually found you, intent on bringing you to the academy. After all, Byron and Mary had agreed to the plan. But then I saw how happy you were, and I couldn't do it. Your happiness meant more to me than our plan, so I left. I thought, if you wanted to lead a normal life, then I would not interfere. You deserved it more than anyone."

"Byron kept trying to talk me out of going to the academy," she confessed. "He said there was no reason we couldn't lie low and live in the forest indefinitely."

"Now that I've met you, I doubt you would have been satisfied with living a life on the run."

"I suppose not," she agreed.

"There's something else you should know."

"Another secret?"

"A confession. Over the years, I've visited you a few times to check in on you. Barbara made a portal at my request—"

"So, you've been spying on me all these years?"

"At first, I wanted to ensure you were safe. That no vampires had discovered you. But after a while...I admit, I was curious. I couldn't stay away."

"So, spying."

"Yes."

She let out a low whistle. It was strange to think he'd been watching her while she'd gone about her simple life, unaware of his existence.

"This explains why your scent was so familiar when you came to the cottage."

"I tried to keep my distance. I wandered through the woods in the hope of seeing you. As time went by, I ventured closer to the cottage."

"Too shy to say hello?"

"I was in awe of you."

A shiver ran down her spine, and her voice grew soft. "Is that your confession?"

"Not quite. You need to know *how* it was that I was able to track you down. After the Revolution, I spent years trying to find you. And it was only possible because of your blood. That night, after Mary and Byron took you away from Wintermaw, I returned to where your other seven selves had been killed. Knowing it would help me locate you, I tasted your blood. Only a drop, but it connected me to you forever. I did it so I could find you, but even so...it felt wrong to do such a thing. Kirabelle, please forgive me."

Kira bit her cheek. She could almost taste the metal in her mouth. "Why track me down at all?"

"Because if the world is to have any hope of regaining balance between all of its creatures—vampires, wolves, witches, and humans—it needs a leader who is strong and pure of heart. You aren't just destined to unite the wolves, Kira. You're the one who can unite us all. Not only are you both vampire and wolf, but your birth was blessed by witches. You have magic in your veins, and thanks to Mary and Byron, you were raised amongst humans and have compassion for them. You're the daughter of all the world's creatures. Our key to restoring peace in the world."

Kira rubbed her face. It was a lot of information to take in.

Too much fucking information.

"And you knew all that, did you?" she asked. "Your fourteen-year-old self?"

"I was nineteen when I first found you. I'd had a lot of time to observe and learn, and too much time watching my father become the ruler I feared he would be. But I never stopped searching for you. By the time I found you, I had a plan in place. But I had help. You see, you were not the first person I saved, and the night of the Revolution was not the first time my father found cause to whip me."

Kira winced. "Your father should not have done that."

She couldn't deny that Henrikk was the true monster, corrupting everything he touched. But not his son. Now that Nathaniel had confided in her, she felt a mixture of relief and regret. Victoria had been right—Nathaniel was not like his father. "So, who did you save?"

"Barbara," Nathaniel said. "After my father finished ransacking the witch covens, I was sent after her to kill her. I had her cornered, but I hesitated, and she escaped. A few nights later...when I was lying in bed, recovering from my father's punishment..." He let out a long exhale.

Kira did not dare ask what the punishment had been.

"Barbara came and found me in secret," Nathaniel went on. "She claimed to be the last witch left in existence, and she had come to ask for my help."

"Do *not* tell me Barbara fucking orchestrated the plan to overthrow Henrikk," Kira growled. She would be furious if that woman—nice as she was—with a head stuffed with wool, had been responsible for the course her life had taken.

"No, it was not Barbara's idea. But she shared knowledge with me over the years, which later inspired me to find a way to set the world right. And you were crucial to that plan. Even though a part of me wanted to let you live your life in peace."

"I wish I'd known all this sooner," Kira said sadly.

"If Byron and Mary hadn't taken you away when you turned eighteen, we would have had more time to prepare. I had hoped to tell you everything. As it is, my thirtieth birthday approaches, and on that same day, my wedding to Gloria."

"Still going to marry her, huh?" She pulled away from Nathaniel and began twisting the fabric of her sleeves.

He rested a hand on hers to steady them. "I'm going to do whatever it takes to support you, Kira. Even the unpleasant things."

"Marrying Gloria is an 'unpleasant thing'?"

"Well...just wait until you meet her."

I don't want to meet her, she thought to herself.

Nathaniel coaxed her hand open, and she didn't resist as his fingers interlaced with hers.

"If I could change the past, I would. But I can't even change the present without your help. So here I am, Princess, kneeling before you. In awe of you. Asking for your help as I strive to be more than what I was."

"Are you actually kneeling?" she asked dryly.

"It was a figure of speech," he chuckled.

She heard him shift his position in the dark so he was in front of her, presumably on his knees, his hand still holding hers.

"Better?" he asked.

"Yes. You were saying?"

"Only you can unite every faction without bloodshed," he continued. "And should you have children one day, your magic will pass to them. You are the witches' only hope of not dying out completely."

"I don't feel like I have any magic," Kira admitted.

"Not yet. But you will. You need only to drink a vampire's blood to awaken your powers."

A strange tremor ran through her, heating her core, and causing her shoulders to tingle. Surprisingly, the thought of drinking Nathaniel's blood was not the worst thing in the world. And the fact that he would want to share it with her felt intimate in a way she couldn't describe.

It was almost...appealing.

She shook her head quickly. "Gross. No thank you."

"It's natural and normal for you to drink the blood of a vampire."

Kira sniffed. "Says who?"

"Says Barbara."

Fucking Barbara.

"According to her, drinking the blood of a vampire will allow you to replenish your magic. The only question is, will you help us?"

"You're giving me a choice?"

"There is nothing I wouldn't give you, Kira. Including helping you discover your magic. All you need is vampire blood. Later, when I feel more recovered, I will happily offer you mine."

More heat pooled inside her at his words, this time accompanied by a longing ache. She wanted that closeness with Nathaniel, but was scared of what that would mean. She sensed he was inviting her to venture into unknown territory, and she wasn't sure she trusted him enough to take that leap.

Which was why, instead of saying 'yes', she made a sound of disgust. "I'm really not sure that this supposed magic I have is worth me drinking blood."

Nathaniel's laugh rasped in her ear. "Oh, trust me, pet, the mere taste of my blood will be worth it."

CHAPTER 7

Truth and Love

KIRA

AFTER SITTING IN THE dark for so long, the daylight blinded Kira as she left the cave with Nathaniel. Mary and Byron were sitting by the campfire, but they scrambled to their feet and rushed over to her. Mary looked as if she'd been crying, her face blotchy and as red as her fiery hair. Byron's appearance reminded Kira of a sad, oversized puppy, his eyes searching hers pleadingly as his strong muscled frame hunched with shame.

As the couple drew near, Kira took a step back out of their reach, and they halted in their tracks.

"Kira..." Mary shook her head in dismay, causing droplets of tears to fall. "Sweetheart, I'm so sorry..."

Kira hugged herself as she faced her foster parents. The former guards had never been good at expressing their feelings, so to see them break down was alarming. But their remorse was etched clear as day onto their faces, and through the pain of their betrayal, Kira was certain that they loved her.

Their unwavering love had been expressed over the years more with deeds than with words, their dedication evident in the time they took to teach her lessons, and their constant patience.

I was the centre of their world, she realised, glancing at Nathaniel.

His expression was pained, but his eyes softened as he leant close and whispered, "It's all my fault, not theirs. Take it easy on them."

Kira suppressed a scoff.

Not a chance.

"Byron," Kira barked, causing the large man to startle. "We need to talk."

Without waiting for his response, she morphed into her two wolf forms and darted down the rocky terrain into the woods below. She heard him following.

She sped up, relishing the feel of the air rippling through her fur and the soft earth beneath her paws. It was refreshing, but it was not a reprieve from the dilemma that pressed on her.

Nathaniel had given her a choice. "If you choose to walk away, I promise I will leave you alone forever."

It was the last thing he'd said to her before they left the cave.

"After you went to so much trouble to claim me? Why?"

"Because I love you."

His earnest words had struck her deep, causing her heart to thrum. She hadn't known how to respond, so she'd turned and walked outside in silence. Now, his words hounded her as she ran through the forest, the dense undergrowth whipping at her face as she played the words over and over in her mind.

Because I love you.

His words drifted back. "I could think of nothing else as I lay awake that night in Wintermaw Keep. I was surrounded by death and destruction, in a room that had once belonged to someone else. I lay there, the son of a celebrated murderer, completely out of my mind, wondering if you made it out alive. Your bravery had already captured my heart."

Chills had swept through her, but Nathaniel had continued, the rumble of his voice causing her to shake. "Kira, I have loved you ever since I found you in that dumbwaiter, and every moment after that. I have loved you from afar, and I fell even harder when you bit my hand. And when you tried to end my life in my office, I thought it really *would* end if I could not have you."

Kira felt a heartsick longing, but she did not trust the feeling. Those words could not—*should not*—make her happy, not when they came from him.

Especially not in light of what he'd said after his confession of love: that he loved her enough to help her rise to be the leader of the wolves, beginning with the Poplarin Pack. His expression had turned pained as he confirmed that her intact virginity would be enough to secure a new initiation ceremony.

Which meant he would support the pack's requirement that she submit to their alphas. It was back to square one, but the cost seemed higher this time. She did not want to inflict pain upon Nathaniel, not really, but he insisted they were running out of time, and that the initiation was the fastest way to propel her through the ranks.

She picked up speed, her muscled limbs sweeping across the ground with a new surge of frenzied energy. She needed to think, and not about his declaration of love, but about the plan.

Nathaniel wanted her help, and she'd promised to give him her answer by evening. But it was already late afternoon by the time they'd left the cave. Time was running out. Her entire future hung in the balance.

The world's future hangs in the balance.

She felt a pang of guilt.

If she ran away, who would help change things? How would the lives of any of the wolves improve?

Nathaniel. He won't give up on them.

The realisation filled her lungs with fresh air, and she couldn't help the admiration she felt for him. Hope seeped into her with each fresh breath she took. No matter what she decided, he would keep fighting. But could he succeed without her?

And what if he failed? An uncomfortable thought stabbed at her. *What if he dies?*

Kira came to a stop at the cottage, morphing back to human form. She clutched at the fence post, breathing hard as Byron caught up to her.

She didn't wait for him to finish transforming before speaking. "You said you found me in the servants' wing. But you failed to mention Nathaniel."

Byron twisted his hands. "He asked us not to, so you could live as normal a life as possible...and so you wouldn't seek him out."

"You should have told me."

Byron bowed his head, and after a long moment, Kira took the spare key from the window ledge and entered the old cottage.

It was obvious Mary and Byron had not been back. There were small cobwebs on the usually immaculate windows, and the dining table was covered in a thin coat of dust. Her favourite cup, from which she'd been drinking tea the night Nathaniel abducted her, was sitting by the sink on the drying rack. The realisation that he'd taken the time to wash it that night was both sweet and disturbing, and she couldn't help but smile as she stepped deeper into the cottage.

She'd only taken a few steps when she stopped dead in her tracks. The familiar sights and smells made her chest grow tight as the memories of her childhood returned. The kitchen where Mary had taught her to cook. The forest mural they'd painted on the once-white wall.

Bittersweet melancholy assaulted her senses.

This was meant to be a simple errand to retrieve her locket, the one she'd hidden in her desk, as well as her chance to berate Byron for letting her down. But standing in her childhood home reminded her of all the good times.

Like the way Mary's jokes would always make them laugh, filling the cottage with joy. The time Kira had discovered Byron's secret stash of honey—mostly because the ants had found it first—and the berating Mary had given him for his sweet tooth. Her gaze lingered on the empty space the couple's bed had occupied. They'd let her sleep there until she was old enough to be in a room by herself.

Until I was old enough to realise that they were not my biological parents.

Tears pricked her eyes as she tried to reconcile the foster parents who had raised her with what she knew about them now.

"Are you all right, Kira?" Byron asked softly.

She didn't answer immediately, trying to push down the emotions that were threatening to make her cry. Without looking at him, she asked, "Did you ever love me?"

His thick moustache drooped as he regarded her with mournful eyes. "Oh, Kira...of course I did. Mary and I, we loved you like our own child."

"And yet you kept the truth from me. Why didn't you tell me who my parents were? And who I really was?"

"You had already suffered so much, and we wanted to shield you from more pain. A part of me hoped you would grow up to lead a normal life." Byron sighed and rubbed the back of his neck. "And we feared revealing your royal lineage could make you a target for Henrikk and his followers. Keeping your true identity a secret gave you an extra layer of protection."

Kira crossed her arms. "I could have kept a secret. Which means...there's something you're not telling me."

Byron bowed his head. "Nathaniel feared that if you knew what Henrikk did to your family, that you would act impulsively and put yourself in danger."

"Would not," she protested, even as hot fury shot through her veins. She wanted nothing more than to tear Henrikk limb from limb...but that was a reasonable thought to have, right? "I am *not* impulsive."

Byron's serious expression shifted slightly, as if he were suppressing a smile.

"I'm not," she grumbled. "Besides, it sure would've been nice to have my magical abilities sooner."

Whatever those abilities are.

"Nathaniel insisted that you be properly trained and prepared first."

"So, it was all about controlling me." It was typical of Nathaniel, but while he may have been at the head of everything, she wasn't about to let Byron off the hook so easily. "You let Nathaniel drag me to the academy. You knew what he would do."

"I tried to talk you out of it. But your mind was set. And Nathaniel is a good man, and a good vampire."

Kira scoffed. *Good vampire* was an oxymoron if she'd ever heard one. Her mind flashed with the memory of the gag and collar Nathaniel had made her wear when he'd arrived at the cottage.

"You could have warned me about what Nathaniel would do."

"Actually...I warned *him* of what you could do to *him*. I understand you bit his hand."

Kira hesitated. She *had* bitten him. Was that the real reason Nathaniel had gagged her when he'd come to the cottage?

He said he'd gagged me for his own safety, but I didn't believe him.

She had no doubt he'd taken pleasure in putting the gag and collar on her, but the realisation that she'd forced his hand by biting him made her reconsider her first meeting with him.

Was it possible that he might never have laid a finger on her if she hadn't fought him?

Whatever.

But try as she might, it was further proof that he might not be the tyrant she'd first thought him to be. She'd already figured out that he wasn't as cruel as he'd led everyone to believe. It was only a ruse to satisfy what his father expected of him, but now, she was finally able to reconcile the two different sides of Nathaniel she'd gotten to know. The one who relished dominating her, and the one who respected her autonomy.

Both of them wanted her to be happy.

Both of them were assholes.

"I'll be out in the garden if you need anything," Byron told her, retreating.

Kira went to her room and shut the door, letting out a long, deep breath as she sank onto the familiar bed.

You have such a nasty bite, Nathaniel had said, his words ringing in her mind like a compliment.

She laughed under her breath. It hadn't occurred to her until now that *she* had been the one to bite him first.

Except I didn't draw blood.

Which meant she still had the higher moral ground.

Sort of.

As for everything else...her hand drifted down to caress her inner thigh. She recalled the time she'd tried to seduce him by going down on him. She'd intended only to distract him for long enough to stab him, but he'd been one step ahead of her. He'd stolen her knife, and she'd ended up sucking his cock until he came in her mouth. And then he'd pleasured her. And he'd pleasured her many times since.

Kira clicked her tongue in frustration. She was getting turned on despite herself. After making sure her door was locked, she scooted back onto the bed so her back rested against the wall. The curtains were already closed, and in the safety of the semi-dark room, she slipped her fingers beneath her waistband. She was already wet, and she let out a soft murmur as she touched herself, remembering the way Nathaniel's tongue had devoured her.

That was nothing compared to everything else she'd experienced with him. The steel plugs he'd made her wear...the water bowl he'd made her drink out of...the lesson he'd given her bent over his desk, his hand delivering sharp spanks as she read aloud at his insistence...forcing her to crawl on a leash...the heady feeling when he'd allowed her off of her leash so she could fetch for him...and, most notably, the rough way he'd fucked her ass in the jewellery shop, as if he were an alpha rutting her.

As if he were claiming her in the most wolfish, animalistic way possible.

Sex with him was degrading, rapturous, and unlike anything else she'd ever experienced, or would likely ever experience again. Turning on her side and nestling into the pillow comfortably, she let herself slip into a fantasy, her hand pumping slowly as she played with herself. Soon, she was pressing her face deeper into the pillow to muffle her moans, wishing it Nathaniel's firm hand clamped over her mouth, or his cock down her throat moving in and out as he took his pleasure from her.

Fuck.

She wanted to relive those moments, and it forced her to be honest with herself about everything that had happened between them. She'd wanted him to do those things. It had been her choice, and that revelation turned everything she'd ever thought about him on its head.

Except for him claiming me.

That thought came as a small, self-righteous victory.

Nathaniel made the first move, not me. He was the one who started whatever this is between us.

But rather than be annoyed at that, a part of her felt glad, because it felt good to be wanted, and it felt good to be wanted by *him*.

Her fingers moved in and out, trying to reproduce what Nathaniel had made her feel, but it wasn't the same as if he'd been here, his cock sliding into her. She let out another soft moan. He'd pushed the head of his cock into her, but never enough to break her hymen, and as she fingered and stroked herself, she found herself wishing he was here right now.

Her skin tingled at the hope that he would knock on her door right now. That he would enter her room, press her down on the bed, and sheathe himself inside her.

She wanted to feel the safety of his strong arms and the delicious bliss of relinquishing control as he ploughed into her. She wanted him to take her virginity, and if he'd been with her right now, she would have kissed him.

Because, as it turned out, she'd been both right and wrong about Nathaniel in the best way. He was dark, and twisted, and dominating. And, while he hid it well, he was also kind-hearted and respectable, and she *wanted* that in her life.

All of him.

Her insides ached as her fingers sped up, and her longing surged as she approached climax.

She was so close.

Sudden realisation doused her desire like frigid water poured over her head, and she sat up, her insides throbbing in protest as she removed her hand.

"Holy shit," she breathed to the empty room. "I fucking love him."

CHAPTER 8
The Locket

KIRA

KIRA RETRIEVED THE LOCKET from the secret compartment in her desk. It was circular in shape and made of gold, with tiny rubies fanning across the surface like nine gleaming tendrils.

Like nine tails.

It hung on a gold chain, hinting at a past she couldn't remember. The locket had an extra gold clasp whose function Kira had never been able to figure out...until now.

She reached up to trace the centre of her ruby collar. She'd forgotten all about the collar. Despite its tightness, it was not uncomfortable. The opposite—it was comforting.

Taking a deep breath, she went outside to where Byron was waiting for her, weeding his abandoned garden.

"Did you find it, Kira?" he asked, tossing the weeds aside and straightening.

She held up the locket, so it flashed in the sunlight. Opening her mouth to speak, she froze. Something new had caught her attention on the locket's surface. Each wave of red rubies was bordered by black, but it was only now that she realised what the borders were: thin rows of black onyx gems.

Black, the colour of wolves. Red, the colour of vampires. And inside the locket, as she already knew, was a tiny clump of dry herbs that smelt like brimstone and magic.

Byron and Mary had given her the locket on her ninth birthday, stating that she was old enough to have it. But now that she thought about it, they'd claimed that the locket had been enchanted to protect her.

If that was the case, why hadn't they given it to her when she was younger?

She frowned. Something didn't add up, and she suspected the locket had only come into her foster parents' possession when she was nine.

It wasn't hard to guess who might have given it to them. Nathaniel was ten years older than her, and he'd said he was nineteen years old when he finally located her years after the Revolution. It couldn't just be a coincidence.

"My parents didn't give you this locket, did they?" she asked.

Byron shook his head. "Not exactly. We didn't have a chance to salvage anything from Wintermaw the night we rescued you. Mary and I left with you; we never went back..."

He trailed off, but his answer had all but confirmed her suspicion.

"Nathaniel went back for it, didn't he?"

Byron nodded. "That locket is one of the last remaining heirlooms of Wintermaw Keep. It was made especially for you, the daughter of Queen Liddia and King Bakker. Henrikk destroyed everything he could during the takeover."

"Why did Nathaniel risk his father's wrath to bring me this?" she whispered.

"Because he wanted you to know that you come from a great line of wolves. That no matter what the future brings, you are the daughter of a king and queen of two great creatures—nine tails wolves, and vampires."

Kira shut her eyes for a moment, recalling her ninth birthday. That locket had triggered a thousand questions that she'd badgered Mary and Byron with over the subsequent years, but it had also solidified something in her—a sense of belonging to something greater.

Removing the gold chain, she used the ruby collar's clasp to attach the locket. It hung like a pendant. The collar had clearly been designed with the locket in mind, because the pattern of rubies and onyxes flowed together seamlessly.

"I wish I'd known all of this a lot sooner. But," she added, holding up her hand when Byron went to speak, "I suppose I was only a child."

"We debated when to tell you about the plan. Nathaniel intended to tell you everything on your eighteenth birthday when he came for you. But I got cold feet. I wanted you to have a choice."

"And we went into hiding for a year."

"That's right. By the time Nathaniel realised you were back at the cottage, it left him very little time to prepare you. I spoke to him when he arrived in Nordokk the evening he took you to the academy. He had decided not to reveal the plan to you after all. He feared that with no time for you to process things, you would not agree to help."

"He was fucking right about that," Kira muttered.

A pained expression crossed Byron's face. "Mary and I love you with all our hearts," he said, his voice thick with emotion. "How could we not? You're Princess Kirabelle. Everyone adored you. But to us...you were the only daughter we ever had. Our little Kira."

"Byron..."

"Let me finish, please. While I still have the words." He cleared his throat. "I need you to know that your parents loved you too. Very much. I should have told you more often. Just like I should have told you the truth sooner. Mary and I argued about it all the time. I can see we left it too late. Please, forgive me."

"I forgive you," she whispered, his honesty prompting her to reveal a truth she'd buried deep. "And I think we both know I would have chosen this path no matter what."

Byron shook his head. "Like a fool, I hoped to talk you out of your plan for revenge." He glanced at her warily. "It is not too late, Kira. The choice is yours. It is not an easy path, and I fear it may not end well."

When she didn't speak, he sighed. "But like any father who loves his child—one who is no longer a child—I will accept your decision. Nothing would have made me happier than to see you leave all this behind. We have often spoken of justice. But revenge is not the same thing, Kira. It can eat at the soul and continue this cycle of destruction we've all been pulled into. If you choose to go on with the plan, remember that."

"I will."

The corners of his eyes crinkled with a smile. "Nothing has made me prouder than seeing you grow up to become the fearless leader you were born to be."

A tear ran down her cheek before she even realised she was crying. "Don't cry, little princess." Byron's rough thumb scraped the tear from her cheek, his own eyes glistening.

Little princess. The name he used to call her when she was young. She'd never realised he'd meant it literally.

"I don't feel fearless," she whispered. "I don't know if I can do this."

His large hand closed over hers and she squeezed it.

"And yet, you are so close. The journey up the mountain is always the most difficult near the top, but keep pushing, Kira. For once you reach the top, the water is so sweet, the air so fresh, that you will never want to leave. That is where you belong. Do not forget that."

"I won't," she said, smiling weakly as she wiped her eyes. Fiddling with the locket at her neck, she searched for a change in topic. "So, err...what about the herbs inside this?"

"Ah. Well..."

Byron rubbed his moustache and mumbled something intelligible.

"Speak up, I can't hear you," she said..

"The magic herbs were intended to soothe your emotions. Nathaniel wanted you to have a source of comfort and stability throughout your life—"

"So, you're telling me the locket regulates my emotions?" Kira interrupted.

"Yes."

"Well...they clearly don't fucking work," she snapped, fuming as she marched towards the woods and morphing midstride.

How dare he!

But she wasn't half as angry as she had been earlier. There were many more important things to consider. The sun was travelling low, and she was ready to tell Nathaniel what her decision was. But first, she was going to give him a piece of her mind.

Byron loped after her.

When Kira arrived back at the campsite, Nathaniel was not alone. Two female wolves sat beside him, one in human form, one in wolf form, both of them gazing at him with admiration as he laughed at Mary's joke.

Jealousy blossomed in Kira's chest, and she stopped at the edge of the campsite, paralysed as she watched Nathaniel help Mary drain the stock from a large black pot.

"See? This is why we've missed you, Nathaniel," the female wolf in human form said, giving a soft melodic laugh that made Kira's insides curdle.

The wolf's laughter died when she caught sight of Kira staring daggers at her.

Nathaniel looked up and met her gaze as he tilted the heavy pot back into place. "Kira, you're back."

He made it sound like he'd been waiting for her all this time. It tempered her jealousy, but only slightly.

She swallowed the lump in her throat. "Yes. I'm back."

Nathaniel approached, and the way he looked at her made her momentarily forget about the female wolves. As he drew close, her gaze darted to his lips. For a second, she thought he was going to kiss her.

Hesitating for a fraction of a second, Nathaniel placed his hand on her back.

"I'm glad you're back," he said in an undertone, guiding her towards the campfire. "Come meet the others. I think you'll get along well."

I sincerely doubt it.

The wolf in human form shuffled over on the log she was sitting on to make room for her and Nathaniel.

As they sat, Kira drew a sharp breath. The wolf had a tan-coloured coat with the faintest spattering of light spots. Kira couldn't see her tails, but she was certain she was of the nine tails bloodline.

Which means we're related.

Meeting another family member of hers should have been a joyous moment, but then the wolf stretched and moved closer to the fire, and Kira caught sight of the wolf's tails—or lack of.

They were missing, with only a small stub at the base, as if someone had...

Her fists curled as grief and anger roared to life.

Who the hell would dock a nine tails?

"Kira," Nathaniel began, "Allow me to introduce Haley and Ana. They have sacrificed much for our cause."

Including their tails, she realised.

She'd already discovered for herself that Henrikk's scarf of eighteen tails was real, from which she'd wrongly concluded that Nathaniel truly had killed Haley and Ana. Except that clearly wasn't the case. The two female wolves were alive in the flesh, minus their beautiful tails.

"Hello," Kira greeted stiffly, eyeing the way Haley—the one in wolf form—ambled over to Nathaniel and licked the back of his hand before returning to her spot.

Mary and Byron chattered away with Haley and Ana, leaving Kira to ruminate in her thoughts with Nathaniel sitting quietly beside her.

She chewed the inside of her cheek as she remembered back to what Susie had said about the female wolves: that they were students of the academy, and had become involved sexually with Nathaniel in the days leading up to their disappearance. It was hard not to ignore the sharp stab of jealousy twisting round and round in her gut, the feeling growing sharper with every assault of Ana's melodic laughter.

She jumped when Nathaniel placed a hand on her knee and leant close. "They were students at the academy."

"Yes, I know." She cleared her throat and swivelled to face Nathaniel head on. *May as well get it off my chest.* "I heard you were quite...*close* to them."

"Ah. Well...appearances can be deceiving."

"Susie said they were your pets. That you had intercourse with them."

Nathaniel raised an eyebrow. *"Intercourse?"*

"Susie's choice of word, not mine," she muttered.

Nathaniel shifted closer, his other hand cupping her face. "I did not have an intimate relationship with Haley or Ana. Or any other wolf or vampire in recent years." He paused, and Kira felt the tension in her chest ease as the words sank in. "It is true that I treated them as pets, and that I had them sleep in my room. But it was a ruse to protect them. When I first discovered their links to the royal family, I approached them with the intention of counselling them to keep a low profile. However, another student grew suspicious of why they never shifted publicly and reported them to the authorities. Fortunately, I found out before my father's men did and helped them disappear."

"But there was a cost," Kira murmured.

"Indeed. I want you to know that they both gave their tails freely so I could present them to my father as proof that I had killed them. It allowed them to flee without being hunted, and it solidified my position at court. It was what led to my father agreeing to crown me king when I turned thirty. He has long wished to abdicate and focus his attention on raising new armies and...other pursuits. My father was built for war, not for sitting on a throne."

"But not you."

"No. I detest war."

"A vegetarian *and* a pacifist," she said under her breath.

"What was that?"

"Nothing," Kira smiled, knowing that he'd heard her just fine. She fell silent, trying to find the words to describe what she felt for him right now. Surprise? Relief? Gratitude? All her misconceptions had come tumbling down, the last of her reservations answered as she stared wide eyed at the two female wolves.

"I had Barbara make their tails into a scarf to satisfy my father's vanity," Nathaniel added. "I hope you do not think less of me for it."

Kira blinked. "No. Not at all."

She couldn't imagine giving up her tails and could only imagine what a harrowing experience it must have been for them all—Haley, Ana, and even Nathaniel. She had a strong feeling that he had been the one to remove their tails.

As the others talked amongst themselves, Kira gave Nathaniel a sidelong look, studying him.

He caught her looking. "What is it?"

She gave her head a small shake and smiled as her fingers brushed the locket. "Nothing. It's just that I'm running out of things to not like about you."

CHAPTER 9

Blood

NATHANIEL

NATHANIEL AND KIRA WITHDREW from the campsite as night began to fall. He led her to a nearby grassy outcrop overlooking the small village of Nordokk. They sat side by side, his arm around her waist as they watched the last of the sun melt into the distant hills in pools of golden light.

"I've made a decision," Kira announced as twilight settled in, and the first stars appeared.

"Hmm?" He pressed a kiss against her hair, unsure if she welcomed the gesture. "And what is your decision?"

"I'll help you."

"Help?" he asked gently. "But I don't want you to *help*. I want you to lead. 'Help' is why you have us."

"Mary and Byron, maybe. And Haley and Ana. But you'll be the King."

"At first, yes. But Kira, I do not intend to be on equal footing with you. You will not be a queen. You will be so much more than that. Once we succeed, there will be no need for kings and queens. There will only be you."

Kira frowned. "That sounds lonely."

"It's always lonely at the top."

"The nights are the loneliest," she said, wringing her hands.

Did she regret her words?

He placed his hand on hers to steady them. "Yes, they are."

But they don't have to be, he wanted to say.

Kira cleared her throat. "So, what will happen after we succeed? I mean...that is, will you stay at Wintermaw? I know you'll be married, but..."

He didn't dare presume what she meant, but he had a strong inkling. "In the evenings, in your private bedchamber, you may be whoever you wish to be, with whomever you wish." He meant to end the sentence there, but then thought better of it. He would lay all his cards down, come whatever may. "If you were in need of company...I would be happy to oblige."

"Good," she said with a hint of mischief gleaming in her eyes. "Oblige me now."

He blinked. "Oh? And how may I be of service?"

Kira turned so she was facing him, her lips inches from his. "You offered me your blood earlier."

He ran his fingers through her hair. "Not only my blood. I'm offering you the whole world."

"The world can wait," she said, holding his gaze. "Tonight, I only want you."

Nathaniel leant in and kissed her, his lips barely brushing hers. They were soft and perfect. "Tonight, tomorrow, forever—that is when I want you, Kira."

Their kiss deepened, their eyes hooded and breaths mingling as they savoured the moment, with all of its promise and uncertainty hanging in the air between them.

When they eventually drew apart, Kira's eyes searched his, and the way she wetted her full lips made him want to go in for a second kiss.

Instead, he drew his hand to his mouth and pierced his wrist with his fangs. Hot blood trickled down his arm, and he held it out for Kira to drink.

She looked apprehensive as she bent her head. Her lips were warm on his wrist. Her expression soon turned pensive as she lapped up his blood, her slender hands tightening on his arm. She let out a soft moan, and he had to subtly adjust himself as his cock hardened at the sound.

He'd had the same reaction when drinking her blood—full mast before he'd even drawn blood—but he'd never known that giving blood could elicit the same reaction.

No one had ever made him feel the way she did.

His body grew warm and his senses hazy, and he smiled as Kira's mind met his in a gentle, hopeful caress. No sooner had he opened his thoughts to her than her hunger and longing surged in, sweeping him away until his head was reeling.

"You taste so good," she said with relish, shifting so she straddled him, her breasts pressed against his chest, the tips of her erect nipples grazing him through their clothes.

He groaned when she rocked her hips against him.

"You are trouble," he croaked, pulling his wrist away from her lips. *"Enough."*

"Already?" she said, sounding disappointed.

"That is all the blood you need, for now. And I am not yet fully recovered."

"Oh. Shit, have I taken too much?"

"No. But I don't have a lot to give right now."

Kira nodded, licking the last trace of his blood from her lips. *"Don't break the connection,"* she pleaded.

Nathaniel tightened his hold on her waist. *"I wouldn't dream of it."* He kissed her, and as her mouth opened, his tongue found hers, the delicate sensation as thrilling as a seductive dance. He grabbed her hips and pulled her close so she would feel his erection.

"I take it you forgive me?" he asked.

"Yes. But I think you could sweeten the deal."

"I can do that."

"How?"

"By treating you the way you deserve."

Chapter 10

The Restaurant

KIRA

THE TASTE OF NATHANIEL'S blood was tantalising. It coated her tongue and mouth, making her fantasise about tasting more of him. She wanted to taste his lips, and she wanted to run her tongue over every inch of him. Her insides burnt for him, and Nathaniel stoked that fire with every soft word, every kiss, every touch, until her entire body was charged with anticipation for what was to come.

It was all so innocent—until it wasn't.

Her veins pulsed with his words—*By treating you the way you deserve.*

"And what is it I deserve?" she asked coyly.

"I have something in mind," he said, running his finger along the angle of her jaw. *"Let me show you."*

Kira knew they were entering another of Nathaniel's memories as blue smoke swirled around them. When it cleared, it was the same starry sky, but she was standing with Nathaniel on a restaurant balcony overlooking a lamplit street. Patrons talked quietly at nearby tables. Nathaniel was wearing the formal attire of a nobleman, whilst she was wearing a red dress with matching heels.

"You look stunning," he said, kissing her hand.

"*Is this another memory?*"

"*Why, no. It's a date.*" He led her to a candlelit table with two unoccupied chairs.

"*A date...?*"

Her lip twitched as she caught sight of his coat tails. Before she could stop herself, she said, "*You look like a penguin.*"

"*Is that so?*" Nathaniel smiled.

Kira cursed herself for the outburst. Truthfully, he looked dashing in the tailored coat, which had an ornate lapel, sharp padded shoulders, and a dark green capelet. He had pinstripe trousers and polished maroon shoes on. His blond hair was combed back sleekly, and the combined effect made her weak at the knees.

"*Is this a memory of yours?*" she asked.

"*No. It's a dream. Is it to your liking?*"

"*Yes,*" she smiled as he pulled out a chair.

Apparently, they could interact with objects in a dream, unlike the memory of the Revolution.

"*Thank you,*" she mumbled, treading carefully in the tall shoes as she took her place.

The atmosphere was pleasant and romantic. Fresh roses adorned the table, and the candlelight softened Nathaniel's features and caused his brilliant blue eyes to sparkle. At any other time, Kira would have loved nothing more than to relax and soak in the evening's ambience with him.

But not tonight.

She struggled to mask her disappointment as Nathaniel passed her the menu. When he'd promised to treat her the way she 'deserved', she'd imagined something entirely different. She had been hinting at...something else.

"*What's wrong?*" Nathaniel asked, watching her with concern.

"*Nothing,*" she smiled, pressing her thighs together to try and quell the throbbing ache there. She could hardly focus on the menu, and when the waiter arrived, she chose the first item on it—Spaghetti Bolognese—before realising that was the only thing on the menu, listed repeatedly.

She glanced at Nathaniel. *"Not a whole lot of variety."*

He shrugged. *"Spaghetti is my favourite. Feel free to order anything you like. It is a dream, after all. You can shape it how you wish."*

Kira handed the menu to the waiter. *"Two spaghettis please."*

"And a bottle of wine," Nathaniel added.

"Certainly," replied the waiter, retreating.

"A bottle of wine?" Kira asked. *"That's not very specific. You didn't even specify a red or a white."*

She'd only ever eaten out at the local pub in Nordokk with Byron and Mary, but even the pub had stocked more than one variety.

Nathaniel laughed. *"It doesn't matter. We can change the details of the dream. So, mine will taste of rum. What do you fancy?"*

"Maybe an iced tea," she said distractedly, tugging her red dress down when what she really wanted was for Nathaniel to walk around the table and strip it off her. No sooner had she thought this than she glanced up at Nathaniel, worried he'd read her mind.

His pupils dilated, and the corner of his lips curved, but he didn't say anything.

Clearing her throat, Kira asked, *"Since this is all in our heads, do you think we'll be able to taste the food?"*

"I don't know, this is new for me, too. I've never been on a dream date before."

"Are you saying I'm your dream date?" she asked modestly, biting her lip.

"Absolutely."

"Well, anyway, it feels pretty real so far." She leant back in her chair, the polished wood cool on her skin where her low-cut dress exposed her back. Trying to be subtle, she rubbed her thighs together to alleviate the hot ache pulsing between her legs.

The food arrived, and it was delicious. The tomato sauce was rich, and the pasta soft and buttery. The wine transformed as she poured it, and it tasted like lime and ginger tea.

"How is your drink, pet?"

"Hang on, I'm not finished," she said.

Shaved ice and a paper umbrella appeared in her glass, followed by a slice of lemon, a wedge of pineapple, a frothy tower of whipped cream, and a dollop of chocolate mousse with wafers sticking out of it.

"Finished?" Nathaniel asked, amused.

"Not yet."

A cherry appeared on top in a shower of colourful sprinkles.

"Don't be greedy, pet," Nathaniel smirked. He canted his head to watch the leaning tower of toppings swaying on her glass.

"This is all essential to the mission," she said.

"I can see that."

The crazy concoction was a good distraction, but she wasn't truly hungry. Not for food, anyway. She had an idea, and spent the next few minutes trying to summon the courage to bring it up in conversation.

Nathaniel patted his face with a napkin. *"I can't help but notice the cheeky smile on your face, pet. What are you thinking of?"*

Kira tried to hold his gaze, but she couldn't do it. His eyes glittered in the flickering candlelight and her heart was beating too fast. She looked down at her plate, took a deep breath and said, *"I'm just wondering if everything else feels as real as the food."*

She twisted her fork in her leftover spaghetti, simultaneously hoping and dreading that Nathaniel would understand her deeper meaning.

His lips curled. *"Let's find out, shall we?"*

Her heart lurched as he stood, strode around the table, bent close and cupped her face. Kissing her deeply and passionately he made her feel as if they were the only ones on the balcony. In a way, Kira supposed they were, but she was still conscious of the patrons' stares nearby, even if they weren't real.

"*Let them watch,*" Nathaniel murmured into her mouth, exploring her lips, her jawline, her throat. Each brush of his lips, and each lick of his tongue, was like hot fire that left her shivery and breathless.

Kira was disappointed when he drew away.

"*Is that all?*" she asked.

"*It is just the beginning,*" he said, holding out a red rose.

She smiled as he tucked the rose into her hair, just behind her ear. It was the same vibrant shade as her dress, and although she suspected it was of the scentless variety, in the dream it was the most enchanting rose she'd ever smelled. Yet, it paled in comparison to the allure of Nathaniel's masculine scent. As he leant close to nestle the flower into place, she inhaled deeply through her nostrils, capturing the musky undertones and warm aroma of cardamom.

"*You're beautiful when you smile,*" Nathaniel praised, causing her own smile to widen.

"*I didn't think you were so romantic.*"

"*If you think I only came over to kiss you, then you are mistaken,*" he lowered himself on one knee.

For a moment, she thought he was going to propose, but then he pushed the skirt of her dress up, spread her legs, and before she could react, kissed her inner thighs. He nibbled her thighs gently, his mouth leaving damp spots each place he marked her. She nearly died from shock and pleasure when his hot tongue swept up along her pussy.

"*Oh,*" she cried, clutching at the edge of the table as he licked her again. Apparently, he hadn't given her any panties to wear. "*Fuck.*"

"*You taste exquisite,*" he told her, grabbing her hips and pulling her against his mouth, spreading her even wider as his tongue pushed into her, delivering hard strokes along her moist folds and making her even wetter.

Kira moaned, her head lolling back as Nathaniel pleasured her.

He reached up to pull the top of her dress down, causing her breasts to spill out over the low neckline.

"Look at you, pet," he remarked as he kneaded her breasts. *"You're so fucking hot. So impatient. I tried to court you properly and bring you to a nice restaurant, but all you want to do is fuck."*

He pushed his fingers into her so suddenly that she jumped, her knee banging the table loudly.

She glanced at the other patrons, but they'd disappeared; she was alone with Nathaniel.

"Fuck," she gasped as he fingered her.

"You're so greedy, aren't you pet?"

"Yes sir," she replied at once, running her hand through his immaculate hair and mussing it up. *"Please, more."*

She was rewarded with a deeper thrust of his fingers, and then his mouth was on her heat once more, his tongue stroking her again and again until she was panting.

"What do you want, pet?" he asked, inserting his fingers again. *"Hmm?"*

Her head was spinning, and she couldn't find the words.

Nathaniel's hand gripped her jaw, his fingers slick with her dampness. *"Answer me."*

"Your cock," she said, so timidly it was almost a squeak.

"Where?"

Kira gulped.

When she did not answer, Nathaniel released her jaw and began to unbuckle his belt.

"Very well—I shall choose."

Suddenly, his cock was in her face in all its magnificence.

"Open," Nathaniel commanded, but gave her no time to comply,

pinching her nose so he cut off her air supply.

The moment she opened her mouth, he thrust his cock inside, filling her with his hard length.

"Suck," he demanded.

Kira did her best to comply, perched on the edge of the chair as Nathaniel stood before her.

"Tell me, are you enjoying yourself, pet?"

Kira knew from experience that Nathaniel expected her to answer, and with his cock still in her mouth, she mumbled a garbled response.

"It's a beautiful night," Nathaniel sounded like he was agreeing to a comment on the weather. *"And you look so beautiful like this—with your mouth full. Is this what you meant by romantic?"*

Nathaniel took hold of her hair, holding her in place as he slowly slid his cock deep down her throat until she began to gag.

"Is this what you wanted, pet?"

Another garbled response as she fought for air, the head of his cock pushing uncomfortably on the back of her throat. She clutched at his thighs, trying to push herself off.

"I can't hear you, slut."

After she answered him more loudly, he removed his cock and released her, leaving her bent over and gasping for breath.

She felt his hand on her head as he petted her. *"Good girl. That will be all."*

She watched, dumbfounded, as he returned to his seat while doing up his trousers. He sat down, laid his napkin across his lap in one fluid motion, and had a sip of rum from his glass.

He was composed and relaxed, behaving as if nothing out of the ordinary had happened—as if she wasn't sitting opposite him in a state of complete disarray. Chest heaving, naked breasts with dark tender nipples on full display. Her dress hiked up over her spread legs, exposing her pussy. Her cheeks were hot, and she felt like her entire body was burning up.

And he'd just left her like this. Aching, wanting.

She stared daggers at him. *"Bastard."*

He didn't reply, and fury surged through her.

"Bastard," she repeated, leaping to her feet. She didn't bother to adjust her dress. *"This is not fair."*

"Why isn't it fair, pet?"

"Because...you can't just leave me like this." A pleading whine had entered her voice.

Nathaniel merely swirled the liquid in his glass, looking remarkably put together for someone who'd had a raging boner down her throat just a minute ago. She would have admired his self-control if he wasn't being such a fucking *bastard* right now.

"Well," he began, regarding her over the lip of his glass, *"Why don't you come do something about it?"*

Kira was one step ahead, and he'd hardly finished his sentence before she seized the table and pushed it sideways, upending it and causing the plates, cutlery, candles, and tablecloth to slide off.

Nathaniel was perfectly still as he watched her move to stand before him, the shadows lending a wickedness to his expression. *"Yes, pet?"*

"We're not finished here," she growled.

"Oh? But I'm quite content to resume our romantic evening...if you prefer."

"No, I do not 'prefer'," she snapped using finger quotes.

She knelt between his legs. He might have been acting blasé, but his erection was obvious through his trousers, and the sight of it sent a thrill through her. Cursing impatiently, she undid his belt, keeping her eyes locked on his as the buckle clinked beneath her fumbling fingers.

Nathaniel waited patiently as she unfastened his trousers and freed his cock.

She drew a sharp breath when it sprang free and slapped her in the face, leaving a trail of precum across her cheek.

"Careful, pet."

"You be careful," she retorted automatically, but she was fixated on his cock. She'd intended to take it out so she could ride him, demanding what she needed from him after his relentless teasing, but now that she was staring at his cock, she had other ideas. She licked her lips as she took in his engorged member. The veins were prominent along his velvety shaft, the head glistening with his arousal, and his balls were large and taut, calling her.

Kneading his sac with one hand, and taking hold of his shaft with the other, she leant forward and kissed the bulging head of his cock, allowing his precum to glaze her lips.

Nathaniel's chest rumbled with approval. *"Kiss it again, pet."*

Kira did as he said, delighting in the way his cock twitched in response to her lips, and glad he was finally telling her what to do. She wanted more direction, but she wasn't sure how to ask for it.

Kira continued to tease him by licking his balls, drawing a low groan from Nathaniel.

"Fuck, pet."

Suddenly, the waiter arrived asking if they would like dessert. And since it was a dream, one of them had imagined the interruption, and it definitely wasn't her.

Kira grabbed Nathaniel by the scruff of his shirt. *"Very funny."*

His face broke into a grin. *"Sorry. I couldn't resist."*

Kira pushed him back roughly in his chair so it rocked precariously before tipping forward. *"Tell him to fuck off."*

The head waiter vanished without a trace, his silver tray clattering to the ground.

"Better?" Nathaniel asked.

"No more interruptions." She climbed astride him. *"And as much as I'm enjoying this date, I feel like you're showing me the things you*

think I want. This is a beautiful restaurant, but if it's truly a dream, the sky's the limit, right?"

"What did you have in mind, pet?"

Kira rocked against him, and as she leant forward, she felt his hard cock against her belly. *"I want to see your deepest, darkest fantasies."* She ground against him, wetting his balls with her damp slit and delighting in his reaction. *"Show me what you really want, Nathaniel."*

Surprise crossed his features. *"Are you sure? I'm enjoying your company, and I'm quite content to continue our evening here."*

She gripped his hair as an animalistic force took over her, lust and hunger driving her to take what she wanted.

"I don't want your contentment. I want your passion."

She pulled on his hair.

"I want your command."

She tipped his head back until his lips parted from pain and his pelvis lifted to thrust up against her.

"I want your dominance."

She whimpered as he ground against her, igniting her being.

"I want you to take me in every way."

Nathaniel's eyes became glassy, his voice hoarse as he regarded her with lust. *"I must warn you...my fantasies are more extreme than you are prepared for."*

Kira lifted her chin. *"Then teach me."*

His eyes flashed with danger. *"Teach you?"*

"Yes. I'm eager to learn."

Nathaniel let out a low, sinister laugh. *"Very well. Let's see if you make for a good student."*

Chapter 11

Teacher and Student

<u>Kira</u>

Dark sapphire smoke surged in so thickly it obscured everything from view, including the restaurant and Nathaniel.

When it cleared, Kira found herself in a deserted classroom. It was dim, and the lights were off. The only source of light was from the small windows set too high to see through. Sunlight filtered in, and dust speckles danced gently like magic sparkles. In front of her was a blackboard and a teacher's desk.

Her arms were suspended above her by chains attached to the ceiling, and her wrists felt sore from the pressure of the smooth metal cuffs. The metal clanged as she shifted to look around. There was only one school desk, which she was sitting on, wearing her school uniform. Long red socks emphasised her calves and plump thighs, and her pleated red skirt didn't quite reach her socks. Her white blouse was unbuttoned, barely covering her breasts. For some reason, her hair was woven into tight pigtails, the twin plaits trailing below her breasts and tied with large red ribbons. She had no undergarments—apparently, Nathaniel preferred her like this.

"Are you ready for your lesson, pet?" spoke a voice behind her, making her jump.

Nathaniel came into view, striding to the blackboard and picking up a piece of chalk. He looked her up and down, his expression scrutinising.

Heat washed over her as she took in Nathaniel's appearance. Everything from his tie and professor's gown to his teacher's cap was attractive, and it made her more aware than ever of the age difference between them. She was self-conscious beneath his piercing gaze, which undressed her and made her clit throb.

"I expect you to answer, pet. Are you ready for your lesson?"

"Yes," she answered.

"Yes, sir."

She nodded quickly, the chains rattling as she did so. *"Yes, sir."*

"Good." He faced the blackboard, his shoulders tight as the chalk scraped. He wrote *Introductions*, underlined it, beneath which he wrote *Sir*.

He turned back and gave her a discerning look. *"And what shall we call you?"*

"Err...pet?" she ventured, taken aback by Nathaniel's seriousness. He assumed the authoritative position so naturally. Combined with the restraints, she felt completely at his mercy.

He tapped the blackboard with the chalk.

"Pet is technically correct, but I think we can do better for this session, can't we?"

Kira racked her brain, desperate to think of an answer that would please him. Suddenly, it hit her square in the chest. Her lips parted, the word on the tip of her tongue, but she faltered at the last moment, a furious blush heating her face.

Nathaniel made a bemused sound. *"Don't be shy. Speak up so I can hear you."*

She couldn't. It was one thing for him to call her that, but to say the word out loud was too much. Even in the dream, she couldn't do it.

Nathaniel rapped the chalk on the board again. *"If you aren't going to speak, I may as well gag you."*

The threat made her pulse quicken, and her insides twisted with fear and anticipation as he advanced on her, standing so close their faces were inches apart.

"I will ask you one last time. What. Is. Your. Name?"

His clipped words sent a chill through her, spurring her to speak.

"Slut," she whispered.

Nathaniel's stern expression gave way to a triumphant smirk. *"Yes, pet. Yes, you are."*

He regarded her a moment longer before turning back to the blackboard. He wrote *SLUT* in large, jagged letters beneath *Sir*.

"And what is a slut like you good for, pet?" Nathaniel asked.

It was the same tone his father, Henrikk, had used when posing the same question. Humiliation seeped through her.

She bowed her head as tears pricked her eyes. It was horrible, in a wonderful way, and it made her skin feel hot and cold at the same time as feverish tingles swept through her.

"You know the answer to this," Nathaniel prompted, the chalk hovering by the board.

Kira gave her head a shake.

"Too afraid to tell me?" Nathaniel asked, *"Or have you forgotten the answer?"*

Silence.

"Perhaps you need a reminder."

Nathaniel set the chalk down with a click, the sound making her flinch.

"It seems we'll be needing this after all," he said, pulling open a desk drawer and producing the gag and collar that she was all too familiar with.

Kira jerked her head back as he approached, but she was chained up and couldn't get away. He placed the collar around her neck and tightened it. Struggling was no use, and the realisation of what was about to happen made her clammy.

"Open wide," Nathaniel instructed.

When she didn't obey, he reached to pinch her nose. She quickly opened her mouth wide.

"Good girl," he said, slowly pushing the ball gag into her mouth.

It pressed against her tongue, her cheeks, her palate, and it forced her to stay open with her teeth resting on the ball. She caught his gleaming gaze and felt her face burn hotter.

"There, that's better." He caressed her cheek. *"Now you look like a real slut."* His hand slid up her skirt and probed her wetness, making her twitch and groan as he inserted his fingers into her pussy. *"So fucking wet and tight,"* he hissed. *"So tight I bet you'll scream when you take my cock."*

Kira's eyes widened at the implication, but she was powerless to speak.

Nathaniel read the question in her eyes.

"Oh yes, slut. The time has come. I can see you're hungry for it, and it's about time I showed you what you're good for." He removed his fingers, leaving her feeling swollen and empty, and undid his belt.

Kira leant forward in anticipation and lost her balance, slipping off the edge of the desk. She cried out as the chains above snapped taut, her wrists taking most of her weight as she stood on tiptoes, her feet barely grazing the floor.

She let out a muffled plea, hoping Nathaniel would help her back onto the desk, but he shook his head.

"We don't need it," he said, placing his heel beside her against the table and kicking it backward.

Kira flinched as the desk slammed on the ground. When she faced back, Nathaniel had taken his cock out and was stroking it.

"I should start you off slow, given this is your first time." He placed a hand on her ass and pulled her close, causing her to swing forward

so her feet no longer supported her, and his cock pressed against her mound and belly. *"I was going to be gentle..."* his tone shifted an octave lower, *"But I've waited far too long for this."*

A cold sensation washed over her.

Was he really about to do what she thought he was?

Even though he promised he wouldn't take her virginity? Even though she had to save herself for Mark?

It's just a dream, she reminded herself.

Nathaniel seized her legs, lifted them high, and wrapped them around his waist.

Kira let out a whimper. She had no way to hold on to him. The chain pulled her one way whilst Nathaniel pulled her another, positioning his cock so it sat at her entrance.

"Ready, slut?"

Her heart thundered in her chest. Was she ready?

If this was a dream, it felt too fucking real.

And real or not, she was scared by how much she wanted this. Was she ready to relinquish complete control? A tiny sliver of her mind said 'no'. The rest of her said an overwhelming 'yes'.

Nathaniel's muscled chest and arms rippled beneath his shirt as he adjusted his grip, positioning her so the head of his cock rubbed against her clit. *"I'm waiting. Are you ready to proceed with your lesson?"*

The burning intensity glazing his eyes gave her the courage she needed. She nodded, and even made an attempt to say 'yes sir' through the gag.

Nathaniel's voice grew so husky it made her shiver. *"I can't wait to feel you stretch around my cock. Brace yourself. Today, I will make you a woman. But do not forget, pet, that you were already my little slut."*

She winced at his words. They cut her, and filled her, stripping her bare and energising her all at the same time. It was humiliation, it was praise, but more importantly it meant she belonged to him.

"*Now,*" Nathaniel continued, "*Spread your legs and take my cock.*"

She tensed as anxiety shot through her, but there was nothing she could do as his strong fingers tightened on her hips. Slowly, purposefully, he dragged her onto his cock, his broad head spreading her lips, pushing through her entrance and stretching her walls with his thick shaft. She cried out in pain as he punctured something that had to be her hymen, but he didn't stop like she expected him to. Instead, he continued the slow slide in until he'd penetrated her completely, leaving her panting and shaking as she adjusted to the fullness.

And then he groaned, a low, lusty sound full of edges as his voice broke with unrestrained pleasure. She could tell he was trying to collect himself as he held himself still inside her. The knowledge that he desired her so badly that he was threatening to come undone sent a rush of exhilaration sweeping through her.

In the brief seconds he held her there, impaled on his cock, she had a chance to admire this incredible man—he was powerful, strict and commanding, but also thoughtful, clever and loving, and she wanted every facet of him. She wanted him to claim her, to make her his, even if she regretted it tomorrow, or the day after, or the day after that.

Fuck the consequences. Fuck the plan.

Just let me have this with him.

It was crazy that this was who she wanted. He was the fucking enemy, but she wanted him so badly it hurt. She needed him in her bed, in her home, in her life. The realisation that these moments were fleeting—that this act between them wasn't even real—made her vision grow blurry as sadness rolled through her.

"*Shh,*" Nathaniel said, wiping her tears. "*Don't cry.*"

Kira remembered with a start that he could read her thoughts.

"*This is as real for me as it is for you,*" he said, his conviction helping ground her. "*And I'm honoured that, at least this way, I will be your first.*"

She squeezed her eyes shut and nodded, her wet eyelashes dampening her cheeks. She was still gagged and chained, the collar tight around her throat, but she knew he felt her gratitude through their mental link.

"I like it when you're grateful," Nathaniel said soothingly, kissing her forehead. *"It's a good quality in a slut."*

She bristled as she realised what was about to happen.

"Now," he said curtly, *"Enough tears, and keep your eyes on me while I fuck your cunt."*

It was the only warning he gave her before he pulled back halfway and thrust deep into her. She yelped as she felt the full force of him ram into her, breaching her tightness and grunting possessively.

Her fingers tightened helplessly above her head. She wished she could clutch his shoulders, but the restraints turned her on.

"Good girl, take my cock," he said, and thrust into her again, giving her no chance to catch her breath as he dealt out another stroke, and then another. Always pulling back slowly before suddenly thrusting back in.

"You're mine, Kira," he said, dragging her closer by her pigtails as if they were reins, causing pain to prick her scalp as he pulled her one way whilst the chains pulled her another. *"Do you understand? Mine. Your mouth, your ass, your cunt, it's all mine, and once I've filled every one of your holes, you're going to carry my seed inside you. And no matter where you go, no matter how many years pass, or who you fuck, you will always be mine. I will find you, and when I do, I will bend you over and fuck you as many times as it takes to cure this heartache because I love you so much it fucking hurts."*

His words broke her apart, and she cried out as Nathaniel sped up, revelling in the pain and pleasure and the feel of him stretching her.

It's a fantasy, she reminded herself. *It's just a dream.*

But it felt real, the euphoria intoxicating, the rhythmic pounding the perfect blend of pleasure and discomfort. Her head fell back to look at the ceiling, and all she could see, feel, hear, were the rustling rattle of chains and Nathaniel's raspy grunts as he fucked her.

Clank.

Clank.

Clank.

Clank.

Clank.

He ploughed into her, pushing her to the brink until all she saw was a galaxy of light and dark and torrents of hot fire as she came hard and fast, burning up like a shooting star. And all the while the chains clanged, her wrists and arms protesting as Nathaniel's thrusts became fast and rough as he lost control. Finally, he yelled out her name, roaring it as he sank his cock into her one last time, driving his shaft deep and holding it there as he pumped her full of hot cum.

The chains disappeared, and Kira slumped, wrapping her hands around Nathaniel's neck. She breathed heavily, trying to endure the violent shudders wracking her body whilst her insides throbbed around his thick member.

Nathaniel held her there until her orgasm subsided, and then he set her down gently, his still-erect cock sliding out of her with a wet sloppy sound. Sticky, whitish-clear fluid dripped from her, coating her legs and pooling between her feet as she swayed on shaky legs.

"Are you sure this is just a dream?" she asked weakly as Nathaniel steadied her. "Because it feels fucking real."

"Real or not, it's amazing." He smiled down at her fondly and pressed his lips to hers. "*You* are amazing. I love your mind...and I love all of you."

Kira was almost ready to say the words back. Almost. But first, she had a pressing question.

"Are you sure I'm still a virgin after all that?"

Nathaniel laughed and kissed the top of her head. *"Quite sure. Well, definitely maybe."*

CHAPTER 12

Her Love

NATHANIEL

THEY WERE BACK ON the grassy ledge at the edge of the woods beneath the starry sky. Kira was on his lap, her soft perfect bottom pressed against him. As she climbed off him, Nathaniel saw that his trousers were ruined, his cum already seeping through to create a dark patch.

He hadn't even been touching himself when he came. He was in love with Kira's mind, body and soul, and he'd ejaculated purely because of how turned on he was by his sexual fantasies with her.

Which was the hottest fucking thing that had ever happened to him.

The bond had allowed him to feel her pleasure, her pain, along with every ache and throb tormenting their bodies, as they came together in a cataclysmic release. He'd never felt so close to anyone before, not by a long shot, and he wanted nothing more than to sink into her for real.

Kira seemed to be of the same mind, because their link had hardly severed before she climbed astride him and pushed him back into the grass. Her thick hair swung down, tickling his face, her golden eyes glowing like low-burning embers.

"Take me," she said, the command laced with desperation. "I want you to."

He gave a strained chuckle. "Believe me, pet, I want nothing more than to be the first man inside you." He twisted her hair around his fingers. "But you would regret it."

"No, I wouldn't."

"Tomorrow, when you woke, you would realise that without the lure of your virginity, the Poplarins would be unwilling to accept you after being with a vampire. It would take weeks, perhaps months of building rapport before you could rise to lead them. And while you are more than capable, we do not have that kind of time. We were meant to have a year to prepare, but instead we have only a matter of weeks before my coronation."

"I don't care, I want you." She rocked her hips over his groin, stroking his erection, which had refused to soften more than a little and was rapidly approaching full mast again.

Nathaniel gritted his teeth as she ground against his damp trousers, tempting him with what he could not have, all with a cheeky smile and a devious glint in her eyes.

"Fuck, pet." His grip tightened in her hair and he pulled her down so she was lying on top of him. He kissed her, long and hard, urging her to feel how much he wanted her. "You make it so hard to resist."

"Resist what?" she asked through sultry, slow-batting eyelashes. Kira gave him a mock pout, her full lips parting invitingly.

Under different circumstances, he would have liked to part those lips even further, making them wrap around his cock and milk every last drop of cum from him.

"Do not play with me," he warned, pushing his hips up so she felt his thick erection press into her thigh. "If I took you now, I would take my time. It would be slow. Sweet. But make no mistake, it would not be gentle, and you would be completely and irrevocably mine."

Nathaniel's voice shook with intensity, his body wound tightly as it threatened to come undone. Kira was soft everywhere he was hard, and he wanted to press and squeeze every curve, to bury his face in her plump breasts and bury his cock in her wet heat. He wanted to make her moan and steal her every breath. And when she knelt for him, she would be doing it for *him*, and not because she was training to serve his father.

That last thought was like an icy fracture of his heart, creating a hairline fracture that travelled all around, weakening his resolve. He ran his tongue over his aching fangs and pushed his hand into her hair. "Do you have any idea how much I want to tear your clothes off and take you?"

Kira's eyes had widened in shock, but then her eyelids drifted down halfway, and she peered at him through her eyelashes again. "Then why don't you?"

Fuck.

He leapt at her, capturing her mouth and coaxing it open, and when she offered her tongue, he brushed it with his, eliciting deep pangs of want and need in his groin. His abs flexed as his desire rose, mounting until he was a breath away from losing control. He cupped her face, staring at her like a man possessed.

"Tell me you don't care about the plan," he rasped. "Tell me you don't care about uniting our people. Tell me you don't care about becoming our ruler and bringing justice to the world." He locked eyes with her, his restraint thinning as his throbbing cock strained against his pants. "Tell me you don't want those things, Kira, and I will deflower you right now and plough you into oblivion until you scream my name. And when you are too tired, I will take you again, and I won't stop until every inch of you is lathered in my cum and the only name you know is mine. Tell me."

She stared at him with her mouth agape.

Nathaniel tried to calm himself, but the growl of his voice betrayed his jealousy as he said, "Tell me you don't want Mark."

"I don't," she mumbled, but she dropped her gaze, and it made his heart ache.

The thought of Mark touching Kira, of his undeserving cock filling and scenting her with his cum, filled him with rage.

"Did you hear me?" Kira whispered. "I said I don't."

"I don't believe you."

She lifted her chin, fire flickering to life in her eyes. "Tell me you won't marry Gloria."

Nathaniel winced. Kira was asking him to give up becoming the king. But as he beheld her determined gaze, he knew he stood to lose something far more precious than a crown. "I won't marry Gloria."

Kira's eyes widened. "You really mean that?"

"Yes. On one condition." He held Kira tight, and he rested his head on her shoulder, because he was too afraid to see her face when she answered his next question. "I will not marry her...*if* you tell me that you don't want Mark."

Kira hesitated, and it was enough to cause the crack lines around his heart to run deeper. He buried his face in her hair, shutting his eyes as he tried to compose himself, fighting the urge to try and compel her to choose him.

Choose me.

"I love you," she said, the precious words filtering into his life like sunlight. "But..."

"But?"

"We have responsibilities." She pulled back, shaking her head in frustration. "This is *your* plan. You started this. And I agreed to be a part of it. Why are you making this so hard?"

He felt a pang of guilt, defeat piercing him like a thousand arrows.

"I know," he said reluctantly. "You're right."

"It's not what I want, Nathaniel. But—"

"I know," he said, drawing her close again. "We need to focus on the plan." Nathaniel stroked her hair to calm her as much as to calm himself. He wished he had the privilege of seeing her wolf forms right now. He would have loved to see them—his beloveds. Not an accidental glimpse, but the honour of her intentionally showing him. That would have completed him in a way that words could not describe.

And he would not have been able to walk away from her.

CHAPTER 13

Her Choice

KIRA

SOMETHING PROFOUND HAD CHANGED for Kira once she'd said those three little words out loud.

I love you.

It had shifted the mood, dissolving a barrier between her and Nathaniel. Suddenly, they could see each other clearly, their hearts laid bare, the love and longing etched into souls stark and undeniable. *This* was what they both craved, this companionship.

The pure strength of Nathaniel's affection was disarming, and it had given her the courage to open up her heart and admit that she loved him too. Yet, it hadn't made a difference, because the outside world was waiting for them, and they couldn't be together without forsaking everything they believed in.

She'd fallen in love with Nathaniel, the person—the *vampire*—who was fighting for justice. Whatever they felt right now, however consuming the heady combination of lust and passion was, it wasn't enough to override who they were, and neither of them could run away.

Which left her feeling trapped by a cause that had once driven her. Her dream of improving the lives of her kin had given her purpose.

Now, that role just felt like a duty. It was something she had to do, regardless of her personal feelings or the pull of her heart.

Because what I want doesn't matter.

A cold helplessness crept in. There was no future for her and Nathaniel, and the limited time they had together was already slipping away.

"It will be all right," Nathaniel soothed, kissing her tenderly. "Try and sleep."

It felt good to be held, and she clutched him tightly, unwilling to waste these precious moments on sleep when she could spend it savouring the warmth of his long, lean body. She inhaled his scent, revelling in its smoky muskiness. She memorised every note that distinguished him, and pressed herself closer, wanting their scents to mingle so he would unmistakably be *hers.*

"I don't want Mark," she declared, breaking the silence. "You're the one I want. I need you to know that."

Nathaniel's arms tightened around her. "I know."

Kira could sense his ambivalence by the tension rippling through his muscles as she stroked his back. He was struggling just as she was, her duty threatening to tear her heart in two.

She hung her head with a defeated sigh. "But it doesn't change anything, does it?"

Nathaniel pulled back slightly to rest his forehead against hers, their eyes drifting shut as he spoke. "Don't worry, pet. I will be with you every step of the way. We will both do what needs to be done."

"And after that?" she prompted. They'd never discussed what would happen once they were successful. "Do you think there's a chance for us then?" Nathaniel's face darkened, and she hurriedly continued, "I know you'll be married, but—"

"Gloria and I will be bound by blood," he interjected. "I will be obligated to defend her, or else to forfeit my life. The possibility of a marital future between you and me will be...an impossible thing."

Her heart fell. Tentatively, she asked, "What is she like? Gloria?"

"Not my favourite person."

"And?"

He shrugged. "She's decent enough that I haven't had to kill her, but cruel enough that I will never love her. But like you, she is strong and fearless. She also has the support of many great vampire families." He rubbed her arms. "Let's not talk about her."

Kira's jaw muscles twitched, but she nodded, her throat feeling tight with the knowledge that she and Nathaniel could never be together. There was only one way forward.

Nathaniel would marry the vampiress, Gloria, and he would become king.

And I'll seduce his father and kill him—if he doesn't kill me first.

The sky began to lighten.

"Let's return to the academy," Nathaniel said.

They returned to camp to bid Mary, Byron, Haley and Ana goodbye.

"Summon us when you need us," Haley said to Kira.

"We are ready to serve," Ana added, baring human teeth in a wolfish grin.

Mary nodded at Nathaniel, but Byron gave him a hard stare.

As for Kira, saying goodbye to the couple who had raised her was strange and awkward. She still loved them, and hoped rather than believed that one day, their relationship could return to the way it had been; easy, pleasant, and full of laughter.

Kira and Nathaniel walked down the gentle incline of the foothills and through the woodland until they reached the portal. Nathaniel's room was visible on the other side, along with the large, ebony bed with its black satin sheets. She stared at it glumly, because it suddenly represented a life she couldn't have.

The night had been incredible, but its events had taken their toll. The knowledge that the best that life had to offer was now behind them soured her spirits. Over the coming weeks, Nathaniel would train her to become the kind of sex slave his father desired.

It left them no room to be their true selves. No more stolen moments with this mysterious, tender-hearted vampire with his dark secrets. No more dreams of love and passion she would not have dared to imagine before meeting him.

He had so much love to give. And so did she.

Even though the world needed them to set their feelings aside, it felt like a fucking waste.

Kira stared through the portal sullenly. "Aren't you worried someone will find the portal?"

"Only we can see it," Nathaniel replied. "It was made with blood magic—yours, and mine. I had Barbara create it after I found you."

A chilling thought occurred to her. "Can your father see the portal?"

"No. But even if he could, he would never guess its significance. He would see a country lane, nothing more."

"How can you be so sure?"

"Because he has a way of noticing everything about a person whilst learning nothing meaningful about them."

Kira chewed her lip worriedly. It was obvious that he was no longer talking about the portal.

How much abuse had Nathaniel suffered at his father's hands growing up? One day, she would summon the courage to ask him how someone so pure of heart could survive in the Vampire King's shadow.

"Ladies first," Nathaniel said, offering her a hand up as he indicated for her to step through the portal.

Always the gentleman.

The sweet gesture made her feel worse, because it made her love him just that little bit more, pining for him when they were both helpless to do anything about it.

Kira didn't move, her shoulders stiff and fists clenched as her helplessness culminated in rage and anguish. "No."

"I beg your pardon?"

"I said 'no'. I don't want to."

Nathaniel placed a hand on her shoulder, but she shrugged him off, her facial muscles stiff as she tried not to cry.

Even though she felt closer to him than ever, she also felt rejected and abandoned. She was angry at the world for the taste of happiness it had given her, and angry at herself for choosing to go against her own wants and desires.

"You're upset," Nathaniel said softly. "What's wrong?"

She locked eyes with him silently, letting him see that her disobedience was completely intentional. It needed no explanation.

Nathaniel's eyes narrowed. "Kira, I want you. You know that."

And then he said those words she'd come to hate, the ones that stripped her of the calm bliss he'd given her when he'd taken charge.

"It's your choice, Kira."

She shut her eyes. More than ever, she hated that it was her choice, because she did not have the courage to turn her back on the people she loved, nor on her dream to make a better world...not even for him.

And yet, if he'd grabbed her arm right now and taken her somewhere far away, she would have followed him in a heartbeat.

But it was not a choice she could make herself. She didn't want to be responsible for all the people who were depending on her to overthrow Henrikk and make the world a better place for every kind—wolves, witches, humans *and* vampires..

Nathaniel's soothing voice echoed through her reverie.

"It's not too late to change your mind, Kira. I am here to assist you. If you wish to back out, no one will hold it against you. I will understand, and I will love you with my every breath. That does not change, no matter what you choose. But if you choose to be a part of this plan, you must return to the academy with me."

Kira opened her eyes but stared at the muddy ground. "Will following through with the plan make you happy?"

Nathaniel stepped closer but did not touch her. "Once we succeed...there will be far less suffering in the world, especially amongst humans and wolves. There will be less inequality. Young wolves will have brighter futures, with prospects beyond being living breathing blood donors. I expect many people will be happier. I suppose, I will be glad of that."

She nodded. It wasn't the kind of happiness she'd been asking about, but he was right. He was fucking right. And she wished he wasn't.

"It's your choice," Nathaniel repeated, his hand brushing the side of her arm like a feather touch.

Kira fell silent. Every fibre of her being urged her to abandon the plan and stay with Nathaniel. But that option wasn't even on the table. Either way, he would continue with the plan, with or without her. Because it was the right thing to do.

It was quiet, the only sound the rustle of leaves as tiny birds searched for breakfast.

Nathaniel waited patiently, his expression stoic whilst she deliberated—or seemed to deliberate. Truthfully, her mind was blank, and the choice wasn't really a choice at all.

"We proceed as agreed," she announced stiffly. Her own words hit her like a punch in the gut. "And you can start your training right now, because I'm not going through that fucking portal unless you make me."

CHAPTER 14

Punishment

KIRA

KIRA'S CHALLENGE HUNG IN the air, buzzing with anger.

"You *will* go through the portal, just like I asked," Nathaniel said in a reasonable tone.

Too reasonable.

If she was going to survive the next few weeks, Nathaniel would have to take control, because it was too daunting to contemplate otherwise.

I need him to take control.

She sure as hell wouldn't make it easy, though. She trusted Nathaniel enough to relinquish control to him, but she was also furious enough to lash out in any way she could.

"I'm waiting, pet. Go through the portal."

She spun to face him, pushing him squarely in the chest. "Make me. You want me to be a good slut for your father, right? Here's your chance to punish me."

Nathaniel looked distraught. "Kira, don't do this."

"Yes, *Nathaniel,* let's do exactly this. Show me what the consequences are for disobeying the Crown Prince." She shoved him in the chest. "Show me *exactly* what the punishment is."

She punched him, but he caught her fist. She swung with her other hand, her uppercut hitting him under his jaw, his teeth clicking audibly.

She laughed in his face, sounding half-mad to her own ears. "I expect I will need correction after that, won't I, sir? For hitting you. For not being good enough."

She hit him again and again, and he just stood there and took it, watching her in concern as her voice grew higher pitched as she taunted him. "Don't just stand there, *sir*. Aren't you going to punish me?" She swung at him again.

Nathaniel caught her wrist. "I *will* punish you if it keeps you alive. My father is not a forgiving man, and what he expects from his courtesans are—"

"*Courtesans?*" Kira half-shrieked, half-laughed the word. "Why not just call me a whore? Or a slut? That's your preferred term, isn't it? There's no need to sugarcoat it. Or will it make you feel better to call me a courtesan when your father is the one who's fucking me?"

Nathaniel flushed red, the veins throbbing at his temple. Kira laughed again, but this time it was a wretched sound, and that's when she realised she was crying, the tears drenching her face and blurring her vision.

"That's all I am, aren't I, Nathaniel?" she sobbed, grabbing the front of his shirt and pushing him without letting go of the fabric, unwilling to truly push him away.

Her sobs cut off as he gripped her chin, his voice deep and menacing.

"You know what you are to me. You are *everything*." He cupped her face, kissing her teary cheeks and mouth. His kisses stifled her sobs as she clung to him, wishing he did not have to let go.

"You are everything to me," Nathaniel repeated, the statement resounding deep in her heart. He pulled back, looking haggard as love and pain flitted across his face. "But the road ahead is dangerous, and I *will* ensure you survive the ordeal ahead. This is not a game. My father expects you to be perfectly trained. So if you wish to avoid a whipping, if you wish to *survive* long enough that he lets his guard down so you can defeat him, then you must be flawless. And I will ensure you make it out the other side alive. Do you understand?"

"Yes," she whispered.

"Because you *will* triumph over evil, Kira, and then you will rule."

His expression changed, the raw tenderness he was showing her slipping away until his features were blank, and she saw a shadow of his father in the thin line of his mouth and the cold stare of his eyes.

"Now, let us begin anew. A fresh slate, a second chance." He paused, as if to let his words sink in. "There will be no punishment if you obey me right now." He paused again, and when he spoke next, there was no love in his words. "*Get on your knees.*"

Kira choked back a sob, shaking her head in fear and denial, as she spoke the only word she needed in order to challenge him: "No."

"No? Think carefully, pet, before you disobey—"

"*I said no.*"

She glared at him, because even though it wasn't his fault, he was the only one she could reveal her inner turmoil to. She was frustrated at how little control she had over her own life and was absolutely devastated that the person she wanted most in the world, the one who could make her heart sing and her soul come alive, was off limits.

Her rage bubbled beneath the surface, injecting her veins with fury until she felt like she'd burst. Maybe it wasn't fair on Nathaniel, but lashing out at him felt good, giving her a fleeting sense of release.

"Kira," he warned, sounding more like himself in that instant than his father as he urged her to obey. "Do not force my hand."

"*I said no!*" she screamed, swinging for his head.

He ducked and grabbed her around the middle, wrestling her to the ground and turning her onto her front. He pushed her face and chest down into the mud as she cursed him.

She struggled, but his heavy weight pinned her, and she was powerless to do anything as he held her down.

"Calm yourself."

"Fuck. You!"

He stroked her hair, offering solace and gentle words of comfort in her ear as her body convulsed with sobs for minutes on end.

Finally, the tears subsided, and it left her feeling tired and numb. She tried to angle her face so she could wipe her muddy tears on her shoulder, but she only managed to make it smear more.

A long silence followed as they lay there in the grey pre-dawn, Nathaniel's hard body firm and heavy as he lay on top of her, his erection growing more obvious by the second as it pressed into her ass.

"Do it," she finally said, because he had no choice, and because she'd given him a thousand reasons to punish her. He couldn't let this slide. They both knew it.

She squeezed her eyes shut as Nathaniel wrenched down her trousers, exposing her buttocks to the cool air.

"I love you," he said.

Kira tried to block his words out as fresh, soundless tears flowed down her face and dripped from her chin onto the mud. She faced ahead so he wouldn't see.

"Kira—"

"Just do it," she sniffed. "Get it over with. Punish me."

Another teardrop fell, but this time, she felt it on the back of her neck.

Was he crying?

She craned around just in time to see Nathaniel lean back and wipe his eyes with the back of his hand.

As their eyes met, his expression grew cold. "Face ahead, slut."

Kira winced and did as she was told, her body tense with

anticipation as she waited for the punishment to begin.

She did not have to wait long.

Smack.

Searing hot pain emanated where his palm struck her bottom, making her feel like a naughty child. It was degrading, humiliating, and—

Smack.

It hurt, but paradoxically, it turned her on, making her feel hot and flushed. Maybe it shouldn't have, but it did. Something about Nathaniel taking charge, about assuming control so she didn't have to *think* or *worry*, was—

Smack.

She gasped. *Liberating.*

Smack.

This time, the slap was harder than the others, and she cried out.

"Quiet," Nathaniel warned, but his hands were gentle as they kneaded her ass cheeks, creating pleasure where there had been pain. "A good slut knows how to take her punishment in silence."

"Y-yes sir."

Smack.

Another hard, cruel hit that stung. It took effort not to cry out.

Nathaniel let out a low moan, as if he were enjoying the effect he was having on her. She imagined his erection and could feel it pressed into her backside, threatening to burst free from his trousers.

The slaps rang loud in the forest as he spanked her ass, making her flinch each time his open hand slapped the sensitive skin. After the first ten strikes, she lost count.

She tried to relax as physical pain rolled through her, washing away the last of her emotions as she receded into an empty, dark place in her mind that was peaceful, and where she felt nothing but a warm, dull ache.

It was cathartic, and she needed it. To escape from everything else, from all thoughts and responsibilities. Being disciplined by Nathaniel was intimate in a way that nothing else was, and she trusted him not to hurt her more than was necessary.

He was panting by the time he finished spanking her.

"Good...slut," he hissed.

Kira lifted her head wearily. Her hair was streaked with mud, her body covered with it. She tried to prop herself onto her elbows, but Nathaniel did not let her get up. Instead, his hand was hard against her back as he kept her face down on the ground. He climbed back over her and kissed the side of her neck, nuzzling her as if he were her partner.

But he's not my partner.

He's not my mate.

He could have been, but he isn't.

Which made her feel all the more confused when she heard him unbuckle his belt.

"Spread your legs," he commanded in a voice she did not recognise, harsh and clinical, devoid of all emotion. "I'm not done with you yet."

"Is this part of the punishment?" Kira asked snidely, injecting as much sarcasm as she could into her voice to mask her nerves.

"Quiet." He forced her legs apart with his knees.

She tensed when she heard him spit, realising what he intended to do. She could imagine him rubbing his saliva over his cock as he stroked it. A moment later, she felt the large, moist head against her asshole, confirming her fears.

"Or is this because you love me?" she taunted in her best *fuck-you* voice.

Nathaniel didn't answer. His hand clamped over her mouth, stifling her outraged scream as he forced his cock into her ass, inserting himself deeper and deeper, pushing and shoving past her tight band of resistance. He ignored her bucking and screaming, not stopping until he had completed his conquest and ploughed fully inside.

"Fucking hell," she choked with a sob.

"Shh. Just take it, slut."

It was Nathaniel's voice, but as he moved in and out of her ass, making her body hurt and twitch and throb each time he drove his cock into her. She wondered how it would feel when his father took her like this. Would he be rougher? She didn't think that was possible.

Nathaniel was beyond rough, each ram of his hips deliberate and forceful, his tight grip and heavy weight keeping her pinned like the prey she was as he took her from behind. If vampires were cruel, then there was nothing crueller than the savage thrusts he inflicted upon her now.

But where there was pain, there was pleasure, and his movements were as sweet as they were sinful, the perfect clash of light and dark, like the rays of sun penetrating the leadlight windows of a dark church.

Nathaniel reached around and stroked her wet clit, and she groaned against his other hand on her mouth as he fingered her, uncaring of how dirty she felt as he fucked her deeper and deeper into the mud. Waves of pain and pleasure swept her up, and he drove her over the crest of each one until she came tumbling down into frenzied, violent whitewash that carried her to shore. Her world flashed white, then dark, and she was coming on his hand and moaning like a whore as throbbing pleasure overtook her senses.

Cloudy satisfaction descended over her, but his rough thrusts did not stop. A minute passed, and then another, and Kira felt a wave of apprehension as she realised Nathaniel hadn't come yet. He was still going, his movements slow and steady now, as if he had no intention of stopping until the sun came up.

He removed his hands from her mouth and clit and sat upright, dragging her with him by the hips so he could fuck her deeper. Too deep. He was too large, and she was too sore. But he ignored her whines of protest, and his low groans rumbled through her.

"Nathaniel," she squeaked as she hovered somewhere between the end of one orgasm and the start of another.

"Say your name. Tell me what you are."

"A slut," she stammered, the words punctuated by her gasp.

"Whose slut?" he demanded.

"Y-yours."

He stilled.

"Wrong," he said, thrusting so deep and hard that she shattered into a thousand pieces. He held her there, letting her feel the full force of his strength as his swollen member spread her ass cheeks, forced her tight sphincter apart, and jutted deep against a part of her that hurt. "Try again." He pulled out completely. "Who do you belong to?"

He must have misheard me before.

"Y-you," she stammered as his colossal cock hovered at the entrance of her ass. "I b-belong to you."

Nathaniel thrust into her again, swift and cruel.

Kira groaned from the impact, blinking back tears. It was another merciless stroke with his too big, too thick cock.

"Wrong. Try. Again."

Her body turned cold like steel as she realised what it was he wanted her to say, the name he demanded that she speak. She clamped her mouth shut.

Her silence was met by more punishing blows, and her entire body shuddered with each thrust. She had sunk so deep into the wet mud now that she had to lift her head to glimpse the forest.

"Answer me, pet."

She shook her head. She wouldn't say it. No way.

Except a new ache was growing in her core, and she wanted badly to reach a second release. As if sensing her thoughts, Nathaniel slowed his assault, reached around and inserted his fingers into her pussy, fingering her as he took her ass slow and steady, making her feel every inch of his engorged cock. He seemed to be in no hurry, drawing out each movement as if they had all the time in the world.

"We are not done until you say it, slut. So, be a good girl and tell me...Who. Do. You. Belong. To?" Each word was delivered with a hard thrust of his cock, causing her entire body to tremble.

Kira held back, panting as Nathaniel brought her closer and closer to the brink. Suddenly, when she was just about to come, he pulled his fingers away from her clit.

Panic seized her, and she rocked her hips uselessly against mud and thin air, whining pathetically like a dog as she sought his touch.

"Say it," he coaxed, pushing his thick cock in and out of her ass, his heavy balls slapping her lazily. "This is important. It lays the foundation for your training, and for your future. Tell me who you belong to."

His fingers hovered over her clit, grazing the wet folds with an unfulfilled promise.

Kira let out a shuddery breath and whispered the word.

"I can't hear you, pet."

She cleared her throat. "Henrikk," she felt something break inside of her. "I belong to your father."

"Correct," Nathaniel said, but there was no satisfaction in his tone, only resignation as he pushed her head down and pulled her closer by the hips so he penetrated her ass as deeply as possible. "You do."

He stroked her pussy, a single touch that lit up sensations all along her folds and right up along her spine. "And now, for the final part of your punishment: You will take my cock in silence, and when I finish, you will take my seed like a good little cumslut. But...*you will not come.*"

Kira felt the life drain from her as the dying embers of her almost-orgasm began to fade.

"No," she cried as Nathaniel fucked her relentlessly, hard and fast, both of them breathing heavily as his balls slapped her clit. He was a tyrant, a monster, but also her lover, and she needed him, now more than ever, to help her reach fulfilment. "Please, sir, I'm so close."

She desperately needed his hands on her heat. When she tried to touch herself, he leant forward and seized her wrists, his grip tight as he pumped into her harder than ever.

"I'm going to fill you up," he hissed, his breath hot against her neck. "I'm going to dump every last drop of my cum inside you. Here's your chance to make me proud: take it like the good little slut that I know you can be."

His groans grew loud, his thick length burning her insides with each rough thrust, and then he choked with grief and pleasure as he came inside her, spurting hot jets of cum into her ass.

"That's it, take it," he growled, pumping her so full that his cum leaked out of her ass and streamed past her clit and onto the muddy ground.

She yelled in frustration, demanding that he help her climax, but Nathaniel kept a tight hold of her wrists, pinning her in place with his body. He groaned loud and deep, pressing her into the forest floor with his cock fully sheathed in her as he drove in and out. Gradually, his movements slowed, his body twitching and spasming with his release.

Finally, he went still.

"Please," she whispered. "Please, I'm so close."

He kissed her neck and caressed the aching folds of her cunt, causing her to shiver and moan from the warm, tantalising touch. He kept her primed and aching like that for what felt like an hour, and in all that time, he stayed inside her, and he did not let her come, not even when he hardened and fucked her once more to welcome the dawn.

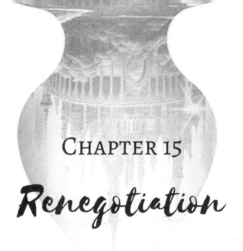

CHAPTER 15

Renegotiation

NATHANIEL

IT WAS PEACEFUL AS he lay on top of Kira on the forest floor, balls deep in her ass. The forest was waking up, birds chirping and fluttering between the trees around them. The sun had begun to rise, and the early morning light streamed through the leafy canopy above, lighting up the autumn leaves with grey light.

Kira was warm beneath him, her soft panting finally subsided after he'd rutted her from behind a second time. His cock was still in her ass, finally deflating after the second round of punishment he'd administered.

She'd begged him to help her reach an orgasm, but he'd resisted, moving her in a way that was hard and fast, and did nothing for her while it felt incredible for him. Her mewls of disappointment were tantalisingly sweet and heartbreaking at the same time, and it took everything in him not to stroke her clit and help her reach release.

It had gone against his moral compass to put his needs before her own, to use her body as if she were a fuck doll, but that was the point: to make her feel as dirty as the mud that coated her. It was a feeling she would have to acclimatise to, and quickly. His father would expect her to be completely broken in, and unfortunately,

Kira was not skilled at playing pretend. She would have to learn to relinquish control in order to be convincing.

"Is that it?" she asked after a long silence, her disappointment palpable.

"Yes, pet. We are done." He kissed the back of her neck before climbing off her. "You took your punishment well. Now, it's time we head back." He offered her a hand standing up, but she ignored it, wincing as she lurched to feet.

Nathaniel frowned and tried to steady her, but she pushed his hand away.

"Don't," she said, her eyes blazing. "Don't touch me." She wiped her muddy hands on her clothes, but it didn't help. Her entire front was covered in mud, her rear smeared and sticky with his semen, and he felt a note of pity for her even as the sight of it aroused him.

Kira eyed his reaction with pursed lips as she pulled up her pants. "I have a new condition," she announced. "If you expect me to help you—"

"We already have an agreement in place."

"I'm renegotiating," she growled.

He tilted his head. "I'm listening."

She jabbed a shaky finger at him. "No more sex."

"Excuse me?"

"Did I fucking stutter? I said, *no more sex*. You want to prepare me for your father? Fine. I'll wear your stupid toys. I'll kneel, and fetch, and call you 'sir'. I'll lick your boots, and sleep on the floor. I'll do anything you ask, but you will *not* put your dick inside my ass again."

She glared at him, exhaling through her nostrils like a wild animal.

A wild animal he very much wanted to mount and tame. She was still so far from broken in.

"Are you quite finished?" he asked.

"No. And another thing: you will not come in my mouth again. And, once I join the Poplarins, you will not touch me, in any capacity, ever again."

"And those are your terms?"

"Yes," she snapped. "Those are my terms."

He considered the prospect of spending the next few weeks in Kira's presence without being able to come inside her. It was disheartening, but she'd left one thing out. Something important that he intended to take full advantage of.

"Very well. I accept."

Kira was obviously itching for a fight, and she looked taken aback by his easy agreement. "You do?"

"Yes, pet. Yes, I do." He advanced, uncaring of how muddy she was as he wrapped his arms around her. Her soft breasts lifted and pressed up against his hard chest. He could tell from her downward glance that she felt his hardness against her thigh. "I can work with those limitations. It will be more difficult for me, and it will not be easy for you. But I think we will manage, won't we?"

Kira tried to shove him off, but he held her tight against him, and after a few seconds of struggling, she craned her neck up and settled for scowling at him instead. "Yes, we will manage, *sir.*"

He patted her cheek. "Good girl."

CHAPTER 16

Aftermath

NATHANIEL

KIRA WAS UNSTEADY ON her feet. Ignoring her protests, Nathaniel scooped her up and carried her through the portal into his bedroom. He took her through to the ensuite and drew her a hot bath, filling it with salts and bubbles. After helping her undress, he insisted on bathing her. Rolling his sleeves up, he sat beside the bath on a stool and lathered her hair with shampoo, taking his time rinsing it with water from a jug.

Kira bore it well, all things considered. The atmosphere between them was intimate but strained, and she didn't speak a word as he washed between her legs with a sponge. She tensed when she felt his fingers on her clit.

"Relax," he ordered, placing a hand on her chest when she tried to sit up. He gently pushed her back so she lay against the bath. When she glared at him, he added, "You promised to do *anything* I asked. So, let me touch you."

Kira looked away defeatedly, and he rubbed her folds in circular motions, working her until her eyes fluttered shut and her head tipped back against the bath's edge.

He leant over the bath to be closer to her, bracing himself with one hand on the edge whilst he inserted two fingers into her pussy. He was pleased to feel her arousal, even through the water. He worked her until she was panting, her small melodic whimpers causing his spine to tingle. She was so beautiful, and he wanted her to feel how much he cared for her, despite what he'd made her endure in the forest.

"I apologise if I was rough with you," he began. He immediately regretted the words because they sounded so inadequate.

"You did what you had to do," Kira replied detachedly, arching her back to try and meet the thrusts of his fingers. "Just keep going."

Nathaniel was happy to comply, but he couldn't help but ask the questioning weight on him. "I hope you can forgive me for the way I treated you—"

"You had no choice," she said with a shrug. "I forced your hand."

It was true. "But even so..."

"Just keep touching me. Please."

Her amenability surprised him, and it was at odds with how upset she'd been with him earlier, but he was happy to do whatever he could to make it up to her now. And if what Kira wanted were not words of apology, but *this*...then he was ready and willing to oblige.

"Do you like that?" he asked huskily, inserting his fingers deeper into her cunt.

Kira's chest rose with a gasp her nipples piercing through the frothy bubbles that had hidden them.

"Yes," she whispered. "I do."

She was getting close to her orgasm, and he sped up, his bicep bulging and the veins on his forearm prominent as he stroked and fingered her pussy.

Suddenly, her eyes flew open, and she clutched his wrist, pulling his fingers deeper into her. "And I hope you can forgive me too," she said through manic, glazed eyes.

He was so enthralled that her words hardly registered. "Forgive you, pet? Whatever for?"

"For thinking of your father now as I come," she hissed, bucking her hips against his hand as she approached her release. "For pretending this is his hand, not yours."

Her sick words sunk into him like claws and tore the flesh from him. That was when he saw the angry sparks in her eyes, hidden amongst her glazed desire. Her passive expression melted away, and she jutted her chin at him defiantly as he went still.

She's goading me.

If her words hadn't struck him so deeply, he would've laughed at her cleverness.

He removed his hand and stood abruptly, leaving Kira unfulfilled once more.

"What's wrong?" she taunted, sitting up so abruptly that water sloshed out onto the tiles. "Was it something I said?"

Nathaniel ignored her. She was trying to rile him up, and it was working. He'd allowed her to sense weakness, to see his vulnerability, and she'd struck like a snake. He dried his hand on a towel and left the bathroom.

Kira's bitter laughter echoed after him.

Nathaniel paced his room, his ears ringing as he imagined his father's hands on Kira as he lay on top of her, hurting her.

His fists clenched, his fingernails digging into skin. The dangers ahead of Kira frightened him, but one thing he had not contemplated was the possibility that she might actually *enjoy* being with his father. It was a ridiculous notion. Beyond farfetched.

Wasn't it?

The possibility was infuriating, and it made his blood run cold with fear.

She's just messing with me.

He knew that. But the possibility remained, however slim: his father was a powerful man, and had a way of getting what he wanted.

He knew how to use force, but he also knew how to make sweet promises that people found hard to resist.

Nathaniel stopped in his tracks and rubbed his eyes. This part of the plan was harder than he'd ever thought it would be.

But it's even harder for Kira, he thought sadly. He admired her courage, and recognised that despite her anger, which was justified, she still trusted him, because she was here, putting her life in his hands. Trusting him to do the hard thing. Trusting him to prepare her for the ultimate showdown of taking down his father.

He sighed and went to the wardrobe, selecting a bathrobe for Kira. There was a time and a place for discipline. Sometimes, all that was needed to foster good behaviour was praise and gentle correction. Being Kira's Master meant knowing what methods to use at the appropriate time—the carrot, or the stick.

Kira appeared in the doorway, beautiful and naked as she dripped water everywhere. Her contemptuous expression confirmed what he'd feared.

This was one of those times when he must use the 'stick'.

CHAPTER 17

The Carrot and the Stick

KIRA

"YOU ARE TRYING TO antagonise me, pet," Nathaniel warned. "That kind of behaviour is not in good faith with our current arrangement."

"Your problem, not mine," Kira said, crossing her arms to cover her breasts and trying not to show how much it bothered her that she was naked in front of him.

She wasn't entirely sure why she was being difficult—it probably had something to do with the fact that he'd fucked her up the ass two times and then left her to suffer through an endless, torturous, incomplete orgasm, twice. She was frustrated beyond reckoning, and not in the mood to be civil.

"Put the robe on, pet," Nathaniel instructed.

She stared at the bathrobe, wrinkling her nose even though the fluffy towel-like fabric looked soft and warm.

"Or remain naked, if you wish," he said, giving her an appraising look.

Point taken.

If she hadn't been through so much already, she might have strutted around naked just to annoy him, but she didn't have it in her. She donned the robe quickly, tying the sash and crossing her arms again.

"Now what?" she asked.

"Go and dry off by the fire."

Kira did as she was told, knowing better than to take his armchair as she sank down on the rug.

Nathaniel gathered a towel and a change of clothes for himself. "You will stay here while I shower, understood?"

"Yes, sir."

Understood. But ignored.

Her mind instantly seized on what she could do with the precious minutes she had while he was in the bathroom. There was nothing stopping her from leaving his room, or from staying and trashing his things to make a point. Something had roared to life inside of her after he'd punished her. Rather than make her more compliant, it had incited her to rebel.

She wanted to push Nathaniel to his limits just like he was pushing her. Because fuck the plan, she wasn't going to make this easy for him. He'd fucked with her—literally—and now she was going to get a piece of revenge, just because she could.

Because life wasn't fair, and the evening had been long and arduous, and she didn't know whether to laugh or cry at its insanity.

Mischief and havoc would bring her solace.

Or...I could use the time to make myself come.

It was a tempting thought. The pent-up yearning was still there like a dull, throbbing ache, the kind that made her want to mew like a damn cat. She was tired, and desperate.

Desperate enough that playing with herself was obviously the most productive, sensible use of her time.

As she sat there considering her options, she became aware of Nathaniel watching her as he leant against the mantelpiece.

Shit.

She raised her chin slowly, adopting an innocent expression. But she was too late. Nathaniel's gaze was sharp, and he must've seen something on her face, because he said, "It seems I cannot trust you to follow simple commands. No matter. You *will* stay here while I shower."

She snarled in protest as he took hold of her wrists and tied them with a length of cord and secured them to the leg of his heavy armchair. It forced her to remain kneeling and bent over on her elbows, facing away from the fire.

Staring at the chair legs sullenly, she spotted a small spider spinning a web. Not that she minded. She wasn't scared of spiders, and it was better company than Nathaniel, even if it had a similar craftiness in how it trapped its prey.

Nathaniel crouched down beside her. He didn't speak, and she knew he was waiting for her to look at him.

Kira sighed. *"What?"*

Nathaniel still did not speak, his gaze intense as he studied her.

His hand slipped under her bath robe and slapped her clit.

She flinched in shock at the sharp sensation. It smarted, and it felt good, and she hated him even as she craved for more.

She snapped her teeth threateningly at him, wishing she could reach his wrist and do some damage, but then her growl turned into a whimper as he dipped a finger inside her and deep longing emanated in her core.

"More?" he whispered.

She nodded weakly.

He stroked her clit. His touch was foreign, unwelcome, but also incredible, and it sent shivery flutters shooting through her.

"More?" he asked.

She exhaled shakily. "Yes."

His hand stilled. "Yes, what?"

"Yes, sir."

His hand grazed her folds but did not slip back in, hovering on the outside, the sensation almost ticklish.

It made her delirious with longing, and it was her only excuse when she whispered: "Please."

"Clever girl," Nathaniel smiled, pushing two of his long fingers into her.

Kira's head fell forward, her forehead resting against the side of the armchair. She was done fighting Nathaniel. If this was the price for reaching an orgasm...for the tight tension coiled up inside her to finally release, then so be it.

She was so close. So, so fucking close...

She just needed him to keep inserting those long, slender, hateful, delectable fingers into her. The pressure seizing her body grew, her pussy swollen and tender as it leaked her juices.

More, just a little more...

"Yes," she breathed, her eyes rolling back. She was on the verge of exploding, right here on the ground, in this demeaning position: Tied to Nathaniel's armchair, forced to submit to his will as he coaxed a fire to lick and burn her insides whilst the fireplace seared her face.

Without warning, Nathaniel took his hand away. "I promise I'll take care of you when I get back."

"Wh-what?" she gasped as he stood and walked away. "Where are you going? Come back!"

She craned her neck to try and see what he was doing.

A moment later, the bathroom door clicked shut.

"Fucker!" she yelled after him.

There was no answer, but she heard the spray of the shower beyond the door. She groaned and let her head drop back against the armchair.

Great.

How on earth was it possible to hate someone while also loving them?

And what had he meant when he said he'd take care of her? Maybe, he meant fingering her, but the ominous shift in his tone had suggested something more significant.

Her stomach did a backflip.

We agreed no sex.

The uncertainty bothered her more than the cord biting into her wrists did. Sure, the cord was soft, but he was still cruel for tying her so tightly.

Kira was almost starting to get used to being restrained by Nathaniel. And if she was being really honest with herself...there was a weird comfort in knowing she had no choice but to stay right where she was.

It quashed the flight of ideas she'd had a minute ago about rebelling.

Fuck.

Here she was, tied to a fucking chair, and she was letting herself give up.

She let out a long sigh. The armchair was too heavy to drag, the cord too tight, and there was no point struggling. It was not the most comfortable position in the world, but the rug was soft beneath her knees, and her forehead was cushioned against the armchair. It was not so bad.

The bedroom was quiet, peaceful. It was their sanctuary, in a weird, twisted way. It was a place that could be wild and thrilling in one moment, and a quiet, safe place the next.

She must have dozed off, because she flinched awake when Nathaniel placed a hand on her shoulder.

He was wearing nothing but a towel around his waist, his washboard abs glistening with water. He looked glorious in the shadows and flickering firelight. It was not a bad sight to wake up to.

Her gaze travelled up.

His hair was damp and tousled, and as he crouched beside her, she had the strong urge to touch it—except she couldn't, because her hands were fucking tied.

"Don't go to sleep, pet," Nathaniel said, petting her head before untying her wrists. "We have a busy morning ahead."

As soon as Kira was free, she sat back on her heels and rubbed her wrists.

"Busy how?" she asked.

"You have school in a few hours, and I have need of you before then."

"*School?*" she exclaimed. She'd lost track of time. It couldn't be Monday already, could it? Then again, it was the longest fucking weekend of her life. At least this meant it was over.

"Yes, pet. And I don't want you to be late. So, I expect you to comply with my orders."

Nathaniel lowered himself into the armchair, his towel parting to reveal a sliver of his muscled thigh. Her heart fell when she noticed the bulge of his erection through the towel.

"And how may I help you, sir?" she said stiffly, making a valiant effort at politeness.

"Can't you guess, pet?" He parted the towel, revealing his legs—long, lithe, and golden in the firelight—and his cock at full mast, as glorious as the heavy balls that hung at its base, taut and full of his seed.

She gulped, unable to tear her eyes away from the length of his shaft, highlighted by the fire's glow.

"You know what I want, pet. Come please me with that pretty little mouth of yours."

Kira snapped out of her daze and shook her head furiously. "No way."

"I'm not asking."

She let out a laugh of disbelief. "Forget it. We had an agreement. You agreed to *no sex.*"

"I agreed to the specific terms you laid out."

"Exactly! So what—"

"You never said I couldn't make you suck my cock."

"Yes, I did!" Kira retorted, feeling a hot blush spread across her face. "I said—"

"You said I cannot come in your mouth. And I will not. But I *do* expect you to suck me off."

"What? No!" She leapt to her feet, staring at him incredulously. "Fuck off. You *know* that's not what I meant."

"What I know, *slut*," Nathaniel said in a crisp voice, "is that we have an agreement, one that I will honour. I will ensure the Poplarins make you their alpha. I will train you to use your magical abilities. I will not take your virginity, nor will I ever come inside you again."

She turned on her heel furiously, but Nathaniel was on his feet in an instant. He spun her around and seized her throat, making her wheeze for air. "Meanwhile, I will teach you to become the perfect undercover assassin to kill my father—but you have a very long way to go, Kira. You are wilful, disobedient, impulsive—and I love you for it. But you are so very far from the perfect whore you need to be. So, you can count on me to use every toy, rope, chain and whip I have at my disposal."

He was breathing heavily, his eyes wild in a way she'd never seen before, and when he released her, she dropped to the ground, panting for air and clutching her throat.

Nathaniel sat down in his armchair. The towel had fallen away, and he gripped his shaft with one hand whilst beckoning with the other. "Come here."

Reluctantly, Kira shuffled onto her knees before him, but she did not touch him. She waited for him to tell her to suck his cock, but he didn't. Instead, he began to stroke himself near her face.

She wanted to tell him to fuck off, but his chokehold had unnerved her.

"Play with yourself, pet."

Kira hesitated.

"Go on," he coaxed, "Make yourself come for me."

Her hand drifted down. It felt so good to touch her clit, even if she felt awkward doing so in front of Nathaniel.

"That's it, keep going," he urged, fisting his cock.

Her cheeks burnt hot as she stroked herself beneath his unnerving gaze. She tried to remember how his eyes had looked earlier, because all she saw now was Henrikk's stark cruelness reflected in them.

"I don't think I can come like this," she said.

Nathaniel smiled. "Oh, but I'm certain you can. And I will relish every second of it. Now, eyes on me, and continue."

Annoyance sparked, but Kira did not stop. She fingered herself, trying to block out Nathaniel's presence, which was impossible when he kept directing her to look at him.

And then, embarrassingly, she grew wetter, and her fingers began to make a wet, squelching sound as she moved them in and out of herself.

Nathaniel smiled. "Do you hear that, pet?"

Kira stilled. "No."

"Don't be coy, and do not stop. I love hearing how wet you are."

Her face flushed even hotter, her ears burning. She opened her mouth to protest, but he cut her off.

"Show me your fingers."

"Here," she snapped, whipping her hand up and thrusting it in his face, giving him the middle finger.

Nathaniel laughed, and she was mortified to see that her fingers were slick with her arousal, the sticky strands hanging between her fingers like honey.

He seized her wrist before she could hide it.

Kira watched, both embarrassed and mesmerised, as he licked the sensitive skin of her palm, before sucking on her fingers one by one.

"You are so delectable," he murmured.

"Am I?" she asked doubtfully.

"Oh, yes. I'm glad we didn't rule eating out your pussy from the negotiation." He smiled wickedly at her shocked reaction.

Kira jerked her hand back at the same time that he released it, and she fell backwards onto the rug, her robe falling open and her breasts bouncing.

Natheniel's pupils dilated with hunger as they swept up and down her exposed body, his lips drawing back to expose his fangs.

"Now, pet...I want you to finish yourself off."

"Fine. But I'll do that in my own room. See you later."

She scrambled to her feet and marched to the door. She'd had enough of Nathaniel's games, or so she thought, but her heart beat wildly in her chest as a treacherous part of her willed him to chase her.

She heard him move behind her, and she broke into a run.

It was no use.

She reached for the door handle, but Nathaniel was faster, and he caught her and lifted her clean off her feet. He ignored her protests as he carried her to the bed, where he tied both of her legs and her left arm to the corner post. He kept her right arm free so she could 'play' with herself, but fuck that.

"I think you need some motivation," he said when she refused to touch her clit. He knelt on the bed behind her head.

"Wh-what are you doing?"

"We will do this as long as we have to, pet," he said, positioning his knees on either side of her head and sitting forward.

She gasped when he rested his balls on her forehead. They were heavy, soft and hard at the same time, the textured sack making her feel things she didn't want to feel. Degradation. Humiliation. And an achy desire in her core that longed for him to pound her cravings away.

And as she felt the warmth of his sack, it became hard to think of anything outside this room, because...

His balls.

On her face.

It couldn't get any worse than this, could it?

It filled her with a hopelessness that was comforting, and she embraced the dark resignation he offered her.

Slowly, her hand drifted down to her clit.

Nathaniel hissed in approval.

"There's a good pet. Touch your filthy little cunt. Show me how you like it."

Encouraged by his praise, and aroused by his insults, she sped up, stroking and fingering herself, no longer embarrassed by his scrutiny as her urgent need to climax took over. She delved in and out of her sopping pussy, gasping for air as her earlier build-up of longing and frustration hit her in full force, the feeling so intense she felt like she was going to cry.

Nathaniel lifted his balls from her forehead.

"Keep going," he ordered, positioning his cock beside her face and swinging the shaft to the side. It sprang back and slapped her across the face.

Slap.

"Hey!" she scowled. She caught a mouthful of his cock as it swung at her again.

Slap.

Tears sprang to her eyes. It was as bad as when he'd rested his balls on her face. Possibly worse.

It was a new low for her. The act was so degrading, and yet, it caused her insides to throb maddeningly with desire, the raging fire inside her hot enough to kill. She was going to come. She was finally,

finally going to fucking come.

"That's it, pet," Nathaniel urged, his eyes wild and gleaming. "Come on your hand like a good little slut."

She shrieked as she pushed herself closer and closer to the brink, hardly noticing each time Nathaniel slapped her with his thick, hard cock.

Slap.

Slap.

Slap.

"Now, pet," Nathaniel said, positioning himself so he was in front of her face. He gripped her hair painfully and tilted her head up. He fisted his shaft with his other hand, aiming it upwards as he lowered his balls onto her lips. "Suck my balls as you make yourself come. Do it now."

She opened her mouth, and he stuffed his balls inside, holding them there as she finally began to tip over the edge.

"Let me hear you moan with your mouth full, *slut.*"

She moaned, the sound choked and muffled through his balls as blazing hot fire rolled through her.

"Louder," he instructed. "Scream my name so everyone can hear what a greedy little slut you are."

She screamed his name loudly amidst a torturous, never-ending wail, her face streaming with tears as she lost herself to pleasure so powerful that it punched and shattered through her like a violent series of explosions.

"*Yes,*" he hissed gleefully, wrenching his balls out of her mouth. "Well done, pet."

Nathaniel's words were hateful and beautiful. They found the darkest corners of her mind and soul and stroked them until she felt alive with his darkness, and her entire body twitched and spasmed against her restraints as a violent orgasm shattered through her until all she could see was pure, blinding white.

CHAPTER 18

All Over Her Face

NATHANIEL

SEEING KIRA LET GO of her pride was a beautiful thing. She screamed like a banshee when she came, so loud that he could have sworn the soundwaves vibrated his balls.

He was confident that she'd woken every vampire in the dorm.

Kira's chest rose and fell, her breasts plump and beautiful, the dark nipples erect, and he kneaded them as she came down from her orgasm. He lifted his balls out of her mouth so she could breathe properly, and when she finally opened her eyes, he smiled down at her.

"Well done, pet."

Kira looked half-comatose with hooded eyes, and she even offered him a tentative smile, but it vanished a second later when he began to jerk off.

"Wh-what are you doing?"

He fisted his aching cock, pointing it directly at her face. "You were so beautiful," he rasped. "Simply enchanting."

"Don't tell me you're going to—"

"Not in your mouth, pet. But all over your face." His movements became more intense, his balls taut and ready to explode as he pumped his cock harder and faster, focusing on Kira's conflicted face as he prepared to spray his cum all over her.

She seemed to settle on anger, and she scowled up at him, her words dripping with acid as she spoke through clenched teeth. "You know...I think I hate you again."

Her expression made him believe it, and the twisted thought of her hating him pushed him over the edge, until his body was rocking with a thunderous, life-changing orgasm and he shot his load all over her face, coating her forehead, eyebrows, cheeks, and even her hair with his thick, creamy cum.

"Beautiful," he whispered, wiping the wet tip of his cock against her surprised lips. "My father will be pleased with you."

CHAPTER 19

Back To School

KIRA

AFTER UNTYING KIRA FROM the bed, Nathaniel instructed her to get ready for school.

In response, she gave him the middle finger as she slammed the bathroom door shut behind her. Letting him groom her was harder than she thought it would be, even if she was the one being difficult. She knew Nathaniel had only punished her because she'd pushed him to, but she was beginning to miss the other side of him—the one who'd held her on the grassy outlook beneath the stars and kissed her tenderly.

With a long sigh, she opened the woven bag of clothes that Susie had packed her.

She felt a pang of guilt—she'd almost forgotten about her friend. Was Susie all right?

Kira had last seen her yesterday, recovering in the sick bay after an unknown vampire had attacked her in the library, draining her of nearly all her blood. If it wasn't for Nathaniel taking swift action to save her, Susie wouldn't be alive.

I have to go visit her... after washing my face.

Nathaniel's cum was sticky on her skin, and he'd even managed to get it on her hair. There was no time to wash it again. Clicking her tongue in frustration, she did her best to comb it out under the running tap. The warm water made it worse—his semen congealed and she spent several minutes trying to detangle her hair.

Fuck you, Nathaniel!

When her hair was finally free of knots and tangles, she began to plait it, mimicking the twin-plait hairstyle Nathaniel had given her in his fantasy when he'd sort-of-but-not-really taken her virginity. It had felt so real that she'd discreetly checked to make sure she wasn't bleeding afterwards.

Plaiting her hair in the same style was a small act of revenge, a way to tease Nathaniel by reminding him of what he couldn't have: to be her first.

Was it cruel? Maybe. But he *did* fuck her ass twice, so...*fuck it.*

She nodded in satisfaction at her reflection. The twin plaits were flattering, emphasising her cheek bones and drawing attention to her large almond-shaped eyes. She was wearing her academy uniform, including the red thigh-high socks that drove Nathaniel wild, the short, pleated skirt in a red tartan pattern, and the white blouse with the red ribbon tied at the collar. The smart navy blazer with red piping and fitted shoulders leant her some authority, at least, but she suspected that Nathaniel would take one look at her and want to bend her over and fuck her.

Too bad.

"Hope you get blue balls, Nathaniel," she muttered to herself as she left the ensuite.

Nathaniel was standing by his wardrobe, preoccupied with straightening his tie. He was dressed like a teacher again: polished shoes, black slacks that clung to his powerful, lean legs, a lilac shirt with rolled up sleeves, and an elegant grey waistcoat that emphasised his broad shoulders and chest.

He turned to look at her and froze.

Kira gave him a mocking smile as his stunned gaze raked her up and down, taking in her sock-clad legs, her skirt, her chest, her face. His gaze settled on her plaited hair, and she was rewarded by the subtle arch of his eyebrows.

"Fuck, pet. What are you doing to me?"

Lifting her chin, she sauntered over to him, leaning into the sway of her hips as she offered him a smile. "Do you think your father will like it?" she asked shyly, stopping in front of him.

A pained expression crossed Nathaniel's face, and she relished his discomfort even as she felt a surge of triumph.

Two can play at this game.

Tension gripped the air as she waited for him to respond.

Nathaniel licked his lips, clearly debating how to answer. He loosened the perfect knot of his paisley tie as if he were feeling hot. His arctic blue eyes searched hers, a hint of what looked like hope blooming at their depths.

Was he remembering their classroom fantasy? She hoped so.

Her breathing stilled as he reached out and lifted one of her plaits, rubbing the glossy strands between his fingers. "I like this," he murmured. "And I know you did it for me."

"Did not."

Nathaniel smiled and tugged her head forward by the plait.

"Hey!" she protested.

"We can argue about it later when you suck my cock. But it's time for school, and I don't want you to be tardy. Now, fetch your collar and leash. I set it out for you on your mat."

Kira swallowed and turned slowly on the spot to face the foot of the bed. Sure enough, the red-jewelled collar bearing her locket was there, with a matching red leash looped beside it. He'd removed the collar when they'd returned to his room, and she'd felt strangely naked without it.

"We can do this the easy way, or the hard way," Nathaniel spoke in her ear. "But if you wish to see Susie before class, I suggest you make haste."

Kira snapped her head back at him in astonishment. "You'll let me see Susie?"

"Yes, pet. I thought you might like to see her. I will escort you to the sick bay, and then to class."

Her anger faded as gratitude took its place. "Yes, sir, I would," she said hesitantly.

"Well, then. Let's not waste time."

Appreciation for his thoughtfulness warred with her opinion of what a complete and utter asshole he was being. But Susie was more important than her personal gripes, and she quickly fetched the collar and leash.

"Good girl. That wasn't so hard, was it?"

She rolled her eyes as he fastened the jewelled collar around her neck, wincing at the sound of the leash clipping onto her collar—it was a significant blow to her ego.

"Did you have that leash especially made for me?" she queried, eyeing the thin leash.

"No. I bought this in a pet shop."

"*A dog leash?*" she hissed.

Nathaniel laughed softly under his breath. "No, pet. It's a cat leash."

No fucking way. She lunged at him, fists drawn. He caught her, but her momentum sent them tumbling out into the hallway. Nathaniel managed to steady them before they hit the floor, and he slammed her into the wall, knocking the breath from her lungs.

"Are you quite finished?" he asked.

"No," she argued, but then she thought of Susie, and reconsidered her answer. "Yes, I'm finished. Sorry, sir."

"That's all right, pet. This is our first walk on leash in public...it is normal to feel nervous."

He placed one hand in the pocket of his waistcoat and tugged the leash.

"Come along, now, pet."

Kira took six reluctant, agonising steps down the hallway before digging her heels in.

"What is it, pet?"

She shook her head furiously. She could hear the sound of vampire students from the kitchen, and was suddenly overwhelmed with the fear of appearing like this in front of everyone. The thought of Nathaniel walking her through the school like she was a dog was too much. It was too public. Too humiliating. "I can't. Everyone will see me."

Nathaniel stepped close and cupped her face. "That is the point. Everyone will see that you are my beautiful, obedient..." he tucked a strand of hair behind her ear, "*submissive* pet. And after these public displays, my father will hear of the progress we are making and leave us alone."

"Have you considered how this will affect my standing with the Poplarins?" Kira hissed.

"It can't be any worse than it is now," he teased, patting her face making her growl. "Trust me, pet. Leadership can be a fickle thing. You will rule over them soon enough. In the meantime, you will do as I say."

"Wow, you've really won me over," she quipped, crossing her arms. "Here's another option: take the leash off, and I'll heel beside you without protest. Deal?"

"There will be no more renegotiations, pet."

"Bastard," she quipped just as a male vampire passed them in the hall.

"I won't tolerate backchat from you in public, pet," Nathaniel said. "But I see you need a little more convincing." He called out to the passing vampire. "Frederick. A moment of your time."

Frederick was larger and beefier than most vampires, and he turned back and ambled over, regarding her with curiosity.

"How may I be of assistance?" he asked.

Kira watched in shock as Nathaniel handed Frederick her leash. "Hold this for me, please. I left something in my room."

She gaped after him as he re-entered his bedroom. "What the actual fuck?" She turned to Frederick, urging him to acknowledge the situation's absurdity.

But the vampire merely frowned. "You're quite mouthy for a pet."

"I am *nobody's* pet," she snapped. "I'm a student here, just like you."

"Quiet," Frederick said. "You'll get me punished, too."

Kira laughed in his face. "Good. I fucking hope so."

Nathaniel returned a few seconds later. "I brought you a little reminder, pet," he said, showing her the sparkling object in his hand.

Her heart fell. It was the steel anal plug—the largest one with the red gem.

"No," she begged. "Please don't put that in."

"I wasn't going to, pet. I figured you must be sore after the ass fucking I gave you."

Kira bristled, glancing at Frederick who quickly looked away.

"But alas, you've left me no choice," Nathaniel continued. A chill entered his voice. "Bend. Over."

"Please," she stammered.

"Frederick," Nathaniel called calmly.

The beefy vampire instantly seized her around the middle, knelt down on one leg, and forced her to bend over his knee.

"Fuck!" she cried, struggling as Nathaniel positioned himself behind her and lifted her skirt.

Smack.

She yelped as he spanked her ass, a single sharp slap that caused her to struggle harder against Frederick's hold.

Smack-smack.

Two hits in quick succession, and then a third—*smack*—that took the fight out of her.

She went still.

"That's better," Nathaniel said.

She let out a string of curse words, her voice rising in panic as she heard Nathaniel spit, and felt his groping hands pull aside her panties. A moment later, the cold, pointed tip of the plug met the tight pucker of her asshole.

"Stop!" she yelled, not caring that her voice carried to the rest of the dorm.

"Quiet, pet, or the gag is next."

She stilled, gritting her teeth, as Nathaniel twirled and rubbed the spit-covered plug, lubricating her asshole.

She waited, body tense and braced for the plug.

A long, drawn-out minute passed as he coaxed the tip in and out, twirling it against her asshole. Having Frederick present made her stomach twist, as if this was no longer between just the two of them. The fact that Nathaniel was going to plug her in front of a stranger was a special kind of humiliation she'd been unprepared for.

"Can't you just get it over with?" she muttered.

"Patience, pet. We're nearly there."

She bowed her head and whimpered as he teased the toy along her crack and against the tight ring of muscle of her ass. He pushed, stretching her torturously, and she drew a sharp, whimpering breath as the large object expanded her sphincter. "Stop, it's too much!"

"Shh," he whispered.

She groaned as the plug slid in further, the bulging body moving past her sphincter. And then it landed beyond, filling her anal cavity. The stretching sensation immediately eased, her sphincter relaxing with relief. She was left feeling heavy and full, as if she had a lead weight in her ass weighing her down.

"How does it feel?" Frederick asked eagerly.

Oh, hell no.

Human form or not, she twisted her head, lunging at the beefy vampire with teeth bared, narrowly missing his collarbone.

"Thank you, Frederick, that will be all," Nathaniel said casually, dismissing the large vampire, who released her.

Her legs gave out. Every part of her body ached and burned with fire and need, and she became aware that Nathaniel had caught her, and she was clutching at him for support.

Kira pushed him away, sniffing as she pulled her skirt back down.

Nathaniel's voice was soft, his words simple yet impactful, "Are you ready for school now, pet?"

She didn't answer.

He advanced, pressing her back against the wall with his body. "What's wrong? Don't you like me taking a firm hand with you?"

She gave her head a shake.

"But you like me plugging you?" His hand drifted down, and she gasped as he reached under her skirt and cupped her pussy through her panties.

"No," she lied in a whisper, even as her body throbbed for him; charged and ready to rush towards completion.

Nathaniel wasn't helping. He fondled her pussy, his dexterous fingers expertly sliding the fabric aside and stroking along her seam. "Well, you must like *something*, because the evidence between your legs says otherwise." He inserted his fingers into her and pumped them in and out.

Kira let out a soft moan, her body slumping in his arms. He held her up, keeping her pinned against the wall as he fingered her.

"I love the feel of your wet cunt as it squeezes around me," he breathed, beginning to withdraw his fingers.

Blinking through her hazy pleasure, an angry retort sprang to her lips. "You know who else is going to love how I feel? Your fath—"

Before she could finish her sentence, Nathaniel rammed his finger so hard into her that he lifted her up the wall until she stood on tiptoes.

"My father," he finished, his eyes livid as his other hand seized the scruff of her collar.

Nathaniel looked hurt, angry, and half-mad, and she suddenly regretted provoking him.

"Since you were kind enough to remind me of my father, pet, let me remind *you* of what is to come."

"Will it involve Frederick?" she asked, unable to help herself.

He ignored her. "Make no mistake: you will serve my father in *every* way. You will bring him food, pour him wine, and attend to him at meetings, if he wishes. You will suck his cock, crawl on the floor, and if he so wishes, you will spread your legs for his councillors, too."

Kira was too shocked to speak as dread welled up inside her. But, as terrible as it was to admit, there was a spark of excitement too, and that made her feel ashamed, especially because Nathaniel was only trying to scare her, and he looked haunted by his own words.

"Kira..." His voice broke, and it took him a moment before he could compose himself enough to speak. "You will be *everything* to me, do you understand? Everything. And almost nothing to my father, and yet, it will be *his* bedchamber you wait in every night." He kissed her mouth forcefully as he stroked her clit, rubbing her wet folds intensely. "*He* will be the one to take your cunt night after night, not me. It will be his cock, his seed that fills you. It will be his kisses that wake you in the night, and his punishments that fill your dreams." His voice shook with barely repressed pain as tears filled his eyes. "So..." He took a steadying breath, "think about *that*, slut, as you come for me. Come for me *now*."

Kira's eyes widened in horror. She wanted to console Nathaniel—the person behind this cold mask—but the heady combination of his command and the brutal thrust of his fingers was too much to bear, and she silently gasped for air as he drove her over the edge.

Pleasure slammed into her as he pushed his fingers further into her, lifting her completely off her feet and sliding her up the wall. He crushed her with his chest, and a ragged sound that was more a squeal than a scream tore from her throat.

The orgasm was gone as quickly as it had come, a fleeting sensation that had robbed her of autonomy and left no satisfaction in its wake.

She stared helplessly at Nathaniel, twitching and pulsing on his hand. She leant close to kiss him, but he was too far away, her lips inches from his.

He did not close the distance, and it crushed her.

Just like she'd crushed him with her taunts.

He kept her pinned against the wall, their breaths mingling as they sucked in deep breaths, both of them craving something the other could not give.

Gradually, her mind began to clear, and the reality of the situation loomed over her.

"You just made me come thinking of your father," she stated.

"Indeed."

It had been one thing to rile Nathaniel up about it his father, but another thing entirely to get off on it.

"I will never be yours," she said, her voice harsher than she'd intended it. It was something they'd both known, and yet, she was only just realising how brutal the finality of it all was.

Nathaniel dropped his gaze, and he set her down gently, letting her slide down the wall and slip through his fingers as if she were a fragile flower. His voice was hoarse as he acknowledged the truth of her words.

"You will never be mine."

Kira's heart beat hard as he brushed a strand of hair that had escaped her plait out of her eyes. She waited for him to speak, wishing he would tease her, challenge her. Tell her what to do.

Even another punishment would have been better than this despondent silence.

But instead, Nathaniel wordlessly dropped the leash and slowly walked away towards the dorm's living area.

Kira blinked as she stared after him, guilt pooling in her chest. Her comment had been cruel—too cruel, and she wished she could take it back.

What the hell am I doing, provoking him like that? I agreed to this arrangement. He's just doing his job training me, but I'm giving him hell for it.

She didn't always agree with his methods, but he was trying to prepare her, mentally and physically, for the mission ahead.

And she was doing everything in her power to sabotage it. Was he making her life difficult?

Yes.

Was her outburst justified?

Probably.

But she'd just had a glimpse of how hard this process was for him as well, and she was acting like a bitch.

Sighing in exasperation, she snatched up the leash and hurried after Nathaniel.

CHAPTER 20

On Leash Training

NATHANIEL

I WILL NEVER BE yours.

Kira's barbed words echoed in Nathaniel's mind as he walked down the hall towards the living area. There were very few things that fazed him, but the truth in her words had wounded him, finding the vulnerable part of him and piercing tender flesh.

Even he had his limits, and the knowledge that he could never be with the woman he loved. That he would soon have to give her up to someone who would almost certainly hurt her, made it hard to breathe.

Just the thought of having to present Kira to his father on his thirtieth birthday left him heartbroken.

"Nathaniel, wait," Kira said, catching up to him and pressing something into his hand.

He halted and stared at the leash in his hands, hardly seeing it.

"I'm sorry for bringing up your father," she whispered, glancing at the vampires who were having breakfast at the dining table nearby before turning her earnest gaze to him. "I didn't mean to hurt you."

Nathaniel nodded, his hand closing over the leash. "There is no need to apologise. It was my fault for pushing you so far." He smiled and caressed her face. "Never apologise for pushing back. Your fighting spirit is one of the reasons I fell in love with you."

Kira returned his smile—a real, genuine smile, full of love and understanding.

"You can fight me, Kira," he told her quietly. "You can even disobey my orders. I can handle that." He pulled her leash until she was standing close and looking up at him. "But I need you to take this seriously. Because the thought of having no future with you has me at breaking point. And I cannot fail, Kira. I cannot break down, because you need me. And the entire world needs *you*. The wellbeing of so many people depends on you, and I would be selfish to keep you to myself." His eyes were hooded and full of resignation as he met her gaze. "So, unless you're prepared to turn your back on everything and…"

He barely managed to stop himself from saying *run away with me*.

He would do anything to protect Kira, and the temptation to whisk her away to a safe place far away from here was strong. They could start anew, just the two of them.

But it would mean leaving everyone they cared for behind, and he could not bring himself to do that.

Kira closed the distance between them and surprised him with a warm embrace. She rested her cheek against his chest. "I want what you want," she whispered.

Nathaniel nodded, even as he tried to decipher her meaning. Did she want the plan to be successful?

Or does she want…a life together?

He was too afraid to ask which one it was, and instead placed his hands on her back. He would stay here, holding her, for as long as she was content to stay.

Kira pulled away all too quickly.

"Ready to go?" she asked tentatively.

He took a deep breath and nodded. If Kira could do this, then so could he. Her bravery never failed to impress him. As did her compassion in his moment of weakness.

And holy hell, despite the fact that he was getting choked up, her kindness turned him on.

They crossed to the dining area. He stayed a few paces behind Kira, subtly adjusting himself as they walked.

Victoria was the only one left at the table, playing idly with her cereal.

"Morning, Kira," she said cheerfully, before looking pointedly at the tent he'd pitched in his pants. "And a very good morning to you, my prince."

"Good morning," he greeted, ignoring the dig.

Victoria jabbed her spoon at him. "I see you've downgraded Kira to doggy status. What's next? Going to make her bark?"

"Bark?" Kira repeated, narrowing her eyes at him as if to say, *you're not going to make me bark, are you?*

He passed Kira a pastry. "We have to get going. You can eat as we walk. Victoria might not care about being late for class, but no pet of mine will be tardy."

"Whatever," said Victoria. "But Kira, before you go..." She leant closer conspiratorially. "Tell me, have you two had sex yet?"

Nathaniel had been about to tug the leash, but he hesitated, curious to see what Kira would answer. Would she count their shared dream of the classroom as her losing her virginity to him? It had only been a fantasy, and yet, it had left a powerful impression on him.

"We're...taking it slow," Kira mumbled.

"Bullshit, I know what's up," Victoria said through a mouthful of food. She gave Kira a wink. "Come to my room sometime, babe. You can tell me all the details."

"Sure...if I'm allowed," Kira answered, casting Nathaniel a wary look.

"You will be allowed free time," he informed her, before tugging her leash gently. "Come, pet."

Victoria watched them go with a glint in her eyes, her voice singing out, "*Bye.*"

"Some rules for you, pet," Nathaniel said, leading her up the stairwell, which was busy with students heading to class. "Tonight, after school, you will wait for me by your locker, on your knees."

Kira bristled. "On my knees? Where everyone can see?" She tried to keep her voice low as they reached the upper levels of the dorm, joining the throng of students heading up to the foyer. The wolves gave them a wide berth, whilst the vampires paid them no mind.

Nathaniel did not bother to lower his voice as he replied, allowing it to echo in the stairwell. "As I said, pet: every day, after school, you will wait for me on your knees, by your locker." He ignored Kira's silent pleas to keep his voice down. "You will spend an hour with me in my office for training. Afterwards, you may have free time until seven o'clock, when you will join me in my dorm for dinner."

"I'd rather eat alone."

"You will eat with me, or you will not eat at all."

Reaching the foyer together, Kira walked beside him, keeping so close they were touching. He smiled as he realised what she was doing—trying to make the leash less obvious to the people around them.

Their earlier delay leaving the dorm had put them behind schedule, and the bell soon rang to signal the start of class. Nathaniel took Kira to the sick bay anyway.

"We're still going to the sick bay?" she asked hopefully as he led her through a stone archway. "I thought you didn't want me being late."

"I mostly didn't want us lingering to talk to Victoria. Besides, visiting Susie is more important than your Potions class."

"It is," Kira agreed, throwing him a grateful smile that made his cock twitch. "Thank you."

"You're welcome." He opened the sick bay door for her.

"Not coming in?" she asked when he didn't follow.

He shook his head, deciding to afford the two female wolves some privacy. "I'll wait."

"Are you sure? I'm sure Susie would like to thank you in person for saving her."

That hadn't even occurred to him, but he smiled and shook his head. "Another time."

He paced back and forth in the corridor, enjoying the peace and quiet. Kira emerged a few minutes later wearing a relieved smile, looking at him with large, happy eyes that made him want to kiss her.

"How is Susie?" he asked as they set down the corridor.

"Good. She seems like her normal self. But Mrs. Bur has decided to keep her for another couple of days, so she's feeling cooped up."

"Does she? Well..." Nathaniel considered this as he reclipped the leash to Kira's neck, noting the subtle way she averted her gaze as he did so. "Why don't you bring her some books to read during recess?"

"That's not a bad idea," Kira said hesitantly, as if not trusting his motives. "You'll let me do that?"

"Of course. You can do whatever you please during school hours."

"Huh. And here I was thinking you were going to keep me on a leash all day."

"Don't tempt me, pet."

His reasons for giving her space were twofold. Not only was it healthy for her to have some time away from him, but the return of her freedom would make it all the more humiliating for her when he took it from her again. It was harsh but effective, and it was only step one of what he had planned for her.

Later, he would strip her down in his office and make her go down on him. His balls ached at the prospect, and he sucked in air to try and cool his arousal.

The corridors were devoid of students now, but he'd taken immense pleasure earlier in the curious stares of the passing students and teachers. Kira was strong, fierce, and beautiful, and he had her on display like a show dog, amenable and subdued, proving that she belonged to him as she walked on leash beside him.

Except she isn't truly mine.

The reminder snaked its way into his head, souring his happiness.

"Are you sure I have to go to class?" Kira sighed.

Her pace had been growing slower the closer they got to the Professor Parna's Potions classroom. Wolves loathed Potions, and it seemed hybrids like Kira were no exception.

"Yes, pet."

"Can't we do something else?" she asked, dragging her feet so much the leash went taut. "Please? I just remembered we're learning how to dissect troggleberry sacs. I can *smell* the pus from here."

"*Suppuration*, pet. Not 'pus'. Professor Parna will expect you to use the appropriate terminology."

"Whatever. It reeks, and the smell is a million times worse for me than it is for you."

"I'll take your word on that."

"Please, there must be *something* we could do instead?"

He halted. "What are you offering, pet?"

She shrugged. "Gee, I don't know. A blowjob? What do you want?"

He burst out laughing, harder than he'd laughed in a long time.

Kira folded her arms. "It's not funny. And you're being rude. I was seducing you."

He chuckled and gave the leash a light tug. "Come."

She groaned in resignation and followed him at a snail's pace. "So, when can I rejoin the Poplarins?"

"Patience, pet. I will approach the pack's leaders soon."

"How soon is 'soon'?"

"Never you mind, pet. The only thing you ought to concern yourself with is how well you suck my cock in the evenings."

Kira's jaw dropped, and it took her a moment to respond. "Oh yeah? Well...at least I won't have to swallow your cum," she shot back.

"Ah, but you will have to swallow it, pet."

"But—"

He jerked the leash, making her gasp and stumble forward.

"I promised I wouldn't come inside your mouth. That was our agreement. I never said I wouldn't scoop it up and make you swallow every last drop."

Kira's jaw dropped another fraction. "You...you..."

She seemed genuinely at a loss on what insult to use, and she finally settled on throwing him a bratty look.

It made his cock harden even more than it already was. If she didn't shut her mouth soon, he would reconsider her offer of a blowjob.

"And my magical powers?" she demanded. "When will you show me that? You promised that if I sucked your blood, it would unlock some supposed powers. Or were you just lying about that so I'd let you fuck me?"

She was running off her mouth again, trying to rile him up—and he loved it.

He tugged the leash firmly. "Keep up, pet. You mustn't dawdle. And I never lied." He lowered his voice to a whisper. "We will discover your powers together. Tonight, I will feed you my cock, and then, when I am satisfied, I will feed you more of my blood."

"More blood?" she sighed, even as she licked her lips. "And then what?"

"And then, we shall see." Nathaniel ran his tongue over the tip of his fangs as he eyed Kira's slender neck. With her hair tied back, her throat was on full display, and he was itching to sink his teeth into her supple flesh. The thought made his fingers tremble and his cock twitch. He forced himself to look away.

Kira gave him a sidelong look, nodding down pointedly at his groin. "Sure you don't want me to go down on you? I'd even pretend to enjoy it."

"You *would* enjoy it," he said distractedly, glancing around the corridor out of instinct as his mind jumped to the possibility of feeding on her. He had to control himself, but it didn't stop him fantasising about pushing her down on the floor and having his way with her in the middle of the corridor.

Fangs, flesh, fuck.

Those three words planted themselves in his mind.

Luckily, they had arrived outside Professor Parna's classroom. His jaw clenched as he unclipped Kira's leash.

"Last chance," she teased. Her tone was flirtatious, but the effect was ruined by the way she wrinkled her nose at the pungent smell coming from the classroom—which even he could smell by now. "We could go back to your bedroom."

"Alas, no. I have business to attend to. But before you go: some new rules. Your education is important, and therefore, whenever you are in school, I expect you to be a diligent student. You will wear a plug every day—"

"Is that for my education?" she interrupted.

He ignored her. "You are not permitted to remove the plug."

"And if I need the bathroom?"

He met her challenging stare. "Then you had better come find me, hadn't you, pet?"

Kira glared at him. "Yes, sir."

"Good. Any more questions?"

She glanced at the classroom door miserably, where Professor Parna could be seen drawing vesicles on the blackboard whilst the wolf students covered their mouths and noses. Even the vampire students looked green.

"No more questions," Kira sighed. "Except...what will you do while I'm at school today?"

She was stalling, and she was standing too close.

"Careful, pet..."

Kira bit her bottom lip, looking sexy as she stroked his hard length through his trousers.

The temptation to pull her aside into an empty classroom was strong.

"Are you going to touch yourself while I'm in school?" she asked.

"No."

Without warning, she cupped his crotch, taking hold of his balls through his trousers and squeezing them ever so gently, causing a rush of sensations to surge through him. "Are you sure?"

"Yes. No." *Maybe.*

Fuck.

"I'd like you to..." she whispered, batting her eyelashes at him. "Touch yourself while you think of me."

Her voice was smooth like honey, and he wanted nothing more than to feel her soft lips wrap around his cock and milk every last drop from him.

Powerless under her captivating gaze he held his breath as she fondled him. Her amber eyes danced with golden sparks. He was seriously starting to reconsider whether his sexual needs didn't take priority over Kira's education after all.

"Go, pet," he rasped. "Now."

Kira smiled mischievously, ignoring his command as she kneaded his balls.

She was just toying with him now.

Suddenly, the door behind them swung open, and Professor Parna cleared his throat loudly. Inside the classroom, the students were whispering surreptitiously as they craned their necks to see what he and Kira were doing. Her body blocked their view, but it was no great secret. Someone wolf whistled.

"Coming, or going?" Professor Parna asked with barely concealed amusement.

"Going," Nathaniel replied, straightening his tie as he turned on his heel and left.

I fucking wish I was coming.

CHAPTER 21

Moving In

NATHANIEL

AT THE END OF the school day, Nathaniel found Kira beside her locker, waiting for him dutifully on her knees. To his surprise, she was perfectly behaved as he led her on leash to his office. If she minded the stares of her peers, she did not show it. And when they reached his office, she did not protest when he commanded her to undress and service him.

He'd been waiting for her all day, and he wasn't prepared to wait a minute longer. As soon as the door was shut, he locked it—something he rarely did—crossed the room to sit at his desk and jerked his head to indicate the floor at his feet.

"Knees. Now. You know what to do."

Kira required no further instructions. She was uncharacteristically polite, well-mannered, and obedient, and she sucked his cock like a trooper, her head bobbing obediently for the better part of the hour without complaint until he finally sprayed his cum all over her face.

Even then, Kira did not glare at him. Her expression was composed and professional, as if they were colleagues who had just completed a business transaction.

It made him pine for the hot, fiery Kira who fought him on

everything, and the submissive side of her that looked up at him with wide innocent eyes full of trust. This new Kira was detached and devoid of emotion.

His training was working, and yet, he found little sense of gratification.

"Can I wipe my face yet, sir?" Kira asked, breaking through his thoughts.

He'd instructed her to sit on the edge of the desk so he could offer her his blood.

"Not yet, pet."

"But it's in my eye," she grumbled.

"Drink first," he said, biting his wrist. Blood trickled from the two puncture wounds his fangs had left.

Kira blew air in frustration, but her reluctance faded as she drank his blood. He gave her much more than he had last time, encouraging her to drink for several long minutes.

When he finally pulled his wrist away, her eyes were glazed, her tongue darting over her stained lips and teeth. Together with her cum-splattered face, she was a vampire's dream come true.

"So, how do I do magic?" she asked. "You still haven't told me what my special power is."

"Influence."

"Influence? As in manipulation?"

Nathaniel interlaced his fingers as he regarded her. "More or less. I have high hopes that you will be able to exert influence on not only wolves, but on vampires as well, to help persuade them to follow your command."

Kira's eyes widened. "No way. You mean I'll have mind control?"

Nathaniel smiled. "Influence, not mind control. If I am correct in my theory, then you will be able to unite both factions with your natural ability to lead. It is also my hope that we could mitigate the need for you to join the Poplarin pack."

"So I won't have to go through the initiation?" Kira asked hopefully.

"That's right, pet." Mark could keep his large oaf hands and small dick away from Kira. "So, let me know if you notice your abilities showing."

"Yes sir," Kira nodded, looking more cheered by the news than he'd expect her to be.

It reduced some of his agitation.

Kira's gaze flickered to the neatly folded hand towel on his desk.

He allowed a few more seconds to pass, waiting for her gaze to return to his before he reached for it.

She sat still obediently as he wiped her face, making no protest as he patted off the excess cum. The rest had already dried, but he dampened the towel with water from a jug and cleaned the film off.

"There, all done," he pronounced.

Kira stood.

"Before you go," he said, "tell me...What's changed? You're awfully well behaved."

She shrugged. "I realised you were right. I need to take your training more seriously. I feel like I've been looking at this dynamic between us all wrong."

"Oh?"

"I should be focusing on what we're trying to achieve, not on a relationship with you that was doomed before it even began."

Her words were light, but he felt the full force of them like a blow to the head.

Kira left his office without a backwards glance, and then everything was quiet and still.

Everything was proceeding perfectly, as planned. And he felt completely and utterly alone.

Nathaniel's loneliness stayed with him that evening, his mood only improving slightly when she joined him for dinner a few hours later in his dorm.

She sees no future with me.

Kira had clearly accepted the fact that they could never be together and moved on. As for him...

I'm just going through the motions.

They sat at the long table eating roast with the vampire students. Kira conversed freely with the others, but she hardly exchanged two words with him, except to politely tell him when he'd asked that she couldn't feel her magic.

When he asked about Susie, however, her face lit up, and she seemed to forget her indifference as she described the books she'd borrowed from the library and taken to Susie.

To his dismay, when he asked Kira about the books, she only gave a vague response. It was as if she was purposefully shutting him out, and she suddenly became interested in a debate between Victoria and Felix.

Nathaniel's heart ached. She'd put up a wall between them. He understood that she was trying to guard her feelings, but the selfish part of him wanted nothing more than to break that wall down and pull her close.

Suddenly, he turned to her and announced, "I want you to move in with me."

The others fell silent, and Kira looked surprised. She covered her mouth as she finished chewing her food, and by the time she swallowed, the others had resumed chatting.

"Really?" she asked.

"Yes. It's the logical choice in order to fast-track your training." It was a feeble excuse, and she probably saw right through it, but he forged ahead. "I can have your things brought over from your room if you agree."

Say you agree.

Please.

She considered this for a moment. "Yes. Sure."

Nathaniel's heart skipped a beat.

She said yes.

Logical choice or not, having Kira move in would give him more time with her. More seconds, which added up to more minutes, more precious hours when they already had so few left. He lived and breathed for those moments he could be near her, even if things between them were tense.

They continued Kira's training that evening in his bedroom. He'd bought her lingerie while she was in class—a concoction of sheer silk with bright pink satin ribbons that looked beautiful against her dark skin. Any colour would have been flattering on her, and it drove him crazy to see her dark nipples showing through the translucent fabric.

For the first half of the evening, he lounged in his chair with his feet on his desk, throwing Kira a ball for her to fetch over and over. She retrieved it each time without complaint, crawling around his bedroom floor on her hands and knees. He'd half-hoped she would morph in order to bring the ball back more easily, but of course, she didn't.

"Good girl," he praised softly as he took the ball from her mouth for the umpteenth time. "That's enough fetch for one evening."

Kira nodded. "Yes, sir. What would you like me to do instead?"

Her tone was formal, her expression carefully blank, as if she were ready to say 'yes' to anything.

It left him feeling sad and uninspired. She was drop dead gorgeous, especially in the pink camisole and silk stockings.

But he missed the real Kira.

As he deliberated, he noticed her subtly massaging her knees. She must have been tired and sore from crawling around.

After another moment's consideration, he said, "Go get ready for bed. Shower, if you wish. There's a towel and pyjamas on the vanity."

Kira blinked, glancing down at her lingerie. "You want me to change into pyjamas?"

"Yes." He hadn't touched her, or himself for that matter. There was nothing in her emotionless expression to suggest that she wanted him to, and her blank apathy was another blow, confirming that she'd shut him out. He cleared his throat. "When you are ready, go to your mat and sleep." When Kira hesitated, he added, "That will be all, pet."

"Yes, sir," she said, giving him a confused look before walking away, the lace of her panties riding up the perfect crack of her ass cheeks.

Nathaniel let out a long exhale.

Fuck me.

He'd never imagined it was possible to be this aroused and melancholy at the same time.

He remained at his desk long after Kira had curled up on the mat, and the hours passed as he stewed in his thoughts, watching the fire burn low.

Finally, he got into bed, which felt large and empty without her. Not even the soft hum of the magical candles could calm his racing heart. He wished he could connect to her mentally. He lay perfectly still, staring at the ceiling as he tried to detect the sound of her breathing, wondering if she was asleep. After what felt like hours, he assumed that she must be.

Until she spoke.

"Nathaniel?"

He drew a sharp breath, the sound of her voice in the darkness invading his heart and tempting him with hope. "Yes, pet?"

When she didn't answer immediately, he sat up in his bed and leant over the edge.

Kira was staring up at him from the mat, her face cast in shadow except for the golden flecks caught by the candlelight.

She didn't say anything. Neither did he.

A long minute passed as they held each other's gaze, both of them unable to say in words what they wanted.

Finally, he beckoned.

Kira rose, slow and graceful, and climbed onto the bed.

The feeling of the mattress depressing as she crawled closer caused joy and longing to radiate through him.

Without uttering a word, Nathaniel wrapped his arms around her soft, warm body and pulled her against his chest, burying his face in her hair and inhaling her scent. She felt like home.

Everything he never knew he'd wanted was right here, and yet he was powerless to keep her. Sooner or later, she would slip out of his grasp again.

Kira seemed preoccupied.

"What is it?" he murmured.

"I'm thinking of your father."

His chest tightened. "What about him?"

Her voice was uncharacteristically timid. "What happens if I can't kill him? What if he kills me first?"

Nathaniel tensed. "I won't let that happen."

"You can't guarantee my safety."

"Yes, I can," he insisted, even though they both knew it wasn't that simple.

Kira wasn't fooled. She touched his face. "If I die..."

Seizing her wrist, his every word dripped with fierce protectiveness. "I won't let that happen."

"But...*if* I die..."

"Then I will destroy him."

"But if you kill him...you'll be cursed."

Nathaniel nodded.

It would be a terrible price to pay, to become an empty vessel with no thoughts or feelings. But he wouldn't hesitate to intervene to protect Kira from his father.

Or in the event of the unthinkable, to avenge her death.

The looming threat of the curse would be of little consequence then; a life without Kira would be full of darkness. Without her, he would be lost, regardless of whether he was cursed or not.

"I won't let anything happen to you," he vowed, cradling her in his arms. The weight of that promise pressed down on him as they clung to each other.

CHAPTER 22

Best Laid Plans

NATHANIEL

KIRA'S TRAINING CONTINUED OVER the following week. Nathaniel had her drink his blood every night, but to both of their disappointment, there were no signs of her magical powers.

By Friday, they were forced to return to their original plan: Kira would have to rise to alpha status the traditional way—by ascending the ranks of a pack.

Reluctantly, Nathaniel promised to speak to the Poplarins to negotiate her membership.

Meanwhile, his training methods intensified. Every day, Kira went to school wearing a plug, and in the evenings, he would have her perform increasingly degrading acts in increasingly revealing outfits—like licking his shoes clean whilst he sat in front of the dorm fireplace with his friends.

Kira was so docile, at least to outward appearances, that he was having to find more and more creative ways to challenge her. She didn't even baulk when he instructed her to lick Victoria's heels clean.

Victoria had protested at first, but he'd insisted, and the vampiress knew better than to disobey a direct order from the Prince.

"Anyway, I'm trying to decide what I'm wearing to your thirtieth, Nat," Victoria was saying as Kira ran her tongue over her bright green six-inch heels. "I'm thinking of my orange jumpsuit."

"Whatever you wear will be fine," Nathaniel said distractedly.

Victoria rolled her eyes. "Whatever I wear will not be 'fine'. It's your coronation, and I want to dress up. Oh, by the way, you missed a spot, sweetie," she said to Kira, pointing to the toe box of her shoe.

Kira didn't bat an eyelid as she licked the shiny green fabric.

Nathaniel didn't like anyone else giving Kira orders.

"That's enough, pet," he said sharply, indicating for Kira to sit on his lap.

"Yes, sir," Kira said, standing and settling on his lap.

Her eyelashes fluttered in surprise when she felt his rigid length through his trousers, and she glanced at him.

"Yes?" he murmured, hoping she would say something.

He would have been glad to see her show any emotion, whether it was anger or lust. He wanted to know if his presence affected her even a fraction of how much she affected him.

Kira had acted aloof all week, but even she could not ignore the tension between them. It was thick, musty, and had given him blue balls every night as he lay awake, holding her as she slept.

He was half out of his mind as he tried to hold onto something that was slipping through his fingers.

Victoria was chatting to the other vampires, but he only pretended to listen. He could tell Kira was hyper aware of him by the goosebumps on her skin, and the way she kept glancing in his direction.

Nathaniel squeezed her thigh, relishing the way Kira's breathing turned shallow. And then slowly, subtly, she shifted, her ass grinding against his erection, the motion stroking his aching length ever so slightly.

"Pet," he warned quietly when she did it again.

"Yes, sir?"

She turned large innocent eyes to him, but she couldn't disguise the mischievous glimmer lurking in their depths, nor the faint twitch of her lips.

He trailed his fingers along her arm, leaving goosebumps in their wake. He leant close to her ear, and when she didn't recoil, he whispered in a gravelly voice, "I need you so badly it hurts."

It was an understatement. He hadn't come in days, and despite his constant arousal, he hadn't had the heart to jerk off.

He needed so much more than a quick release. He yearned to reconnect with Kira, to lavish her with love and affection, and to be everything she needed too.

Kira had said she loved him on the grassy outcrop. Was it still true? *Or have I lost her heart forever?*

He lifted his hips ever so slightly, pressing his cock against her ass as he spoke in a low undertone. "Take me out of my misery?"

Kira was pretending to listen to the others' discussion, but she tilted her head towards him and whispered, "Is that an order, sir?"

"No, it's not. But I need you." Her mouth, her clit, her ass, her hands. Anything and everything. He needed it now.

Kira turned her head to look at him dead in the eye. "I need you too." His heart leapt, but only for a moment as she added, "I *need* you to arrange an initiation with the Poplarins."

Nathaniel tried to hide his disappointment—and his guilt. Truthfully, he'd been putting off the meeting; once Kira became a Poplarin, she would cease to be his. Their cherished nights would be over. His bed would be cold forever.

"Well?" she prompted.

"I'm working on it."

"How much longer?"

He arched an eyebrow. "Why, pet...Don't tell me you're looking forward to the initiation."

"No," she retorted immediately, "You know that's not why." The first sign of hurt he'd seen flashed in her eyes. "But my magic hasn't returned, and we're running out of time. And this is part of the plan. You agreed to talk to the alphas about—"

"Shh," he said under his breath, "not in front of the others."

"They can't hear us," Kira replied as a loud peal of laughter broke out from the vampires. "See?"

She had a point, but just to be safe he leant back in his armchair, pulled her close, and whispered in her ear.

"Actually, pet, I already met with the alphas this morning. They have agreed to initiate you tomorrow night."

Kira froze in his arms.

"T-tomorrow?"

"That's right."

"When did you find out?"

"This morning."

"And you're only telling me now?" she accused.

Yes, he wanted to say.

I wanted one more evening with you. One more night of holding you in my arms, feeling your warmth, and your gentle breathing as you drift to sleep.

Just one more perfect moment.

Except he didn't want just one more. He wanted all the moments.

"Forgive me, pet," he spoke softly, stroking her arm. "It is not so easy for me to let go of you."

Kira drew a sharp breath, and they stared at each other for a long moment.

Nathaniel's heart beat faster as he waited, hoping she would say something. But what could she possibly say? *We're in too deep...*

"Is it...all twelve alphas I need to submit to?" Kira asked cautiously.

He'd known she would ask that, and yet, hearing her voice it out loud caused a cruel doubt to stab him, planting the thought that maybe, just maybe, Kira wanted to lay with all twelve. Was it completely absurd to think that she might enjoy it?

It *was* absurd, but he couldn't shake the image of her sitting naked on a dusty gym mat as the twelve bastards lined up for their turn.

His fists clenched.

"Nathaniel?" Kira asked, peering at him with concern. "Are you alright?"

"Just Mark," he croaked, his eyes locking with hers. "You need only lie with Mark."

Kira's lips parted in surprise. "How did you manage that?"

"I negotiated."

"Meaning...?"

"Meaning I threatened to claim the next batch of first year virgins for myself if they did not agree."

It was an empty threat. After Kira, there would be no one else for him. But the alphas had taken his threat seriously, and the prospect of losing access to next year's cohort had made them willing to agree to his terms.

Which had brought him no joy. But he'd promised Kira he would arrange the initiation to go ahead.

And he'd delivered.

Kira did not respond the way he expected. She looked shocked...and angry.

"What is it?" he asked.

She exhaled through her nostrils. "I feel a little jealous," she admitted.

Before he could process that, she asked, "How did you convince them I'm a virgin, anyway?"

"I didn't. They can scent your heat a mile away, apparently. Their words, not mine."

Even with her dark bronze complexion, he could see the glow of her blush, and thought her rather pretty.

"What are you two lovebirds whispering about?" Victoria interrupted loudly. "Get a room."

The others laughed.

"This room is adequate," Nathaniel said, his gaze never leaving Kira's. Without raising his voice, he said, "Leave us."

A hush fell throughout the common room. Everyone filed out with haste, even the students in the kitchen, leaving him alone with Kira.

"Are you sure you want to go ahead with the initiation?" he asked.

Say 'no'. Tell me you only want me and I will make love to you right here by the fireside.

"I don't *want* to go ahead with it," Kira said softly, as if he were the one who needed consoling. "I *have* to go through with it. Apparently, I don't have a shred of magic in me, so..."

"So, this initiation is the only way you can become the Poplarins' leader. By ascending their ranks legitimately."

"Exactly," she whispered, her answer barely audible this time.

Don't do it. Stay with me.

Be mine, forever.

Words swirled round in his head. Just as he began to speak, Kira asked "Does this mean it's our last night together?"

Nathaniel blinked, and it took him a moment to focus on his question. He'd been on the cusp of urging her to abandon everything. "Yes," he answered. "Tomorrow night, after the initiation ceremony, you will officially be a Poplarin. I will lose all claim to you."

He tried to gauge how Kira felt from her reaction, but her face was carefully blank.

"So...do I meet them in the gymnasium after school?" she asked.

"No, pet. I will escort you to the initiation myself. It is not at the school's gymnasium."

"Oh?"

"It was one of my terms. You deserve to be wooed and bedded in luxury. So I've arranged for a suite at the Haxby Hotel in the city."

"Oh, wow," Kira said. "That's...nice. Thank you, I guess...?"

He smiled sadly. "I wish I could have taken you there myself. If we had more time...there are many things I would have liked to show you."

Kira returned his smile. "I would have liked that."

Together, they took a deep breath and let it out slowly. Their eyes met. The urge to kiss her was strong. His body immediately responded to that hope, his abs aching, his chest tightening, his breathing turning shallow. But did she want to be kissed?

He leant forward, but Kira chose that moment to slip off his lap and kneel by his feet.

"Kira, what are you doing?"

"Given that this is my last opportunity to train with you, sir...perhaps I should demonstrate all that I've learnt?"

The soft 'sir' made his hair stand on end, his body sizzling with streaks of lightning as she slid her delicate hands along his thighs.

He did not protest as she took his cock out.

She handled it carefully, her hot tongue sliding along his semi-hard length divine strokes that soon had him at full mast.

Even though his heart ached as the last of their time together slipped away, he surrendered himself to the moment, gripping her thick lustrous hair as she began to suck.

CHAPTER 23

The Haxby Hotel

KIRA

THE HAXBY HOTEL WAS a tall building in the heart of the Capital. Its cool halls and opulent furnishings offering respite from the bustling streets outside.

The suite that Nathaniel had reserved was on the top level occupying half the floor, with tall windows offering a stunning view of the evening sun as it dipped below the horizon. Golden light bathed the west-facing rooms, causing the polished tiles, rich furnishings and gilded decorations to glow. Everywhere Kira trod, soft plush carpet caressed her feet, which were bare except for her white silk stockings.

She didn't dare ask how much the suite had cost, and could only stare at the luxury in awe as she explored the rooms. There was a bathroom with a deep tub and a selection of lotions and oils, and a balcony full of exotic-looking plants and a loveseat.

Out of nowhere, a yellow-crested bird fluttered onto the balcony and began to sing.

"Do you like it?" Nathaniel asked, appearing behind her as she stared at the balcony.

"I do," she nodded eagerly, momentarily forgetting why she was here as she turned to Nathaniel. "This is amazing."

"The birds are trained to do that. Sing, that is."

Kira had not known that, but she laughed and gave him a playful push. "Not just the bird. *Everything.*" She gestured at the suite, pulling him along by the hand. "All of this. It's absolutely incredible."

Her excitement petered out as she spotted the bed, a grand four-poster draped in cascading layers of deep burgundy and gold silk that pooled onto the polished mahogany floor. The headboard bore intricate carvings of twisted vines, and the corner posts made her mind jump to the fantasy of Nathaniel tying her to them.

Except it wasn't Nathaniel who would take her here. She bit her lip and frowned.

"What's the matter?" Nathaniel asked with concern, resting a warm hand on the small of her back.

"*I wish it was just us,*" she nearly said, but managed to hold the words back. Tonight would be hard enough without having second thoughts. Now that she'd made a decision, she just had to follow through. Once it was over, the rest of her life could begin. Finally, she would be back on track to her initial goal when she'd first stepped into the academy: to become an alpha.

She would work to unite all the packs, just like she'd always planned. With Nathaniel's wedding fast approaching, she would soon be presented to Henrikk, and they would need the shifters' support once she assassinated him.

Just one step at a time. First, she had to get through this ordeal with Mark.

"I'm fine," she added, offering Nathaniel a smile.

Meeting his gaze just made it worse. He was breathtakingly handsome, his icy blond hair golden in the sunset, his face angled, his eyes soft as they drew her in.

Kiss me, she thought, suddenly craving his touch, his lips, the safety of his arms.

"You're nervous," he said, caressing her cheek.

She leant into his hand, closing her eyes against the warmth of his palm. "I'm glad you're here."

It couldn't be easy for him to witness what was about to happen, and if she'd been braver, perhaps she would have insisted she was fine to be here by herself. The fact that he would be here to protect her, to ensure nothing went wrong, gave her the strength to go through with it. Even if the thought of just seeing Mark made her gag.

"Champagne?" Nathaniel asked. "It might help settle your nerves."

Kira nodded. "Yes, please."

They drank several glasses on the balcony, sitting close beside each other on the bench as they watched the sun go down. In Nathaniel's easy company, she could almost forget her troubles, but the nervous butterflies dancing in her stomach made her feel on edge and nauseous. As the last of the light faded, Nathaniel set his glass down with a clink and turned to her, his expression serious.

"I have to tell you something, Kira."

"Oh?" Her stomach tingled with butterflies, even though there was a note of finality to his words.

"Yes.

"I need you to know that I love you with all my heart. You are my soulmate. No matter what happens, no matter what we endure and who we wake up beside in the future, there will never be another for me." He cupped her face, leaning close. "There is only you. And if I could ask for an entire lifetime with you, it would not be enough."

Her breathing hitched as his lips grazed hers. She was on the precipice of losing him, and the words came easily. "I love you too, Nathaniel. You're the only one I want to be with. It took me a while to figure that out. But I respect you, and I trust you enough to follow you anywhere."

And this is not what I want.

If only he would bite her, then he would hear her thoughts and know her heart. Then maybe, he would talk her out of this ridiculous task she'd set her mind to.

"Nathaniel," she began, her voice small and pained.

He closed the final distance between them and kissed her, the intense press of his lips feeling both desperate and final. He pulled her into his chest, gripping her tight as if he was afraid to let go. Despite his tight embrace, Kira could feel a heartbreaking chasm opening up between them, threatening to wrench them apart.

And then a knock came from the suite door.

"They're here," she squeaked as fear and nerves spiralled through her like a hurricane. She clutched Nathaniel's shirt, burying her head against his chest, seeking warmth and safety.

Seeking his protection.

It made her confess what she really felt. "I'm scared," she whispered.

Nathaniel drew back and appraised her.

"You can do this, pet. You're the strongest person I've ever met. The fiercest wolf that ever existed. I'll be here, and I won't let anything bad happen to you. Everything will be all right." He hesitated. "Do you want me to help you?"

She knew what he meant by 'help'. To take over, dominate her, to take the stress of choice away as he ordered her to do his bidding. It was a huge thing to entrust him with in a moment like this...but it was the only way she would be able to follow through without puking all over the carpet.

Her eyes welled with tears.

"Yes," she said, flinching as the knock came at the door again, louder this time.

"Shh, don't worry about them," Nathaniel said, brushing away a tear as it rolled down her cheek. "Look at me."

She took a shuddery breath, and felt an instant calm as the blue pools of his eyes drew her in, his voice unwavering as he spoke.

"Go into the bedroom, remove this robe, and wait on the bed. When Mark enters, you will spread your legs for him and take his cock like a good slut. And you will do so without protest because I asked you to. Can you do that for me?"

Kira drew a deep breath, her lungs filling with air as Nathaniel's calmness and strength steadied her.

All she had to do was follow his orders.

I can do this.

She met his gaze.

"Yes, sir."

CHAPTER 24

Her Virginity

NATHANIEL

NATHANIEL OPENED THE DOOR. Mark and Chelsea entered, looking uneasy as they stepped past him. At his request, Mark had brought a bunch of flowers for Kira, but it was a paltry offering of semi-wilted marigolds, and not the thoughtful bouquet she deserved.

Nathaniel's jaw flexed. When Mark nodded to him in polite greeting, Nathaniel returned the courtesy by not killing him.

He couldn't breathe, and every step he took in leading the pair to the hotel bedroom was like a rusty nail dragging across the flesh of his back.

Breathe.

He had to keep it together—for Kira. This was what she needed to do for the greater good. It was what they both needed to do, to put aside their personal desires. Plus, a wolf shifter like her deserved to be part of a pack. He'd robbed her of that opportunity the first time he'd bitten her. He wouldn't ruin her initiation again. It wasn't fair, and she didn't deserve that, not from him.

Even so, his feet felt like lead, and he faltered at the bedroom door.

"Is she in there?" Mark asked eagerly, brushing past him into the room.

Chelsea gave Nathaniel a look that he couldn't quite decipher—Hate? Disapproval? Pity?—before following Mark in.

Nathaniel hesitated a moment, his ears ringing as he heard Mark speak.

"There you are, Kira. Wow, you look incredible."

Nathaniel licked his lips and entered, his chest tightening as he spotted Kira.

She was wearing the outfit he'd bought her: a sheer white lace corset that hugged her every curve. It lifted the swell of her breasts to emphasise her cleavage and barely masked the dark circle of her nipples. Thin white stockings travelled up to her thighs, and she'd donned the silver stilettos he'd packed. She looked like an angel, and no one who saw her could doubt her innocence as she sat with her legs squeezed together and her hands fidgeting nervously in her lap.

"Is it just the two of you?" she asked.

"I'm the only witness," Chelsea explained. "The other alphas are not required to be here."

By which she means I made them stay away.

The initiation would be degrading enough for Kira without the whole pack ogling her.

"Let's begin," Mark announced, already taking off his shirt.

The fucker hadn't even bothered to wear a blazer.

Kira looked green as she watched Mark pull down his trousers and step out of them.

"Hope you're wetter than last time," Mark said, his cock swinging half-mast as he pushed down his boxers and approached Kira. "Lie back, let me get in there."

Fuck.

This was happening too fast.

The urge to run to her, to throw Mark out of the room and tear him a new one was strong.

Nathaniel bit his cheek and tasted blood. His helplessness was agonising as it clawed up his throat, making it impossible to breathe as he watched Mark push Kira's legs apart. No foreplay, no conversation, and no regard for her feelings whatsoever. Just a clinical, impersonal ritual.

The air left the room, and Nathaniel strode to the balcony and pushed the doors open, drawing a breath as he reeled with dizziness.

I can't do this. I can't.

His heart thundered in his chest, and he clutched at the railing tightly, his knuckles white.

This was wrong. It all felt wrong. That was *his* mate, the love of his life, and he was just standing by as another man took her.

What the fuck was wrong with him?

This is what needs to happen. The initiation is important for Kira.

Suddenly, Kira screamed, a painful cry that shattered through him. He whirled around in time to see Mark cheer in victory as his muscled body hovered above her. His large arms splayed on either side of her body, his ass cheeks clenching as he forced himself into her.

Kira's face was contorted with pain, the sheets scrunched up in her fists, and her entire body jerked as Mark rammed himself into her all the way.

"Fuck, you feel good," the alpha said, drawing back and thrusting into her again. "You like that, Kira? I bet you've fantasised about my cock."

She didn't reply, but Mark didn't seem to care, or maybe he mistook her whimpers for pleasure, because he thrust into her again.

Even Chelsea looked uncomfortable as Mark repeated the action, grunting louder each time he rammed into Kira.

Nathaniel was in hell, his entire body shaking as he watched from the balcony. He felt the last of his sanity disappear as he watched that piece-of-shit screw the woman he loved.

He clutched at the doorway as the room began to spin, red-hot anger obscuring the edges of his vision.

The sound of Mark's laboured breathing, along with the repetitive shifting of the bed as he rutted Kira, was torture.

Nathaniel felt as if he would crumple in on himself. If he intervened, Kira might never forgive him. But he would never live with himself if he didn't do something to stop this madness.

Jealousy and anguish consumed him as stood in the doorway, watching Kira's body jostled carelessly as Mark sped up.

Nathaniel's head dropped in defeat, his shoulders rising and falling with heavy, angry breaths.

"Stop!"

Kira's voice broke through the grunts.

Nathaniel's head snapped up. Her voice was so timid he wasn't sure if he'd imagined it...until he heard her call out again, her voice breaking into a shriek.

"Mark, stop!"

But the alpha did not stop.

"Hang on, darling, I'm nearly there," he panted, increasing his pace and causing the whole bed to shake. "I'm going to fill you up right now."

CHAPTER 25

Mark's Conquest

KIRA

MARK WAS NOT ROUGHER than Nathaniel had been. His cock wasn't even as large. But he was a selfish pig, and even though she'd tried to ready herself beforehand so she wouldn't be dry, he'd still shoved it in without any consideration to how it would make her feel.

"Look at your virgin blood on my cock," he drawled. "You'll never forget this night." He lowered his barrel chest onto her.

Kira gasped for air. His full weight was crushing, the proximity stifling, and the feel of his slimy cock moving in and out of her was disgusting.

She tried to bear it, but as he sped up, grunting and staring straight ahead at the headboard as if she wasn't there, a part of her shrivelled and died.

"Stop!" she stammered, unable to take the indignity any further. Nothing was worth letting this happen to her. Nothing.

"Mark, stop!" she shouted, trying to push the large man off.

The bastard only sped up, making her breasts bounce and the bed shake around her. The thought of him coming inside her made bile sting her throat, and she threw her head around, looking for

Nathaniel.

She'd glimpsed him before on the balcony in her peripheral vision, but she'd been too embarrassed that he would see her like this to look at him directly. But now, she needed him. Searching for him, she prayed that he would pull Mark off her.

But the balcony was empty, and the sight of it made her blood turn cold. Nathaniel was gone. He'd left, and she was alone.

I don't blame him for leaving...

The sheer wretchedness of her situation set in as her body shook from Mark's back-and-forth thrusts. She didn't know whether to cry or throw up.

"Hang in there," Chelsea comforted her anxiously, squeezing her hand.

Kira pulled her hand away, choking back a sob. She did not want the female wolf to see her cry. She shut her eyes and covered her face.

I just have to endure.

Soon, Mark would finish, and then the initiation would be over.

Just another minute. As soon as he comes inside me, I can go shower.

Every second felt like an excruciating eternity. Mark's body pressed down on her, sweaty and soft where Nathaniel's had been hard, his cock making her feel empty and used in a way Nathaniel's never had.

Nathaniel had always made her feel special. Even when he was punishing her, including the time he'd fucked her ass in the woods, driving her into the mud and not letting her come. He'd left her in no doubt of his desire, whispering in her ear and showering her with affection. The way he purred that she was his pet, his girl, his whore... Each time he called her 'cumslut' made her shiver with delight, the word hot and filthy in the best way. Like his mouth on her pussy, reminding and reassuring her that she was *his,* and that only she would carry his seed.

Nathaniel had never made her feel like a sack of potatoes.

"Fuck, here I come," Mark said, and she felt his cock harden.

She tried to think of other things, but she was all too conscious of every slide of his cock, the squishy press of his hairy balls, and his hot breath on her neck.

The realisation that Nathaniel had left her, that he wasn't coming to help her, made her feel alone and abandoned.

Without warning, Mark began to morph. His face became a weird distortion with human eyes and a wolf snout, and his broad shoulders sprouted fur. His large cock transformed too, feeling slimier as it elongated, the head changing in shape and growing more invasive...

"I've decided to knot you, Kira," Mark announced with a grin, huffing hot air and flecks of drool onto her face. "I'm going to keep us joined together for the next hour. Would you like that?"

Hell no.

"No," she croaked.

Mark laughed. "You'll love it. Now stay still, I'm nearly there."

Kira was too horrified to scream as she felt Mark's cock pulse and grow inside her. He was about to come, and the bastard had shifted into a grotesque form of half-man, half-wolf, just so he could knot her and extend the torture. It meant that she wouldn't be able to shove him off once he was done. They would be joined for whoever knew how long.

Nausea flooded her senses. The thought of having to lie here, to have to *feel* him inside her for an agonising long hour was too much to bear.

She would rather be fucking dead.

At least Nathaniel wasn't here to watch.

"Here we go, darling," Mark announced, his eyes glazed as his weight rocked back and forth on top of her. "One fresh hot batch of cum is coming right up."

His bulging cock head grew larger as he neared his climax. Panicking, Kira tried to push him off, but he was too heavy, and the large, muscled wolf seemed oblivious to her struggle.

Fuck.

Any moment now, Mark would shoot his seed into her and knot her.

No, no, no.

Suddenly, Mark's weight suddenly lifted off her. Her eyes flew open, and she saw him fly backwards off the bed.

What the...

She pushed herself onto her elbows in time to see Nathaniel drag Mark away, his hand on Mark's fur-lined throat.

Her heart fluttered with shaky relief at the sight of Nathaniel.

He's still here. He didn't leave.

Nathaniel's fangs glinted as they protracted in a snarl, his face contorted in fury, and he lunged, biting Mark's throat and causing him to shriek.

Chelsea screamed, apparently too distressed to shift.

"What the fuck?!" Mark shouted as Nathaniel withdrew his fangs, leaving two red puncture wounds on the wolf's neck. "You didn't even let me finish!"

"You're finished," Nathaniel hissed, dragging him out of the room.

"I hadn't even come yet!"

"I promised you her maidenhood, nothing more," Nathaniel snarled. "That was our agreement. Now, *get out!*"

Kira stumbled out of bed, her legs weak as she crossed the bedroom. She reached the entryway just in time to see Nathaniel throw Mark out into the corridor.

Chelsea had already gone. Nathaniel slammed the door shut after them. A trail of blood dotted the carpet, and it glistened on Nathaniel's chin.

Kira stared at him in shock. He was shaking, his shoulders rising with heavy breaths. He stared at the door a moment longer before spitting Mark's blood onto the carpet.

He turned slowly and froze when he spotted her.

Their eyes locked and Kira felt the breath leave her. Admiration surged in her chest. Nathaniel had saved her. He was vicious, protective, and a predator...

And I love him.

"Nathaniel," she whispered, gasping as her knees nearly gave out.

Leaping forward, Nathaniel crossed the room in two strides, scooping her up in his arms. He carried her through to the bedroom, and all she could do was lie limply in his arms, blinking up at him in wonderment. His icy eyes looked crazed in their intensity, and he never once looked away as he gently lay her on the mattress.

"I've failed you," he apologised, lying down beside her. "Forgive me, my love."

"You haven't failed me. There's nothing to forgive."

"I should have put a stop to this before it began."

She shook her head. "That's not fair. Don't blame yourself. I'm a Poplarin now. This is fine," she added, unsure who it was she was trying to convince.

"Mark doing that to you was *not* fine," Nathaniel growled. "No one will ever do that to you again."

"But, what about your father—"

"*No one,*" he repeated, his harsh tone carrying a finality to it, "Except me. You are mine. From now on, the only one who touches you is me. Understand?"

Before she could question him, he stopped her mouth with a kiss, urgently coaxing her mouth open as he claimed her. Their lips explored one another, seeking, tasting, their mouths open and their tongues flicking together sensually.

"I want you," she said, breaking the kiss and hastily helping him unbutton his shirt. Nathaniel shrugged out of his clothes, but as he leant back, he paused to stare at a small patch of blood on the bed sheets. She saw his nostrils flare as he inhaled, and she felt a sharp jolt as she realised it was her blood.

Nathaniel met her gaze, the depraved energy darkening as he undid his belt. "Mark might have been the first person inside of you," he began, taking his cock out, "but mine will be the last. I'll be damned if Mark is the last person to use your cunt. So spread your legs, pet. Welcome your master as he reclaims you."

Kira was too stunned by his aura to disobey. She shuffled back onto the bed and spread her legs. The magnificent sight of his rigid cock had her nervous with anticipation.

Nathaniel hitched her feet over his shoulders and leant forward, brushing the bodice of her lace outfit.

"You are so beautiful," he breathed, before his expression hardened. "And you're mine. My cum is the only seed you will carry. Is that understood?"

"Yes, sir."

"Show me you understand."

Kira eagerly took hold of his cock and guided the head against her entrance.

Tension thickened between them, as taut as the pressure primed and ready to ram through her entrance.

Nathaniel cupped her face tenderly. He held her gaze with hooded eyes, studying her reaction as he pushed his body against hers, his large cock thick and insistent as it pushed through her tight folds and eased inside.

Kira gasped as he slid deeper, stretching her apart.

"Feel me, pet," he commanded hoarsely, thrusting himself deeper. "Feel me inside your tight wet cunt. This is what you deserve. Isn't that right?"

"Yes, sir," she gasped.

Nathaniel didn't stop until he'd penetrated her fully and the entire length of him filled her. He held her there, pressing against her deepest part like a predator who'd caught his prey, and they groaned together, holding each other as their bodies joined.

"You feel so good, Kira," he said, trailing kisses along her jawline, his lips moist and teasing, his fangs agonisingly close to the throbbing vein at her neck. "You're so fucking tight that you're squeezing the life out of me."

"Good," Kira giggled. "Better than our fantasy?"

Nathaniel's expression remained serious. "Every moment with you is a fantasy."

With her legs lifted high, he folded forward and pushed his cock as deep as it would go.

She cried out and lifted her hips to meet him, wanting him, needing him to reclaim her.

He grinded his hips against her, ploughing her in a way that felt surprisingly different to when he'd taken her ass. It was deep and sensual in a whole different way. There was less pain, although Nathaniel knew how to exert just the right amount, his cock hitting her deep spots slowly and with expert precision until she felt sore. Just when she thought she couldn't take any more, he would pound those deep spots fast and hard for good measure until she had tears in her eyes.

"You are mine forever, Kira."

He claimed her, driving his cock in and out of her like a piston, using more force than Mark had. "There is no escape now. You will be on your hands and knees every morning and every night, waiting patiently for me. You will beg me to give you my cock, and I will use your body if and when I see fit. On those occasions, I will fill your slutty pussy like the cumslut that you are, and you will thank me for the opportunity. Won't you, pet?"

"Yes, sir," she gasped, clutching his shoulders as he thrust into her deep, repeating the action again and again.

"What is it you will say, pet?"

"Thank you."

"Louder, pet."

"Thank you," she cried, her voice growing steadily higher pitched as Nathaniel's brutal thrusts caused waves of pleasure to blossom through her.

She was getting close.

"I'm going to fuck you until you scream, pet, and then I'm going to fill you to the brim with my seed. And, if you would allow me to bite you...if you would agree to let me drink your blood..."

"Yes," she said breathlessly, "but as you suck my blood, I want you to come inside me at the same time."

"*Fuck.*" Nathaniel growled as he nibbled the sensitive skin at her jawline. "Pet, do you know how much I've wanted that?"

Kira angled her neck to give him better access, brushing her hair out of the way. "Then what are you waiting for?"

With a hissing growl, Nathaniel seized her shoulders and pushed his cock deep inside her, whilst extending his fangs.

She gave a silent gasp and arched her back, raising her hips to meet him.

He gave a guttural groan and thrust into her violently. Kira squealed as he leant close and sank his fangs into her neck.

Sharp pain emanated from where he had bitten her, and then she only saw stars as he drank her blood, lapping at her throat as he fucked her with his thick, swollen member. He took her slowly and jealously, pounding the deep spot inside her that Mark hadn't reached.

She shuddered from pleasure when Nathaniel's mind reached for hers, grazing her thoughts like a sensual touch whilst his hands intertwined with hers.

"*I want you to come at the same time as me, pet,*" he spoke in her mind. "*Come on my cock as I taste your blood and pump my seed inside you.*"

"*Yes,*" she cried, screaming the word out loud even as she whispered it in her mind. Her body throbbed with every blow, and Nathaniel drank hungrily, gripping her hair and pulling her head back to give him better access to her exposed throat.

She was trapped. But it was exactly where she wanted to be, pinned by his body and unable to move as he drove himself further into her, fucking her hard and slow as he fed from her.

"*Look at me, slut,*" he said, drawing his mouth back.

Kira opened her eyes and met his gaze. His lips were stained red as he brushed her lips, and his eyes met hers with burning intensity, holding a jealous, deranged fire that seared her.

"*It's time for your punishment, pet.*"

"*What?*" Her heart sank. "*For what?*"

"*You let another man touch you. You spread your legs for Mark and let him take his pleasure from you. If I hadn't intervened, he would still be inside you.*"

Kira's face grew hot with shame and she looked away, hot tears sliding down her face to damp the pillow.

"*Shh, don't cry, pet. There's nothing to be ashamed of.*"

"*Isn't there?*" she asked bitterly.

"*No. Not at all. In fact, I am proud of you.*"

"*You are?*"

"*Yes. But that does not mean there aren't consequences.*"

Dread filled her as she stared up at this dark, ruthless side of Nathaniel. His expression was hard, and she knew there was no escaping the punishment he had planned for her.

"*Do not look away,*" he warned as his hand closed over her throat, tightening on her airway and making it hard to breathe.

"*Yes, sir,*" she wheezed.

Holding her gaze with his steely eyes, he rammed his cock in as deep as it could go, hitting the sensitive parts of her. He repeated the motion, studying her response, patting her cheek in gentle slaps to remind her not to look away.

"Again," he said, punching his cock in again.

He was hurting her, but she didn't shy away from his gaze, nor from his slow, deliberate thrusts.

"You deserve this," he crooned, and she whimpered as she felt the full force of his possessiveness, and the barbs of his twisted love. *"Don't you?"*

"Yes, sir!" she gasped.

"You were a bad pet. But I'm going to make it all better. Do you understand?"

"Yes sir," she cried as his cock pummelled her.

Nathaniel wasn't just punishing her. He was reclaiming her. As he took her harder and faster, she realised she needed this as much as he did. There needed to be repercussions for what she'd done. She desperately needed him to wipe every last trace of Mark from her memory, to fuck her until her entire body ached.

She had hurt Nathaniel by letting Mark use her, and now he would hurt *her* so that they could both forget what they'd done.

And then a more terrible realisation hit.

He's not just punishing me. Nathaniel's punishing himself. He's letting himself become the person he hates—his father—to do it.

Her husky moans filled the room as she clung to him, this man who was more Henrikk than himself in this moment. She moved to meet him as he took her, sinking into her again and again. He devoured her with a primal hunger as his teeth sunk into the other side of her neck, and she couldn't get enough of him as he sucked at her essence.

"I'm so fucking close, slut. Look at what you do to me."

"I'm close too, sir."

"I know, I can feel you clamping down on me. Let me hear you scream my name."

Kira screamed, both out loud and in her mind.

But she didn't scream Henrikk's name. She screamed Nathaniel's, because there had to be a distinction. He was not his father, and he wasn't truly even like his father, and she needed him to know that.

She screamed his name as he roared hers. Their bodies moved as one as he held her down and rammed into her tight, wet hole again and again until his cock was flooding her with his thick, creamy seed, and she was sobbing as her orgasm caused tears to run down her face and her entire body quaked in his arms with agonising release.

"Take it, pet," he groaned as his movements came to a still and the last spurts of cum filled her. "Take it all."

CHAPTER 26

Showering Love

NATHANIEL

THEY LAY TOGETHER ON the hotel bed. It was still dark outside, the city lights below mirroring the stars. The suite's candelabras had sprung alight with tiny vermillion flames, casting a soft glow around the lavish bedroom.

Kira was draped in nothing more than a thin sheet, which bunched at her waist, emphasising the curve of her hips and hinting at her perfect, naked form underneath.

Nathaniel had one arm wrapped around her, and she was nestled close, resting her head on his chest where she belonged.

She let out a contented sigh. "For fear of sounding romantic...I wish this night never had to end."

Nathaniel smiled sadly as he traced her arm. The night would end sooner than either of them were prepared for, the hours before dawn slipping away too fast.

"I'm sorry," he said quietly.

Kira glanced at him in surprise. "What for?"

"For failing you tonight."

"You've already apologised—"

"It's not enough. I shouldn't have left the room. And I should never have allowed Mark to..." his fists curled. "For letting that happen..." He couldn't get the words out, his grief instantly replaced with anger that charged his muscles. The punishment had cleansed them, but he couldn't let go of the guilt that crept back in to tighten his chest.

"Shh," Kira soothed, adjusting her position so she could prop her chin on his chest—such a wolf thing to do. "You're being too hard on yourself. You did not fail me. This was *my* choice, and I agreed to it because it's essential to our plan."

"*My* plan," he corrected, feeling annoyed with himself. "I should have put a stop to it the moment I met you."

"I don't understand. What's changed?"

"Everything."

Nathaniel loved Kira with all his heart. But the fact that he was grooming her bothered him greatly. This was not how a male vampire was supposed to treat his mate. Growing up, he'd had so few examples of honourable behaviour, but that was no excuse.

Barbara had told him enough of what vampires had once been like—what many were still like outside his father's court—that he should have known better.

Nathaniel had even met some of them. Such good-natured vampires typically lived in the countryside far from the Capital and were nothing like his father's courtiers. The royal court was rotten to the core, but once destroyed, there would be hope for the rest of them to live better, kinder lives.

"Nathaniel?" Kira prompted. "What's wrong?"

He let out a long sigh, but it did not relieve the tension he felt. "Vampires have similar but different values to shifters. Wolves, as you know, rely on a strict pack hierarchy, where members obey orders without question like soldiers. Vampires, however, place more importance on family structures. We don't have a choice in the matter because these are reinforced by blood ties. There is nothing more important to a vampire, especially a male one, than honouring one's family. Tonight, I let you down by not protecting you." He cupped her face, and she leant into his touch. "My love. I will do better by you."

"We both did what we had to," Kira whispered, shutting her eyes as a tear ran down her cheek and wetted his hand.

Nathaniel's jaw clenched. He was starting to lose his nerve, and his mind struggling with the impossible dilemma of what to do. How could he follow through with the plan? The first phase—situate Kira so she could raise a secret army of wolves—was all under control. But as for the second phase, how could he give Kira up to his father? Especially knowing the abuse she would undoubtedly suffer at his hands. His stomach twisted and knotted sickeningly.

"We've come so far," Kira whispered, "Don't back out now."

Nathaniel didn't say anything.

Kira sat up suddenly. She placed her hands on his shoulders and sat astride his lap. "I have an idea," she said with a forced cheerfulness he suspected was for his benefit, "Of how we can be together."

He forced himself to smile as well. "Go on."

"We'll continue with the plan, just as we agreed. I'll do whatever it takes. And when all of this is over...and your father is slain...and you're married to Gloria..." her voice wavered ever so slightly, "I will rule. My life will belong to the people. But my heart will belong to you. I will be your mistress."

Nathaniel flinched. Whatever names they used in the bedroom—even publicly—was between the two of them.

"You deserve better than that," he croaked. "You deserve love."

Kira smiled at him coyly with a raised eyebrow. "And I have it, don't I? Your love?"

A smile crept across his face. "Yes, pet. You certainly do. Now, and forever." He lifted her hand to his lips and kissed it as he met her gaze. "I love you with every breath."

"And I love you." Kira interlocked her fingers with his and squeezed them tightly, as if she had no intention of ever letting go. "Although, technically, I'll be the ruler, so that will make *you* my mistress."

"I have no problem with that," he smiled, even though the guilt welling up in him was almost too much to bear.

She gave him a kiss on the cheek, the light-hearted peck drawing another smile from him as she touched his face. "Promise me something, Nathaniel. That when all of this is over...we'll be together. Please, tell me that much is true, because if I know that, then I think I can endure just about anything."

Nathaniel forced himself not to grimace. He knew perfectly well what it was Kira was nervous about enduring—his father's advances.

"I promise," he said stiffly, hating himself for the hardships ahead of her.

Kira's eyes were bright with hope for the future, but he couldn't stop the dread eating away at the edge of his happiness.

"Hey," she whispered, smoothing back his hair. "Everything will be all right."

Her expression was soft, and her encouragement coaxed a smile from him. "I should be the one reassuring you."

"We can reassure each other. Now, stop moping. I want to play."

"Do you, now?"

"Yes." Her eyes lit up with mischief as she settled onto him, a move that squished her naked breasts against his chest.

And then she leant her head against the side of his neck and nuzzled him, the gentle graze of her face against his throat igniting a wild roaring flame. A soft groan escaped him as she licked his throat, a long, damp swipe that instantly made his uneasiness vanish.

Kira grinned at him as she grinded her clit against him, wetting his thigh.

He couldn't help it, he was already hard. He groaned again as she ran her hands through his hair, mussing it as she rubbed herself against him again, this time coating his balls.

"*Fuck,*" he gasped.

Kira grinned at him, and before he knew it, she'd hopped off the bed and was prancing across the room, looking lighter and happier than he'd ever seen her. "I'm going to have a shower."

Nathaniel was stunned.

She's leaving me here? Like this?

His hardened cock ached from her denial.

"Think twice before you leave the room, pet," he warned.

Kira slowed her steps, but she did not stop. Instead, she continued towards the bathroom, humming as she swayed her hips and strutted away without so much as a backwards glance.

Except when she reached the bathroom door, she stopped, tossed her thick mane of hair, and then slowly, ever so slowly, she glanced back at him over her shoulder.

He gave her a warning look that made her squeal and disappear into the bathroom.

He chuckled, pumping his aching cock once before sliding off the bed and prowling after her. The hunt was on.

The bathroom was steamy, but she was easy to find, and when he grabbed her, he found her willing. He made her kneel to suck his cock, and her eagerness to service him made it almost impossible not to come in her mouth.

A sad thought held him back. When all was said and done, Kira would be his lover, his friend, and his companion.

But not my wife.

Those were the words that haunted him, even as he pulled Kira to her feet and opened his mouth to devour hers.

Not my wife.

No matter how passionate their kisses were.

No matter how deep he moved inside her as he made love to her against the slick wet tiles, he could not rid himself of the melancholy words that repeated themselves over and over again in his mind.

Never my wife.

And he realised then, though he did not have the heart to tell Kira, that there *was* an alternative to the plan. One where she could still become the ruler they all needed, and more importantly, one where she wouldn't have to suffer any abuse as his father's sexual plaything: he would destroy his father.

It was not a new idea, but it had not seemed feasible until now. The thought of being cursed to walk the earth as a mere shadow of himself had always chilled him to the bone, just as it did now.

But I will do it for Kira.

He had to. Because what kind of partner was he to send her to do his dirty work for him? What kind of vampire did that make him? Not an honourable one, like his ancestors had been, but a cruel one like his father. He exhaled through his nostrils. Henrikk was his father, he was his responsibility.

"Is everything all right?" Kira asked as she sponged herself with soapy water.

They had been standing beneath the water—set to a lower temperature to cool their hot skin—washing each other.

Nathaniel took hold of Kira's chin and lifted it to meet this gaze. "You are mine, Kira. I've said it before, but I was a fool to think that I could ever give you up. No one else will ever touch you again except for me."

This time, he would not let her talk him out of it.

She blinked. "But what about your father? The whole point of grooming me was so I could kill him."

"We'll find another way. I will hide you and keep you safe."

"You can't hide me," she said softly. "Who will kill your father?"

I will, he thought to himself. *Once I have married Gloria and become king, my father will forfeit the magic that protects him...and*

I will kill him. Even if it means I will be cursed, for at least then you will be safe. Living a cursed life will be better than knowing I allowed you to do my dirty work and be harmed by my father.

Kira could not hear his thoughts, but she must have sensed something in his countenance, because understanding flashed in Kira's eyes.

"Nathaniel, *no.*"

"No?" he tried, feigning ignorance.

"You can't."

"I didn't say anything."

"Well, your thoughts were very loud. I could hear you."

"You could?" *Interesting.* Their mental link wasn't even in place. He pulled back to study her. Had she really heard his thoughts? Or was it simply intuition?

She looked aghast, her face reflecting deep worry. "You can't kill your father. You said so yourself—you'll be cursed."

Nathaniel didn't say anything. He lifted Kira up into the air, wrapped her legs around him, and pinned her against the tiles, his erection pressing at her entrance.

"Stop trying to distract me," she snapped, fixing him with burning eyes.

"Is it working?"

She shook her head.

"Are you sure?"

Kira's lips parted in a silent moan as he pushed his cock inside her in one, slow, smooth motion, until he had penetrated her to full hilt.

There was a slight tremor to her voice as she spoke. "*Promise* me you won't. I can't live without you."

He drew his cock out slowly but didn't answer.

"Nathaniel, please. Answer me."

He thrust into her, hard.

"Please."

He thrust again, harder.

"Nathan—"

"I promise." It was a lie, and he hated himself for that. But to let her go ahead with this dangerous mission was unthinkable.

One small lie...in exchange for her wellbeing.

He thrust again. "I will find someone else to kill my father."

Another lie.

If not Kira, then it has to be me.

Even if his father lost the magic protecting him, Henrikk was too careful. Only someone who he explicitly trusted—or underestimated—would have half a chance of succeeding.

Which made Kira the perfect candidate.

And it made him an even better one.

"And if you can't find another way?" she asked, her eyes glazing as she shuddered from the impact of his cock.

He offered her a grim smile. "Then that's a lack of imagination on my part, isn't it?"

"That's not funny."

There would be no convincing her, but his duty to protect her was too strong. The kingdom's need for a just ruler like Kira too great. She was strong, pure of heart, and stubborn as fuck, and if she ever discovered her magic, she would be truly formidable.

That was why she had to survive. What happened to him was of little consequence where the rest of the world was concerned. With Henrikk slain, they needed a ruler to unite them—otherwise, there would be anarchy.

Which was why he found himself lying to the woman he loved. If his greatest purpose was to protect her, then he would do so now, and die with some semblance of honour, even if the curse condemned him for killing his own father.

A white-hot determination rushed through him as he pounded Kira against the slick, tiled wall, the water trickling fast down their faces and hair obscuring their vision.

He lost all sense of time as his brooding thoughts consumed him, and he let Kira feel the full force of it.

He would tell a thousand lies if he had to, because the thought of his father whipping her perfect, unmarred back as he bedded her made him sick to the stomach.

His mind was set, his heart heavy with grief, but at least he no longer felt guilty. Finally, he would do right by Kira.

The plan would remain the same, only that he would cut Kira out of it...At least until he'd dealt with his father. And then she would be free to rule.

In the meantime, he still had to marry Gloria in order to become king. It was his father's condition, introduced to prevent revolt, and it was a sensible one.

Henrikk may have dubbed himself King after the takeover, making Nathaniel the Crown Prince, but deep down, every vampire knew that Gloria was the rightful heir to the throne. She was the daughter of Vampire King Dmitri, who had died several years before the Revolution, and Vampire Queen Liddia, who'd died immediately after the Revolution. Henrikk had given her to his men, and she'd died a slow, humiliating death. 'A traitor's death', Henrikk had called it, using Liddia's death as a warning to other vampires as he banned marriage between vampires and other races.

"Where are you?" Kira asked, breaking through his thoughts.

"Here," he said, opening his eyes and squinting through the heavy downpour of water. He kissed her, long and slow, before continuing his movements. "I'm always here, with you."

Kira gasped for air as his movements grew ominously slow, the force of his cock slamming into her and pushing her up the wall, causing her legs to squeeze around him.

Should I tell her?

He doubted Kira knew how her mother had died, and perhaps

it was better he spared her the horror of it. The mode of Liddia's execution was widespread knowledge amongst older vampires, but it was rarely spoken about, and few people of Kira's generation even knew who Liddia was. It contradicted Henrikk's rule too much.

There was another thought weighing on Nathaniel. Since Gloria and Kira had the same mother, it meant they were half-sisters. The dilemma of when to tell Kira had been gnawing at him.

Even if he did, there would be no heartfelt reunion. The two women were nothing alike. Gloria was thirty-years-old, as he was, and had been raised at Wintermaw Keep by Henrikk, the man who'd subjected her mother to a slow, humiliating death.

Growing up as a political hostage in Henrikk's court had not been easy for Gloria, and she'd grown to become as cruel as the courtiers around her. The vampiress had never lost her supporters, who had infiltrated Henrikk's court and secretly supported her right to rule, and this made her dangerous.

A danger that will be neutralised if she marries me.

Thinking of Gloria at a time like this was cooling his ardour, and he pushed his worries aside as he focused on the beautiful wolf in his arms.

Kira was wildly different from her cold half sister. Kira was passionate and full of life, her spirit burning hot as it drove her from one goal to the next. She was also watchful and reserved, speaking out only when confronting an injustice.

And when she was angry, fiery sparks flew that brightened the darkest of nights and seared a lasting impression on his soul.

Soon, I won't have a soul at all.

Once Nathaniel killed his father with his own hands, he would become a soulless, pitiful creature. Unable to love, or to feel the sun on his skin. Doomed to feel nothing at all. It was a lot like what he imagined being married to Gloria would have been like.

Shit.

Once again, stress had turned his thoughts back to his father and his dreaded wedding night. Couldn't he just enjoy this final night with Kira without thoughts of his father tarnishing it?

And yet, with his decision to cut Kira out of the plan, a weight had been lifted off his chest.

He'd been panting for air as he fucked her, but now his lungs could draw air properly.

This was it. This was what he should have done all along, and he was only ashamed he hadn't had the guts to do it sooner. But it was not too late to be the man Kira deserved, at least while he still had a soul.

In the meantime, for these last remaining hours in the hotel room, he would make love to Kira with every fibre of his being. He would worship her, and he would fuck her in every way he knew how, teaching her all the ways to satisfy him as he revelled in the tight needy dampness of her cunt. Because once he was cursed, he would lose her and himself in every way that mattered, and he would never feel love again.

For Kira.

Resolve empowered him, hardening his mind, his muscles, and even his cock. Kira felt it too, because she gasped, a half-smile of surprise lighting up her features.

"You were brooding again," she murmured, caressing his face.

He swallowed the lump in his throat knowing how much he would miss her touch.

"I was. But you have my full attention now." He set her down. "On your knees, pet."

Kira looked eager but tired as she lowered herself onto the wet floor.

"Bend forward onto your hands. Good girl." He knelt behind her, fisting his cock and pumping it several times. His entire body was charged, ready to fuck, bite, and feed. "Now, spread your legs, pet...you know what happens next."

She did as she was told, spreading her legs and presenting the perfect swells of her ass. She made no protest except to wail like an animal as he forced his fat, heavy cock through the tight pucker of her asshole.

It was just the head of his cock, but it felt so good, and she was already writhing like a bitch in heat.

He held still, enjoying seeing her like this.

"I love your moans," he said, leaning over her so his chest was flush with her back. He held her throat with one hand while reaching around to cup her pussy. She twitched, and then she squirmed as he inserted his fingers into her pussy, filling both holes at the same time.

His throat rumbled with approval. "I love your tight, wet cunt and the way it yearns for my cock." He shoved his fingers in deep, an impressive feat given how little room there was inside her. "Can you feel how tight your cunt is with my cock in your ass, pet?"

"Yes, sir," she exclaimed in a wavering voice.

He wished she could see what he could: the way he had her spread, her tiny asshole stretched impossibly tight around his enormous thickness. His engorged cock was almost purple in shade as it slid in and out of her, invading her ass again and again in torturous strokes.

He relished the way she trembled, and he took her slow and steady, inching his cock in so she could appreciate the full length of him. Each time, he drew out almost all the way, his bulging head stretching and magnifying her poor sphincter, causing her to cry out as her fingernails scraped the tiles uselessly.

"Nathaniel," she gasped. "It's too much—"

"Shh."

He stayed where he was, teasing the deep forbidden space of her ass with tiny thrusts.

The next time he drew out, his cock head forcing her pucker wide, he paused.

"Be ready, pet. I'm afraid this will hurt. But it will feel good for me."

Without warning, he sheathed himself in one deep stroke with a grunt. Kira's body jerked forward, eliciting a perfect gasp of pain from her perfect mouth.

Nathaniel didn't give her a chance to catch her breath. He bore down on her, pummelling the depths of her ass the way his father would have, in hard, punishing strokes. And this time, there was no excuse for why he did it.

He was no longer grooming Kira for his father. There was no longer any pretence of training.

He was hurting her because it made him feel good. And bizarrely, Kira wanted him to.

"Moan for me, pet," he rasped. "Moan for me like a bitch in heat."

She moaned with pleasure, her throaty cries echoing around the bathroom in an orchestra of noise.

"Louder. Show me what a horny animal you are."

"Yes, sir," she said, peering over her shoulder at him. Her normally voluminous hair hung flat in dark wet sheets, and her amber eyes were pure gold now. That was when he noticed the crackling glow of magic shimmering over her body. "I will show you exactly what kind of animal I am."

He froze.

Did she mean what he thought she meant?

Was she morphing...for him?

Chapter 27

Whipped

NATHANIEL

HOLY SHIT. NATHANIEL COULDN'T believe it. This was it. Kira was morphing. His heart leapt, and he was so stunned by the prospect of her transforming for him that he pulled out. Sitting back on his heels, he watched in wonderment as golden light ravelled around her, glowing brighter and brighter until he could no longer see her human form.

Within seconds, the dazzling lights disappeared. Two breathtaking, majestic wolves sat before him, their dark fur drenched and rippling beneath the pitter patter of water. They blinked radiant golden eyes at him, and in that instant, he had a profound feeling of being both lost and found.

"You honour me," he murmured as both wolves nuzzled him. He petted them, his hands lost in the thick, wet manes of their necks. He'd never felt so humbled, so helpless, and so in love in his entire life.

One of the wolves pulled back, canting its head to the side as it appraised him. Without warning, it pounced. Its large paws hitting his chest, pushing him back to sprawl on the ground.

He didn't try to sit back up. Instead, he lay perfectly still as the two wolves sniffed his body, exploring. One of Kira's forms ran her tongue up along his upper thigh, travelling dangerously close to...

He jerked as if lightning had struck him when she licked his balls, the incredibly long tongue wrapping around his sack and sliding tantalisingly, teasingly, causing his cock to twitch over and over.

"Fuck me," he breathed dropping his head back to hit the tiles, blinking up at the ceiling as he surrendered to her. She began lapping at his balls, coating them in thick slobber.

It was too good. It was too fucking good, and it was torture.

Luckily, Kira's impatience soon got the better of her. She was demanding in her hybrid wolf forms, and he was soon at their mercy as she dominated him in ways he could not have imagined.

The hybrid who had been nuzzling him used her whip-like tails to restrain his wrists, whilst the other used its long, rough tongue to lick his erection.

Minutes passed in complete, breathtaking bliss. The hybrid restraining him by his wrists nudged him persistently, demanding that he scratch her ears at all times. Even though Kira couldn't speak while transformed, he was a fast learner—and the lashings of her whip-like tails were a good motivator, leaving red marks across his chest and abdomen.

"More," he rasped.

She flipped him so he was on his knees, keeping him bound and upright as she whipped him harder. His back soon stung from her lashes, his blood staining the water pink. His body coursed with the heady concoction of pain and pleasure, and it served to bring him close to the edge several times.

"You...are a delightful creature," he gasped as she whipped him into submission. He groaned with unfulfilled need, and every part of him ached, none more so than his cock which was throbbing painfully and bursting for release.

Kira prolonged his suffering, and the bathroom echoed with his desperate, ragged moans.

She licked his wounds, easing the pain there.

And then she whipped him some more.

He loved every second of every moment, including the painful sting of her tails, and the dreaded moments in between where he waited for them to fall.

The one whose hot tongue had caressed his cock lifted her head and gave him a long intense look before slowly turning and facing away from him. She lifted her tail and presented herself.

Holy fucking shit.

Before he could begin to question her motives, the one restraining him bit his neck. The tip of her long, savage teeth pierced his flesh and ripped through his soul as their minds connected.

No vampire had ever bitten him before, and shock rushed through him as he realised she was sucking his blood.

He was prey. And he was hers.

He eyed the hybrid before him, her pink asshole surrounded by soft, white fur.

"Do it," she whispered in his mind, her voice both commanding and pleading. *"I want you to."*

He wanted that too, and he dragged the hybrid wolf closer and plunged his cock into her without a second thought, gripping thick, wet handfuls of fur as he thrust into her like a madman.

He'd never beheld creatures so beautiful, and he made sure they knew it as he took first one of Kira's forms, then the other. By some wild miracle, he managed not to come until he'd made them both howl in ecstasy. Their combined orgasms shattered through all their minds simultaneously, and then he was coming inside one of them—he no longer knew which one—grasping thick fur as he pulled himself deeper, roaring as he buried his chest in her fur, his cock pumping agonising loads of cum into her tight wet space. And all the while, he felt the encouraging lash of whips stinging his back as his cum drained out of him.

When Nathaniel opened his eyes, he was lying on his side on the bathroom stall, not entirely convinced that he hadn't blacked out.

"I think you did black out," Kira laughed.

Where was she?

He groaned softly as he peeked an eye open. He felt sore and exhausted in the most wonderful way, and he was perfectly content to remain lying where he was, enjoying the shower of lukewarm water from above.

Eight paws entered his vision, and he forced himself to tilt his head to meet two sets of amber eyes.

"I'm not done yet," Kira growled, her tone sounding sulky as her wolf forms whined. *"More."*

It was his turn to laugh, a spluttering sound as he choked on water. *"I don't think I can."*

One of the wolves lowered her head and nudged him hard, turning him onto his back. She crept closer, her snout hovering near his shoulder.

"Feed from me," she offered. *"And then we'll go again."*

Nathaniel burst out laughing, his body shaking as he covered his face against the onslaught of shower water.

"I'm serious," Kira pouted. *"I want you. I want more."*

He seized the thick fur at her neck and tugged her closer.

"Then let me deliver."

He sank his teeth into her neck, and after he drank his fill, he sank his cock into each of them and filled them both once more.

CHAPTER 28

Happiness

KIRA

KIRA'S COILED TAILS SWISHED in happy, lazy wags as she lay on the bed, one of her wolf forms on either side of Nathaniel.

"That tickles, you know," he smiled with eyes still shut.

"I know."

She trailed the furred ends of her tails along his chest, stomach, and hip, continuing all the way along his lean legs to the tips of his toes.

He chuckled and pulled her close, one wolf in each arm, and buried his face in her fur. He inhaled deeply, and she adored his contented groan.

In fact, she adored every part of Nathaniel, and it was bizarre to think she'd once loathed him. Somewhere along the way, she'd fallen hard, and now, she was dangerously and irrevocably devoted to him.

What she felt for him was more than words could describe. It went far deeper than the Master/pet relationship the academy tried to instil between its students.

Her heart had never felt so full, nor had she ever felt as safe as she did in Nathaniel's presence. It was a crazy feeling, being in love—especially with a vampire—but there it was.

Never mind that she was half vampire herself. That was a revelation she still hadn't fully processed. She was still hung up on the fact that this cold, ruthless vampire, with his icy heart, wasn't so ruthless after all, and that far from wanting to kill her as she had once feared, he loved her. Really, truly, desperately loved her, enough to trust her with his darkest fantasies and relinquish control.

Just as she loved him.

It gave her the sense of belonging she'd never known she needed. Who would have thought that being this vulnerable with another person could feel so good? The readiness with which Nathaniel had opened his heart and mind to her had given her the courage to do the same.

The road ahead would be arduous and messy, but they were a team, and one way or another, they would find a way to come out the other side and be together.

Sort of.

Gloria would have Nathaniel, but Kira had his heart, and that was enough to sustain her, at least for now. Nathaniel had promised her they would face the future together, and she trusted him to be honest with her. He valued her as his partner, and they were a team.

A pack.

Lovers.

It was why she'd finally felt ready to morph in front of him. Showing him her true form like that was a huge deal.

It wasn't that she was shy—had she not been keeping her true form a secret, she would have had no qualms wandering through the school in her wolf forms like some of the other shifters did. But in the intimacy of the bedroom, when it was only them, it was different. Private, somehow.

It didn't matter that Nathaniel already knew what she was, or that he remembered a time when she'd had nine selves.

For a female wolf, shifting meant something more.

A lot more.

Just as Nathaniel had equated biting her more than once to loving her, letting him see her true selves, to touch and feel her intimately, was like showing him a part of her soul.

From Nathaniel's reaction, she could tell he'd understood the significance of her gesture: she had chosen him as her mate.

With her personality laid bare, with every strength and flaw apparent, she'd waited for him to choose her back. She'd had no expectations that he would want her in her transfigured forms. Would a vampire want her in that way when she appeared as a creature? Would *he* think her the monster? A beast to recoil from?

She didn't think so, but her vulnerability had caused doubts to creep into her mind.

Nathaniel's heartfelt response, however, had laid those fears to rest. His revered gaze had made her heart beat faster, and he'd soon convinced her that he wanted her in every way—*especially* this way, in her most natural, true forms.

It meant far more to her than her virginity had, which besides the power it had given her in choosing a pack, was not something she'd been particularly attached to. While Mark had taken her virginity like he was taking something from her, Nathaniel had given her himself and made her whole; his love and acceptance mending the tender edges of her heart.

She hoped the feeling would last.

CHAPTER 29

Cake and Love

KIRA

HER NEWFOUND HAPPINESS MADE returning to her human form and leaving the hotel room difficult. After Nathaniel checked out at the front desk, Kira prolonged the inevitable by dragging him into the hotel's downstairs restaurant and ordering everything on the breakfast menu.

She savoured each bite slowly, and ordered a second helping of a creamy vanilla cake, which was the best thing she'd ever tasted.

Nathaniel had long ago set aside his cutlery, but he seemed content to watch her eat as he drank his coffee.

"I never took you for a vanilla girl," he said in amusement as she softly moaned her way through delicious spoonfuls of buttercream—she couldn't help it. The frosting melted in her mouth.

She rolled her eyes at the innuendo as she swallowed her food and said, "Yeah, well...you never *took* me vanilla before. Until last night, anyway."

His eyes gleamed in response, and she could tell he was recalling their missionary pose. "No, I don't suppose I did."

She bit back a smile. "I liked it though."

Nathaniel set his mug down on the table. "So did I."

A teasing thought occurred to her. She focused on her plate. It probably wasn't a good idea, but the words slipped out before she could stop them. "You should have that at your wedding."

The air shifted between them like a cool breeze.

"Have what at my wedding, pet?"

"Vanilla cake," she said innocently, popping another spoonful in her mouth before glancing back up. She had the dreaded feeling she was tempting fate, but...why not?

Nathaniel had frozen still, his eyes boring into hers.

With each passing second, she regretted having spoken. She'd meant her comment as a light-hearted dig, but it hadn't come out that way.

When Nathaniel eventually spoke, his voice was flat, but she felt the barb all the same. "There will be cake."

She immediately registered the double meaning: there would be literal cake, the kind she was eating now... And then there would be Gloria, waiting for Nathaniel to perform his duty in consummating their marriage.

Her heart dropped.

What if he enjoys it?

What if he likes her better?

"Pet," Nathaniel said softly, trying to call her back.

It was too late. An image flashed in her mind of Nathaniel leaning over a white bed in a fine suit, his head buried between the thighs of another woman in a wedding dress. It made her stomach queasy, and her food turned to ash in her mouth. She had a strong urge to spit it out, but she forced herself to swallow.

"Pet." Nathaniel was reaching across the table, his hand extended.

She didn't take it. Instead, she cleared her throat as she busied herself with patting her mouth with her napkin. "And are you looking forward to having your cake and eating it too?"

For fuck's sake, Kira...

Pain flashed across Nathaniel's face, and her question hung in the air, her fragile heart beating too fast as she waited for him to answer. She'd set the trap for herself. Now, she waited for the plummeting fall.

"Well?" she demanded, digging at the remainder of her cake with her spoon, burying her spoon as she buried herself deeper. She was no longer hungry, and was hardly aware of the delicate frosting she was wrecking.

Nathaniel's voice was steady. "Kira. You, and only you, are the one that I love."

"Yes, well...I'll try to remember that when you hand me over to your father."

Damn it, Kira. Just shut the fuck up.

Just shut the fuck up!

She hadn't meant her words to come out so negatively, but she couldn't help it. She was so jealous. So...so sad that this was it.

That it was all ending.

It was worse than simply jealousy or sadness. Those were fleeting and temporary. The emotion she felt looming over her had an ominous finality to it: resignation.

No.

No!

Better to be jealous and petty than to accept defeat and feel *nothing*.

So, she embraced the insanity of it, and her quiet jealousy roared to life into something beautiful and untameable. It was like a sleeping dragon that she'd accidentally woken, and she purposefully dragged it out of its cave to face stark daylight. It thrashed about and seethed with thick smoke, ready to destroy everything in its wake.

Thankfully, Nathaniel was calm. He rose from his chair and walked around to her side.

"Pet."

She didn't respond.

Unleash the dragon? Make a scene? Break some shit?

So tempting, even if it would solve nothing.

"Pet."

Another infinitely calm, steady word from this beautiful man.

She sighed and rose from her chair, letting the dragon retreat in thick cloudy smoke as she leant against Nathaniel's chest.

He enveloped her in a tight embrace and did not let go. His fingers tangled in her hair, and she heard him draw a deep, relieved breath. Or maybe it was a sad sigh. She followed suit, trying to calm the residual embers searing her veins.

He didn't pull away, and he didn't seem to care about the other diners or hotel staff as he held her. She loved that about him, his steady patience. After a minute, she'd composed herself enough to pull back and give him a smile.

"We can do this," she said, holding back from adding, *"can't we?"*

Nathaniel closed his eyes and tipped his head until his forehead touched hers. "Yes, we can."

He sounded earnest, but Kira frowned as she sensed a fragmented thought emanate from him. There were no words, only a feeling, but they echoed a terrible sadness that contradicted his outward optimism.

CHAPTER 30

Magic

KIRA

THE FIRST MORNING BELL to signal the start of classes had not yet rung when they arrived back at Volmasque Academy. They attracted curious glances from other students as they walked side by side up the school's drive, but Nathaniel's only response was to place his warm hand on the small of Kira's back.

Kira felt a burst of pride at the gesture, and she smiled at him. She wasn't even annoyed by the leash swinging from her collar anymore, not knowing that once he unclipped it, she would belong to the Poparlins and would never wear a leash again. She was simply glad that it was Nathaniel holding the handle.

He returned her smile, his eyes aglow with warmth. It sent her heart aflutter, helping soothe some of the doubt that had crept in earlier.

She'd watched him attentively on their walk, on alert for any more fragments of thought he might have projected, but she'd detected nothing amiss. Nathaniel halted at the top of the steps and pressed several soft kisses against her neck.

"Everyone's watching," she whispered. By everyone, she meant the dozen or so students in uniform sitting on the steps and lawn, enjoying the morning sun before the start of class.

"Are they now?" he asked, his hands running along her waist and up her back as he placed an open-mouthed kiss on her neck.

She shivered as she felt the tips of his fangs on her skin. "Don't tell me you're going to bite me," she said, even as she arched her neck to give him better access.

He nibbled gently, causing wicked tingles to streak through her.

"Do you want me to?"

"Yes," she answered immediately, eliciting a chuckle from him.

He pulled her close, so their bodies fit together and his growing erection pressed into her stomach. "Right here, in front of everyone?"

"Yes," she said breathlessly.

"Don't tempt me, pet."

"Please?" She wrapped her arms around him tightly.

Nathaniel flinched in response, and she released him immediately.

"Oh, I'm so sorry." She'd forgotten all about the whip marks her tails had left on his back. Most had been pink and red marks that had faded, but there were several welts from when she'd gotten carried away.

"Don't be sorry," he said hoarsely, crushing her against his chest. "I love it. I've never been claimed by anyone before."

"You haven't?"

"No, pet. You are my first...and my last."

Kira didn't know why those words sounded so foreboding.

"Are you going to remove the leash now?" she whispered.

Nathaniel tilted his head in consideration.

"Not just yet. Grant me a few more minutes."

"Why? So you can make Mark jealous?" she asked, genuinely curious.

"Fuck Mark. Because I'm having trouble letting go."

Kira swallowed hard, her heart fluttering—at least until

Nathaniel's hands drifted lower and slipped underneath her skirt. She gasped when he tapped the plug.

He'd made her wear it just before they entered the school grounds. To her chagrin, he'd ordered her to hold the wrought iron bars of the gate as he rutted her, and he'd ploughed her ass to his content as the helpless security officer and passersby looked on. Then he'd inserted the plug.

Nathaniel's eyes became glassy as if he was remembering it too.

"You were so good for me earlier," he said, pushing on the plug so she felt the pressure even more.

"Maybe I should have made *you* wear it today," she scowled.

"You'll have to be faster if you want to plug *me*, pet."

Kira groaned and pushed him away, but he seized her arms and drew her close again, giving her the same smirking grin he'd worn when he'd first brought her to the academy in the carriage. She'd wanted to strangle him then, much like she did now, but mostly, she was smitten with him.

Or, she would have been, if he hadn't been teasing the plug in and out of her ass.

"Nathaniel," she pleaded, throwing a wary look around at the students. At least there had been no students around earlier, only city folk. Now there were more than a few students glancing their way, and a couple of male wolves on the front steps were leering unabashedly, their expressions disgusted even as their pants bulged.

"Yes, pet?" he asked innocently.

"Stop it."

"Stop what?" He kept teasing, in and out, in and out, stretching her sphincter to painful proportions before sinking the plug back in.

She stifled her moan and hissed, "For the record, this does *nothing* to keep your cum inside me."

Despite the bulging toy, she'd been all too aware of the squelching motion happening back there each time she took a step. And as they'd walked along the drive, she'd felt the slow wet ooze of his cum inside her crack, down her thigh, and even near the hem of her sock.

"And *this* isn't helping!" she added, batting his hand away.

Nathaniel's smile widened, revealing sharp fangs.

"Don't look so pleased with yourself," she chastised.

"Mostly, I'm pleased with you." He grabbed her ass cheeks and squeezed, shifting the plug and causing a fresh drip of cum to leak from her.

"You're a bastard," Kira snapped. She could feel her face burning, and she was sure that every single person in the vicinity had stopped what they were doing to watch them.

"You love it."

Yes, well...that's not the point.

"It's like you're trying to make my first day in the Poplarins difficult. They'll smell you on me." They would have smelled Nathaniel on her regardless. Shifters had an excellent sense of smell, and they would detect his scent clinging to her for weeks. The smell of his fresh, wet cum coating her insides would be a slap on the face for the alphas.

"Good," Nathaniel said roughly, leaning in for a kiss.

Kira laughed indignantly and stepped out of reach, retreating as far as the leash would allow. "No, not 'good'. The alphas won't like it." Not that she gave a shit about what Mark thought, but it would make fitting into the pack more difficult. "I'm surprised they even want me after you claimed me."

Nathaniel tugged on the leash, forcing her close to him again. "I am confident you will have no trouble bringing them all to heel."

"Just like you've tried to bring me to heel?" She purposefully used the word 'tried', a thinly veiled challenge.

His expression darkened. "There is no 'try', pet. There is only 'do'. And right now, I want to *do* bad things to you."

Her throat went dry as heat exploded in her core. "Like what?"

"I'm considering asking for a kiss."

The air left her as she analysed his meaning, and stammered, "On the lips?"

"No, pet. You know where."

The glint in his eye confirmed her suspicion. *On his cock.*

"Here? In front of everyone?"

Class was about to start, and most of the students were headed inside, but some lingered to enjoy the morning sun.

Or to watch the show.

Nathaniel nodded. "Right here. Right now." He tilted his head. "Your mouth on my cock."

Pausing for a moment, he added. "It's your choice, pet."

My choice?

Her knees grew weak.

But if it wasn't an order...

"And if I don't?"

Nathaniel chuckled. "It will be a lost opportunity for you to please me, pet."

Kira licked her lips as she considered it. Before she knew what she was doing, before she was even aware of having made a decision, her knees began to bend. She hadn't decided whether she would actually go through with it, or whether she was just teasing him, but she enjoyed the triumph and surprise that flared to life in Nathaniel's eyes.

Suddenly, a voice called out.

"Oi, lovebirds!"

It was Victoria, and Kira hastily straightened out of her half-stooped posture as the vampiress left her friends and made her way over.

She was wearing her school uniform, the formality of the blazer offset by the glossy nails she was sporting—bright yellow with pink polka dots. They matched her yellow headband, which failed to keep her thick fringe out of her shadowy eyes. What would have looked absurd on anyone else looked chic on Victoria, and Kira felt in awe of her.

"You're both looking smitten," Victoria said, pulling Kira into a hug. "Congratulations on your initiation, babe. I heard you're one of the Populars now." She winked. "Guess that means you're off limits to feeding?"

Kira couldn't tell if she was joking.

Victoria narrowed her eyes at Nathaniel. "But I see you're still playing with her, Nat. Feeding too, by the looks of it." Her gaze flickered to the bite marks on both their necks, and she pursed her lips disapprovingly. "Feeding from *each other*? Nat...your father won't like it."

"I can handle my father," he replied tersely.

"I know. But we don't need any more conflict between the packs and the vampires at school. Everyone was just beginning to get along after Kira's friend got attacked. The number of wolves willing to let us feed on them dropped off. I had to *share* someone the other night."

"That's unfortunate," said Nathaniel without a hint of emotion.

Kira knew him well enough to realise he was deflecting.

Victoria rolled her eyes and held up her hand, her thumb and forefinger almost touching. "I'm *this* close to raiding your food cupboard for those dried mushrooms."

"They're a good source of protein."

"But then, I figured I'd rather fucking starve." She rolled her eyes again, this time at Kira. "Can you believe him?"

Kira shrugged her shoulders, trying not to show how much this conversation unsettled her.

"Anyway," Victoria said, returning her attention to Nathaniel. "I heard you sent Mark packing. What happened? Got jealous? Also, the Haxby Hotel? Why didn't we get invited?"

Her question was met with stony silence, and Kira appreciated that Nathaniel wasn't discussing their personal affairs with anyone else.

Victoria waved dismissively. "Whatever. Kira will tell me later, won't you, sweetie? We're long overdue for a catchup, and I'm dying to know all about your secret love affair."

"We're not in love," Kira said carefully, resisting the urge to glance at Nathaniel.

Back at the hotel, they'd decided to keep their feelings for one another a secret, lest Henrikk found out.

Victoria seemed to see through their denial. "I *knew* it," she hissed. "You two are *actually* in love. Ew!"

"Actually..." Kira began, but Victoria placed a hand on her shoulder.

"Listen, honey, you're great and all, but at the end of the day, you're a wolf, and Nathaniel is a vampire. You both deserve to be with your own kind. And Nathaniel, you know better!"

He didn't reply, which seemed to irritate Victoria. She swiped her fringe and turned to Kira. "And if I were you, sweetie, I wouldn't tell anyone about your feelings for Nat."

"I didn't," Kira said through gritted teeth.

"And I won't tell anyone either," Victoria nodded to herself. "Sex is one thing, but those love bites?" She gave them both another disapproving look. "Nat, aren't you worried what Henrikk would do if he found out his son, the soon-to-be-king, is not only giving his blood to a wolf—I'm sensing a pattern here, by the way—but to a wolf he *loves?*"

"Keep your voice down," Nathaniel admonished sternly, even though everyone else had already gone inside.

"Did you even stop to think that Henrikk might punish Kira just to make an example out of her? I mean, I take responsibility for encouraging you, but I didn't think you'd actually *fall* for her. And look, I get it, Kira's a cool chick, but she's a *wolf* for crying out loud. Unless you're feeding or having sex, she's off limits. That's it. What the hell were you thinking, Nat? Because—"

Victoria cut off as Nathaniel advanced, his expression darkening. She took a hurried step back.

Just then, the school bell rang. Victoria threw her hands up, fingers apart as if she had wet nails. "Whatever. You're right. It's none of my business." Her gaze travelled to Nathaniel's neck. She shuddered and hurried up the academy steps with her hands still raised. "Ew, ew, ew." She paused at the top step and called back, "Come to my room sometime, Kira. I still want to hear about the pre-sappy era when things were *hot* and less stupid."

She disappeared through the front doors, and Kira and Nathaniel exchanged a shrug before following her. Despite Victoria's drama, Kira couldn't help but smile as she jogged up the steps.

"I'm pleased to see you smiling again," Nathaniel said, linking his arm with hers as they entered the foyer. "Feeling better?"

"Yes," she said distractedly, scanning the large hall which was bustling with students hurrying to their first class of the day.

There was another reason for her newfound happiness, and it was something she hadn't even told Nathaniel yet. Gradually over the last few hours, she'd felt a change come over her. And while she'd been unsure of what that feeling was at first, she was now all but certain: her magic had returned.

She'd felt the glimmers of it as they left the hotel and walked back to the academy, like sparks of potential emanating from the people they passed. Here in the crowd of students, she was growing increasingly certain of her theory. Each student radiated life and energy, like fonts of possibility waiting for her to latch on.

She halted in the middle of the room, her breathing shallow as she attuned herself to the low melody of her body which thrummed with magic. She could feel her power unfurling inside her, flexing like a new muscle.

Finally.

Just when she'd begun to lose hope that she had any magical talent at all, it had awakened inside her. She'd felt the first tingle of magic last night at the hotel, but she hadn't recognised what it was at the time. There had been glimmers of it since, and with each passing minute, there was more of it.

Kira didn't know why her magic was returning now. Was it because she'd let her guard down so completely with Nathaniel?

Maybe it was just Nathaniel's blood starting to take effect.

Or, maybe it's the sex, she thought wryly, recalling the way she'd ridden him through one soul-shattering orgasm after another. Her vision momentarily went black as she toppled off him onto the mattress in pure ecstasy. He'd barely caught her before she toppled off the bed, both of them laughing as they clutched each other.

Yeah...no. The last thing Nathaniel's ego needs is for him to think he has a magic cock.

"What is it?" Nathaniel asked beside her. "Why have you stopped?"

"Wouldn't you like to know?" she replied, flexing her magic once more. Like a baby foal who could walk within hours of being born, she had a feeling she already knew how to use her magic intuitively.

The only way to find out was to take that first brave step.

"Now, I definitely have to know," Nathaniel said, regarding her with his head cocked. "You've got that mischievous look about you."

Kira felt her smile widen as she prepared her magic, coiling it as if wrapping her hair around her fingers. Her senses grew hyperaware of every single person in the crowded foyer, including the students on the stairs and the landing above.

It works, she thought happily. A part of her had assumed that she would only be able to use magic in her wolf forms, but she was wrong. And without being able to explain how, she knew exactly what her magic was and how to use it.

She let out a low laugh of disbelief as the pulsing strength of her magic increased in intensity until her extremities ached just like sore muscles after a long run.

"Kira?" Nathaniel asked, a small frown appearing on his brow and a question half-formed on his lips.

Her only answer was a mysterious smile as she let her magic fly, the invisible tendrils bursting out around her to touch and capture the minds of every single student and teacher in the general vicinity. Her magic even touched Nathaniel's mind, but it was only a gentle brush to make him aware of her.

Nathaniel drew a sharp breath as the bustling foyer went still and quiet. It was as if everyone had been stunned. No one spoke or moved, at least for a few seconds.

She hadn't harmed them in any way, nor could she control them, but she had a direct line of communication to each and every person around her, and that was powerful in itself. It was as if she'd given them all a hard, mental tap on the shoulder.

She drew back her magic slightly, reducing the intensity until it was a subtle touch on their minds. She had been careful to ensure no one besides Nathaniel was conscious of her presence to avoid arousing suspicion.

But that did not mean the students were completely oblivious that something had happened. Judging by the flurry of muddled thoughts she sensed in the room, no one could tell what she was doing, or that it was even magic they were experiencing. They were simply startled, their minds primed and ready for instructions.

Kira shut her eyes, soaking in the feeling of being interconnected with so many people at once. It was noisy and confusing, but it felt right.

She was curious to see how far she could take it.

Look up, she whispered, her subtle suggestion radiating down each and every link like a bead of light.

Nearly everyone looked up. Some who were stronger-willed resisted, and that was fine. They *considered* looking up at the ceiling, which was a small victory of its own.

Time to wrap it up, Kira thought to herself as people began looking around as if searching for the source of what they'd felt. Some laughed nervously, others exchanged hushed tones.

Kira repressed a smile. Everyone looked so unnerved by her intrusion that it was tempting not to shout 'boo'. It would have been funny to see if she could make every person in the room jump at the same time.

She shared that last thought with Nathaniel, who gave his head a firm shake.

"Don't. Come away, pet."

Kira gave an exaggerated sigh. "Fine." She released her hold on everyone's minds, her invisible magic whipping back to make her whole again.

After a few seconds, people began to move about again, shrugging off the experience as a figment of their imagination.

Nathaniel turned her to face him, his hands on her shoulders as he searched her face with sparkling eyes. "I'm very impressed. Truly. However...you need to be more discreet."

"I was," she insisted.

"I know. But *more* discreet than that, pet." He took hold of her arm and pulled her in the direction of her history class.

Just before they passed through a large archway, Kira halted, ignoring the tug of the leash as she glanced back at the foyer. The hall was full of its usual loud chatter again.

She had the strangest feeling that someone was watching her, which was a bizarre thing to feel with so many people milling about.

"What is it?" Nathaniel asked.

Kira gave her head a tiny shake as she scanned the room,

searching...

Her heart jumped.

She'd caught sight of Victoria from across the room, silhouetted against a grand circular window. Although it was hard to be sure with the glare from the sunlight, it looked as though the vampiress was staring at them with her head tipped to one side as if scrutinising them.

Kira's view of Victoria was blocked when someone stepped into her line of sight. She craned her neck to catch sight of the vampiress amidst the shifting crowd, but Victoria was gone.

CHAPTER 31

Special Privileges

KIRA

ON THEIR WAY TO History class, Nathaniel took a detour, guiding Kira up an endless winding staircase. They reached an empty classroom at the top of the North Tower.

This must be Professor Zott's classroom.

The other students had described the pristine room in horrified whispers, but it was only now, as she gazed around, that she realised they hadn't been exaggerating about the feature wall. It was painted black and lined with whips, paddles, riding crops, and other punishment equipment. The leather and steel twinkled ominously in the early sunlight, and she felt a chill as she stared at the vast collection. They were pristine, but for all she'd heard of the suffering Zott subjected his students to, they may as well have been covered in blood.

Only Nathaniel would have dared come here.

He shut the door and sat in the large chair behind the teacher's desk, his demeanour calm as he advised her on strategies for exploring her magical powers.

Kira sat on a chair opposite him listening attentively, but she soon grew bored of the magical theory lesson. It was based on information

Nathaniel had learnt and memorised from Barbara long ago in the hope that he could one day pass it on to her. She appreciated his thoughtfulness but didn't find any of it particularly useful.

Her magic felt much more intuitive than words could describe. The charts Nathaniel was drawing on the sheet of parchment between them were making her head spin. She might have been half vampire, but when it came to learning, she was all wolf, and would have much preferred to be outside than looking at graphs of hyperbolas and other squiggly lines.

The only tangent she wanted to see was Nathaniel's cock between her curved breasts, an act she'd found both bizarre and arousing last night when they'd done it.

And now I'm thinking about his cock.

"These two foci are the wellsprings of magical energy," Nathaniel was saying enthusiastically, his quill drawing bold lines that seeped into the rich paper. "These energies converge at the centre, which is called the nexus point. Do you see?"

Kira blinked and nodded politely, but all she could think of was how attractive his hand was as it drew deft strokes across the page, and how pleasant the low rumble of his voice was. She loved that he took the time to share this with her, explaining it so patiently. She did her best to pay attention, she really did, but her mind simply didn't work the way his did. Try as she might, she was soon lost in thought as she played with a loose thread on her skirt's hem.

His countenance was gentlemanly, pleasant, and radiating intelligence, and she found it so alluring. It was such a contrast to how serious he'd been last night as he fucked her, slowly and possessively.

Nathaniel stopped talking when she stifled a yawn.

"Am I boring you, pet?"

"No, not at all," she answered quickly. "I'm just having trouble following all this. I don't see magic the way you—or

Barbara—describe it."

Nathaniel considered this. "Perhaps I'm not explaining it in the best way."

Kira laughed. He was too polite to say what everyone knew: that wolves usually made for terrible students, at least in the classroom. They were restless, hot-blooded and quick to act up. But with the exception of Potions, they excelled in practical tasks, and they dominated the sports field in everything except badminton—partly because it was favoured by vampires, but mostly because hitting a shuttlecock was stupid.

"Perhaps, some mental stimulation would be helpful," Nathaniel suggested softly.

Kira froze, the loose thread she'd been playing with slipping between her fingertips.

"Something that might hold your interest," he continued, "and keep your mind engaged."

She gulped, her heart beating faster. "What do you suggest?"

"Come now, pet. Use your initiative."

She avoided the urge to lick her lips, but her gaze drifted down to the crotch of his trousers—not that she could see it from the table in between them.

Nathaniel remained very still, waiting.

Waiting for her.

Well, it's better than learning about hyperbolas.

Shrugging, Kira slid off the edge of her chair and rounded the table. Nathaniel's chair scraped back to make room, and she knelt at his feet. The ground was hard and not exactly clean, but Nathaniel shrugged out of his jacket wordlessly and lay it on the ground.

"Thank you, sir," she murmured, adjusting the fine velvet jacket beneath her.

"You are welcome, pet."

He leant back, looking relaxed with his hands resting loosely on his thighs as she unbuckled his belt. She loosened the fastenings and took his cock out. The rest was becoming routine in the best way, which somehow made it feel more taboo—after all, it was just a Master being serviced by his pet.

A few weeks ago, she would have been mortified by the prospect. Now, the directive to suck his cock made her entire body shudder with pleasant tingles.It was an opportunity.

A privilege.

A duty.

She was reduced to the very thing she'd once despised—an obedient pet—and she couldn't have been more thankful. Because right now, she didn't have a care in the world. The only one who existed was *him*, her protector.

But the real power lay with her.

Nathaniel made a low sound of appreciation as she slid her tongue along his length. She repeated this several times, smiling to herself as she teased him, relishing the way he twitched from her touch. When she finally took him in her mouth, he let out a long, slow exhale.

She touched his mind with her magic.

"So...you were saying?"

He peeked an eye open. "Hmm?"

"The lesson. You were saying something about gravitational pull?"

"I...don't recall."

Kira smiled as she sucked the head of his cock, breathing through her nose. Then she stopped and lifted her head.

"What is it?" Nathaniel asked, a note of exasperation entering his voice.

Kira didn't answer straight away. She licked the end of his cock thoughtfully, the tip of her tongue playing with the opening where his precum had gathered. *"I was also wondering...what the hell is a jarroscope?"*

Nathaniel looked confused for a moment. *"Gyroscope."*

"*Yes,*" she licked the rounded glans before her tongue darted across the tip again. "*That. I didn't understand when you were explaining—*"

"Pet."

He said the single word out loud, with enough volume and seriousness that she froze and looked up.

"Yes?"

"Suck. My. Cock. In. Silence."

She shivered under his stern gaze and did as she was told, lowering her mouth to take his rigid length and sucking it the way he'd taught her.

"*So much for taking my magic seriously,*" she grumbled in mock-humour.

"*I do take it seriously. Just look at how well you are communicating right now. This is good practise.*"

"*Yes, well...I'm glad you're prioritising my education.*"

"*Always.*" His hand curled in her hair as he guided her deeper onto his cock. "*I have to tell you, pet, that seeing you use magic back there was incredible. You were magnificent.*"

He teased her with an extra half inch of his cock, working himself deeper as she tried not to gag.

"*Truly spectacular,*" he continued. "*But it bears repeating: it is imperative that no one detects your use of magic.*"

"*I'll be careful.*" She sent the thought slamming into his mind in the most unsubtle way she could, just to prove she knew the difference.

Nathaniel flinched as if she'd shouted in his ear.

"*Sorry, too much?*"

He gave a low laugh and pushed her further down onto his cock. She gagged, but he didn't stop until he'd pushed his cock down her throat as far as it would go, and her lips pressed against the base of his shaft. "*Too much? You tell me.*"

Gagging again, her entire body jerked in response to his large cock pressing deep into her throat. She tried to push herself off, but Nathaniel held her in place by her hair, her scalp stinging sharply as she struggled.

"Well, would you look at that," he murmured out loud. "It's a day of firsts for you, isn't it, pet? First you learn to use magic, and now you're deep throating my cock. I'm so proud of you."

He released her, and Kira fell backwards onto the ground, wheezing and spluttering as she threw another coil of magic at his mind.

"Fuck. You."

His lip twitched. "I find it so delightful that I can hear your thoughts in my mind now." He motioned for her to get up. "Come now, slut. Sit on my cock."

Kira wiped the drool from her lips as she glared at him.

"No."

Her collar tightened as Nathaniel tugged the leash. He'd retained a hold of it all this time.

"Magic is no excuse for disobedience," he growled, dragging her to her feet. "Sit. Down."

Her panties were already off; he'd made her remove them earlier and had dumped them in Professor Zott's drawer, where it had joined a collection of blue-feathered quills, as well as a sample essay titled *Ten Ways To Positively Reinforce Pet Behaviour*. Kira had not gotten the chance to read any further before Nathaniel shut the drawer, but it suddenly sprang to mind.

Ignoring Nathaniel's orders, she reached past him, jerked the drawer open, and held up the summary page.

"Rewards and incentives," she read out loud. "Special privileges. Thank you notes. These are many ways you can encourage good behaviour from your submissive without resorting to punishment."

"Some submissives need regular correction in the form of

punishment," he said with a relaxed smile.

"Positive affirmation," she continued, raising her voice. "Use positive affirmations and encouragement to boost self-esteem and reinforce good behaviour. Say things like, 'you are so responsible and helpful'."

"*Pet.*"

She flinched at the sharpness of his tone.

"Professor Zott will be here for next period soon," he continued in a low, dangerous voice. "So, unless you wish for me to demonstrate the reverse side of that page to the entire class, you will sit on my fucking cock and ride it like I told you."

Kira froze.

Slowly, she turned the page over.

"*Ten Ways to Correct Unwanted Behaviour,*" she began. "*Modes of punishment may include verbal reprimands, time-out, and physical punishment such as spanking...shit.*"

She dropped the parchment, letting it float to the floor.

Nathaniel raised his eyebrows at her expectantly, his smugness irking her as he pulled on the leash, the tension on her collar increasing.

"Come on," he coaxed, dragging her forward until she was standing between his legs. "Hop on."

Kira crossed her arms. "Not until you offer me a special privilege. My choice of dinner, for example."

Nathaniel's eyes flashed, and they were intense and unblinking as she'd ever seen them as he dragged her head down until she was bent awkwardly and they were eye to eye. "Riding my cock *is* a special privilege. Do not take this opportunity for granted."

She finally yielded, climbing astride him with her legs dangling on either side of the chair as his cock pushed through her wet folds. She was embarrassingly wet, and she groaned as his girth pressed against the bulging plug in her back passage. It felt as if his cock was in both her holes at the same time.

"Fuck," she moaned internally down their link.

Nathaniel smiled in response. "Oh, pet. You are so wonderfully tight. Feel how much I've stretched you."

She whimpered in response. She was too full—his hard length at the front, the large plug in her rear, and his chiselled muscles trapping her in all their glory as he grabbed her by the hips. He lifted her and drove his cock up to hit the deepest part of her. "Feel how I fill you, slut."

Kira nodded absently, her eyes unfocused as lusty fog clouded her senses. Nathaniel pulled her close, and she made a soft sound as she draped her arms over his shoulders and let her head loll to one side, shutting her eyes and savouring the sinful feeling of having him take control like this.

Even though she was on top, she felt too high on euphoria to move, and despite his early instructions to ride him, Nathaniel seemed content to do most of the work as he rocked against her.

"I used to take this class, you know," he said conversationally as he took her slow and steady. "And I always dreamt of a pet as obedient as you."

He held her hips tightly and thrust up like a piston, lifting her high on his cock. "Someone to teach."

Another thrust. "To praise."

Again. "To fuck."

Each impact caused shockwaves to reverberate through her core and left her feeling clammy as she gasped for breath.

"Someone to own," Nathaniel continued, his grip tightening as he rammed his cock into her again, faster this time.

"Someone to lick my work shoes clean in the morning. Someone to await my return every evening in my bedchambers."

His profound words shook her senses. "Nathaniel," she gasped. "I'm close."

"Not yet," he growled, lifting her as he stood and set her onto the edge of the desk. He planted a hand on her chest and pushed her back until she was lying on the tabletop, staring up at the dark rafters.

Nathaniel lifted her legs over his shoulders and dragged her closer by the hips, spearing her pussy even deeper and jostling the plug as his bulging cock head forced its way past. "Not until I say so."

He squeezed her breasts, his touch the perfect blend of rough and sensual.

"Holy shit!" she cried.

Nathaniel grinned as her cry of pleasure travelled down their mental link, and she clamped her mouth shut to prevent it echoing in the classroom.

The last thing she wanted was for someone to discover them. She had a feeling that despite Nathaniel's earlier threat, this was a line even he would not cross—having sex with a student in a classroom.

"Out loud, pet," he urged, gripping her hair with both hands and folding his body over so his face was close to hers. The action lifted her legs so high they were vertical, her knees nearly touching her head. It also brought him deeper than he'd ever been, and she was acutely aware of every tiny movement he made. "Let me hear you moan."

"Someone will hear us," Kira protested.

"You need not be loud. You may mew like a cat, or grunt like a wild boar, if you wish. It makes no difference to me, so long as I hear you enjoying yourself as I fuck you."

"I'm not going to grunt like a fucking pig," she snapped, but there was no bite to her words as he pressed his cock deep, causing a moan to escape her.

"Oh, but you already are, pet." His eyes glinted with amusement. "Just listen to you."

He slowly pulled back, then drove in again, drawing another deep guttural sound from her as he made her feel the full force of his cock.

"I hear you, Kira, and I see you. You're a wild animal begging to be tamed."

Fuck.

The words were like an insult and compliment rolled into one, especially with the fondness with which Nathaniel spoke them. It was pure insanity just how much his words gripped her, causing her aching heat to throb.

"*Now* you may come," Nathaniel announced.

"Go to hell," she retorted, but it was too late. She was coming, her body obeying his command over her own self will. She was loud like a boar as she moaned all the way through it, her body arching against Nathaniel's muscled frame.

Fucking hell.

How many orgasms was that today?

She was losing track.

Nathaniel looked pleased as he tucked her hair behind her ear. "Very good, pet."

Her chest swelled with pride even as her body shuddered, her fluids leaking all over his cock.

"And if you are in need of further positive affirmation..." He leant close and murmured, "Thank you for being so responsible and helpful earlier when you were sucking my cock."

Her jaw dropped as she realised he was teasing her with the summary she'd read earlier. "Great. Are we done? I'm meant to be in History class."

He chuckled. "Oh no, pet. I'm far from done with you. I have yet to fill you."

"Oh."

Kira felt sheepish. She'd assumed he'd come too, and the prospect of him pummelling her for any longer made her giddy.

Nathaniel scooped her up and carried her around the desk, making her feel as light as a feather as he moved to the wall. Holding her up by her legs, he pressed her back flush against the blackboard, pinning her with his cock.

"You are so beautiful," he breathed, pressing a long kiss to her mouth. "Now, hold on to me. I'm going to fuck your cunt and fill you like the slut that you are."

His harsh words reached into the depths of her soul, touching and probing her pride, and sullying her dignity.

Before she could react, he pressed her into the wall and shoved himself deep into her.

"Fuck," she gasped as a jolting ache shot through her.

"Yes, slut. Feel me."

His intense gaze locked on her as he repeated the motion, swift and hard.

Kira's head lolled back with a groan.

Nathaniel grasped a handful of her hair and pulled her head forward. "Eyes on me. You will watch as your Master pounds your ungrateful little cunt."

Kira was speechless as he delivered another slow, deliberate thrust that made her vision dance with stars. She blinked rapidly, her vision refocusing with effort on Natheniel's sharp gaze.

"Are you watching, pet?"

"Yes, sir," she croaked.

"Hold on tight."

His expression darkened as he sped up, his thrusts fast and erratic, drawing small involuntary shrieks out of her with each thrust.

"Fuck," he groaned, the sound echoing from his chest and making her body shake. "You are so fucking perfect."

His strokes grew faster, wilder, bordering on insanity as he drove her closer to the brink, his deep grunts mixing with her yelps as the blackboard vibrated behind her.

Kira felt his cock stiffen to epic proportions, the delivered strokes hurting as he approached his climax.

"I'm going to unload my cum into you, Kira darling," he said, his tone shifting to be more like his father's. "Hot and fresh, so Mark knows you're mine."

He slammed into her, the force of the impact making her pussy ache. "He'll smell your cunt. He'll want it."

Another thrust. "But it will be my cum dripping down your legs."

He shoved his cock in deeper. "And everyone will know that you're mine, ready and eager for me. My pet, my slut. Mine to fill and mine to use as I please."

He kissed her neck, nibbling and licking a trail up to her lower jaw. "And they will know your secret—something I've known from the moment you bit me in that cottage."

He leant back, his expression etched with hunger. "That deep down, you wanted me to tame you. You dream of great things, Kira, but your truest ambition is to be a cum dump for my seed."

Her body, which had been burning up with desire, convulsed as the truth of his words hit her like a tidal wave, jarring her mind, quenching her pride, and causing her pussy to seize up and grip his cock like a vice.

"Fuck," he growled. His darkened gaze fixed on her as he finished rutting her, smiling in victory as she screamed down their mental link and he pumped her full of cum.

Afterwards, he held her suspended in the air, kissing her softly. "You know, I have the strangest feeling, pet," he began, "that you intended for me to take you against the wall. Did you plant that idea in my head?"

"Shh," she smiled, pressing a finger to his lips. "Let's just enjoy this."

He held her against the wall, warming his cock for several more minutes until the school bell rang and brought them abruptly back to reality. They hastily separated and left before Professor Zott arrived for the second period.

CHAPTER 32

Alpha

KIRA

KIRA SPENT THE REST of the school day testing her powers on her classmates. She was starting to get the knack of connecting with someone else's mind, and was getting better at influencing her classmates to do as she suggested.

Both wolves and vampires were susceptible to her magic, and even her professors were not immune. She managed to convince Professor Parna to add ten teaspoons of clownwood powder to his laughing potion instead of two. The result created fumes so potent that the entire classroom became delirious with laughter. Eventually, Headmaster Arken was called to investigate what had happened.

"I've never heard you laugh this much before!" Susie commented at lunch time as they sat on the lawn eating sandwiches. "It's a nice change."

Kira lay on her side clutching her stomach, her sandwiches almost untouched beside her. "It hurts."

The uncontrollable laughter had finally subsided, but she was still prone to laughing fits, and the smallest thing could set her off—like when Susie chewed her ham and cucumber sandwich a little too loudly, or when an acorn fell to the ground beside them.

"I won't tell you my knock-knock joke then," Susie winked, but kept a straight face.

"Don't you dare." But it was too late, she couldn't stop herself from grinning ear to ear as giggles erupted from her throat.

"Just wait until Nathaniel sees you like this," Susie smiled.

"He...fucking...better not," Kira gasped. "He spends...half the time looking smug as it is."

Susie gave her a sidelong look. "How are things going between you two, anyway?"

That made her laughter fade in an instant. "I don't know what you mean." She sat up and seized a sandwich, taking a bite while she still could. "He claimed me, remember? I don't have a choice in all this."

Susie gave her a knowing smile. "I see the way he looks at you." She leant closer. "And I see the way you look at him."

Kira might have tried to deny it, but even without the laughing potion's effects, it was hard to resist returning Susie's smile. Plus, she didn't feel comfortable lying to Susie.

"I do feel something," she admitted. "But...it's complicated. I'd prefer if people didn't know."

"Of course, I understand. Don't worry, I won't tell anyone. And I know I told you to stay away from him when you first arrived at the academy...but I take that back. And not just because he saved my life," she added quickly. "I like how happy you seem around him."

Kira swallowed. She was touched by Susie's earnestness, and for a moment, didn't know what to say. She'd never had a friend like Susie before, someone she wanted to confide in. "Thank you...for saying that."

"Of course," Susie pulled her into a hug that squeezed Kira's insides. "I'm here for you. If you ever need anything..."

"Actually, there is something I need," she said as she caught sight of the Poplarin Pack in the distance talking to a group of first years. "The Poplarins are holding an initiation tonight...and I need your help."

Susie followed her gaze to where Mark was crouched down beside a female in wolf form, flirtingly running his hand along her back. "Why, what are you going to do?"

Kira's jaw set. "It's time for a change in leadership."

Susie's eyes widened as she sucked in a breath of air. "Good."

It was the middle of the night when Kira and Susie slipped into the dark gymnasium. Ever since Nathaniel had interrupted Kira's initiation, the Poplarins had been smarter about when they held the ceremony.

Smarter, but not smart.

Perhaps just plain arrogant, because they still used the same location. They were even playing basketball, which rang with the loud bounce of the ball as they played. A single light illuminated one end of the court, but the rest of the lights were off, so there were plenty of shadows for Kira and Susie to blend into to avoid detection.

Unlike her own initiation, the curtains on the stage were open, and Kira could see several first years lined up on the stage. They sat silently, glancing anxiously at the alphas playing basketball below as they waited for the initiation to begin. Despite the late hour, everyone wore their school uniform.

Kira did a quick head count—there were ten students sitting on the stage, nearly one for each of the twelve alphas. Nine of them were female wolves she recognised as first years with black thigh-high socks—no longer virgins. But the other, she was surprised to see, was a male vampire. He was tied up and gagged, and he was almost certainly here against his will.

It gave her a bad feeling.

Susie, who had snuck into the gymnasium with her, murmured her agreement. "That's Devon, he's a first year too. I reckon they took him as retaliation for what happened at the hotel."

Kira nodded grimly. Whilst she and Nathaniel had been close-lipped, Mark had not, and he'd loudly complained to anyone who would listen about the 'fucking vampire' who'd robbed him of his right to come. It had infuriated Kira to overhear Mark talk about his 'right' to have her that way, but mostly, she'd been angry at herself for ever seeing anything in him.

"If we keep to the shadows, we can get to the stage," Susie whispered.

Kira shook her head. She had no intention of hiding. She was here to confront the alphas. And she'd even dressed for the occasion.

She wore pointed shoes with low heels that she'd borrowed from Victoria—the lowest in the vampiress' collection, anyway—and a killer black dress that Victoria had complained was too big for her petite frame. It was strapless, slashed in the middle, and fit Kira like a glove, the silky fabric clinging to every curve.

"Sweetie, you look *hot!*" Victoria had gasped. "Are you sure you're not a vampire?"

Little did the vampiress know that her comment was half true. Victoria had assumed Kira was dressing up for Nathaniel, and she had not corrected her.

"I've got this," Kira told Susie, before turning her attention to the noisy end of the gymnasium where one basketball team was trying to score.

She took a steadying breath, sending out her magic in a gentle wave to graze the minds of every person present. No one reacted, oblivious to her power.

Smiling, she suddenly wished Nathaniel was here to see her. She'd insisted on coming alone. This was something she needed to do by herself.

Even so, Nathaniel had escorted them to the gymnasium and was waiting outside.

"Just in case," he'd assured her, crossing his arms and leaning into the building's shadow.

Kira had nodded her thanks, but she knew she wouldn't need his help.

This was her destiny.

The Poplarins cheered as one of the female betas scored a goal.

Lifting her head high, Kira strode forward. Her heels rang through the gym, whilst the daring thigh-high split of her dress parted to reveal her dark-skinned leg. A hushed silence fell as she came to a halt on the painted centre circle. The basketball rolled away, forgotten.

"Kira," Chelsea sneered, their recent truce apparently forgotten. She'd been bitchy ever since the hotel incident, as if to save face. "I see you made it after all."

"She's come to watch," Mark answered with a glower, "Haven't you, darling?"

Kira shrugged a shoulder lazily, aware of how the wolves followed her elegant movement and the way it rippled her dress. "I doubt there's much to see. From my experience, anyway."

Mark's eye twitched from the insult, whilst the rest of the pack listened in stunned silence. "Well, maybe if your parasite, blood sucking *boyfriend* had let me finish what I started at the hotel, you would address me with more respect—"

"Enough," Kira interrupted. "You're boring me. Just like you were boring me then."

Mark's jaw dropped. By the time he closed it, Kira had shifted her attention to the rest of the pack, sending a gentle, persuasive thought along her tendrils of magic.

"Look at us," Kira said. "We are wolves, but look at what we have become. We are meant for so much more than..." she gestured at the first years sitting on the dusty gym mats on the stage, "...Than this. We have allowed ourselves to be kept under the thumb of vampires...to be their food, their playthings. Some have done so willingly. Others have had no choice."

She thought of Susie's relationship with Professor Arken and the reprehensible way it had started. Squaring her shoulders, she continued. "I stand before you all, not to judge you, but to remind you of what we wolves have forgotten: that we are meant for much greater things."

The pack listened, entranced.

Some of them were so moved that they'd morphed into wolves, and at least one of the alphas was erect. He adjusted himself through his trousers, and Kira had to conclude that his reaction was a good sign, even if it wasn't the kind of arousal she'd intended to cause with her speech.

To her surprise, the first person to speak was not an alpha, but Chelsea. She slow-clapped as she approached Kira, coming to a standstill before her. "Wow. That was a lot of awkward bullshit you just served."

Well, maybe not so surprising.

"Where's your Master, *pet?* Does he know you're in here giving big speeches?"

"Yes," Kira answered simply.

"A little hypocritical, don't you think?"

"I am proud to be a vampire's submissive," Kira said firmly. "Just as I am proud to be a wolf. It makes me no less deserving of either respect or greatness."

Chelsea scoffed, but she was amongst the few. Like Kira, most of the shifters present had been intimately involved with a vampire at one time or another, and more than a few seemed roused at her words.

"You're new to the pack," Chelsea continued, "And you skipped our induction meeting this morning, so let me clear something up.

You are nothing, and you do not give orders. You are the lowest of the low, and once our initiation is complete, you will still be the lowest of the low. I will make sure of that."

Kira drew a deep breath, then exhaled slowly, regretfully. "I didn't want to do this..."

Chelsea's eyes narrowed. "Do what—"

A bolt of magic struck Chelsea's mind, causing her to leap backwards with a yelp. She looked around her wildly. "What the *fuck* was that?!"

Kira hadn't harmed Chelsea, only scared her. She'd learnt through her experimenting that her magic was most effective when used subtly—just like Nathaniel had recommended. Gentle persuasion was by far the most effective way to influence others. Whereas a strong burst of magic was about as useful as shaking somebody by the shoulders—it had the opposite effect to what she intended.

Still, the burst of magic had shocked Chelsea, momentarily shattering her offensive stance and putting her on guard.

"What did you *do?*" Chelsea cried, jabbing a finger at Kira.

"I didn't do anything," she replied, emulating that thought so it resonated in the rest of the pack members' minds. *"Chelsea is overreacting."*

"Chels is overreacting," someone muttered.

"This bitch is crazy!" Chelsea exclaimed, looking to the others for confirmation, but they exchanged uneasy looks behind her back.

"Overreacting," Kira pressed.

Her words echoed softly in the wolves' minds, duplicating like a rippling pond until each person repeated the thought of their own volition.

Mark rested a hand on Chelsea's shoulder. "Let me handle this, Chels."

Chelsea bristled and retreated, crossing her arms unhappily.

"Kira, you can't just come in here behaving like an alpha," Mark began, making an obvious effort to sound reasonable, but he stopped talking as a wolf brushed past him.

And another wolf.

And then another.

One by one, the majority of the pack moved to stand by Kira. She gave Mark a helpless shrug before pivoting.

Leading the pack members to the gymnasium's exit, she noticed the eager ones trotting close at her heels. Some of them panted eagerly, others whined anxiously, but none stayed back except Chelsea, Mark, and a couple of alphas.

Kira smiled to herself. She hadn't even gotten around to asking the pack to join her.

She didn't have to.

Her powers and strength were all it took for the Poplarin Pack to be disbanded. They weren't quite her pack yet, but they were ready for a new leader—and she was ready to lead them.

"How'd it go?" Nathaniel asked, pushing himself off the wall.

Kira gestured at the crowd of wolves filing out behind her. "As you can see."

"Indeed," Nathaniel murmured. "Very impressive."

Kira turned to Headmaster Arken, who had been waiting outside with Nathaniel at Susie's behest.

"The alphas are all yours, headmaster. And Susie's inside with the first years. You should also know that there's a first year vampire too... he's tied up, and he doesn't look like he's in good shape."

"Tied up?" Arken snapped. He scraped his silvered hair back angrily as he stalked inside the building.

Kira wondered if he would expel the alphas for breaking school rules, or simply suspend them. Either way, she had a gut-wrenching feeling that he would feed on every single one tonight.

While privy to the alphas' thoughts, Kira had been mortified to discover that they had indeed been holding Devon prisoner as a sick form of revenge against vampires in general. It was revenge of the worst kind—an eye for eye mentality, which would only create suffering with no hope of improving life for either race.

Even worse, the alphas had captured Devon two days ago and kept him locked in a storage room backstage.

"What's wrong?" Nathaniel murmured, touching her hand which had curled into a fist.

Kira's nostrils flared. "I think both sides are really messed up—vampires, *and* wolves."

"Good thing we'll have you to steer us on a better course."

She harrumphed. "Yes, well...I can see I'll have my work cut out for me. It's going to take a miracle to unfuck everything your father has done."

Nathaniel nodded gravely. "Indeed."

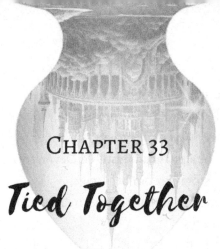

CHAPTER 33

Tied Together

KIRA

NATHANIEL'S JOINT BIRTHDAY, WEDDING, and coronation at Wintermaw Keep was looming close, which meant their time together would soon come to an end. He still didn't have a bride—something they would rectify tonight when they visited Gloria.

Kira didn't know exactly how Nathaniel wanted her to help in convincing the vampiress to accept his proposal, but she had a suspicion. Everything he'd told her about Gloria painted a picture of a compassionless woman that Kira would have probably been better off not knowing.

And then he'd unveiled a shocking revelation: that Gloria was her half sister.

Kira wasn't sure how she felt about that. She'd always thought her own family was Byron and Mary, so to discover she had a half sister...

She wanted to be excited by that. To be overjoyed. Though she hadn't even met Gloria yet.

And I'm plotting with Nathaniel to help trap her in marriage with him.

Nathaniel's answers to her questions about his plan for the

evening had been cryptic, although it was obvious it would involve coercion of some nature. She'd pressed him for information as they got dressed in his room, but he seemed uncomfortable with the subject.

That makes two of us.

The thought of Nathaniel marrying her half sister was strange and confusing, but she would have felt more distraught if the whole situation didn't seem so surreal.

Instead, Kira felt calm and even a little excited, as if she were going to a party with Nathaniel. She wore a tight, gold minidress that glittered, with matching earrings and tall black heels that made it almost impossible to walk. They were not exactly comfortable, and she was unsure about the black straps that criss-crossed from her ankles up to her calves, which she felt were sexy to the point of indecent.

"Forget it, I'm not wearing these," Kira said, reaching to undo the strap but losing balance.

She wobbled dangerously on the stilettos until Nathaniel steadied her.

"Leave them on," he said huskily. "I like seeing you this way."

"What, helpless?" Kira grumbled as he helped her sit on a chair. "I'd rather shoes I can walk in."

Nathaniel leant over her, a hand on the armrests either side of her, trapping her in. "I'd rather shoes I can fuck you in."

"No problem," she snapped. "*You* wear them then."

He laughed and made to stand, but she seized his necktie, which was silky black and striped with sparkling gold.

"Was this intentional?" she asked, holding him in place.

"Is what intentional, pet?"

"Your necktie. It matches my dress."

Nathaniel frowned and glanced down. "Frankly, I hadn't noticed."

"Oh." The fact that he'd unconsciously coordinated his outfit with hers was sweet. But although it made her glad, she had to put their mission objective first. "Maybe you should wear a different tie."

"Oh? Why's that?"

"Well, are you trying to make Gloria jealous, or piss her off?"

He blinked in surprise, then locked eyes with her.

"I'm trying to make her my wife. So..." His gaze flickered down to take in her gold dress, which was clinging to her curves, roving unapologetically before snapping back up. "What do you recommend?"

Kira swallowed as he lowered his head, the silk tie slackening in her hold as his lips came within inches of hers. "Well, I..."

She couldn't form the words. His arctic blue eyes were unnerving, his chiselled face too distracting.

A smile tugged at his lips, and he tilted his head and kissed her neck, his mouth sensual as he trailed hot touches with his lips up to her jawline.

Kira's breathing turned shallow, the silk tie slipping through her fingers as her head dropped backwards.

"You were saying?" he asked.

"Um..."

She gasped as Nathaniel hiked up her short dress, pushed her legs apart, and knelt in between them to kiss her inner thigh.

"Yes, pet?" Nathaniel murmured, pressing kisses up along her leg until he reached her clit, his breath hot and inviting.

She wasn't wearing any panties—Nathaniel's orders—and she felt exposed and vulnerable as he gripped her thighs and slid his warm tongue around her clit.

"Fuck," she said, her head lolling back as his open mouth explored her, his tongue delving into her slit to ravish her. A deep rumbling built in his throat, so low she hardly heard it except for the way it made her body quake.

"I asked you a question, pet," he growled, pulling back and delivering a long, wet stroke with his tongue.

It took her a moment to remember what they'd been talking about, and then she twitched as he dipped his tongue back inside her.

He lifted his head, his eyes intense and unreadable as he studied her. "Well? Shall I change my tie to a different one?"

Kira shook her head, because she didn't know the answer. She did, but she didn't. If the matching tie implied they were a couple, however, then she wanted him to leave it on.

"Cat got your tongue, pet?" Nathaniel teased.

"*No,*" she shot back. He knew she hated any mention of felines.

His lip curled, revealing his long fangs as he began untying his tie.

"What are you doing?"

He didn't answer as he took hold of her hands and bound them tightly with the black and gold fabric.

"Nathaniel?"

His lower jaw clenched in concentration as he pulled the fabric tight in one swift motion.

It dug into her wrists, and there was zero wiggle room as he tied a bow.

"You're right, pet," he said, reaching past her to open the dreaded drawer of his desk to take out the collar and gag. "We don't want Gloria to think you're a threat."

"No," Kira protested as he unclipped the collar he'd given her—the one studded with onyx, rubies, and bearing her locket—and strapped the black leather one on instead. "I don't want to wear it."

Nathaniel hesitated. "I know. But it would be in our best interest if Gloria grants us a private audience without her cronies present. She has a bedroom at the back of the club. If you arrive gagged and collared, with all outward appearance of the perfect, docile pet, then

Gloria will lower her guard."

"You make a strong case," she said sarcastically. "Did you think that up just now, or were you always planning on making me wear this thing?"

Nathaniel smiled. "I had not planned on using my tie to restrain you, but...yes, it was premeditated."

She huffed. "Figures."

"Be flattered, pet. You've inspired me."

Kira rolled her eyes, then glanced down to where her legs were still spread. The hem of her dress barely covered her cunt, at least to her own eyes. Nathaniel no doubt saw every inch of her, glistening and yearning for him. She was throbbing with need, and she was ready for him to finish what he'd started.

Nathaniel's eyes glinted as if he read her mind. He pushed the ball gag into her mouth. "Soon, pet. But not yet."

CHAPTER 34

The Nightclub

KIRA

KIRA WAS SECRETLY GRATEFUL for the carriage Nathaniel ordered to take them from the academy to the nightclub. She was struggling to manage in the ridiculously tall heels, which she was sure even Victoria would have been hard-pressed to pull off. She was forced to rely on Nathaniel's arm for balance, which she soon came to realise had been his intention all along.

He'd offered to carry her up the seven winding staircases from the dorms to the foyer, but she'd insisted on climbing up herself.

No way am I letting him carry me like a damsel in distress.

By the time the door to the foyer came into sight, her feet were sore and her hair had stuck to her sweaty forehead, making her regret her stubbornness. In hindsight, it had been pointless. She hadn't saved face at all—for once, there had been no one on the stairwell except them.

Having her wrists bound before her had not helped matters, and the gag in her mouth made it difficult to breathe. At least she wasn't wearing a leash, but she'd spotted him pocketing it earlier, and it made her wary.

She resented Nathaniel for insisting that she lead the way up the stairs, knowing it gave him a perfect view of her ass. She couldn't even tug the hem of her skirt down with her hands bound, but at least he'd been there to catch her in case she fell backwards.

"I need a drink," she said mentally when they finally reached the top, letting him feel how parched she was and how much the shoes were killing her feet for good measure. They could both suffer together.

"There'll be water in the carriage," Nathaniel promised as they entered the foyer.

To her horror, the hall was full of parents and teachers sitting at tables. She'd forgotten about the parent-teacher interviews that were being held for the fifth years tonight.

Everyone stopped talking to look their way.

Great. Just when she'd thought she was becoming used to public humiliation, her embarrassment reached new heights.

Her face grew hot, her feet frozen in place.

No one said a word.

"Come, pet," Nathaniel said loudly, whistling low as if she were a dog.

"You did not just fucking whistle at me!" she gasped, hurrying to keep up with his stride. Her heels echoed loudly, and she felt more degraded than words could say as she clacked past the appalled parents with her mouth stretched taut around the ball and her skirt ridden up to expose her ass.

She wasn't even wearing fucking panties.

"I'm going to die from embarrassment," she moaned.

"Not until I fuck you in this dress," Nathaniel shot back with a grin.

Headmaster Arken nodded in approval as they passed, and he gave Nathaniel a knowing wink as he stroked his short beard.

Kira bristled when Nathaniel nodded back, as if he and Arken were exchanging some secret gentlemen's club message at her expense.

"Acknowledging your conquest?" she snarled.

"Yes," Nathaniel replied simply as the front doors opened for them.

She was relieved when they were outside in the open air. There were no students to be seen, at least.

She threw the dirtiest glare she could at Nathaniel, although she suspected the ball gag ruined the effect, which forced her jaws open and her lips parted and stretched.

"I like seeing you like this." Nathaniel looked pleased with himself as he led her towards the waiting carriage in his elegant gentleman's coat. "It reminds me of our first carriage ride together."

"It reminds me how much I loathed you."

"Loathed?" he whispered. "Past tense, pet?"

She didn't trust herself to answer, and settled instead for letting him feel her anger through her magic.

He chuckled in response and pulled her closer by the elbow. "You know, one of the limitations of using the gag was that you couldn't answer my questions. Now that you can respond to me with your magic, I see no reason why we couldn't use it on a daily basis."

Kira had been about to get into the carriage, but she hesitated, not because of the threat of the gag, but because of the emptiness of that threat.

With only a few days before the wedding, 'daily basis' held little meaning. There was no guarantee they would be able to see much of each other in the coming weeks—it was traditional for a vampire couple to take a month-long honeymoon, and Kira had a feeling she wasn't invited.

The prospect of being left behind while Nathaniel travelled all over the world with his new wife left her feeling bitter and hollow, even though she knew it wouldn't be easy for Nathaniel, either.

He seemed to read her thoughts, because he helped her into the driverless carriage without another word and rapped on the ceiling.

It lurched forwards as the horses set off with loud clip-clops down the drive and through the gates into the city.

The late afternoon breeze was pleasant, the hearty smells wafting from restaurants enticing. If Kira's stomach hadn't been queasy with nerves, she might have enjoyed the city sights more. Nathaniel encouraged her to lean out the window and 'take it all in', which she thought was nice of him, at least until he appeared behind her and lifted her skirt.

Before she could ask what he was doing, he pushed something hard and cold between her ass cheeks.

Icy panic flashed through her as she tried to twist away, but he wrapped one arm around her waist and held her in place, her elbows propped on the open window's ledge.

"What—?"

"Hold still while I plug you," he murmured in her ear, easing the object in deeper.

Kira squirmed, but she was powerless to stop what was happening. As the pressure built uncomfortably, her body seized up, and the edges of her vision went murky with an overwhelming, nauseating, carnal desire.

"There," he announced once it was fully seated.

"You're an assho—"

Her voice cut off as he tapped the plug sharply, making her wince.

"You were saying?" he mused.

Kira inhaled a steadying breath and fixed him with a glare. *"Ass. Hole."*

He laughed and leant back on his seat with an arm stretched lazily over the backrest, looking as pleased as a cat who'd gotten the cream.

Kira sank slowly back onto her seat, trying not to let it show on her face when the plug inevitably pushed up into her.

Nathaniel's lip twitched as if he knew. It wasn't long before he had her sitting back on his lap.

"I'm sorry the plug doesn't match your dress, but the steel has significance. One day, perhaps I'll give you one made of gold."

Kira snorted through the gag.

"That's what you're sorry about? Material choice?"

"I'm sorry about a lot of things," he whispered in her ear, pressing himself close so she felt his erection pressing against her rear. "But never about plugging you."

The sun was setting when they arrived at the club. The multi-storey building had a plum-coloured exterior and tall, shuttered windows with seductive, bright red trimmings.

There was a long line of people waiting to be let in, most of whom were vampires in glamorous outfits. The few wolves present were scantily dressed, and most were kneeling on the ground or sitting obediently in their wolf form.

"It seems I overdressed you," Nathaniel mused as they passed a shifter wearing nothing at all except a ball gag that was eerily similar to hers.

"You wish," Kira scoffed. Secretly, she was grudgingly grateful for the dress Nathaniel had chosen for her; it was much more on par with what the vampires were wearing than the daring strips of leather some wolves wore.

Deep music pulsed from within the building, making Kira feel even more jittery and anxious. She still had no idea how Nathaniel expected her to help win Gloria over. Did he expect her to use her magic to make Gloria fall in love with him? Because even if such a thing was possible, she wasn't sure if she'd be able to bring herself to do that.

Whatever he had planned, Kira hoped she would be up to the task. She was trying to ignore the jealousy and hurt welling in her chest, but her heart beat rapidly, outmatching the steady blood-pounding music.

"There are a lot of people here," she commented. The prospect of

joining the back of the very long line was not appealing.

"Most of them won't be allowed in," Nathaniel replied. "The club is very exclusive. Come."

He led her to the front of the queue, where a muscled wolf bouncer was standing with arms crossed and a bored expression. His beady eyes widened when he recognised them.

"Prince Nathaniel," he greeted, hurriedly unclipping the red rope barrier from the bollard.

He bowed low as Nathaniel passed, Kira following close behind.

"Nice," she said, wishing she could remove the gag just to smirk at Nathaniel. *"That was quite the reception. Guess you're a regular here."*

Nathaniel didn't take the bait, but at least he had the courage to meet her gaze, if only for a moment. *"I used to be."*

Kira's heart plummeted, even though there was nothing wrong with what he'd said. *Of course* Nathaniel had come here. As per his father's wishes, he'd courted Gloria for years. She would like to have reassured herself that it was in the past, except here he was, dressed in his finest with a ring box tucked away in his inside pocket.

Kira squeezed her eyes shut as bitter anger swirled inside her like acid, shielding her mind and suspending her magic so Nathaniel wouldn't feel how utterly wretched that made her feel.

Keep your shit together, Kira.

The nightclub was dark and eerily lit with magical lights that floated through the room like gold and purple fireflies. Rather than one single, open area like she'd expected, there were several rooms, all connected in a long twisting series by open archways and darkened, hairpin corridors.

Black-and-white checkered floor tiles added to her disorientation as they moved from room to room, ignoring the tight, circular stairwells with gold bannisters in favour of continuing deeper through the maze.

The rooms were tastefully decorated with sheer curtains, ivy plants, and metallic brocade wallpaper that glinted in the soft light.

Each room contained upholstered furniture, including plush sofas, lavish beds, and leather benches. There was also oddly-shaped furniture Kira didn't recognise bearing metal chains, leather, and other crude features that made her shiver.

Some of the furniture had people strapped into them, including a portly male shifter in human form wearing an underbust corset and a toy in every hole. An older vampiress in an elegant cream dress and a silver-haired updo circled him holding a flogger with purple tails. Each time she struck, the vampires watching hissed with excitement, some sipping wine, others touching themselves.

Several couples were having sex in alcoves or darkened corners. Some activities weren't limited to two people, which Kira found out the hard way when she accidentally wandered into a crowded room where a wolf orgy was taking place.

"Stay close to me, pet," Nathaniel said after he'd dragged her out of the throng of naked bodies and fur.

"*I'm trying,*" she retorted. "*You could have warned me this was a sex club.*"

"Is there any other kind?"

Kira was taken aback by the sight of so many people fucking, and the contrast of formal attire with leather whips and revealing undergarments made her head spin.

"You cannot say I didn't prepare you back in my room," Nathaniel murmured, pulling her aside and pressing her against the wall.

Kira lifted her chin to meet his gaze. "*Are you referring to the half-assed way you went down on me earlier? If so, you could have finished what you started.*"

Nathaniel's eyes narrowed. "Would you like me to touch you?"

"*Well, someone ought to.*"

"Be careful what you wish for, pet."

He'd called her bluff. She didn't dare answer, and she drew a sharp breath as his hand slipped under her skirt. His fingers fondled her clit, and her eyelids fluttered shut as he pushed them inside her.

"So wet," he whispered, working his fingers deeper. "So tight." He pumped them in and out with a steady rhythm. "So needy." He kissed her neck slowly. "I love it when you're gagged like this. It does things to me like you can't imagine..." He sucked on her earlobe. "And it makes me want to do such bad things to you. I'd love nothing more than to sink my cock into you right here...right now. Or maybe you'd like me to strap you to that contraption in the room behind me."

Kira peeked one eye open and looked over his shoulder. She didn't know what the hell was in that other room—some sort of saddle with stirrups and a backrest—but a stupid reckless part of her wanted Nathaniel to do exactly that.

"Yes," she replied before she could stop herself. *"I want you to."*

"I know you do, pet."

She tried to press her body closer to feel his erection, but her bound hands were in the way.

Nathaniel laughed low and kissed her temple.

She whined in protest as he removed his fingers from her pussy and held them up to catch the light.

"Don't tease me!"

He sucked on them slowly, and words failed her.

"I promise I will see to your needs later, pet. But I'm afraid we're on a timeline." He clipped the leash to her neck. "Come on."

Kira hadn't noticed him reaching into his pocket for the leash. She grumbled down their link as she followed him, her knees weak and her legs wobbling from more than just the spindly heels. Her core throbbed with despair; her heartache momentarily suspended for a deeper, more urgent craving. She was sick of Nathaniel tormenting her, and she was so disorientated from the endless puzzle of darkened rooms and colourful lamps that she'd almost forgotten why they'd come.

They turned a corner into a quiet corridor, leaving behind the clamour of laughter and moans. The pumping music was not as loud, but Kira could still feel the bass thumping her heart.

They walked down the long corridor and turned into a grand antechamber illuminated by red flame torches. A set of closed, pristine, white doors with jewelled handles stood before them, manned by two burly vampires dressed in black.

"Your Highness," they bowed, each taking hold of a handle and opening the doors, revealing a sitting area and another door beyond.

Kira made to enter, but the taut pull of the leash stopped her. She looked at Nathaniel in confusion. *"What is it?"*

He nodded to the floor. "On your knees, pet."

Her jaw dropped. *"You're kidding me."* She gestured at her skimpy gold mini dress as best she could with bound hands. *"Is this not enough?"*

"It's club policy," Nathaniel said.

The guards spoke up in unison: "Wolves beyond this point must be leashed and kneeling at all times."

Kira glared at them. She was about to use her magic to impress upon them just how stupid that policy was, when she felt the sharp tug of the leash at her neck.

Nathaniel gave her a warning look. "Pet. Do not make me discipline you."

One of the guards pointed to a black metal post of wrought iron driven into the ground. "You can tie her up if you prefer to leave her outside, sir. We'll keep an eye on her."

"Like hell!" she cried.

"Then kneel," Nathaniel answered down their link.

"Nope."

Nathaniel's head turned towards her so slowly she felt chills. He stepped close until they were toe to toe and cupped her face. "Well, then. What do you say, pet? Would you like to wait outside with these nice gentlemen?"

"I can give them orders to entertain you," he added down their link.

"Ha."

He was just joking, obviously.

Hopefully.

"I need your help, Kira," Nathaniel whispered, the quiet sincerity making her skin tingle.

She sighed, or tried to, but the angle of her head and the gag propping her open caused saliva to dribble at her feet.

Just fucking great.

Still, they'd come this far, and they both knew she had no choice but to enter with him. She was only prolonging the inevitable by being difficult.

Kira exhaled through her nostrils. *"Fine. Help me down."*

Nathaniel took hold of her bound hands and helped her to her knees. *"That's it, pet. Now crawl."*

Kira sat back on her heels and scowled up at him. *"Untie my wrists first. I can't crawl like this."*

Nathaniel gave his head a small shake. "Come, pet. We don't have far to go."

"You are a fucking piece of work, you know that?"

She had no choice but to half-crawl, half-hobble on her hands and knees, trying to keep up as he crossed the sitting room. At least he was walking slowly, but it was all so fucking awkward and humiliating. Her hair was in disarray, hanging across her face and obscuring her vision. Her skirt had ridden up to expose the plug in her ass. She could feel the guards' gaze on her backside as she crawled along the ground, and was glad when the double doors shut behind them.

Nathaniel opened the next door and ushered her through.

Kira was too focused on her own miserable state to take much notice of her surroundings, but as she crossed the threshold, she finally lifted her head.

But then she caught sight of Gloria in the room beyond, and she realised with a heavy heart that her humiliation was just beginning.

Gloria was angelic.

Pale skin. Large blue eyes.

Wavy golden hair that cascaded down her bare shoulders.

A long, pale blue dress that flowed like liquid around her slender form, translucent enough to emphasise her generous breasts.

She was lying on a large bed decorated with cream florals, and the numerous glass coffee tables were covered in fucking lace doilies.

This was not at all the evil blood-soaked lair Kira had envisioned, and Gloria was not at all the blood-thirsty ice queen she'd imagined. Instead, she was perfect.

There's no way we're related, Kira thought to herself as Gloria sat up, her glossy hair shimmering of its own accord.

"There you are, Nathaniel," she cooed, her voice sweet and musical.

A sad realisation came over Kira as she gaped up at the goddess.

Gloria was perfect.

And she was not.

CHAPTER 35

Gloria

KIRA

GLORIA GESTURED LANGUIDLY AT a white fur coat hanging on a nearby hook. Kira recognised it as the fake fur coat that Barbara had made.

"I received the fur coat you sent me, Nathaniel. I assumed it was a wedding gift ..." A sharp edge entered her polite tone, "Since it did not come with a note."

Nathaniel gave a low chuckle. "You must have drawers full of my notes from over the years. Unless you burnt them all?"

Gloria's lips curved in an unearthly smile, and the effect was like watching a delicate crack-line travel across smooth porcelain—on the precipice of shattering the entire veneer. "I kept some."

"Don't lie." He shrugged out of his coat, draping it over the back of an armchair as if making himself at home.

Kira realised with a lurching feeling that he had been here many times before.

"Make yourself comfortable, pet," Nathaniel said gently, sweeping his hand to indicate the various poofs, ottomans and armchairs decorating the room.

Gloria's eyes narrowed, and she made a show of behaving as if she'd only just noticed Kira kneeling on the floor. Gloria sat up, her serene expression becoming strained. "Nathaniel, what is this?"

"*This* is Kira," Nathaniel said, stepping behind Kira to slide the door's bolt shut to lock it. "And *she* is my pet."

Gloria blinked angrily, and there was a flash of jealousy before her composed smile return. "A pet? Without consulting me? But Nathaniel..." she tittered, "you *know* I prefer cats."

Nathaniel gave another good-natured laugh and placed his hands behind his back. "I was not aware I required your permission."

Gloria smiled—a perfect curve of her luscious lips. "I'm your future wife, dearest. We should discuss these things together, since it affects both of us."

"We are not married," Nathaniel reminded her.

"Oh, but we will be, I'm sure. Very soon."

"Hmm." Nathaniel tapped the glass table beside him, as if trying to gather his thoughts. "Indeed. That is what I have come to discuss. But no matter what we decide..." Kira felt the mood in the room shift as Nathaniel placed a possessive hand on her head and patted her. "Kira stays."

Gloria's eyes flashed, her smile freezing as new cracks began to form in her countenance. She held that phony smile as she said, "We'll talk about it later."

Nathaniel did not argue, and he motioned for Kira to stay before advancing to the bed. Kira half expected him to get down on one knee, but he pulled the ring box from his jacket pocket and tossed it on the bed beside Gloria.

"Gloria, will you consent to be my wife?" Nathaniel asked, his voice so flat and lacklustre it was barely a question.

Gloria's eyes darted between the ring box and Nathaniel. "What, no roses? No chocolates? Whatever happened to wooing me?"

Nathaniel tilted his head to one side with a nonchalant smile, his tone soft and ominous. "You've received all manner of chocolates and roses, *dearest*. I have played your games, and now, my patience has run thin. We can do this the easy way, or the hard way. Either way, we both know you will become my wife."

A dangerous silence filled the room.

Kira stared at the ground. She couldn't believe what she was hearing, but she stayed silent, pretending she was no more significant than the furniture around her.

Finally, Gloria spoke. "You may be 'Prince' Nathaniel, but you are in far more need of me than I am of you. We both know the Crown needs my family's connections to secure your *tenuous* claim to the throne. Your father certainly knows it, given he killed my mother to get to where he is."

The melodic quality of her voice was gone, and she all but spat her next words. "Your father remains unchallenged because he is everything a vampire should be. But there are many who doubt your claim—after all, my mother and father were the true rulers. Pure-blooded vampires of royal blood. Without me, you risk revolt." A cruel smile appeared on her lips as she added, "And assassination."

Nathaniel bowed his head in acknowledgement. "It is true. And furthermore, if I may add, we both know there is no small number of vampires who believe that you, *dearest Gloria,* should succeed my father instead of me. Which *does* make me question the value in keeping you alive."

Kira baulked at his threat, as did Gloria, who suddenly looked scared.

"You wouldn't," she breathed.

"Have you never considered that?" Nathaniel asked. "After all this time, did you not realise that failing to marry me would render your existence intolerable to my father?"

Gloria's face grew paler as Nathaniel studied his fingers as if inspecting them for dirt.

He glanced up, his gaze hard with the icy shards of a heart long broken. "Or did you just assume, as you do with everything, that I was a toy you could play with indefinitely?"

The air felt dense, and Kira could scarcely breathe. She was shaken by the regret and disappointment behind Nathaniel's words. His emotions radiated off him, hinting at a past history with Gloria that Kira could only guess at.

"Your father expects you to marry me," Gloria said without emotion.

Nathaniel shook his head. "My father can hardly expect me to marry you if you are dead, can he? And what do you think would happen then?" He advanced on Gloria, who scrambled away to the other side of the bed. He seized the end of her long dress so she couldn't get away. "Once you are dead, do you really think he would deny me the crown then? He has no other heirs, and your loyalist supporters will have no alternative than to support me."

He cocked his head at Gloria, who was trying to back away, blinking up at him in horror as he kept a hold of her skirts. Sadness pooled in Nathaniel's eyes. "Oh, Gloria. I am sure not a day has gone by in your life where you did not play through every scenario in your head. But did you truly not realise you were playing chess with a stalemated king? You have no moves left to make. Your only option is, and always has been, to marry me. Only then can my father be sure that you pose no threat to his legacy."

Gloria was petrified, too stunned to scream as Nathaniel dragged her closer by the hem of her dress.

"The lure of your family's connections is the *only* reason my father kept you alive. But my offer stands, as it always has. Accept my proposal. Marry me. I swear I will never lay a finger on you. And," he continued, his eyes drifting shut for the briefest of moments as if the words he planned to say pained him, "I swear I will make sure my father never touches you again."

Gloria's fearful expression vanished, but rather than warm to his words, her eyebrows pinched together in fury. It was the only warning sign before she leapt at Nathaniel, striking his throat.

He reeled back, clutching his throat.

"I don't want your protection, Nathaniel! You could not protect me then, and you cannot protect me now. Your promises mean *nothing!*"

Nathaniel recovered in time to block her kick, grabbing her foot and swinging her violently to the ground.

Gloria screamed as she rolled away, her dress ripping as Nathaniel stomped on the hem with his foot. She was back on her feet in an instant, leaping at Nathaniel with sharp jabs, chops, and strikes to his jaw with the heel of her palm. He was stronger, but Gloria was faster, more agile, and her fury might have given Kira a run for her money.

Kira had never seen vampires fight before, but she was stunned by the speed with which they attacked each other. She leapt to her feet, watching uselessly as she tried to track their quick motions.

Nathaniel nearly overpowered Gloria several times, but she always slipped away at the last instant.

Suddenly, the vampiress delivered a spinning heel kick that caught Nathaniel's jaw with a smack, sending him stumbling backwards.

Gloria advanced with quick steps, hand slicing through the air in a deadly strike.

Nathaniel side-stepped, caught her by the throat, and slammed her against the wall. Gloria clawed at his hand. Her legs kicked as she struggled, but he held her there, breathing heavily as he stared, waiting.

"Kira." Nathaniel growled her name, his gaze still fixed on Gloria as he hissed with the effort of keeping her pinned.

Kira tensed as she realised Nathaniel was waiting for *her*. *This* is why he'd needed her to come here tonight. He could not fight Gloria alone.

Nor could he resolve this peacefully. Gloria would not marry him willingly, nor out of fear. Which only left two options: killing her or forcing her to marry him.

Kira felt a strange sense of relief that he wasn't resorting to murder. Gloria was her half sister. They shared the same blood, and Gloria probably had memories of their mother. Maybe, one day—and it was a farfetched idea, but maybe—Gloria would share those memories with her.

"Kira!"

Nathaniel's ragged voice shattered through her mind, and she jolted back to reality in time to see him narrowly avoid Gloria's knee to his groin.

And I'm standing around like a fucking idiot.

She morphed, the gag and collar vanishing as her human form dissolved. Her wolf forms darted forward, teeth flashing and coiled tails whipping the air.

They split up. One wolf pulled Nathaniel off Gloria whilst the tails of the other wrapped around the vampiress' wrists and neck.

"What is *that?*" shrieked Gloria as she stared at Kira's wolf forms.

"I thought she would know about me," Kira said to Nathaniel, projecting her thoughts across their link. *"If she's my half sister, shouldn't she remember me?"*

"Gloria is missing most of her childhood memories," he explained. *"It's her mind's way of protect her from trauma."*

"It's hideous!" Gloria scowled at Kira as if she were the dirt on her shoe.

Fuck you too, sis.

Kira threw Nathaniel a weary glance. *"Where do you want her?"*

"Here will do," Nathaniel said, his expressing darkening as he undid his belt. "Make her kneel."

Gloria's face grew alarmed. "Wh-what are you doing?" she demanded as Kira forced her down onto the floor.

Gloria opened her mouth to scream, but Nathaniel clamped a hand around her mouth. "Shh," he soothed. "This is what you want, remember? You told me so many times. I was a fool to think you wanted chocolates and poems. Oh, how you laughed. You led me to believe you wanted romance and kindness, and yet you mocked my attempts behind my back. Who would have guessed? That all along, the proud, icy princess craved the very thing she despised?"

"No," whispered Gloria, even as her head dipped in a nod.

"Yes," Nathaniel breathed. "Deep down, I knew. We both did, didn't we? That *this* is what you wanted."

Kira's gut twisted with shock as a wave of dread washed over her. She'd known this was a possibility—no, a probability. But now that the moment was here...

Her stomach churned.

Is he really going to force himself on Gloria?

"Nathaniel, what the fuck?" she yelled down their link, her voice fearful.

He gave her a wary look.

"An archaic vampire law," he replied. *"One that Gloria has hinted at many times. She even read the scripture to me once. Essentially, any female vampire who was successfully forced into submission by a male vampire was then required to marry him."*

Kira blanched. *"That's horrible."*

"As I said," Nathaniel continued. *"Archaic."*

"But...how could she want this?"

"Gloria has had a difficult upbringing as a prisoner in my father's court. She has grown up in an isolated world where cruelty is rewarded, and it's given her a warped view of the world."

Kira gave a low whine. She knew almost nothing about Gloria, but she couldn't help but feel a twang of guilt as she restrained her.

"Let's get this over with," Nathaniel muttered out loud as he knelt down and positioned himself behind Gloria.

Gloria struggled against the bondage of Kira's tails as Nathaniel ripped away the last of her sheer skirt and pressed himself against her.

Sickened, Kira looked away, wishing she could block her ears as the vampiress—who was her half sister for crying out loud—let out a muffled scream as Nathaniel entered her.

Disbelief hit Kira.

Unable to stop herself, she used her magic to touch Nathaniel's mind, and immediately wished she hadn't. She was met with the physical pleasure of his cock throbbing and tensing from the tight pressure of being compressed by Gloria's tight cunt.

Holy shit.

Kira cut herself off from Nathaniel's magic and bent over, praying she wouldn't throw up as she wheezed for air around the gag, feeling light-headed. All this time, she'd been in denial. He had implied this was his plan, but she'd convinced herself that he was exaggerating, that this would never happen—could never happen.

It's just a bad dream.

And yet, here they were, in a secluded backroom of Gloria's nightclub, the loud, wet slaps of Nathaniel's balls ringing in her ears.

She tried not to watch, she really did, but in her peripheral vision, she saw it all: the way he drew back in a slow, patient movement, before thrusting forward again, the wet squelch as he impacted Gloria making them both flinch.

"Consent," Nathaniel hissed, drawing back, "to be my wife." He slammed into Gloria again, a punishing thrust that caused the vampiress' body to jolt forward against Kira's restraints. "Consent," he repeated, beginning the process all over again.

It was cold, brutal, and deliberate, and Nathaniel was ruthless as he fucked Gloria. His expression was both detached and predatory in a way Kira had never seen before.

A hard truth settled over her as her gaze drifted back to Nathaniel. He was forcing himself on her sister. And she was a fucking accomplice.

Kira's gaze darted to Gloria with concern, but her guilt faded when she heard the vampiress' soft moans, and noticed the way she pushed her hips and ass back to meet Nathaniel.

Kira watched in astonishment.

Gloria's urging him on. She's fucking enjoying this.

What kind of twisted person *wanted* this to happen to them?

Someone like me, Kira realised a split second later.

Her eyes unfocused. Maybe she and her sister were not so different after all. And despite initial impressions, Gloria clearly wasn't perfect.

Nathaniel was breathing heavily, his hands gripping Gloria's hips as he took her in slow, hard, jerking motions.

Kira stared openly now, but he seemed intent on avoiding her gaze, or perhaps he was too absorbed by Gloria to notice her.

Sadness filled her at that thought.

Nathaniel had been at it for at least a quarter of an hour with no sign of coming. The sweat poured off him, and both his and Gloria's eyes had shut as if they were lost in the moment.

Kira was lost too. But unlike Nathaniel and Gloria, she was alone. An outsider, looking in.

She could no longer tell if the vampiress was enjoying herself, or just waiting for it to be over.

Feeling glum, she withdrew her tails from Gloria, who clearly no longer needed to be restrained. Her wolves lay down, ears lowered as Nathaniel took the vampiress.

Hot jealousy surged through Kira's chest, stinging the back of her throat with bile and causing tears to well in her eyes. She licked her snouts anxiously, watching helplessly as the man she loved move inside another woman.

The minutes passed, and she felt smaller and smaller as Nathaniel kept up his slow, steady thrusts. His grunts had grown more anguished, and he looked like he was in pain rather than enjoying himself. Meanwhile, Gloria still hadn't said 'yes' to his proposal.

A realisation hit Kira with shocking clarity.

Nathaniel was struggling. Somehow, he had maintained an erection, but he wasn't able to finish what he'd started, and Gloria was too stubborn to give in.

He needs me.

They needed to break her willpower before Nathaniel lost his.

Her wolves recombined as she morphed back into her human self. The collar was tight around her neck, the gag and plug large and intrusive, but her tight dress and strappy heels made her feel slutty and powerful.

She focused on Nathaniel and Gloria, her insides now boiling with jealousy. Her eyes swam with unfallen tears. She was miserable, her heart aching with betrayal. But the humiliation of being sidelined and made to watch this act also turned her on. She was involved in what was happening to Gloria...

And I can decide how this plays out.

"*Nathaniel,*" she whispered as a heavy tear rolled down her face. "*Nathaniel, look at me.*"

Nathaniel's head slowly turned towards her, and she was startled to see the shame on his face. Not just shame. Regret. And also doubt, the fear etched on his face so plainly she understood his unspoken thought perfectly: *I can't do this.*

"*Yes, you can,*" she said mentally. "*I will help you.*"

She held his gaze as she sat back onto her bottom and spread her legs wide to give him a full view of her pussy. Using her bound hands, she began to stroke herself. "*Watch me,*" she urged, "*And don't look away.*"

Surprise flashed through Nathaniel's eyes, and he watched her with wild, desperate eyes, never looking away as he rutted Gloria—as if Kira was his lifeline throughout all this madness. As if it was her he was taking from behind.

Kira opened her mind to her magic, letting Nathaniel feel her pleasure as profoundly as she did as she touched herself. She shuddered as her fingers grazed her wet folds. She was extremely sensitive, and the feel of her fingers as she pushed them into her swollen slit felt so good that she choked out a sob. She wished it was Nathaniel. His fingers, his mouth, his cock.

"I need you," she said, opening her mind up to his thoughts, his emotions, his sensations, until she keenly felt every ounce of pleasure and shame. She embraced it all—the ragged gasps, the guilty pangs, and each forbidden thrust culminating to something grand and colossal that she couldn't even begin to understand.

And she let him feel her pain. Her heartache. Her love, both pure and imperfect. Her earnest affection messy with hopes and fears.

"I need you," she said again, because he hadn't believed her the first time, and she needed him to hear it. Needing him to believe that she loved all parts of him. Not just the shadow who emulated his father. And not just the kind man hiding underneath who was trying to save the world. But all of him. Even the man who was forcing her sister.

"I need you too," he choked, pushing his cock into Gloria, his deadened gaze growing hungry as he watched her stroke her sopping clit.

The vampiress lifted her head with a scowl. "Who are you talking to?"

"No one," Nathaniel said, pushing her head back down. "Be silent."

His eyes refocused on Kira.

She sent him a new wave of emotion through her magic, letting him feel her anguish and yearning as she worked her fingers in and out. And then she did something new, something she hadn't known she could do: she conjured the memory of how he'd taken her in the hotel, of the sweet and hot moments, and the taboo ones too, and sent the flash of images to his mind.

Nathaniel drew a sharp breath, his eyes losing focus as the scene played out in his mind, sharing his thoughts with her. His movements grew more intense, his breathing heavier as he drew closer to his orgasm, fucking Gloria with fervour even as he pictured Kira.

Gloria ruined the moment when she caught sight of Kira fingering herself.

"Control your disgusting pet," she snapped.

Nathaniel slapped his hand over her mouth. "I warned you to be quiet."

The moment his hand covered Gloria's mouth, the vampiress began to come, her throaty moans causing sickening jealousy to seep into every corner of Kira's heart, dousing the embers of her orgasm. The euphoric moment between her and Nathaniel was gone, and they exchanged a weary look of disappointment.

Nathaniel had no choice but to continue, and as the minutes passed, Gloria was rocked from one orgasm to the next, and still, neither he nor Kira had climaxed. As exhaustion began to set in, their concentration began to slip, as did Nathaniel's facade.

Suddenly, Gloria looked to the side and caught sight of Nathaniel—who was staring at Kira.

The vampiress shrieked in outrage, her eyes blazing as she wrenched her mouth free of his hand. "You're looking at *her* instead of me?"

She tried to buck Nathaniel off, but he held tight, riding her as if she were a wild horse, keeping his cock embedded in her pussy the whole time.

"Why are you looking at her instead of me?" Gloria asked in a whimper so sad that it made Kira feel for her.

Nathaniel leant close to her ear, his voice gentle. "It's something you will grow accustomed to in our lengthy marriage, *dearest*."

"But she's just a wolf! A worthless, mangy mutt—"

"She *is* just a wolf," Nathaniel agreed, his voice dangerous and soothing. "And yet...I'd much rather be fucking her."

"*What?!* How dare you? Get off me—"

Nathaniel's hand clamped over her mouth again, his gaze snapping to Kira. "Play with yourself, pet. Let me see you."

He gripped Gloria's mane of hair and spun her around so they both faced Kira, giving him a direct line of sight as he ploughed into the vampiress from behind. "I will come inside you, Gloria, if and when my slut comes too."

He removed his hand when Gloria tried to speak.

"That is how much she means to you?"

Nathaniel chuckled darkly, his disinterest so convincing it made Kira's insides tighten. "Oh, no, dearest. That is how little *you* mean to me."

That he would rather fuck a wolf than his own kind.

The harshness of his words made Gloria fall silent, but he covered her mouth all the same, his movements growing more intense as he delivered stroke after stroke.

Kira could only imagine how sore the vampiress would be afterwards. She vividly remembered what it had felt like to have Nathaniel punish her like that in the woods. Granted, he'd been in her ass then, but he was being no less gentle now than he had been then.

"Pet," Nathaniel barked. "Come on your hands for me."

Kira tried, she really did, but she couldn't, not with the venomous look Gloria was giving her. It made the build of her potential orgasm shrivel.

"Pet," Nathaniel repeated sharply, waiting until she looked at him before continuing. "Eyes on me."

Kira felt a jolt. He looked and sounded so much like Henrikk in that moment, especially with his cold eyes boring into hers. A terrible dread came over her as she realised what he was going to do: make them both come by any means possible.

"Now...look at Gloria," he commanded, seizing the hair hanging in the vampiress' face and pulling it back tightly. "Are you watching her, pet?"

"*Yes, sir,*" Kira thought in resignation.

"Watch how I fuck her. Think of how that makes you feel."

"*Like shit.*"

If Nathaniel felt any empathy for how he was hurting her, he hid his reaction well.

"What else, pet?" he grunted, saying 'pet' as he slammed full hilt into Gloria.

"*Jealous.*"

Meanwhile, Gloria seemed oblivious to their conversation as she wailed her way through another orgasm.

Nathaniel's face was as cold and emotionless as she'd ever seen it as he went on. "I know you're jealous, slut. I know it pains you to watch. And I know you'd give anything for me to be fucking *you* right now." His voice grew ragged as he repeatedly rammed Gloria. "But I'm going to finish inside her cunt. I'll pump Gloria full of my cum and you will stay there on the ground and watch, wishing it was you."

The harsh words sent a cruel shiver down Kira's back, like a blade slicing through all her nerve endings.

"*No,*" she cried, even though a part of her wanted this. Nathaniel wasn't trying to hurt her. He was fulfilling a dark fantasy she'd never dared voice out loud. Her mind was an open book, her forbidden thoughts flowing through her magic, tinged sweet and sour with hundreds of 'yeses' and 'noes'.

"Yes," Nathaniel growled, his eyelids lowering as his eyes grew glazed. He thrust into Gloria over and over again. "Oh, yes."

It was like he was trying to convince himself he was enjoying this, and she could feel him battling for that glimmer of release on the horizon. Curious, she dipped deeper into the pools of his mind and was left breathless when she realised he was imagining her again. They were alone together in a sunny field, the reality of Gloria's bedroom causing the edges of the fantasy to peel.

"I'm here with you," Kira said through their link.

"Yes," he breathed, getting closer to the edge. "Come on your fingers, pet. Do it now."

Kira withdrew as a painful reality hit. He was going to spill his seed inside Gloria to claim her, just like they'd planned.

And there's nothing I can do to stop it.

Misery, humiliation, and heartache dragged her down, suffocating her, and in that darkness, she felt a hunger like she'd never known, licking her hot core inside out like a hot wet tongue. Pleasure exploded inside her, and tears streamed down her face as she watched Nathaniel groan against Gloria.

Kira broke, coming hard on her hand as she tumbled down into the abyss.

She screamed.

"Yes, pet," Nathaniel gasped, thrusting so hard now his balls slapped against Gloria like thunderclaps.

Kira was weak and groggy as her pussy shuddered on her fingers. She forced herself to lift her head, and immediately wished she hadn't.

Gloria grinned at her—a cruel, smug smile of victory—as Nathaniel bellowed and slammed into her one last time, throwing his head back and emptying his load inside her.

Kira blinked.

No. No, no, no...

She tried to get to her feet, but her legs wouldn't cooperate, and the heels made it impossible. Instead, she fell back down, staring in disbelief as Nathaniel's movements slowed.

A foolish part of her had believed he wouldn't come inside Gloria. She'd hoped that he would stop himself at the last minute, abandon Gloria, and walk over to her and finish inside her instead.

Even though that probably wouldn't have satisfied the old vampire custom, on some level, she'd truly believed Nathaniel would only allow himself to come inside *her*.

And now his seed was inside another woman. Her sister.

Jealousy returned like glowing hot lava to consume her.

"Nathaniel..." she pleaded, not sure what it was she was asking, exactly. To deny what had just happened. To deny that he'd just forced Gloria, using her body to make himself come. Kira didn't give a shit that it was part of their plan. Right now, she yearned for him to reassure her that he cared nothing for Gloria. That he still loved her.

However, as Nathaniel came down from his orgasm, he avoided her gaze. He pulled out of Gloria, grasped her chin, and forced her to look up at him. He did not speak a single word, waiting.

"I consent," Gloria finally said, her voice serene and satisfied, "to be your wife."

CHAPTER 36

Engaged

KIRA

NATHANIEL RELEASED GLORIA, HER head lolling as her body slumped in exhaustion. He turned to Kira, his voice emotionless. "It is done."

Kira returned his stare, her heart thundering.

Nathaniel was engaged to Gloria.

His haunted expression was a storm of emotions, his jaw hard set. She grazed his mind with her magic and was startled by the raging battle tormenting him.

Guilt. Fear. Regret.

It was not the post-orgasm bliss she'd expected to find.

He's disappointed in himself, she realised. *But I'm not.*

She was upset, of course. How could she fucking not be, after what had just happened? They'd crossed every line and twisted them until all three of them—her, Nathaniel, and Gloria—were tangled in it. Their fates were intertwined.

Except Nathaniel would marry Gloria, leaving Kira on the outside looking in.

He was shaking his head. "This was a mistake."

Kira sucked in air. *"No it wasn't."*

"I hurt you."

"No. We endured something difficult. We both made sacrifices."

He gave her a long, hard stare as if he didn't believe her.

As if he was once again being too hard on himself and taking on all the blame and responsibility. Even though they were in this together. Her heart swelled with sympathy.

"I'm proud of you," she said, enveloping him in her magic so he felt the sincerity of her words.

His brooding expression softened, his facial muscles relaxing as the pain in his eyes receded slightly. He held out his hand, offering her a hand standing up.

Kira shook her head in silent refusal. She was transfixed by his still-erect cock, which was magnificent and terrible at the same time as it gleamed wet with cum—his, and Gloria's.

"Sir," she whispered, waiting expectantly.

Nathaniel's eyebrows were drawn in concern, but they now arched in bewilderment. "Yes, pet?"

"Don't 'yes pet' me. You know what I want." She wanted this moment with him, to love him, console him, to nurse the strained bond between them until it was as strong as when they'd been when they entered the nightclub together.

As degrading as the act she was contemplating was, it was the only way they could move forward.

By acknowledging what had happened.

By accepting it.

Embracing it.

And by showing Nathaniel that they could both rise above this.

Her mind was set. She would lick his cock from base to tip, dutifully and wholeheartedly, as if she were licking his wounds.

She waited for his order, cringing from the prospect even as she secretly desired it.

Something forbidden.

Something to make her toes curl and her throat gag as she pushed herself to her limits.

Something to make the bond between them stronger than ever.

"No, pet."

"*Yes.*"

"No. That would be too cruel. I cannot allow you do that."

"*I want to. Please.*"

Silence.

"*Please.*"

This wasn't about submission. It wasn't even about forgiveness, because there was nothing to forgive. No, this was about accepting each other and their place in this hot, messy, imperfect situation. And she could tell by the way his eyes briefly softened that he understood what she was offering.

Finally, Nathaniel caved. "Very well. If you are sure."

"*I am.*"

Kira sat straighter as he removed the gag from her mouth. She wetted her dry lips, relieved that the ball that had pried her jaws open for so long was finally gone. She didn't bother wiping the drool from her chin, Nathaniel liked it.

He'd liked the messy, imperfect parts of her from the moment they'd met.

Nathaniel stared down at her with a hard expression, fisting his cock and aiming it at her face. The last of his cum oozed from the tip, and Gloria's wetness coated his length. His eyes locked with hers, his voice calm as he gave the order. "Be a good pet and lick me clean, slut. Then, we shall go."

Disgust and excitement shot through Kira, causing her insides to tingle with anticipation.

She opened her mouth eagerly to accept his cock.

CHAPTER 37

Before the Wedding

NATHANIEL

IT WAS LATE AFTERNOON on the day of Nathaniel's wedding night. It was a vampire tradition for it to take place after sundown, and this was no exception. There was less than an hour before he and Kira were due to leave his dorm room.

To say that he was nervous would have been an understatement. *More like dead inside.*

He felt as if his insides had turned to ash. The wedding attire did not help. It had once belonged to one of the vampire princes of yesteryear, selected by his father to help him look the part.

He stood before the mirror adjusting his neck scarf with numb fingers that wouldn't cooperate. He wore a three-piece suit: a maroon vest embellished with gold floral thread; dark pants, and a matching coat with sharp accent shoulders, large, folded cuffs, and a jagged swallow tail trailing down to his mid-calf. His icy blond hair was slick with oil and combed back so it lay completely flat. He frowned at his reflection. There was not a hair out of place, and it lent a severity to his face that reminded him of his father.

He flinched when a hand touched his shoulder.

"Sorry, didn't mean to startle you," Kira said with a reassuring smile.

"It's fine," he said, clearing his throat and turning to her.

"Just lost in thought."

Kira nodded slowly. "Me too. Here." She reached up to adjust his neck scarf before giving him a strained smile that didn't brighten her sad eyes. "You look very handsome."

"Thank you. And you are stunning...as always."

She was wearing an elegant cream dress with a fitted bodice of intricate lace that hugged her upper body and emphasised her slender waist. The V-shaped neckline was embroidered with royal blue butterflies, and a voluminous skirt of layered tulle emphasised her long shapely legs. She wore blue, closed-toed heels, and underneath the dress, she wore satin lingerie in the same vibrant blue colour.

"Thank you," she said with a shy smile, looking so much like a blushing bride that he wanted to throw his arms around her and never let go.

Little does she know that my father chose the dress...no doubt for the very purpose of rubbing salt in the wound.

Dressed like this, Kira was a vision of beauty, and it was easy to imagine that this was *their* wedding, and that she was the one he was going to marry.

The thought pierced his heart.

If only.

She stood silently before him, her eyes watchful. She was normally never this quiet, and he hated that they were spending their final moments together grieving for what they could never have.

He caressed her cheek, tracing the curve of her face and feeling the softness of her brown hair. He would miss her sorely in the weeks to come, and then forever after that.

He knew that Kira was counting the days when he would return from his honeymoon with Gloria and she could see him again...but he wasn't. There wouldn't be a honeymoon. This would all be over tonight.

"You're awfully quiet," she murmured.

"So are you."

Last night, they hadn't slept a wink, and had only held each other in the darkness, their hearts racing with the dreaded wedding drawing nearer.

"Happy thirtieth birthday," she'd whispered at midnight, cuddling close and kissing his cheek. "You're officially eleven years older than me, old man."

"Only for a few weeks," he'd pointed out.

"I'm glad you'll be back in time for my birthday," she'd said with forced cheeriness. "I thought we could go out to dinner with our friends. Invite Susie and a few people from my class. And Victoria and Felix, of course."

The guilt had nearly overwhelmed him as he'd listened to her plan a future he could never be a part of.

They both tensed when a knock sounded at the door.

"No," Kira groaned. "It's not time yet. I'm...I'm not ready to—"

Kira cut herself off and took a steadying breath.

Nathaniel could practically read her mind. He wasn't ready to say goodbye either. Especially as it would be their last goodbye.

He kissed the top of her head softly. "Whoever it is, I'll send them away."

"Why, hello," sang Victoria, waving her black-gloved hands at them. Her bottle green dress was almost plain except for the bright pink sash around her waist. "Are we ready?"

"Not yet," Nathaniel murmured, blocking the vampiress' way when she tried to enter. It didn't stop her strong rose-scented perfume from filling up the room.

"I just want to ask Kira a question. Is she here?" Victoria leant past him. "Ah, Kira. Do you want to ride in our carriage with me and Felix?"

"Er, I think I'm alright," Kira said, glancing at Nathaniel. "I'd rather go with Nathaniel."

He nodded. With so little time left, every minute mattered.

Victoria pursed her lips and lowered her voice. "It might better if the two of you say goodbye now, before we leave the academy." She hesitated, giving them both a pitying look. "It might be easier. And it would avoid a scene at the wedding. Henrikk will be waiting for you, Kira. I know it isn't easy, but—"

"Thank you, Victoria," Nathaniel said, cutting her off as he began to close the door, "But we will meet you there."

Victoria clicked her tongue. "There's no need to be so rude—"

The door clicked shut.

He and Kira both let out a collective breath.

She hugged herself, and he went to her, wrapping his arms around her and resting his head on hers.

"I've been wondering something," she said as he held her.

"Hmm?"

"When we were at the nightclub, you threatened Gloria. But I don't understand, if that was always an option, why *didn't* you simply kill her?"

"Because it would solve nothing," Nathaniel said, pulling back to meet her gaze sadly. "Whatever Gloria's faults may be...she's still your sister by blood. Your last remaining relative. After all that you have lost...I would not be the one to kill her. Besides...she is a victim in all of this. Life has dealt her a cruel hand. She has known little kindness, and she rejected the few people who dared love her."

Kira nodded slowly. She'd asked him many questions about Gloria that he'd struggled to answer. Gloria had never let him close enough to get to know her.

He and Kira had reflected on the events at the nightclub. It had been a difficult conversation. The night had shaken them both, and Nathaniel was keenly aware of how conflicted Kira's feelings were towards Gloria.

Kira had tasted her sister's juices on his cock before she'd so much as hugged her or shaken her hand—not that Gloria had been particularly civil to Kira, but the memory drove the guilt deeper into his chest.

Together, they'd crossed a line that should never have been crossed, and yet, the plan had been successful: the next day's morning paper had officially announced his engagement to Gloria on the front page, and the school was now abuzz with talk of the wedding. Few students were invited, but Victoria and Felix had both made the guest list, which surprised Nathaniel as he hadn't invited anyone.

Kira had read the newssheet's announcement quietly over his shoulder, her body rigid, before giving a firm nod. He knew she was trying to be brave for both their sakes, but he could see the toll it was taking on her, and his inability to console her was killing him.

He hoped Kira and Gloria could mend the bridge between them one day. Perhaps, once Henrikk was dead, the kingdom would finally be able to heal. But that would be out of his hands.

He became aware of Kira trembling in his arms, silent tears rolling down her face to dampen his jacket.

"Oh, pet," he sighed, his heart threatening to tear in two. "Everything will be all right."

She sniffed. "Will it?"

He tried to mask his nervous swallow. "Yes. And look. The sun is shining."

Through the window, the lane was basked in golden sunlight as the sun grew low in the sky.

"We should get going, shouldn't we?" Kira asked. "You don't want to be late to your own wedding."

"Soon," he agreed, "But not just yet. Come, let's sit outside for a moment." He placed his hand on the small of her back and guided her to the window. Outside, birds were fluttering in the trees overhead.

"They're singing," a tentative smile crossed her face as she looked up at the trees.

"So they are." He helped her climb through the window, steadying her as she balanced her high heels on the rough ground.

The mud had dried, and neither of them commented on the last time they'd been here, even though there was an obvious depression in the ground of cracked earth where their bodies had stirred it up.

"I really wish you would tell me the plan for tonight," Kira said as he climbed through after her. "I have all the wolves in the academy at my disposal. Some of the vampires, too. It's not too late—just say the word and I'll ensure they all show up at your wedding. We have the numbers. We could deal with your father tonight, and then...I won't have to sleep with him."

With Kira facing the birch trees where blue birds fluttered, he stepped close so his chest was against her back and kissed her neck. "I promise you won't have to do anything with my father."

Kira made a worried sound. "You can't guarantee that. There are too many variables. For all you know, your father could take me away in the middle of your wedding, and how will you stop him? He's still king until you say your vows and have your coronation."

He kissed her again, inhaling the scent of her one last time before taking a step backwards.

"I'll deal with him."

"Deal with him? What do you mean?"

He didn't answer, taking another step backwards as he pulled a feathered quill crusted with old blood from his pocket. Barbara had reluctantly given it to him when she'd first made the portal at his request.

"Nathaniel?" Kira began, turning towards him.

But he was already back in his room, staring through the open window at Kira's thunderstruck expression.

"Nathaniel? What are you—?"

"I love you," he mouthed, his throat too dry to make a sound as he snapped the quill.

"No, wait. *Stop—!*"

Kira's scream cut short amidst a loud whooshing as the portal collapsed, and his view of the country lane vanished. He stared at the dark, blank wall of his bedroom. Even the window frame was gone.

Blood rushed to his head, the room deathly silent except for the pounding in his ears.

She's gone.

A guttural sob tore from his throat as the anguish he'd been fighting to conceal tore free. His head fell forward, his forehead banging against the cool wall.

It was not the goodbye he'd wanted. But at least Kira was safe and hidden from danger...for now.

He would do everything in his power to ensure she stayed that way.

Jaw clenching, Nathaniel straightened his wedding jacket and strode to the door, his body cold and empty.

His heart.

His love.

His hopes and dreams...he'd left them all in the country lane with *her*.

CHAPTER 38

Betrayal

KIRA

"*No! Nathaniel!*" Kira screamed, launching herself at the portal as its opening wobbled like jelly before shutting abruptly in a splash of plasma.

The windowsill vanished into thin air, and she flew through where it had been and landed sprawling on the ground.

"The curse," she groaned, picking herself up and dusting dried leaves off her dress. Panic coursed through her as she scanned the lane around her.

I'm such an idiot. I should have realised he was planning to be the hero. I should have stopped him.

She let out a shaky breath, too paralysed with shock to cry.

He promised me he wouldn't do this.

Nathaniel's hollow eyes haunted her. They were the last thing she'd seen staring out from his bedroom before the portal shut. It explained his odd mood in the last few days. She'd assumed he was nervous about the wedding and the dozen other dangerous things they had planned—she certainly was.

I had no idea he'd given up. That he would sacrifice himself for me.

Her breathing became strained as she paced the spot where the portal had been, her agitation increasing with every second that passed.

I have to stop him. I have to find a way.

The crack of a twig made her spin around. A short woman with blonde hair and forest green eyes emerged from the treeline.

"Barbara!" Kira exclaimed, watching the witch approach. "What are you doing here?"

"I was sent to babysit you. Or, more accurately—" she wrenched her paisley skirt free of a twig that had snagged it, "To detain you. Nathaniel's orders."

"And are you?" Kira asked guardedly, although if the witch was going to capture her, she would have done it by now.

Barbara batted the air dismissively, as if she'd asked a stupid question. "I tried to talk him out of it. Told him he's making a mistake. But he was stubborn as usual. I gave him what he needed to shut the portal, after giving him a piece of my mind, mind you. Haley and Ana were meant to be here too. They were supposed to babysit *me*, of all things. Ha!" She smiled in satisfaction as she came to a stop near Kira. "But I took care of them."

Took care of them?

Kira scanned the treeline, sniffing the air, but there were no signs of the female wolves. "Where are they?"

"Detained," Barbara said cheerfully, "In a vat of goo, if you must know." She dusted her hands on her frilly apron, which was stained yellow with what might have been sulphur. The witch tilted her head curiously. "How are you doing?"

"Not great," she said stiffly, risking a glance behind her to where the portal had been, while keeping one eye on the witch. "Nathaniel and I had a plan for the wedding...but he's cut me out of it."

"Don't be too hard on him, dear. He only wants you to be safe."

Kira nodded. "I know. But he can't always be the one who saves people."

"You're worried for him," Barbara observed.

"Of course, I'm worried. Who's going to save *him*?" Her voice was suddenly thick, and she blinked furiously to stop herself crying. "I can't stay here, Barbara. I have to help him."

Barbara smiled, her bow-shaped lips radiating warmth. "I knew I was right about you." She sank down on a nearby log, as if she was growing weary. "You are just as kind-hearted as our Nathaniel."

"I don't think so," Kira mumbled. Especially not after what he'd done tonight, taking on the burden of killing his father to spare her from what Henrikk had planned for her. It would leave him cursed, and his life as he knew it would be over.

And mine with it, Kira thought sadly, because how could she go on without him? There would never be anyone else for her, not while he was alive and doomed to never be happy.

I have to stop him before it's too late.

But she wasn't entirely sure what to make of the witch. Would she help her? Or was this a trick?

Barbara gave a soft groan and massaged her neck, which cracked audibly.

Kira studied the witch more closely—the last time she'd seen Barbara, she'd been an old woman on her deathbed. Then she'd been revived and transformed by Nathaniel's blood into a young woman. Now, she looked to be in her early forties. The years had made her more attractive, and there was a subtle hollowness to her cheeks and a generous criss-cross of crow's feet at the corners of her eyes.

She's been exerting herself. She's definitely older than the last time I saw her.

Kira did not want to make the mistake of underestimating Barbara, however...she had no time to lose. "I have to get to the wedding. Nathaniel needs me."

"That he does," Barbara agreed pensively.

"Will you help me?" Kira continued, growing exasperated with each passing second. "Please?"

"Of course, dear, that's why I'm here." She rose to her feet, pulling a long dagger with a cruel, jagged blade from her belt. "Always happy to help a friend of Nathaniel's."

"Wh-what are you doing?" Kira gasped, trying to back away, but her heels had sunk into the ground and she lost her balance and fell.

Fear rippled down her spine as Barbara advanced, her eyes manic as she twirled the knife threateningly. "I've been waiting a long time for this moment." She lifted the knife high, ready to plunge it down into Kira's chest. "I knew the day would come when I spill your blood in these woods."

This witch is fucking crazy.

Kira freed one heeled shoe from the earth, but the other was entangled in fine tree roots that wouldn't let go, snaking up her leg of their own accord.

Fuck, fuck, fuck!

Her gaze snapped back to Barbara as she tried to block the blade, but it never came. Instead, Barbara lowered it, grabbed her wrist, and cut a tiny slit onto the top of her forearm.

"Today was foretold," Barbara said, her excited face inches from Kira's.

"What?" she stammered, watching a bead of blood trail down her arm.

"I had a dream many moons ago—a prophecy, if you will—that I would reopen the portal for you. Although in my dream, it was your palm that I cut. That would be more poetic, don't you think? But I find cuts on the hand are such a nuisance; they take forever to heal. Still, blood is blood, and you know what they say about blood: better out than in! At least when it comes to magic, anyway."

Kira was still staring at the witch in horror. *"I thought you were going to fucking kill me!"*

Barbara frowned. "Nonsense, deary. I've always had back

trouble..." She lifted her arms again, grasping her wrist this time as she stretched them above her head, the dagger glinting in the orange sunlight. "The portal is the best way."

"Next time I'll walk," she snapped as the roots that had been trapping her receded with a giggle.

"*Walk?* Goodness, no. Wintermaw Keep is on the other side of the Capital. You'd never make it in time, not even in your wolf form."

Kira sucked in a breath of air, relieved she was still alive.

Barbara began to chant words Kira did not recognise, her hands trailing bright blue plasma as she moved them in patterns through the air.

Awknisi ohkisa vaskezak zsemlelmesz.

Baylhk amayn.

The plasms formed a rectangular frame where the old portal had been, but through it, Kira could only see the birch trees beyond.

"Now, deary. This is not a permanent portal, so it will only be open for a short while. Now, I need your blood to help activate it. Just let a few drops trickle onto the ground beneath it. Yes, that's it, there you go—"

No sooner had the first drop of blood landed on the dry leaves than a loud whoosh sounded. The air distorted violently, whipping Kira's hair back and lifting the tutu-like hem of her dress as the portal flashed white, then blackened. A split second later, an image appeared of Nathaniel's room.

Kira stared through it in wonderment and relief, wishing her magic could reach him across the distance.

I'm coming Nathaniel. Hold on.

Meanwhile, Barbara had not ceased talking, even though the effort of keeping the portal open was obviously causing her great effort.

"—he cheated in order to beat me in the Wizarding Championships," Barbara continued. "Alfonso was his name. I never liked him very much, but then I accepted his marriage proposal. So what does that tell you? I suppose, if you live long enough like I have, you learn to love your enemy. Or not. Which is probably for the best. *Oh!*" She snatched Kira's wrist as she made to climb through. "Deary, before I forget. Byron and Mary left a few hours ago and are on their way to Wintermaw Keep. They wish to help you, dear, but no one can pass through the portal except you and Nathaniel, so they will meet you there."

Kira's heart clenched in fear. Mary and Byron were finally coming out of hiding? After all these years?

"But it's dangerous," she protested. "If—"

"Eh, they'll be fine. They know the layout better than anyone. Oh, and they said to meet them under the east bridge."

"Under the east bridge," Kira muttered, recalling the map of the castle she'd been studying in the academy's library. "That's the one with the stream flowing beneath it, right?"

"Probably. Come to think of it, Mary might have said the west bridge. But I'm quite sure she said east. In any case, I'm sure you'll figure it out once you get there, dear."

Kira pressed her lips into a thin line to stop herself from saying something she'd regret. Barbara was her ally, and was well and truly old enough to deserve her respect. Even if she was bonkers.

Barbara continued with a steady stream of chatter as she held the buzzing portal in place. "Also, what would you have me do with Haley and Ana? Sweet girls, but they were prepared to keep you here against your will for your safety. Gave me quite a bit of backchat when I tried to stop them! 'Nathaniel's orders', they said. To which I said 'pish posh, you're both old enough to think for yourselves!'. Although, Nathaniel can be quite authoritative when he wants to be, as you've no doubt noticed. I suppose that's to be expected when you're a prince, isn't it? And come to think of it—"

"Release them," Kira commanded, grabbing hold of the windowsill and hoisting a leg up. She was conscious of the time they were wasting—and the way Barbara's magic was ageing her with each passing second. She paused and looked back. "And Barbara? Thank you."

"You're welcome, dear," Barbara said, her voice growing croaky as silver streaks shot through her hair. "And good luck."

The portal zapped shut behind Kira, plunging her into darkness.

She exhaled. It felt good to be back in Nathaniel's room. The task of returning had seemed impossible, but now that she was back, the way ahead seemed no less daunting. The bedroom was dark, and unusually, even the magical lights had gone out.

Nathaniel never turned those off.

I guess he has no intention of returning.

Panic surged, but she forced herself to focus and sniff the air. She detected Nathaniel's scent, deep and smoky, tinged with an odd flowery smell that was familiar but out of place. His scent was several minutes old.

He must have left the moment he shut the portal.

She glanced at the clock. It was the only source of light, its magical face aglow. Her heart leapt. She'd been gone less than ten minutes. There was a small chance that Nathaniel would still be here at the academy. If she hurried, she might make it to his carriage.

Or maybe I can ride with Victoria and Felix, they're probably still here.

The vampiress was always the first to be ready to go anywhere, but the last to arrive.

I'll try Victoria's room first.

It was on her way. If the vampiress wasn't in, she would morph into her wolf forms and race up the stairs to the front of the academy, and never mind who saw her.

She'd never been to Victoria's room, but Felix had said it was the door with the purple lilies on it. Kira found herself desperately hoping that the vampiress would be there. It wasn't safe to go to

Wintermaw Keep alone. Even though she'd studied the layout of the castle, she wasn't sure how much practical help it would be. Wintermaw was infamously heavily guarded. But, if she had the help of a vampire like Victoria who could sneak her into the castle, that would simplify things greatly.

Especially when that vampire has a wedding invitation.

They could potentially waltz right through the front doors.

Unlike Victoria, Kira had not received a wedding invitation, even though Henrikk expected her to be there. She had a feeling it was Gloria's doing. She now understood why Nathaniel hadn't corrected the oversight. She'd thought he was trying not to rub the wedding in her face, but she was wrong.

He never intended for me to attend.

Kira stumbled forward in the darkness, circling the bed as she felt her way through the large room. Even in her human form, her night vision was exceptional, but she wasn't used to wearing heels, and for some reason, the floor was littered with all manner of items: socks, chains, sex toys, pillows from the bed, tangles of sheets, books. It was as if someone had searched the room.

She froze on the spot, dread filling her.

She was not alone.

Someone was here.

If she hadn't been in such a hurry, she might have sensed the stranger sooner, and would have smelt the significance of the sickly-sweet perfume reeking of roses.

She stopped breathing, ears strained for any possible sound as she sent her magic pulsing through the room.

Not one stranger, but two. Her shoulders relaxed as she recognised who the intruders were: friends.

She should have rushed for the door. But like a fool, she trusted them, even though she was fucking confused about what they were doing here.

And then it was too late to run.

She screamed as rough hands seized her from behind and dragged her across the room. A moment later, the fireplace roared to life with green flames as she was wrestled to the ground.

She jerked her head up, teeth bared as she glared at the woman sitting in the tall-backed armchair, her legs crossed, and slender arms draped across the armrests.

"*Sweetie*, there you are. I was beginning to worry."

Kira snapped her human teeth at Felix who was holding her down before snarling at the woman. "Victoria...What. The. Fuck?"

"We're going to take a little trip to Wintermaw Keep," Victoria said, dangling the heel of her shoe near Kira's face. "I'm going to ensure Henrikk receives his wolf toy. That's *you*, sweetie."

Kira tried but failed to hide her shock. "Why? I don't understand—"

"Henrikk and I are soon to be an item," the vampiress said happily. "I slept with him when he visited the academy the other week—I would have told you all about it if you'd hung out with me more—and he made me an offer I couldn't refuse. I'm super excited."

"You *slept* with—?"

"Yes. *And* I reassured him. He was concerned Nathaniel wouldn't follow through on his orders to deliver you to Wintermaw. Nathaniel's always had a soft spot for wolves."

"So Henrikk asked you to make sure I get to the wedding," Kira said through gritted teeth.

"Yes, exactly!" Victoria smiled, clapping her hands together. "In return, he promised to make me his wife."

"He's a little too old for you, isn't he?" Kira growled, trying to mask her shock.

Victoria shrugged. "Thirty-two years my senior. But I always did prefer them older."

"It doesn't bother you that he wants to have *sex* with me?"

"Nope. He wants to breed you. But he needs a *wife*. Someone he can respect, like me."

Kira's mouth dropped. She had not realised Victoria was so ambitious. Kira had thought her friendly and cunning, but not conniving. "And you want power."

"What I *want* is to bring my family honour. And can you imagine? I'll be Queen Consort Victoria. Ugh, I'm beyond excited. Oh, and Henrikk said you could be our ringbearer."

Fuck that.

"And Felix is fine with all this?" Kira asked sceptically.

"Felix understands, don't you honey?" Victoria said, without waiting for him to answer. "After all, we're talking about the Vampire *King*. I mean, Henrikk will abdicate tonight, but we all know he holds the real power at Wintermaw. I'm looking forward to spending lots of time with you, sweetie. And look, I have a gift for you."

Kira's heart lurched as the vampiress held out a large metal toy.

"Do you know what this is?"

"A steel plug."

"Wrong. The plugs Nathaniel had made for you were made of steel. I know—I checked. The jeweller was very talkative once I bit his neck."

Kira tensed. "Is he alive?"

"Probably. Who cares? He's a human," Victoria said irritably. "My point is, Nathaniel was ordered by his father to plug you with *silver*. And as the myth goes, wolves are sensitive to the metal. Nathaniel was meant to keep you plugged with silver so you wouldn't be able to use any magic." Her eyes narrowed. "But as I saw in the foyer the other day, he's been slack."

Kira's stomach knotted as Victoria rose.

"Wh-what are you doing?" she snapped, her blood freezing as Victoria walked around her. She sent out her magic, connecting to

Victoria and Felix's mind, thick gentle persuasion that coaxed them to see things her way.

Victoria paused. "I am so sorry, sweetie. I know this is not what you want. But you'll come round."

Shit.

It wasn't enough.

Victoria waggled her index finger at her. "Ah-ah-ah. No more magic for you. Now, hold still while I plug you. We're already very late. You don't want to miss the moment when Nat and Gloria say, 'I do', do you?"

Kira struggled against Felix's hold, focusing her magic on him. His hold loosened, and she almost managed to throw him off, but Victoria was fast and precise in her movements as she darted behind Kira and pushed the plug in. It was lubricated, and although it slid smoothly into her ass, the pressure felt wrong, and the cool silver seared her insides in a way the other plugs never had.

Kira cried out in pain and despair as her insides burnt, her magic disintegrating as if it had never been. As Felix dragged her up, she tried but failed to morph.

It was over.

CHAPTER 39

Deception

KIRA

KIRA TRIED TO THINK rationally as Victoria led her up the stairs with Felix bringing up the rear. The couple had fed on her before leaving Nathaniel's room, and it left her feeling tired as she trudged up the steps.

They'd warned her not to shout, and Victoria held the gag Nathaniel had so often used on her in warning.

"It's such an ugly thing," she said regretfully, "But I don't want any hiccups."

"I won't cause trouble," Kira assured her quickly. "I'll come quietly, I promise. I want to go to the wedding too."

She had to find a way to remove the plug, or any opportunity to get away from Victoria. Once she was gagged, she'd lose her ability to talk, as well as any chance of talking herself out of this situation.

Thankfully, Victoria only made her wear the collar, the ball gag hanging threateningly from it.

Kira followed Victoria quietly up the dorm stairs, resisting the urge to call for help from the students they passed. It was a sad testament to the way wolves were treated that no one questioned the black eye Felix had given her or the fresh bite marks on her neck that still oozed blood.

Victoria was in good spirits after feeding, at least, and as they reached the wolf dorms, Kira sensed an opportunity.

"Victoria, wait."

The vampiress sighed and stopped. "What?"

"I can't go to the wedding like this. Look at my shoes. They're so muddy."

"Quit stalling," said Felix.

Kira ignored him, focusing her attention on Victoria, who seemed conflicted as she eyed her shoes.

"Please, it's so embarrassing," she added, adopting a polite tone she'd almost never used with Nathaniel, "May I change them? If Henrikk sees me like this, he might not want me, and you don't want that. Not if you want to be Queen Consort."

Victoria's face paled, her expression calculating. She was too smart to think that Kira wanted to be with Henrikk, but her ambition overruled her reason.

"Fine," Victoria snapped, following Kira deeper into the wolf dorm. "But be quick. It smells like dog in here. Which one is your room?"

"This one," Kira stopped outside Susie's room.

"So drab," Victoria said, looking at the plain door with the calendar pinned to it. She gave an exaggerated sigh, glancing around the dorm and making it clear she didn't want to be here. "Alright, go on. Chop, chop. And leave the door open!"

Thankfully, Susie almost never locked her door, not even since the attack. It was unlocked now, and Kira opened it and slipped inside, swinging the door half shut.

Susie had evidently just had a shower; she was standing by the bed, wrapped in a towel while drying her hair with another. She looked up in surprise.

"Kira—?"

Kira pushed Susie out of sight behind the door, covering her mouth to muffle her question. Susie stared at her wide eyes.

Pressing a finger to her lips, Kira pulled Susie into the wardrobe, closing the double doors behind them.

She hurriedly filled Susie in on what had happened.

"Do you think Headmaster Arken will help Nathaniel?" Kira asked.

She knew the headmaster and Nathaniel were friends, but she did not know if that friendship transcended Arken's loyalty to the Vampire King.

Susie nodded determinedly. "Of course. We'll help both of you. I'll go find him now."

"Thank you," Kira said gratefully. "Stay here until I leave."

She cracked the wardrobe door open, but Susie gripped her arm. "Be careful."

Kira nodded. "I will."

Kira climbed out and shut the wardrobe behind her. The damp towel Susie had been drying her hair with lay on the ground. Kira hurriedly used it to clean the worst of the mud off her shoes, before dabbing at a dirt mark on her cream skirt. It wasn't pristine, but it would have to do.

"Kira, can you hurry up?" Victoria called, popping her head in.

Kira froze, but managed a half-convincing smile. "Nearly ready!"

Victoria glanced around the simple room, unimpressed, before ducking out.

Kira let out a soft breath. She was tempted to morph now, but fighting Felix and Victoria wouldn't help her get into Wintermaw Keep. Her captors were conveniently taking her to the very place she wanted to go. It was risky, but she didn't have time to waste. Nathaniel needed her, and she needed to stop him from killing his father before she lost him for forever. The thought of him becoming cursed was unbearable.

And I need to stop the wedding.

Pretending to be an obedient pet was her best chance of staying on Victoria's good side. But she eased the plug out of her ass anyway, grimacing silently as the bulging toy stretched the tight band of muscle. Not wanting to piss off Victoria in case she checked, she left the plug in the seat of her panties where it sat heavily. The silver was still contacting her skin, the metal inhibiting her magic. She would find a subtle way to get rid of it later.

As long as it doesn't drop on the ground in front of Victoria.

She rejoined the vampires in the corridor, shutting the door behind her.

"It's amazing what a little water can do," she said brightly to Victoria, showing off her blue heels.

"It *is* amazing," Victoria agreed, drifting behind Kira and lifting her skirt. "Oh, sweetie, look! The plug's come out!"

Kira winced as the vampire lined the plug up with her asshole and shoved it back in.

"That's better. Ready to go?"

In the carriage, Victoria insisted on feeding from her again. Despite Kira's protests, she didn't take 'no' for an answer.

"I'll be in such a mood all night otherwise," Victoria explained, shuffling beside Kira and pushing her head back. She traced a finger along Kira's throat. "You know, you taste different to Arken's plaything. What's her name?"

"Susie," Kira whispered, as the horrible suspicion she'd had became a full-blown reality.

"Yes, *her*." Victoria tittered. "Poor little thing seemed so bored in the library."

"You nearly killed her."

Victoria gasped. "Kira! Don't say that. I wasn't trying to kill her! And don't look at me like that. I didn't mean to drain her. Besides, I really am sorry about that. And I *did* tip off the librarian. I'm the reason anyone found her."

Kira's jaw clenched. "Why did you do it?" she asked, because even though it was obvious, she had to hear it from the vampiress who she'd mistakenly thought was her friend.

Victoria shrugged. "Everyone knows she belongs to Arken."

"And what is that supposed to mean?"

"Look, what do you want me to say? I have a thing for feeding off the pets of powerful men." She hovered closer to Kira's neck, her fangs extending. "The question is, do you belong to Prince Nathaniel...or King Henrikk?"

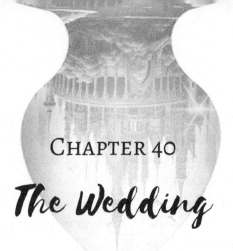

CHAPTER 40

The Wedding

NATHANIEL

WINTERMAW KEEP, THE ANCESTRAL home of royal wolves, had once been a relatively modest castle, a sturdy building with only two storeys made of stone. Wolf shifters generally did not like stairs, or anything that was in excess. The second storey was, therefore, a rarity that was deemed necessary only to distinguish the royal household from the rest of the castle's residents.

Since Henrikk had overthrown the wolves, he'd radically expanded the castle, adding sprawling wings, towers, and a multitude of storeys made of timber that stretched to the heavens. There were more mirrors in the castle than people, and more staircases than there were rooms. There were banquet halls for breakfast that faced the rising sun, the westward facing ones to watch it set, and north facing ones to suit any occasion. Some parts of the castle had no function at all, except to add complexity and glamour to the king's vanity project.

Despite the grandeur of the updated castle, Nathaniel found it all lacking, which he supposed was a trait he shared with his father, albeit for different reasons.

It had taken Nathaniel several years to form a strong opinion about the keep, but he'd finally come to a conclusion around the same time he'd found Kira when she was nine years old: he did not like the Keep's new additions one bit. It had pained him to realise that most of Springcreek forest had been ripped up for the undertaking, and at least two species of animals were suspected to be extinct as a result.

His father let nothing get in his way, not even nature. Although he'd been unable to stop the erosion that deforestation had caused. The foundation of the new north wing, where his Throne Room was located, required constant repairs due to instability. Human architects and builders might have been able to improve the foundation, but his father was too proud to allow humans to build his fortress.

Nathaniel's wedding and birthday were to be hosted in the Throne Room, which was crowded with affluent vampire nobles, none of whom seemed concerned by the slope of the uneven floor, or the way the high table was no longer high, giving the throne a sagging appearance that brought King Henrikk almost at eye level with the guests.

Nathaniel had slipped into the Throne Room discreetly, keeping to the shadowy edges of the room where rose-covered columns blocked him from view. But as he approached the not-so-high table to speak to his father, the herald spotted him.

Trumpets blared.

"Announcing the guest of honour, His Royal Highness, Prince Nathaniel, the illustrious son of our beloved sovereign, King Henrikk. May all within these hallowed walls receive him with the utmost reverence and respect. We extend our most heartfelt birthday wishes to His Royal Highness."

Nathaniel groaned internally as he gave an obligatory smile at the aristocracy standing near him as he ascended the dais, ducking beneath a hanging garland of red roses.

There was no sign of Gloria, for which he was grateful. He was not yet ready to face her.

Henrikk wore a blood-red robe embellished with gold and draped in ermine. He did not rise from his throne when Nathaniel approached, nor did he smile.

Nathaniel bowed low. "Your Majesty."

A tense silence passed as he waited for his father to acknowledge him.

"Prince Nathaniel...I see you did not bring Kira."

Nathaniel straightened. "No, I did not." He braced for his father's reaction. He had dreaded this moment, but had faith his father would swallow the insult in order for the wedding to continue as planned. Henrikk craved the loyalty of Gloria's supporters, and Nathaniel hoped that lure would overrule his disappointment in Kira's absence.

His father's milky pale eyes stared at him for a long moment. "Well, no matter. These things happen."

Nathaniel waited for his father to go on, to express his disappointment in his failure to bring Kira, and to call him soft and weak. But his father seemed strangely unperturbed.

"Your best man is also absent."

Nathaniel smirked in response. "Arken has a tendency to be fashionably late. He was in his cups when I left. He'll no doubt arrive during the reception, completely stewed and in search of more drink."

Henrikk rubbed his chin thoughtfully, his lips curling in a condescending smile. Nathaniel hid the resentment he felt for his father's obvious pleasure in Arken's lingering afflictions. Henrikk had been exploiting Arken's vulnerabilities for years.

It was fitting, really, that the one to take Henrikk's place would be Arken. He would be a better ruler than any one of them—Kira excepted. It was why he'd asked Arken to stay back at the academy with Susie tonight. There was no telling how bloody the aftermath of Henrikk's death would be, and he did not want his friend caught up in any deadly brawls. As for Nathaniel, he would be incapacitated—the curse would grip him almost instantly. He therefore needed someone he could trust to look out for Kira once he was gone. Perhaps, Arken would become her royal advisor. Nathaniel retained a small hope that maybe, Arken would rule, and Kira would opt for a normal life away from the volatility of court life.

"I regret that Arken is delayed," Henrikk said dismissively, not sounding sorry at all. He rose and embraced Nathaniel, a grand gesture that was for the benefit of the courtiers. He raised his voice. "Happy Birthday, son."

The courtiers erupted into applause.

As Nathaniel took a seat in a smaller, but no less ornate chair beside his father, the crowd resumed its chatter.

"I have a wedding gift for you," Henrikk announced.

Nathaniel went still. A gift from his father could not be a good thing. "What is it?"

"It's a surprise."

Henrikk did not say anything more, leaving Nathaniel to try and appear relaxed even as cold sweat broke out across his forehead.

Without warning, an organ began to play a bridal chorus, and the room fell silent as the Throne Room's double doors swung open.

Nathaniel's head whipped to his father, but the King didn't look at him, merely smiled as bridesmaids began to file into the room. He couldn't believe it. There had been no preamble, no 'are you ready?' before the biggest, most dreaded event of his life began.

"Try and look pleased with your bride, Nathaniel," Henrikk said lightly without looking at him.

Nathaniel forced his gaze to Gloria, who was entering the Throne Room wearing a traditional vampire wedding dress—a red monstrosity of gauze and silks that blended with the carpet.

She was every male vampire's fantasy, but not Nathaniel's. On some level, he knew that by marrying her, he would prevent his father from killing Gloria and the threat she posed to his reign. That fact might have made the prospect of the wedding a little easier to bear, had there not been a thousand reasons not to marry her.

Like the fact that Gloria was not a kind person. Or that the marriage was a betrayal of his heart, which beat only for Kira.

Or the fact that none of this matters, because I'll soon betray my own blood line.

As Gloria drew closer, Nathaniel spotted the sequins, which gleamed like droplets of blood. Her blonde hair was gathered high in loose curls, and her ears were studded with rubies, which matched the engagement ring Nathaniel had given her. She blushed prettily, and as her eyes met Nathaniel's, he felt a pang of guilt at the hope that lay there.

Gloria was many things, but this was her wedding day, and all her hopes were pinned on him.

Nathaniel rose, his legs numb as he strode down the dais and led Gloria up the steps, an easy feat given the slope of the room.

"Nathaniel," Gloria greeted, sounding so nervous and happy as she clutched his hand that he forced himself to smile at her.

A priest approached, making Nathaniel's insides seize. It was starting. The wedding was starting, but he wasn't ready. He wasn't even really here. His heart and soul were far away, in a country lane that was quiet, unassuming, and held everything he needed to be a very happy man.

But his body was here, and although this night would end with the King's crown on the floor and a knife in his father's heart, the part of him that lived and breathed was screaming at him for ignoring what he so desperately wanted. To leave this place and find Kira.

"Are you both ready?" asked the priest cheerfully, glancing between him and Gloria.

"Yes, we are ready" said Gloria, before turning at him with a small frown. "Aren't we, Nathaniel?"

He gave a stiff nod as bile crept up his throat. He could not bring himself to smile or speak.

He could scarcely breathe.

"Dearly beloved," began the priest, his words ringing in Nathaniel's ears.

He could hardly hear a word over the pounding of his chest, but he was powerless to slow down time. A few minutes later, he jerked out of his stupor when Gloria turned to him, holding his hands tightly, and said, "I do."

"Very good," beamed the priest. "And do you, Prince Nathaniel, take this woman—"

"Stop," called Henrikk lazily, causing the priest to flinch. "I have a wedding gift for my son. I have been waiting for an appropriate time to present it." He snapped his fingers. "*Now* seems good."

Nathaniel frowned as Victoria and Felix emerged from a side door near the dais, dragging a woman with bronze skin and dark brown hair between them.

His blood turned cold when he recognised Kira. Her normally glowing brown skin was dull, her legs unsteady as she walked. Her expression was taut as she gazed around blearily. Her eyes widened as she took in the large audience. As she turned her head, white-hot anger sparked in him as he saw her blackened eye and the bite marks on her neck.

"What have you done to her?" Nathaniel demanded furiously, releasing Gloria as he ran to Kira.

"Nathaniel?" Kira gasped, spotting him for the first time.

He leapt off the dais and shoved Felix away, pulling Kira into his arms. "Shh, everything will be all right," he whispered, kissing her forehead as fear pooled inside him.

"I've done nothing to her—yet," Henrikk said loudly, giving a dismissive wave. "What you see is merely some minor damage from transit. Victoria had my permission to sample the goods, didn't you, my dear?"

"Yes, Your Majesty," Victoria said.

"You did so well to bring her to me." Henrikk patted the seat beside him. It was the chair that a queen should have occupied, one that had sat empty for many years. "Come, sit by me."

Victoria released Kira and leapt up the dais steps nimbly and sat down, her eyes shining as she smiled in satisfaction.

"The plug," Kira whispered, clutching at the front of his shirt. "It's silver. They plugged me."

Horrified, Nathaniel's hand darted around to remove it. How dare they hurt Kira? How dare they—

His fingertips brushed the plug, but before he could get a hold of it, Henrikk's guards seized them and wrenched them apart.

"Nathaniel!" Kira screamed at the same time that he yelled her name.

"Star-crossed lovers," Henrikk said fondly to the audience. He rose from his throne and swept his ermine cloak back as he approached. "How romantic! Nathaniel, you have my full blessing for your marriage to Gloria, as well as your coronation. But before you rise to manhood and become our new glorious leader, allow a father to impart a final lesson of wisdom to his son."

Nathaniel's body turned cold like stone as his father's hands parted his robes and began unbuckling his belt.

"F-father?" he gasped, realising exactly what the king had in mind.

Henrikk glided down the steps, removing his belt and undoing the lace fastenings of his trousers. "I was disappointed to hear you circumvented my orders. I have heard several disturbing reports from Victoria on your conduct. Sharing your royal blood with those beneath you. Becoming overly attached to wolves—*this* female in particular."

"Her name is Kira," Nathaniel growled.

Henrikk's eyes flashed. "She is a pet, designed for feeding and fucking, nothing more. It is time you learnt that lesson, my boy. It is a mistake to fall in love with a creature so inferior."

Nathaniel's insides burnt with fear and rage as he struggled against the guard, an anguished yell tearing from his throat as the guards holding Kira forced her to the ground.

"Father!" Nathaniel shouted, wishing desperately that he would show mercy. But he knew his father well enough to know that he considered mercy a weakness.

Henrikk glanced back, fisting his cock with one hand as he hovered above Kira. "I am at my wits' end, Nathaniel. I have warned you before. But I am confident that this is a lesson you will never forget. You will thank me for this one day."

"No!" Nathaniel shouted, his muscles screaming as he threw himself forward. The guards jerked him back, and a fist collided with his temple, causing his world to go black.

Nathaniel woke to the sound of the courtiers' hushed whispers rippling through the room, and he peeked an eye open to see the crowd vying close so they could see better. He groaned.

What happened? What...

Fear hit him as his memory returned.

Kira!

Henrikk spoke near him. "Is he awake? Good. Ensure he watches. I will begin now."

Nathaniel's eyes flew open to the disturbing scene of his father kneeling behind Kira, his hand clamped over her mouth as he positioned himself behind her, fisting his cock.

Kira let out a muffled whimper, and he felt utterly powerless as he met her amber eyes, which were fearful and teary.

"Look at me," Nathaniel begged desperately. "I'm here, Kira. I'm right here. You'll be all right—"

One of the guards shoved a cloth gag into his mouth, stuffing it in and tying a strip of fabric around his head to keep it in place.

Henrikk gave a low, sinister laugh. "You will learn better if you watch this lesson in silence, son." He turned his attention to Kira, his hand still on her mouth. "*You*, my dear, will be silent as well. That is your challenge." He caressed her face. "Every sound you make will result in a lash of my whip when I am done. My men are listening and counting, so I suggest you take your punishment quietly."

He turned his empty eyes to Nathaniel. "Let this lesson be my wedding gift to you, son. May it serve as a reminder throughout your reign."

He thrust his hips forward, the sound of his cock entering Kira horribly audible. The sound of her strangled cry as her body twitched turned Nathaniel's blood to ice.

Nathaniel watched in outrage as his father drove his cock inside her, all while wearing a satisfied smirk as he held his gaze.

White-hot pain clawed at Nathaniel's insides and he yelled through the gag.

No, no, no, no, no. Kira!

Time stopped as his father pulled back slowly, commanding the attention of every guest in the room. Hovering behind Kira as he cackled menacingly, drawing out the suspense as he prepared to enter her again.

An excruciating second passed as Nathaniel beheld Kira, beautiful and vulnerable as she silently pleaded for him to help her. His heart was ablaze with agony as he fought the guards restraining him.

Without warning, his father slammed into her again. Kira gasped in pain, her eyes losing focus and her skirt flaring around her as her body jerked forward from the impact.

Nathaniel struggled against the guards' hold. His words intelligible as he urged Kira to lift her head and look at him as he cursed his father for daring to hurt her.

The guards hit him again, and the gag loosened enough that he could spit out the cloth. *"Kira!"* he roared, the sound tearing from his throat. *"Kira!"*

CHAPTER 41

Pounding Silence

KIRA

EVERYTHING WAS DARK. KIRA had shut her eyes so she wouldn't have to see the vampire nobles crowding around, craning their necks for a glimpse of what Henrikk was doing to her. Some jeered, others cheered, whilst some sipped their wine with apathy, as if this was normal. Maybe, in Henrikk's court, it *was* normal.

How many other shifters had been raped in this hall?

It was hard to comprehend that this was happening to her. She'd tried to prepare herself mentally on the carriage ride over, but Victoria's second feeding had left her little time or energy to think. By the time they arrived at Wintermaw, Kira was woozy as she stared up at the daunting structure of stone and timber. She was in the wrong headspace, groggy and unable to think, meaning her plan was half-formed and tenuous at best.

The buzz of the crowd grew louder until her ears rang with white noise, until suddenly, she couldn't hear them at all. A peaceful silence enveloped her as she blocked them out, and all she could hear was her own shallow breathing and the muffled thud of Henrikk's cock as it pummelled into her.

Nathaniel had shouted her name, fighting to get to her. But the made vampires were stronger. They gagged him again and punched him in the stomach, causing him to double over.

That had been a while ago. Now, there was only silence as she pretended she was someone else, that she was somewhere far from here.

Henrikk's evil whisper in her ear brought her back to reality. "You feel good, *slut*. Aren't you glad Victoria brought you tonight?"

Before she could even consider refusing to answer, Henrikk gripped her hair and wrenched her head back, causing pain to erupt on her scalp. "Answer me—promptly."

"Yes, sir," she gasped as fresh tears pricked her eyes.

He held her in that position, yanking her hair so her back arched as he thrust into her with force.

Kira tried not to cry out, dreading the whip he'd threatened her with. He was hurting her, and he was taking his time doing it. She'd lost track of how long they'd been here, and her arms were shaking from supporting their combined weight as he took her from behind.

Everything about the King felt wrong. His voice, his scent, his cock, which she'd glimpsed earlier—it had a length to rival Nathaniel's, with an ugly head and a wicked curve that reached up and into her. His heavy balls squished and slapped her, the coarse pubic hair scratching her sensitive folds. His arms were strong, his hands cruel as he gripped her hair like a rein as if he were breaking in a wild horse.

There was something methodical about his assault. The way he fucked her for mere sport. He seemed in no hurry to finish, as if he was intent on drawing this out for as long as possible.

He certainly wasn't trying to give her any pleasure.

Suddenly, she understood where Nathaniel had learnt it all from. This was not the first public demonstration his father had held—the crowd's eager reaction as they watched her assault unfold had all but confirmed that. But unlike his father, Nathaniel had never done this to her before: subjected her to forced sex for the entertainment of others.

That's what Henrikk was doing. Making an example of her. He moved in and out of her swiftly, pounding deep into her cunt, the crowd gasping with delight each time she yelped or shrieked. To her dismay, she spotted the tally a guard was keeping on a chalkboard. She counted thirteen tally marks.

Thirteen.

Had she truly cried out that many times?

She'd tried so hard to be quiet...

Time passed slowly, the sunset basking the hall with golden light. And then the hall was dark, the flicker of candles casting an eerie glow, distorting the gleeful expressions of the guests.

Henrikk changed his pace, taking her slowly and deeply, one hand supporting his weight on the ground as he leant to the side so he could peer at her. He was gauging her expression, his thin lips curved in a cold smile as he watched her response to every inch of flesh he gave her.

"*Yesss,*" he hissed, pushing his thick member deeper into her cunt until he bottomed out and held her there. "Take it, *slut.* Feel my cock. Remember this night. Remember how everyone watched you fall."

His caustic words burnt through her like acid, eating every hope and dream in their wake. Soon, all that would be left of her was an empty shell. How fitting, that if Nathaniel ever killed his father, she would be just as lost as he would from the curse. That was how she felt. The fight had left her, and if this continued, she wasn't sure if there'd be anything of her left to salvage.

Her one attempt to fight Henrikk had ended with a sharp backhand to her face, and she'd been compliant ever since.

Please, make it stop.

"It would have been a shame for you to miss the wedding," Henrikk said conversationally, his voice raised so that the nobles could hear. "I had you brought in at the perfect moment. Gloria had just said 'I do'...and Nathaniel had been on the cusp of saying it too." He gripped her chin, forcing her to look at Nathaniel, who was staring at his father with icy rage in his eyes, his mouth gagged and lips split, his hair dishevelled and falling across his forehead, and his face covered in bruises. "See how he stands by and does nothing. He is an attentive student, a grown man...but he can still learn a thing or two from his father, can't he, slut?"

"Yes, sir," she said, her words barely audible.

"Have no fear. I will ensure you have the best seat in the room when the moment comes for him to say his wedding vows—I will sit upon the throne, and you will be on my lap, with my cock stretching every inch of your tight cunt."

Nathaniel lunged, and Kira squeezed her eyes shut as a guard punched him in the throat, leaving him wheezing and spluttering.

Several long, endless minutes passed during which Henrikk moved inside her, sometimes fast, sometimes slow, and always, always reminding her that he was there.

Suddenly, he dragged her up by the hair so she was upright on her knees, her back against his chest. He fondled her breasts with his other hand as he hissed quietly in her ear.

"You might be half vampire, Kira, but make no mistake, you are completely and undeniably a wolf, and little more than a whore for breeding. Once you have provided me with gifted offspring who share your talents, that is how I shall use you—"

He moved his cock in and out, "—Every night, and every day."

He thrust hard. "Because that is all you are good for, slut. Taking your master's cock."

He released her hair, pushing her back forward so her palms hit the floor. He rammed into her. "And once I have grown bored of you, I will give you to my guards. Let them take from you what they will."

Tears flowed freely down her face.

"Do you know how many guards there are in Wintermaw Keep, *slut*?"

"No, sir," she whispered as she took another rough thrust.

"Over four hundred."

She whimpered.

"Oh, yes. Some of them are made vampires who helped me seize the Keep. Their lust is insatiable, and they never tire of fucking—they are not truly alive, as you surely know. By the time they have all had a turn, you will be spent. In fact...you will not survive the night. Do you know how I know?"

Kira shook her head. Her 'no sir' was inaudible, but Henrikk did not reprimand her.

"Because," he said, easing his cock in and out of her gently, "It was how your mother, Liddia the Vampire Queen, died."

Horror and rage gripped her, lighting a flame that burnt through her misery, breaking her out of the helpless stupor she'd surrendered herself to.

"Oh yes, the guards took her to the stables," Henrikk continued, his voice excited as he resumed his hard thrusts, pounding her mercilessly. "My men saddled her up and rode her like a horse. She lasted until the morning. I doubt you will last half so long—you are weaker than I expected you to be. Already, there is no fight left in you."

The anger that had been boiling inside her surged as her charged muscles sprang forward, but Henrikk held her tight. She hardly got more than an inch away before he slammed her back onto his cock again. He laughed triumphantly as she struggled and bucked, and her howls only made the tally on the board double.

The audience echoed Henrikk's laughter, the mocking sound echoing through the hall.

"*There* she is, there's the bitch I was waiting for," Henrikk said gleefully, slapping her face three times in quick succession. "Feisty, just like her mother was."

Tears, despair, grief... none of those would help her now. Neither would fighting. It became apparent that no one was coming to help her.

I can't give up. I can't.

"Do you like that, slut?" Henrikk asked, gripping her by the hips as he aimed his cock high into a deep, intimate place inside her. "Did my son do this to you?"

Come on, Kira.

Pull yourself together.

Rage coursed through her veins, and it was with great effort that she feigned nonchalance as the Vampire King pumped his cock back and forth. She shrugged. "Nathaniel did it better."

Henrikk stilled. "*What* did you just say?" he asked in a dangerous tone.

"Nathaniel did it better," she repeated. "I can tell you're trying, but I hardly feel a thing."

Deathly silence filled the room. Even those down the far end of the hall who hadn't heard her knew better than to speak. It was so quiet that Kira could practically hear the veins throbbing at Henrikk's temples as he leant over her, his lips brushing her ear as he spoke.

"Is that so?"

Kira resisted the urge to swallow, knowing her nervous gulp would give her away. Trying to channel Victoria's blasé attitude, she said, "Yeah. But...no offence."

Pain erupted on her scalp as Henrikk tightened his hold, but she'd been expecting his reaction. She gritted her teeth and braced herself for the hit or slap or thrust that was to come.

But Henrikk did not strike.

Instead, he did exactly what she'd hope he would do.

"I'll show you how it's done, *slut*," he said, pulling his cock out of her and releasing her with disgust. "You won't be so dispassionate when I'm fucking you up your ass." He seized the end of the plug, his fingernails cutting the rim of her asshole as they dug in and yanked it out of her. He threw the plug aside where it clattered and bounced across the timber floor.

Kira drew a sharp breath as she felt for her magic.

Come on...

If it was there, she didn't detect it. The silver had poisoned her, clinging to her arteries and filling her mind like a fog.

How long would it take for her magic to return?

Minutes?

Hours?

Days?

Please, please let it be soon.

Henrikk was already lining his cock up, the fat heavy head resting against her asshole. It felt...dry.

"I wiped your juices off," Henrikk said, as if reading her mind. "Let us see if you have trouble feeling my cock now, slut."

He gave her no more warning than that before he thrust.

Pain ripped through her as he forced himself into her ass. There was no stifling her scream now as his unlubricated length dragged her insides. His low hiss betrayed his own discomfort as he struggled to get his cock deeper, but if it was uncomfortable for him, it was hell for her.

She clawed at the smooth floorboards, the pain driving all other feelings from her until her vision turned blinding white. In that agonising emptiness, she found it. A glimmer of her magic in the distance. She reached for it, cursing as it slipped through her fingers.

So close.

Henrikk heaved a heavy grunt as he succeeded in embedding half his length into her. "Feel that now, slut?"

He leant close, and Kira dropped her head so he wouldn't see her anguish.

"Not...yet," she growled.

Henrikk drove his thick cock in another inch, causing her core to flare in protest. "How about now?"

Another wisp of magic appeared in the realm of her mind. She grasped it, but it was feeble, disintegrating between her fingers.

"Not...yet," she repeated, choking back a sob.

Henrikk pushed, his hard body invading her more.

Please, let it stop.

"How. About. Now?"

Kira drew a ragged breath, her answer dying on her lips.

"Well?" Henrikk gloated. "Have you had enough?"

The dry friction of his cock burnt her anal cavity, which was raw and tender from the silver plug. She couldn't take any more, and the wisps of magic drifting around her simply weren't enough to do anything with. She bowed her head until her forehead hit the floor. "Yes, sir."

Henrikk did not relent, and he drove the final inches of his cock deeper anyway, ripping the last of her composure to pieces.

Her mind spun, and her body was a clammy, trembling, numb mess. She hardly heard the King as he addressed his guards, and she caught a brief glimpse of Nathaniel, slumped but conscious in the guards' hold.

"Watch as I ruin her, boys," Henrikk announced. "*This* is how you fuck a wolf. With authority, and with a firm hand."

He slapped her ass. "With intention."

He slapped her again. "It is our right as the superior race."

Kira braced for another spank, but it didn't come. Instead, he stroked her hair, his touch so gentle it momentarily reminded her of Nathaniel.

She couldn't help it—she burst into tears.

"Don't cry," Henrikk said softly. "I intend to fill you many times in these coming years...beginning now."

Keeping his cock wedged in her ass, he lifted her with surprising strength and carried her up the dais steps. There, he set her down beside the throne, and with his cock still inside her, he commanded her to grasp the padded armrest. Her legs were shaky as she stood, half bent over the throne, her fingers splayed across the rich velvet as Henrikk began to move lazily in and out of her ass. Every grating movement burnt.

"This is where I will finish," he said, gripping her hips as he increased his pace, "With you bent over the throne before the court." His panting grew louder, his cock a terrible thing as it destroyed her from the inside out.

Kira couldn't stay quiet anymore, her wails of protest growing louder with each punishing thrust as pain and magic blossomed, clinging together so she couldn't tell which was which.

"Watch as I fill her, Nathaniel," Henrikk called. "Hear how she screams. Did she ever make this noise for you? Not like this, I'll wager."

Nathaniel roared against his gag, but his gaze wasn't fixed on his father. He was looking at her.

He's urging me to fight, she realised dimly. *To not give up. Oh, Nathaniel, I'm trying.* The magic around her was as difficult to capture as sunlight in water, the golden rays promising but elusive.

"We will proceed with the wedding shortly," Henrikk announced, "But I think we shall delay my son's coronation until the morning." She felt his breath on her neck. "Because we're having too much fun, aren't we, *slut*?"

Kira had no words of reply. She was barely conscious as the middle-aged vampire who was her senior by thirty-two years fucked her, forcing himself on her as if she was nothing, the audience cheering him on.

"You are weak, and pathetic," Henrikk said, "And far from the prettiest wolf I've had the pleasure of using. In truth, I was disappointed when I first laid eyes on you. But at least your cunt was satisfactory."

She barely heard him.

She wasn't even there.

She was floating in her magic, her body almost pain-free as it carried her along a gentle river.

Henrikk groaned louder, gripped her tighter, and slammed into her over and over again.

Smack. Smack. Smack.

It was the sound she heard as he took her with rough thrusts, his heavy cock pushing and stretching her repeatedly.

Smack. Smack. Smack. Smack. Smack.

And faster.

Smack-smack-smack-smack-smack—

His massive cock stretched her for miles, the bulbous head pounding her where it hurt, his hard body claiming her as he reached his climax.

He roared as he came, the sound just as barbaric as his final thrusts were, his hardened cock lengthening as he spurted thick jets of cum inside her.

He's filling me, she realised, her chest tightening as her skin crawled with disgust. She could feel the swell of fluid surging deep in her ass, and she was powerless to do anything but grip the throne's armrest and take it as he tore her apart. Henrikk's seed coated her insides, hot and creamy, marking her and tainting her as he delivered wet stroke after wet stroke.

And he wasn't finished. There was more—much more. Another spurt, another load, and he pumped back and forth until his cum filled her ass.

"You're mine, Kira," Henrikk said. "My filthy whore."

His movements slowed, and then stopped, but he held her there, keeping her on display for the audience's benefit. She could feel his cum leaking out of her ass, trailing down her legs and dripping audibly on the tiles in gentle pitter-patters.

"There," Henrikk pronounced. "Full, like the slut you are."

The river of magic flowed faster carrying her faster towards a raging waterfall. Kira's head lolled, and as she went over the waterfall. She was vaguely aware of Henrikk giving a speech while he was still sheathed in her ass.

She plunged into the deep pool of water below, letting go of all thought and feeling as blue and gold magic washed over her. It was refreshing, the rippling energy sweeping her up and jolting her back to life.

Suddenly, she was hyper aware of every detail in the room. The faces of the nobles gathered at the foot of the dais, the sea of unsympathetic faces beyond. The guards assembled on either side of the dais and throughout the hall. Gloria, standing awkwardly to the side like an actress waiting to be called upon the stage. The way Henrikk's cock twitched in her tight rear as he called a toast in honour of his son's wedding day. The clink of many glasses.

And Nathaniel himself. Every cut, every bruise she would remember. His eyes were sad and livid, full of apology and regret. His tortured expression hurt her more than anything Henrikk had done to her, and she seized the pain and anger that had built inside her, wrapping it in vibrant magic.

Kira's power exploded outward, the invisible streams of magic reaching for every single person's mind in the room.

Everyone except for Henrikk's.

She could not bear to feel his condescending thoughts any more than he'd already subjected her to. She would deal with him another way.

With her magic wrapped around the minds of the room's guests and Henrikk still inside her, she morphed.

CHAPTER 42

Finale

NATHANIEL

NATHANIEL WATCHED IN AWE as Kira morphed, silently cheering her on even as he feared for her.

She morphed slowly, as if she was distracted, the golden magic swirling around her body and making her skin glow.

"*Yes,*" Henrikk exclaimed, cutting himself off mid-speech and staring at her with relish. "Transform for me, *slut*. Let us see your true form."

Fur began to swirl across Kira's neck and shoulders, visible where his father had half-torn her dress off. He did not wait for her transformation to complete before he began rutting her again.

"*Yes,*" he groaned, pushing his hips against her in quick succession.

Kira's skirt lifted as long, fur-tipped tails appeared, reaching behind her to wrap around Henrikk's middle. Rather than wrench him away, however, she held him bound against her, the whip-like tails preventing Henrikk from taking his cock out.

"Ha," he bellowed, increasing the intensity of his thrusts as he invited the audience to laugh with him. "Behold, the tamed bitch. See how she wants it? See—?"

It all happened so fast. Kira's controlled transformation from human into wolf.

But even Nathaniel had forgotten about her other wolf form, and its appearance was delayed, held in time and space for those extra few seconds, long enough that Henrikk let down his guard.

Her second wolf form materialised behind Henrikk. Its hackles raised and fangs bared in a snarl, her growl so deep it was inaudible except for the tremors it sent through the room.

No one in the room moved to stop her, as if they were entranced...

Or influenced not to.

As the other wolf whimpered beneath the Vampire King's assault, the second wolf leapt into the air and seized Henrikk's neck, its long fangs clamping down on his throat.

Crunch.

The wolf shook him violently, creating a series of clicks and crunches as bone snapped, before she released him.

Henrikk was dead before he hit the ground.

Panting heavily, its fur raised aggressively, the wolf circled the one that was whimpering on the ground protectively. Licking its muzzle once with its own bloodied tongue, before turning bright golden eyes at Nathaniel.

No, not at me.

At the guards.

Her harsh command radiated out into the guards' mind with so much force that Nathaniel heard its echo in his: *"Release him."*

The guards dropped him at the same time that the double doors at the far end of the Throne Room burst open.

Byron and Mary stood in the doorway wearing faded guard uniforms from a bygone era. Their faces were stricken, their hands wielding deadly scimitars.

Behind them were wolves—at least a hundred of them. Perhaps more.

Students.

Those loyal to Kira had come to her aid. She must have sent them before Victoria captured her.

Kira's wolf forms rose: one fierce, one timid—both a force to be reckoned with. Her harsh command swept through the room, making every person cower as they reached their target.

"*Kill the vampires,*" she ordered.

Mary and Byron charged forward with swords raised, the wolves in hot pursuit as they attacked the unsuspecting guests.

Meanwhile, Nathaniel swung a fist at a made vampire beside him, and Kira's wolf forms killed the others, making short work of the undead abominations.

Victoria and Felix were nowhere in sight.

Gloria screamed and tripped on her red train, scrambling to try and stand as Kira descended on her.

"No! Get back you vile beast!"

Kira's head bent down and clamped over her dress.

Nathaniel froze, and it took him a second to realise that Kira hadn't bitten Gloria. She'd seized the puffy sleeve of her dress and pulled the vampiress to her feet.

"*Leave,*" she said, and Gloria hastened out of the side door that Kira had been dragged in.

Kira watched her go, her fur receding as she morphed. Her two wolves converged into a single woman with a torn dress and dishevelled hair, golden sparkles of magic sliding off her dark skin and floating to the ground like snow. She swayed where she stood, and Nathaniel leapt forward, catching her as she fell and lifting her in his arms.

"You saved her," he was unable to hide his awe of the terrifyingly powerful, beautiful, and merciful woman in his arms.

"I had to," she whispered. "She's my sister."

Nathaniel kissed her. Words were inadequate for what he felt. His sorrow, his relief, his admiration for her.

In the background, vampires snarled, hissed, and screamed, most of them too much in shock to defend themselves.

Nathaniel pitied them, but he felt no regret. He would not miss them. His father had surrounded himself with vampires of the same ilk as him.

Suddenly, the earth trembled beneath their feet, the chandeliers casting flecks of light around the room as the entire building shook.

"What's happening?" Kira cried, clutching his arm as she peered around wildly.

A second later, the entire floor of the Throne Room collapsed, along with the dais and throne.

They all fell, but only a few feet. Nathaniel managed to shield Kira from injury as he took the brunt of the fall, holding her close as he landed on rubble.

Their bodies quaked with violent tremors as the earth shook. And then, as quickly as it had started, the room became still once more.

Large plumes of dust filled the air, obscuring everyone from view. He and Kira coughed, barely able to see more than a few feet in front of them as the dust swirled.

"What happened?" Kira asked.

"I don't know," he admitted. Whatever had caused the earthquake turned the tide in their favour. The wolves were sure-footed, whilst the vampires were not, and the fighting had quickly ended.

It was quieter now.

Wolves roamed the halls, sniffing amidst the rubble and dispatching the last of Henrikk's supporters.

The sound of a woman cursing made him and Kira turn. Behind the dais, the wooden wall had collapsed, along with the blood-red banners of Henrikk's reign. An old woman in green robes stood silhouetted in the swirling dust, surrounded by twinkling magical lights that floated in the air.

She was holding a broomstick with a gnarled handle, and as the dust cleared, Nathaniel recognised the witch. Her hair was silver with hardly a hint of blonde, and she looked tired as she approached, lifting her green skirt as she stepped gingerly across the broken ground.

"Barbara," Kira said in surprise. "What are you doing here?"

The witch looked pleased with herself, and she smiled at them happily, the expression deepening every wrinkle on her face. "You didn't think I'd let the two of you take on great evil without me, did you? Well, here I am. Although…" She scratched her head as she peered around the room, frowning as she realised the fighting was over. "Oh dear. I only meant to knock Henrikk off his throne, but it seems the building wasn't very strong, was it? I've gone and knocked the whole court off their feet!" She chortled. "Anyway, did I miss much? I'm sorry I'm a touch late. I left as soon as I could, but these broomsticks weren't designed for old bones—"

Nathaniel placed a hand on her shoulder. "Thank you," he was sincere, because however ill-timed the magic had been, it had nipped the fighting in the bud. "We couldn't have done it without you."

Kira pressed her lips together in a thin line, giving the witch a nod before looking away.

His insides seized, wishing he could reverse the events of the night. Wishing that somehow he could have spared Kira the torturous ordeal she'd gone through. He stepped close and pulled her into a silent embrace.

There were no words to express how he felt.

As he bit his wrist and held it to her mouth to drink, their mental connection filled the emptiness of his soul, and neither of them needed words.

They were one.

CHAPTER 43

The Empress

NATHANIEL

Three Weeks Later

Having defeated Henrikk, Kira was the new ruler, and Nathaniel was satisfied being prince consort, and relieved he no longer needed to marry Gloria.

Henrikk's Throne Room had been demolished, and Kira held court where her father, King Bakker, once had: in the Great Hall. The old hall was located at the heart of Wintermaw Keep and was made of sturdy stone and rustic beams, restored to its former glory.

Kira sat upon the throne that had once been her father's—a tall seat carved into the Great Hall's northern wall, which was made of grey stone. Polished timber steps led up to where she sat overlooking her court.

Nathaniel sat at her right on a slightly lower seat, murmuring advice when she requested it.

The assembled courtiers were a mix of unlikely creatures that had not peacefully shared a room in more than a decade.

Wolf shifters stood shoulder to shoulder with vampires—a dispersion that was obligatory by Kira's decree. She did not tolerate a room split in two, and she dismissed those who thought themselves too superior to stand near another faction. This had been met with apprehension, but after only three weeks of rule, the new courtiers had quickly adapted, with the early signs of new friendships and alliances showing promise.

Hopefully, old wounds would mend, and they could look to building a better future with equal opportunities.

Humans were present in the Throne Room too, and were the only faction permitted to stand in groups, and to bear arms.

Witches had returned, much to his surprise and delight. Over fifteen years ago, when Henrikk had tried to wipe out the witches, Barbara had managed to save one of the covens, mainly because they'd been away during Henrikk's invasion. Some of the witches and wizards had been in a portal world called Spring Plane—another one of Barbara's closely guarded secrets.

"They were celebrating the Winter Solstice," Barbara had explained as the court watched the robed witches and wizards enter the Throne Room in single file. Most of them appeared old, and seemed a cheerful party, with more than one who was ruddy-faced. "I sealed the portal after them during the attack. They've been trapped over there for years! Not that they've got anything to complain about. They've been drinking and feasting all this time, and taking goodness knows what substances. You should see the state of Spring Plane, it's a mess! If you thought the Throne Room was bad—"

Kira tensed at the mention of the Throne Room. Her response was so imperceptible that Nathaniel only noticed it from the way her chest went still mid-breath, as if she'd stopped breathing.

Nathaniel steered the conversation to safer waters, placing a gentle hand on Kira's shoulder. She looked up at him, and they exchanged a small smile.

Oblivious to their reaction, Barbara continued talking. "...but once this lot have detoxed, you can put them to work, Kira, dear. Oops, I meant, Your Royal Highness."

"The correct address is *Your Imperial Highness*," the herald interrupted.

"Thank you, Bromley," Nathaniel said. The new title reflected not only Kira's expansive rule over multiple factions, but over multiple territories. Kira was not the Queen of a mere kingdom. She was the Empress, ruler of the newfound Vulpire empire. She had quickly eclipsed Henrikk's leadership, masterfully uniting the wolf territories, vampire enclaves, human settlements, and the budding witch covens harmoniously and effectively.

"Your Imperial Highness," Barbara said with a low sweeping bow that was almost elegant but slightly off-balance. "We are at your disposal."

"Thank you," Kira said. "Your support is greatly welcomed. May we grow stronger together."

"May we grow stronger together," the entire room echoed, repeating the new royal motto.

Barbara did not take the hint and continued to chatter away as Kira's eyes glazed over. Nathaniel stroked her arm with his thumb, wondering where she was. Her daydreaming was frequent, and he wondered if they were happy thoughts that brought her respite, or if she was remembering recent events...

His hands clenched into fists. He should have done more to protect her, which haunted him. He would spend his entire life making it up to her, if she would let him. Even so, he wasn't sure if he would ever forgive himself for failing her.

A hush fell over the assembled courtiers as Kira rose from her throne.

Today's agenda included discussions to elect a political leader for the humans. Several lords were present, but if they hoped to leave with a crown, they were mistaken. For all Nathaniel had seen of Kira's fiery temper, she was calm and unhurried in her decision-making. She seemed to weigh up the magnitude of the responsibility she held, and had taken his advice to heart: sometimes, the best decision a leader could make was no decision.

Kira had always been serious and reserved, but she was quieter now, and not as outspoken. It was as if she'd aged quickly in a short span of time. Her inner fire burnt low and steady, without crackling flames and flying sparks that had lit up the darkness. Now, her amber eyes were muted. Often, Nathaniel looked into their depths, searching for the golden flecks that had once brightened them. Sometimes, when he held her at night, he could coax a laugh from her, and witnessed a flicker of hope and optimism reflected in her eyes.

Although Kira was not ready to talk about it, Nathaniel was certain his father's assault had triggered her change in disposition. The man was gone, but the trauma remained, and it had changed their relationship too. Their moments together were careful, every touch soft and gentle, their words loving. Soon, he hoped, Kira would open up to him.

He was content to wait.

For her, he would wait forever.

For his part, he was still too numb to grieve and even be angry. After his father's death, his strategy had been to distract himself by focusing on Kira and helping her assume power. Sooner or later, though, it would hit him: that his father was gone, leaving a heavy responsibility on their shoulders. That he had been a cruel and arrogant man, unsympathetic to vulnerable persons. That the last memory he had of his father was the way he'd brutalised Kira.

When the time came, when he finally crumbled, he knew Kira would be there.

In the meantime, he served her in every way. He stood by her side dutifully, wearing elaborate court clothes, including a turquoise coat, puffy breeches that reached his knee, and silk stockings with pointed buckle shoes.

Kira had jokingly asked him to adopt the current fashion, and he'd done so without argument—an experiment that had resulted in her laughing at him for minutes on end in the privacy of their bedroom and ended with his cock in her. It had been one of the only 'normal' moments between them, but he was glad of it.

There was something else he wore for her: A long stainless-steel plug with knots along its length. The dynamic of their relationship had changed, and there were times when Kira took control in the bedroom.

At his suggestion, she had first plugged him before the court in the Great Hall. They had made a ceremony of it, a public act that was brief but heavily symbolic.

The gesture was supposed to be brief, at any rate, but it had led to them fornicating before the whole court. Which, he supposed, helped to reinforce the symbolism of uniting wolves and vampires.

The act of Kira plugging him had sent shockwaves through the audience, which had been the whole point: to shatter their misconceptions and open them to a new way of thinking.

Nathaniel didn't mind wearing a plug, aside from the eternal erection it gave him. He'd rather enjoyed the experience of submitting to Kira publicly. There was no shame in it. She was everything he wanted, and he enjoyed kneeling at her feet as much as he'd ever had dominating her.

Sometimes, at night, Kira asked him to be rough. Those were deep moments, and he was always very careful to ensure he didn't hurt her. Afterwards, he was attentive, nurturing her and helping her to feel safe. That was what he truly yearned for: the gentle moments.

He snapped out of his reverie as a gust of air blew through the open balcony doors, causing the new white flags to swirl majestically.

Nathaniel and Kira stared at them long after the fabric had settled. It was the new royal colour; white. Kira had initially wanted black on the grounds because it was not a colour, and it was therefore not excluding anyone.

Nathaniel had pointed out that black was officially the colour of wolves, and adopting solely that colour could inadvertently send the opposite message, suggesting favouritism of shifters whilst excluding other factions.

Seeing Kira's disappointment, he hurriedly added, "But, if you're aiming for full inclusivity, may I suggest white, instead? It encompasses all the colours of the spectrum, and it could symbolise unity between all your people."

The old Kira might have argued her point, but the new Kira quietly considered his suggestion for several moments before nodding. "White," she'd agreed, and the order had promptly been placed with the royal artisans to craft new banners, flags, guard uniforms, and all manner of fabrics.

The craftsmen had worked diligently, and by the end of the first week, the luxurious white banners decorated the halls. Together with the updated furnishings, which included wolf-friendly mats by the fireplaces. The transformed Wintermaw Keep represented hope for a brighter future.

It was only in the quiet early hours of dawn when Kira had woken from a nightmare that she'd confessed what she really thought of the new banners. It was with a sinking heart that Nathaniel had listened to her describe the milky white of Henrikk's eyes and the way they'd blended with his pale irises.

Her words had stayed with him. Now, as he stood by her throne, the proud white banners were a haunting reminder of his father. Now, every room in Wintermaw Keep, every bannerman, and every flag mounted on the battlements reflected his father's eyes, and he could no more unsee them than Kira could recall her words.

He leant close. "Are you sure you wouldn't like to change the colour?"

"Don't be ridiculous," Kira scowled without looking at the banners. "These are fine."

"Are you sure? If they remind you of my fath—"

"They do. But they also remind me that he is dead, and I think that should be our focus."

Nathaniel nodded. "So...is that a 'no' to fuchsia pink?"

Kira poked her tongue out in mock-disgust, and his heart leapt. She had almost smiled, and it was another small victory for their relationship.

Nathaniel hoped that in time, once the events of his birthday were no longer so fresh, that it *would* be fine.

Time would heal, or so he hoped.

Mary and Byron had stayed for the first two weeks of Kira's rule, helping her deal with the aftermath of Henrikk's death. Their previous status as guards had helped inspire more wolves of their generation to come out of hiding, as well as others who had remained loyal in their hearts to King Bakker. The rift between Kira and her foster parents had mended, but the scars would always be there.

The scars I'm responsible for.

Mary and Byron were due to visit again next month. It would be good for Kira to see them again. She needed their support, now more than ever.

The Poplarins had been eager to help Kira, and visibly ecstatic that their new leader was also now the empress of all the lands. The pack members had reluctantly returned to the academy to continue their schooling at Kira's behest, but all of its alphas had been invited to return yesterday to swear fealty. Even Mark had been invited, although he was now a lower-ranking member of another wolf pack. While seeing Mark publicly kneel before Kira had brought Nathaniel some satisfaction, for the most part, he was glad to see the back of

Mark when he left again.

Gloria was another complication that Kira had to deal with.

"She's my family," Kira had argued privately with him. "I want to get to know her."

"She's your estranged half sister who would slit your throat in a heartbeat for the chance to wear your crown."

"The crown? Ha. She can have it," Kira had grumbled.

"It doesn't work that way. Besides, I would not like to see her with that kind of power. No one you love is safe so long as she resides within these walls."

"She's my family," Kira had repeated. "I will *not* have her executed. Nor will I imprison her."

"Then send her away. I can recommend a man to watch her."

"Exile? Another kind of prison."

"Fresh air, nature, and a taste of life away from the Capital."

In the end, Kira had conceded and sent Gloria away to live in the mountains with a personal guard that Nathaniel had recommended.

Watching Gloria leave had been a source of torment and relief for both of them.

Meanwhile, Kira had sent Victoria and Felix to Volmasque Academy, along with the other students. Nathaniel had been surprised that she did not have them arrested.

"They weren't doing anything wrong," Kira explained, her voice even as she rapped the armrest of the throne. "It was the world that Henrikk created that was wrong. Victoria and Felix were just living within that system. I cannot punish everyone, it's not realistic. Victoria and Felix simply need to learn a new way of living, as do many of us."

"Victoria was hungry for power and authority," he reminded her.

"Susie will keep an eye on her," Kira said calmly. "And I think Victoria will consider her new room a dungeon."

Kira had not closed down Volmasque Academy, nor had she burnt it to the ground. In fact, she still referred to the primary aim of the institution as rehabilitation. She hadn't even banned feeding, focusing instead on maintaining the natural balance between witches, wolves and vampires essential to sustaining each other. Strict rules to ensure ethical conduct during feeding and other intimate activities were brought into place, and there was a large focus on teaching equality and informed consent in all classes. *Pet Obedience Training* still existed, but they were no longer taught by Professor Zott, who had been encouraged into early retirement with a generous severance package that included not losing his head. In the new curriculum, it was no longer assumed that wolves were the submissive, and the results had been interesting.

There were other positive changes at the academy.

The cursed pike erected on the school steps had disintegrated into a neat pile of metal shavings, which brought both Susie and Arken an immense amount of relief.

The lower vampire dorms were now allocated based on seniority, regardless of whether the students were vampires or wolves, and the lower portal leading to the beach cove was open for use by all students.

On Kira's behalf, Nathaniel had commissioned the wolf dorms to be renovated to improve the living standard. Only one of the rooms remained untouched. It was Susie's old room, which was allocated to Victoria, who'd reportedly complained to anyone who would listen that it was a quarter of the size of her previous suite, and that to live there was a 'prison sentence' in itself.

One afternoon when Nathaniel was visiting the academy, he happened to pass Victoria in the corridor, where she was being consoled by a first year, surrounded by bags and boxes of clothes, shoes and hats.

"Victoria," he said stiffly.

"Oh, Nathaniel! Great, you're here. I have so much I need to tell you."

He half expected her to apologise, but she seemed too distressed to get the words out.

"What's wrong?" he asked, as Victoria sank to the floor on her stilettos, disappearing amongst the waist-high pile of sparkling frocks.

"There's no room for all my stuff! What am I going to do?"

"Your stuff," Nathaniel repeated, quashing his disappointment as if it were nothing. He should have known better than to expect Victoria to feel remorse.

"I've already given away so many of my belongings to those less fortunate, but what will I do with the rest?" She kicked a hat box closer to him. It contained a wide brim purple hat with an ostentatious feather that he was sure he'd never seen her wear. "I can't just give this away, what if there's a ball? And look...these suspenders—"

"You don't wear suspenders," Nathaniel pointed out, trying to keep his tone level when in actual fact, he could barely restrain himself from tearing her to shreds. But he would leave that to Susie—the wolf shifter had a score to settle just as much as he.

Victoria didn't like that answer, and she clutched the suspenders close and burst into tears. "But I could if I wanted to. I had the opportunity to...but now, if I let them go..." She wiped her face. "I suppose they don't take up a lot of room," she said, flinging the rainbow-coloured suspenders into the room. She sniffed and ducked to pick up a box of hair clips, hair bands, and other girly things. "Nat, help me decide which of these to keep. I—"

"I'm not doing this," Nathaniel said, pivoting and striding away as fast as he could. Despite Victoria's self-centredness, he found himself appreciating Kira's judgement. Victoria may have been many things, but she was not malicious, and she certainly didn't belong in the dungeon. He sincerely hoped the academy's new classes and teachers would be enough to steer the school and its students in the right direction.

He'd fired half the faculty and had spent several days interviewing new potential staff members. One of them was a human called Mr. Paypin, who Nathaniel had considered a brave man, as well as interesting: he suffered from a terrible affliction that caused him to turn into a terrifying, blood-thirsty beast beneath the full moon. But he had a kind heart, and was eager to adopt the academy's new policies for fostering positive interrelationships between wolves and vampires. The blood-thirsty beast part they would figure out how to manage later. With multiple staff vacancies, student safety was a top priority, second only to filling the teaching positions.

Kira had not yet had the opportunity to visit the academy, and now, it seemed she wouldn't have a chance for a while to come. She had insisted on visiting all corners of the empire to familiarise herself with the people, and Nathaniel had greatly approved of the plan. It was a chance for her to broaden her horizons beyond what she had experienced in the sleepy village of Nordokk and the vampire-dominated Capital. It was also an opportunity for the people to see their new ruler with their own eyes.

Kira had hoped to improve the prosperity of the kingdom, which Nathaniel suspected she would achieve by simply redistributing the wealth more evenly amongst the people. It also involved restructuring the job opportunities available to humans and wolves, as well as improving access to education, something that Henrikk had not deemed important. He had falsely spread the results of erroneous studies conducted by vampires on the reduced intelligence of humans and shifters. Kira was determined to prove that this was not true and was investing a portion of the treasury to build more schools throughout the empire.

Kira, Nathaniel had decided, was determined to do a lot, and quickly. It was probably why she was so tired all the time.

She had even made time to remember her friends, and had seen to it that Susie received a massive luxury spa bath in her dorm room, which Susie and Arken had found to their joint satisfaction. Susie had also received a calendar from Kira for the new year in the new royal colour—white. At first glance it did not seem striking for a calendar, but the sheets had a pearly sheen, and the edges were embossed with real gold that bore the new royal crest. Kira had also stamped the pages with her paws using gold glitter—real gold flakes. It was one of the only times Nathaniel had seen her smile since his birthday, probably because it was one of the only things she'd done that had some semblance of normalcy.

Though Kira bore it well, the task of ruling an entire empire she'd seen very little of must have been overwhelming. Sometimes, the cracks in her armour showed in the littlest things—like the way she agonised about ensuring Susie's calendar was perfect.

"I wish I could deliver the calendar in person," Kira had sighed, clicking her tongue as she tried to fold the wrapping paper over the calendar. She'd sat at the private desk of her study, rewrapping the calendar over and over again. She waved the steward away when he tried to help. "Thank you, but I prefer to wrap it myself."

"Of course, your Imperial Highness," the steward said kindly. "And I may venture to say that it's the thought that counts." He retreated from the room.

"The thought that counts, huh?" Kira muttered. She looked to Nathaniel warily, something she did often of late, as if she trusted no one's opinion except his.

Even for matters related to gift wrapping.

He cleared his throat with his fist over his mouth to hide his amusement. It was ironic that she was having difficulty with this seemingly small task when only yesterday, she'd deployed soldiers to revolting cities without batting an eyelid. But he understood. This was more than a distraction from the pressures of court. It was also a desperate attempt to cling to her past, the safety and familiarity of an old life. Susie was one of the few people Kira had trusted who'd come through for her, and amidst the isolation of court life, Nathaniel sensed she was terrified of losing her friend.

"I think Susie will appreciate your gift immensely," Nathaniel soothed, pressing a kiss on top of her hair. "She knows how busy you are, and she's looking forward to seeing you as soon as you return from your travels."

Kira nodded. "I wish she could come with me."

They both knew Susie could not.

She was the head of the residential advisors at the academy, and during this time of upheaval, they were relying on her support to ensure a smooth transition. Arken was still the headmaster of the school, and despite his history of feeding on students, he had taken the changes in his stride.

Arken was the reason the wolf students had come to Kira's aid on the night of his and Gloria's wedding. Nathaniel had been curious how the Capital's security officers had failed to stop the students from reaching Wintermaw Keep—so many wolves in a large number would have immediately drawn attention. It turned out that at Susie's urging, Arken had accompanied the students to Wintermaw, allowing them to travel under the guise of a school excursion.

Upon arriving at the castle, Arken had explained that the wolves had been granted a very rare opportunity to view the coronation, and his authority was such that the perplexed guards began debating whether to let them into the foyer. Taking advantage of their distraction, the wolves made mincemeat of the guards at the Keep's entrance, and the ones in the courtyard had soon followed.

So, at least for now, Nathaniel was content to keep Arken on as the headmaster, and Kira had accepted his advice on that front.

She sighed as she gave up on tying a bow over the gift. "I'll miss her."

"I know," Nathaniel said, kneeling down beside her. "But...in the summer, we will take a holiday." He pointed to the map lying beneath the wrapping paper, his fingertip resting on a southern island. The main land's coastline was three hours by carriage, and from there, the tropical island was two days by ship...but with magic portals, paradise was only a breath away. "We'll take a proper holiday, one that does not involve long carriage rides, or crowds of people..."

"Or speeches," Kira interjected, waving the steward over so he could help her wrap the gift.

"Or speeches," Nathaniel grinned. His fingers tiptoed over the map surface and rested on her hand. "Just you, and me, and whoever you wish to invite."

Kira smiled. "Can I invite Gloria?"

He blinked rapidly, unable to tell if she was serious.

"It was a joke," she said softly, "But now that I've said it out loud..."

"Maybe a café for reconciling with your sister would be more appropriate."

"You don't want to be trapped on an island with both of your brides?"

His lips pinched. It was an uncomfortable topic, and a very fine line Kira was skirting. But if this was her way of dealing with things, then he would be as accommodating and chipper as she needed him to be. Still, there were some things he could not joke about, and he swivelled her around on her chair so he could cup her face.

"There is only one bride for me." He let the words hang in the air, expecting no answer in return, and receiving none.

Only three weeks had passed since his father had done what no person should ever do to another. It was a time of upheaval and change, and even positive changes could take their toll. He had a feeling they were both on the verge of tears, because surely, it was not normal to be so numb to all the pressures weighing down their shoulders.

Especially the pressure on Kira. She'd had no downtime to truly process any of it.

That night, Kira went to bed exhausted, and Nathaniel held her tight. Like every night, he was mindful of her emotional state, never instigating more unless she did so first. Like tonight, when she pressed herself close, and kissed him with an urgency that was desperate and new. He returned her kisses with the same fervour, pulling her close in a wordless promise to never let go.

They made love, and lost themselves in each other, escaping the world as they healed each other's wounds. Together, wrapped in sheets, they could just *be* and that was enough.

Afterwards, Kira lay on her side facing the open window of their bedroom. A gentle breeze rolled in, and she shivered and nestled closer back against him.

A dangerous move, as her soft ass pressed against his groin, but he was distracted by the pale moonlight edging the elegant lines of her arms and waist.

Kira broke the silence with a gasp. "Shit. Wait. Nathaniel, are you still wearing the plug?"

He chuckled. "What do you think?"

She gasped again. "I forgot! How long have you been—"

"Since last night. And I must say, it made my meeting with the Provincial Taxation Assessment Panel interesting today."

"Oh my gosh, I'm so sorry!"

He laughed again and pulled her close so her back pressed against his chest. "Don't be sorry," he whispered in her ear. "But perhaps my mistress would permit me to remove it...?"

"Yes, of course!"

He winced as he removed the plug and tossed it in the direction of the bathroom. On their first night, there had been a white-gloved servant who they forgot all about standing there, and he'd caught the plug in his hand, making them laugh so hard they'd had to dismiss the servants from their private bedchamber.

"I hope you don't intend for me to wear it again tomorrow. I'm meant to ride out to one of the estates on horseback."

"We'll see," Kira giggled, giving him a smile that dispelled the shadows of the past.

As Nathaniel began to drift, the echo of her melodic laughter lulled him to sleep, filling his dreams and brightening the stars above.

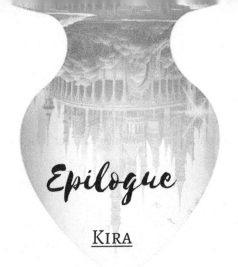

Epilogue

KIRA

Twelve Months Later

EMPRESS KIRABELLE ENTERED THE royal suite and firmly shut the door behind her. The rooms were dark except for the crackling fireplace, and the stars outside the window twinkled brightly in the night sky. The suite was lavishly decorated, but that was not why she loved it.

This place was her sanctuary. There were no guards, no servants, and—mercifully—no councillors. It had been a long day of council meetings and she was exhausted. More often than not, her position as ruler of the Vulpire Empire was dull and boring, and she'd quickly learnt that those were the better days.

Today's list of affairs had unexpectedly concluded with excitement and turmoil, meaning that this was one of those days where she wished for her ordinary life back.

Kira let out a long sigh, shrugging off her heavy ermine-trimmed cloak and letting it drop onto a sideboard. The gold crown followed; a jewelled spectacle finally retired for the evening.

Nathaniel was in his office, and he set down his quill when she leant in the doorway.

"Hello," he greeted.

She gave him a tired smile. "Hello."

"How was your day?"

"The trade delegation returned this afternoon."

"And?"

Kira groaned. "Fucking witches."

"Let me guess...they imported more pumpkin carriages?"

"No, I wish. *Legumes.*"

"Legumes?"

"*Beans*, Nathaniel. They planted a fucking beanstalk. A giant one." She explained, throwing her arms in the air in exasperation.

"Interesting."

"In the middle of Wayside Channel."

"In the middle of...?" Nathaniel raised his eyebrows.

"The beanstalk is smack-bang in the middle of the channel, growing out of the fucking water and into the sky. No ships can get in or out of the harbour."

"Ah." Nathaniel scratched his nose. "That is an expensive problem."

Kira scowled. "Don't laugh."

"I'm not." But his lip twitched, his shoulders shaking with silent laughter.

"I said *don't laugh!*" But she was laughing too. It was so fucking stupid. "What am I going to do with them? I've got more important things to worry about than babysitting witches. I know I promised to allocate positions in the castle equally between races, but...*argh.*" She rubbed her face.

Nathaniel let out a low chuckle. "Come here."

With a low groan, Kira traipsed across the room and sat on Nathaniel's lap. She wrapped her arms around his neck and settled against his chest, breathing in his smoky scent.

This. She needed more of this.

"What am I going to do?" she asked.

"Promoting diversity and being inclusive was—"

"My idea, I know." She rolled her eyes.

Under her leadership, the first twelve months of her rule had been peaceful. New systems had been implemented by people she trusted—loyal, competent people of various races, including wolf shifters, vampires, and humans. The only people not on her staff were witches and wizards, and that was mostly because despite their good intentions, they were, on the whole, an unreliable sort. There was even a saying for it:

Give a witch a seed, and you'll get a pumpkin carriage. Give a witch a carriage, and you'll find it wrecked within a mile of the nearest tavern.

The proverb meant that witches were dreamers, and generally made for terrible chauffeurs. Paperwork was not their forte either; nor were they to be trusted with weapons, lest they accidentally injure those around them. These traits disqualified them for most positions on the household staff, the Royal Guard, and the council.

They were highly skilled at magic, of course, but they were almost too efficient at enchanting the various structures throughout Wintermaw Keep. Kira had tried to keep the witches occupied, but it had taken them no time at all to complete their assignments. There was not a door in the capital that did not open of its own accord (sometimes at inconvenient times), nor a saddle that did not scrub and polish itself after each ride (to the increased pleasure of the still-mounted rider).

Kira had simply run out of useful things for the witches to do, especially when the result sometimes decreased the overall functionality of things that had once worked perfectly. Out of desperation, she had handed a bag of gold to each of the seven eager, young-faced, three-plus-century-old witches, and sent them on a trade delegation across the sea.

This mission had solved the problem of what to do with the witches, and gotten most of them out of her hair for a few months.

Until today, when the ship had returned missing half its sailors, the vessel's timber and sailing masts coloured a pretty shade of pink. Furthermore, the witches had seen fit to unload their cargo halfway into port, much of which had sunk into the ocean. The magic beans—which apparently had been purchased with a great quantity of Kira's gold—had instantly found roots in the muddy soil of the channel, the thick trunk shooting up through the brackish water and growing so high it disappeared into the clouds.

No ship could navigate around the large trunk, and the channel blockage had caused a supply chain disruption for the empire—and a serious migraine for Kira.

The pounding of her head somewhat eased as Nathaniel massaged her neck and shoulders.

"Who did you leave to deal with the crisis?" he asked.

"The steward. He's summoned every woodcutter within ten miles of the capital to try and bring it down."

"Why not ask the witches to solve the problem they created?"

Kira raised her eyebrow. "I did."

"And?"

She turned her head to look at him. "Do you really want to know how that went down?"

"Please, I'm intrigued," Nathaniel said, his eyes twinkling with humour.

"They summoned a giant to uproot it. Which seemed like it might work, except the giant seemed more interested in climbing. It proceeded to fuck off up the beanstalk and out of sight." Kira's voice was deadpan.

"So, the situation is...unresolved?"

"I've detained the witches in the tearoom. So, I consider the problem half solved."

"Which tearoom?" Nathaniel asked curiously.

"The one with the self-refilling cups."

"I like that room."

"*Nathaniel!* You're not helping."

"Sorry." He pressed a kiss to her temple. "Try not to worry about it now. Relax."

"I want to, but I can't stop thinking about my schedule. I'm double booked to visit two estates at once in the morning. *Two!* How can I be in two places at once? And—"

"Shh," Nathaniel whispered. "Tomorrow can wait. Just breathe."

Kira took a deep breath and released it slowly. "But what really frustrates me—"

"Again," Nathaniel commanded.

Kira took another breath, this time filling her lungs fully, the tension starting to seep out of her.

"That's it," Nathaniel said softly.

She took another calming breath. "I just want to not *think* for a while."

A pause.

"Perhaps..." he began, then paused again.

"What?"

"There is a way, pet."

Kira stilled at Nathaniel's tone. The sweetness was gone, the timbre deepening until it made chills creep up her spine. She scarcely dared breathe at his silent offer. It had been so long since he'd called her that: *pet*. Not since the evening of his thirtieth birthday when his father, Henrikk, had assaulted her before the court.

Everything had changed after that.

She had changed, and though Henrikk was dead, she sometimes still saw him when she looked at Nathaniel.

She loved Nathaniel with all her heart, but in the months that followed, their relationship had been different, their words as sweet and careful as their love. He had been so patient with her, so considerate.

And she knew he was having a hard time too. No matter how she tried to reassure him, the guilt had been eating him alive. She could taste the tang of it in those rare moments when she brushed his thoughts with her magic.

But it wasn't enough.

She wanted more.

She wanted to be the person she'd been before his father had touched her.

She wanted...

"I don't know what I want," she whispered, her head bowing. She'd been numb for far too long, entrenched in her new role and never stopping to take a breath.

Nathaniel tilted her chin up. His icy irises had melted into pools of midnight blue that danced with the reflection of the hearth's orange flames. "It's up to you, *pet*. Whatever you need, I am at your service."

She licked her lips. Swallowed nervously. Exhaled again, slowly. Meanwhile, her pulse thrummed with excitement.

Suddenly, it was clear.

She knew what she wanted.

"I want to be at *your* service," she said, slipping off his lap and lowering herself to kneel on the floor at his feet.

Nathaniel's pupils dilated in surprise. "Are you sure?"

"Yes." Kira gazed up at him, touching his mind with her magic in a way she hadn't done in a very long time. Nathaniel shivered beneath her mental touch, his lips parting as he felt her thoughts.

She was scared of so many things, but not of him.

A look of understanding passed between them, and a new certainty blossomed. The dark desires residing deep within them were as special and right as they were forbidden; a secret place that they—and only they—could visit together. No one could come between them, and while they were forever changed, they would heal together, just as they would feel pain and pleasure together in the castle they called home.

Despite what she'd been through—or maybe because of it—the things she now wanted were wilder and more shocking than anything she'd ever imagined. And yet, this was a return to normal for both of them. Nathaniel's mind was a beautiful thing, a polarising mix of hot passion that washed over her, and cold steely authority that sought to control her, both of which were a comfort to her.

But he needed comforting too. Kira interlaced her hand with his and lifted it to her lips, pressing a kiss to his knuckles.

"I've been dreaming of this," Nathaniel murmured. "But I wasn't sure if we would ever—"

"Yes," she answered. It was the only word that mattered, the one that led to a world of possibilities they'd shut themselves off from. "*Yes* to everything with you."

She needed not just the warm side of him. There was more to them than dreams and soft words.

She needed his nightmares as well.

Nathaniel bit his lip as he studied her, searching her face. "Are you sure you're ready?"

"Are you?" she whispered.

His eyelids drifted low as simmering passion appeared in his eyes. "Am I ready for this beautiful, strong, hot-tempered wolf who once tried to stab me—?"

"I *did* stab you," she corrected with a smile.

"True. Well, all I know is this..." He cupped her face, and she leant into his touch. "You have every piece of my heart. I, too, want everything with you. Not just Kira the Empress, but the parts you keep hidden as well. But...after what you went through..." His voice broke, and tears sprang to her eyes. "After what my father—"

"Shh." It was her turn to shush him, pressing her finger to his lips. "I am not the broken creature you think I am."

"Oh, Kira. I would never think that of you."

"Then don't treat me like I'm wounded. Yes, it traumatised us both. But this is not how I want to overcome it—by pretending it never happened. By never talking about it. I'm so tired of us tiptoeing around each other. Please, Nathaniel."

It wasn't about escaping the darkness inhabiting them, nor about finding the light in the darkness. It was simply about them being honest enough to embrace the dark desires within them, and the joyous bliss that came with its sweet surrender.

"Please," she said, wiping the corners of her eyes. "I want something that's real. Even if it's not perfect. I've missed *us*."

Nathaniel bowed his head in quiet contemplation.

When he lifted it, his voice was paradoxically soft and brittle, like chalk that was ready to snap. "Are you absolutely sure?"

Kira wriggled where she sat, conscious of his hardening length through his trousers. "Yes, sir."

Nathaniel shut his eyes for a moment, as if he'd been longing to hear those words from her for as long as she'd been wanting to say them.

"Well, then..." He eased himself back in his chair, planting his feet apart as he spread his legs. "You know what to do, pet."

She did. Slowly, she shuffled forward to kneel between his legs, her worries dissolving as she reached to unbuckle his belt. He was rock hard, his shaft smooth and velvety beneath her fingers as she took him out.

Before she could place her lips on his cock, however, Nathaniel spoke. "One more thing..."

She swallowed in nervous anticipation, hoping he would say the terrible, unforgiveable, liberating words that had lived locked up in her treacherous heart ever since his father had abused her. The words that could set her free, at least for a little while.

"Yes?" she breathed when he didn't speak.

He stroked her cheek with his thumb in a rough caress that made her body tingle.

And then he said them—those beautiful, dark words she'd been too ashamed to ask for. The ones that had haunted her nightmares and inspired her dreams.

Nathaniel's voice grew raspy. "I want you to imagine that it is my father's cock you are sucking. And when you taste me, you will think of him, and moan his name. Will you do that for me?"

"Yes, sir," she gasped, her lips a tantalising inch from the head of his cock.

"Good." A slow, cruel smile spread across Nathaniel's face—one that was so convincing that she had no trouble imagining the ruthless vampire who had once bent her over the throne before a jeering crowd and fucked her until her legs shook and his cum seeped down her legs.

Except this time, she was safe, with the man she loved and trusted with all her heart.

Nathaniel stroked her hair, his eyes glimmering. "You may begin, *slut*. Let us see what you are good for."

Well done for finishing, pet. You did very well. But stay where you are...I am far from done with you.

—NOT READY TO LEAVE THE WORLD OF VOLMASQUE ACADEMY?—

Continue the adventure with *Plug and Drain*, a forbidden romance featuring Susie and Headmaster Arken.

ORDER NOW ON AMAZON

Release Date: March 31st 2024

Plug and Drain: An addictive Teacher-Student Steamy Dark Paranormal Romance

Plug and Drain is the prequel to the *Plug and Claim Duology* and takes place before Kira arrives at Volmasque Academy. There are elements of BDSM, sweet romance, dubcon and noncon blended together as both Susie and Headmaster Arken navigate a darker era at Volmasque. (Also, Nathaniel appears as a side character. Just sayin'.)

◆**Vampires crave more than blood when they visit students' beds. Refusing a vampire student is dangerous. but Refusing the headmaster? Impossible.**◆

Plug and Drain is the gripping <u>prequel</u> to the *Plug and Claim Duology*, unveiling a tale of paranormal fantasy and dark romance with forbidden love, taboo spice scenes, and addictive fast-paced chapters to keep you turning the pages aching for more.

As night falls, Volmasque Academy transforms into a dark realm of forbidden desires, where wolf shifters like Susie are forced to succumb to the dark will of vampires. When the headmaster unexpectedly arrives to feed on a vulnerable female student, Susie has an overwhelming urge to shield her and finds herself standing at the crossroads of morality and survival. To protect another, can Susie muster the courage to invite the monster into her room—and into her bed?

Haunted by his dark past, Headmaster Arken seeks solace in drink to numb his pain, and trudges through the daily grind at the academy. Until a student captures his eye, breaking his monotony and offering a glimmer of hope for the future. Inspired by Susie's ambition to transform the academy for the better, Arken finds himself craving not only her blood, but her companionship as well. But to win her heart, he must contemplate the toughest challenge of all: transforming himself.

♦ TROPES ♦
- Very Spicy with BDSM
- M/F Dark Romance
- Teacher / Student
- Paranormal College Academy
- Age Gap (19F / 39M)
- New Adult (18+)
- Praise / Toys
- Dom / Sub
- Slow-burn romance
- Morally Grey MMC
- Strong FMC

Don't miss another book release. Sign up for my newsletter:
linktr.ee/darcyfayton
Want to beta read my books and help shape the story as I write?
Join my Patreon: patreon.com/darcyfayton

Afterword

Wow, thank you for reading my debut series, the *Plug and Claim Duology!* I hope you enjoyed it.

As an indie author, I would be so grateful if you could please consider leaving a voluntary review online on **Amazon, Goodreads, and Bookbub.**

Easy links at linktr.ee/darcyfayton

WANT EARLY ACCESS TO MY STORIES?

Join my Patreon for:

- **Early Access to new stories and chapters every week**

- **Early Access to Cover Reveals**

- **Auto-approval for ARC Team**

- **Watch me write & Beta Read to help shape the story**

- **Bonus Content, Exclusive Polls, and more!**

Darcy Fayton's Books

PROMISING YOU DARK FANTASY ROMANCE WITH HOT SPICY SLOW BURN ROMANCE. ALWAYS.

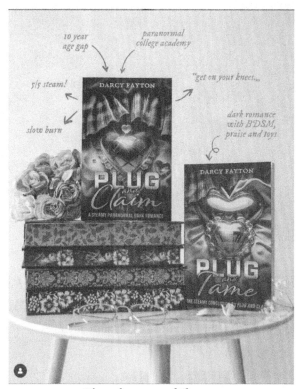

Photo by @tata.lifepages

PLUG AND CLAIM

She was ready to fight. She was ready to resist capture. But she was not ready for *him*, nor the collar he placed around her neck.

The complete Plug and Claim Duology featuring Kira and Nathaniel. A dark fantasy romance with BDSM themes including 'on your knees' vibes, pet play, and a quest for revolution.

PLUG AND DRAIN

Vampires crave more than blood when they visit students' beds. Refusing a vampire student is dangerous. Refusing the headmaster? Impossible.

A spicy duology featuring a forbidden romance between wolf shifter student Susie and Headmaster Arken. It is also the gripping prequel to the Plug and Claim Duology.

Book 1 Release Date: Mar 31st 2024

PLUGGED AT THE GATES

It is forbidden for vampires to fall in love with their pet wolf. Public displays of rutting, however, are not only acceptable, but encouraged, especially in the context of punishment.

A spicy short story featuring Kira and Nathaniel. It's a standalone that can be read by itself. It also serves as a bonus spicy chapter in Plug and Tame.

Available on Amazon, Patreon & my Newsletter

Acknowledgements and Praise

PATRONS:

A very special thank you to all my Patrons. Your support is hugely appreciated and has helped make this story possible!

To my **Good Pets**, thank you for being so good to me.

And as for my **Bad Pets**, you've been especially bad. Yes, you know who you are, and now the rest of the world does, too:

bookish.adventures.of.p
Christine Powell
Carla
Danielle Coon-Davis
gloriaoxford
Shauni Breen
Katie
Melissa

KICKSTARTER BACKERS:

A huge thank you to everyone who backed the Kickstarter for *Plug and Claim*. It was such an awesome thing for me to experience as a debut author.

Ruthenia (Ruth) Dillon
Sarah Freedman
redfishguy
Adriane
MCC
Danielle Williams
Karla V.
Christine L. Powell
Jessica Michalski
Diane Wagoner
Elisha Bryant
valen grimes
Maike ten Dam
Cherelle Hopper
Bianca Tatjana Višić Ritorto
Alexandra Varin Thiel
Zyra Kenzi Bosa
Vicky Salas
Cyynder
David Riedinger
Ltz
Brittany Szwaczkowski
Keema
phoenix_17
Amy Wendt

Kimmer Ann
Leticia Henriksen
Abby Adams
Nekia T
Morby
Kara Sanders
Tionna
Alana
chester

EARLY READERS WHO HELPED PROOFREAD THIS DUOLOGY:

This series has benefited from not only two professional editors, but also a group of wonderful readers who took the time to help polish the story and pick-up last-minute typos and errors. As an indie author, I'm so grateful to every single one of you. I did my best to reach out to everyone I could, so if you don't see your name on this list, please know how much I appreciate you.

Charlie Foley-Friend (The Book Hangover)
Aisha Prentice @the_bookish_cave_of_wonders
Schuyler Marina
Ellie Greenslade @ellies_littlelibrary
Taylor Wittman
Kez Marie
Tabitha Orr
Stacey's Bookcorner
Tallulah @lulahisreading
Morby

And finally, a huge thank you to everyone who has read my books and encouraged me to continue writing! I love creating stories so much and I hope you'll join me on my next

adventure.

~ SUPPORT MY WRITING ~
REVIEW MY BOOKS & JOIN MY PATREON FOR EARLY
ACCESS TO MY STORIES
LINKTR.EE/DARCYFAYTON